samedi's knapsack

samedi's knapsack

gaylord dold

thomas dunne books
st. martin's minotaur ≋ new york

THOMAS DUNNE BOOKS.
An imprint of St. Martin's Press.

SAMEDI'S KNAPSACK. Copyright © 2001 by Gaylord Dold. All rights reserved.
Printed in the United States of America. No part of this book may be used or
reproduced in any manner whatsoever without written permission except in the
case of brief quotations embodied in critical articles or reviews. For information,
address St. Martin's Press, 175 Fifth Avenue, New York, N.Y. 10010.

www.minotaurbooks.com

Library of Congress Cataloging-in-Publication Data

Dold, Gaylord.
    Samedi's knapsack / Gaylord Dold.—1st ed.
      p. cm.
    ISBN 0-312-26643-X
    1. Roberts, Mitchell (Fictitious character)—Fiction. 2. Private
investigators—Haiti—Fiction. 3. Haiti—Fiction. I. Title.

PS3554.O436 S26 2001
813'.54—dc21   2001019145

First Edition: May 2001

10 9 8 7 6 5 4 3 2 1

historical note

*t*he rule of the Duvaliers over Haiti ended in 1986 when "Baby Doc" fled with his millions in loot to the south of France. His father, "Papa Doc," had invented the original paranoiac style, imposing his power through a combination of voodoo rhetoric and Tonton Macoute ruthlessness. The departure of Baby Doc ushered in a period of violence hitherto unknown even in that turbulent and tormented country, a restless political urge that saw citizens hunting down the Macoute, the Army backing various generals, coups by the bucketful. This period, the "dechoukaj," or uprooting, was characterized by "necklacing" (the burning of victims with oil-soaked rubber tires), torture, and revenge.

Reliable sources say that upward of 700 million dollars' worth of cocaine passed through Port au Prince each month in those days. Army officers received a reported 10-percent cut.

Part 1

Vodun is the supreme factor in the unity of Haiti. It came to crystallize, in the dynamism of its cultural manifestations, in the past of the African on native soil, his martyrdom in the colonial hell, the heroism of the knights in realizing the miracle of 1804. It sublimates the tragedy of the Haitian masses.

—François Duvalier,
L'Évolution Stadiale de Voudou,
1944

1

*r*oberts lay in the dark, his mind running clocklike in nearly perfect and meaningless circles. On the floor beside his single bed was a leather suitcase bound by three leather straps, secured with a beautiful brass lock. He had packed the night before, five pairs of jeans, some hiking and fishing shorts, a pair of moccasins, one suit and a single dress shirt, assorted socks and underwear, two ties, now slightly soiled, his shaving kit and utilities, several paper novels, including most of Beckett in Pan editions, a Glock 9-mm pistol stripped into six sections, each section well oiled and wrapped in heavy newspaper, each wrapped part then twined inside black plastic. He had broken down his rod and reel and had stored them in an olive-green carrying case, all of it ready for the long flight to Miami.

How long had it taken him to pack? Fifteen minutes, maybe less?

After packing, he had sat in the near dark and drunk a good quantity of Black Velvet, having bought a cheap bottle of Algerian champagne, some Irish stout. Sitting in the dreary basement flat, he tried to drive the cold from his mind, tasting the sweetish Velvet, then a second time in an aftertaste that was as lamentable and misty as his three years in London had been lamentable and misty. The Black Velvet remained inside his mouth, a bad guest, refusing to depart.

Rolling onto his right side, heaving a sigh, his face turned from the shapes and specters of his sitting-room basement, he hurried through the stages of his paltry grief, the initial convulsive shock of the breakup, the despair, the slowly building anger, the ultimate acceptance and resignation, and now the flight, using the phylogeny of these mental states the way a television director might cut through shifting images to impart a feeling of rapid movement to film. Bad video indeed, he thought.

Back on his left side in a continuation of the toss-and-turn, he saw the glass of Velvet on his nightstand, half-empty, a ring of dried foam on its rim. He flipped on a table lamp and stared at the room, seeing it for what it was, perhaps ten square feet of caged uncertainty, a tapestry on one wall, tie-dyed batik on another, one desk, a single tattered easy chair in which he had spent many hours reading, a small black-and-white unlicensed television, a coil ring in one corner on which to heat canned soup and a cheaply made, massproduced shepherd's pie. Some nameless tenant years before had constructed a washbasin and toilet in another corner.

He decided to get up and wash his face and hands, using the basin. He soaped and toweled his body, shaved with a disposable razor, combed his hair, then put on some chinos, a flannel shirt, hiking boots, and prepared to go. It was just past seven in the morning, and a thin thread of sunshine leaked through the high windows at ground level.

He spit into the washbasin and lit a small black cheroot. He was tempted for a moment by the half glass of Velvet but, gathering his rods and his suitcase, he walked out the door and up three stone stairs to a walled garden floored with old brick.

As usual, the thunderless London sky was the color of a rat. He sat on a bench, quietly hating the Sunday silence, the steadfast bourgeois dullness. He despised the long rows of chestnut trees poised pointlessly to link Kensington Park Road with the inner realms of Nottinghill Gate, all the dark windows of the detached houses capturing each nuance of gray until the glass shimmered with a ghostly nothingness, white plaster walls caked with industrial grime and soot, not a bus, not a car, not a single jet streaking toward Heathrow, certainly not a single human being in sight. In this vast city of thirteen million, the noiselessness of Sunday morning was like an underwater explosion, first an awesome bulge, then zillions of tiny bubbles rising surfaceward, the shock wave undulating through successive layers of liquid. Roberts lofted cigar smoke into the chilly autumn air and waited.

In a concentrated burst of energy, he thought of Amanda for the last time. He probed her body, touching every part, his tongue tasting her nipple, roaming the dark mole alongside it. He placed his ear on the inside of her right thigh and rested his head between her legs, feeling the heat of her. With his right hand, he gently touched the bottom of her right foot. Above him, her belly arched like a risen moon, and he watched it float and fall with the slow pace of her breath, growing and waning as night passed. She breathed her breath into him and he caught it, sending it back, their corporeal semaphores incongruent, proverbial ships passing in the night. He explored her ear, no cave at Lascaux more densely spiritual or more hauntingly articulate. He examined the rich texture of her voice, the raspy Amanda who'd had too much whiskey and who'd smoked too many cigarettes on Saturday night, the pouty Amanda whose feelings had been hurt, the professional Amanda lecturing him on the ins and outs of Eliot's poetry, a sound down just one register from the others. Her auburn hair covered him and he became the rich soil of an autumn hillside. Her green eyes bored into him like smoking diamonds, her fingernails creased his back with pleasure and desire. She tattooed him with her anger and buttered him with her song. She howled in the night like a hunting cat, she barked like a dog, she crawled through the gutters of Shepherd's Bush on her hands and knees begging for sex. She whispered, she scolded, she screamed epithets and endearments, she chattered gossip and slurred the vilest filth. She covered his mouth with hers, his tongue with her tongue. He slicked himself with her fluids.

And then he let her go. She drifted away like milkweed on a strong breeze.

Roberts turned his suddenly quiet mind to Miami, Flight 1045, the first step toward home. Every long journey began with a single step, didn't it?

And then, for some inexplicable reason, he thought of Bobby

Hilliard, an old friend in Miami—the man tall and gangly, with Popeye forearms and a fiery gleam in his eye, the strange acne-clawed face glazing his memory. In a matter of five seconds, Roberts had chewed the memory of Bobby Hilliard with his mind and had spit it out, a piece of tasteless gristle if there ever was one.

2

*t*heir last night together had been like a silent movie. Grainy and spiderwebbed with flaws, each frame of film unspooling as if calculated to unnerve and disturb its audience. Choppy movements, stilted dialogue, a senseless melodrama played out against a background of rainy dark.

He had sat on the white sofa. Behind him were the park and the trees and the dark shape of motionless clouds. Amanda sat across from him on the floor, splay-legged, tapping her cigarette ash into an empty teacup. The room, high-ceilinged and cold, smelled of joss stick and boiled lamb. The windows were filled with rain. Tiny prisms of light caught and reflected the traffic on Kensington Park Road. Amanda had just come home from a Saturday-night reading at her literary magazine, and she was dressed in brown wool and paisley silk, high leather boots, her hair sheeny with the cold weather and the damp.

More than anything in the world that night, Roberts wanted to drink alcohol, make love, to rant and rave his exhaustion and his desire.

"When is your flight?" Amanda asked for the third or fourth time that week. "Have I asked you before?" she continued haltingly.

"I've canceled it," Roberts said. "I'm staying. We're getting married and we're having ten children. I'm going to work down at the docks as a warehouseman."

"Really?" she said, starting. "You shouldn't joke about such things."

"No, not really," Roberts said. "My flight is at eleven." He thought of lying about the time in order to avoid a morning scene. The evening scene was bad enough. "The radio taxi is coming a couple of hours early."

"You'll need the time at Heathrow."

"It will be fine. I'll make it, don't worry."

The wind groaned in the chestnuts. Brown and gold leaves shuddered down like tiny mittens.

"Don't let's be sarcastic," Amanda said. "We'll have a storm tonight."

These nonsequiters were like signal markers in a disastrous conversation.

"It's amazing what telling bullshit comes out of people's mouths when they've had a failure. One thing is for sure." Roberts looked away at the windows. At nothing. "I'll never forget you."

"Don't say you'll write," Amanda told him. She finished her cigarette and immediately lit another. "It's so uncommonly silly to say we'll remain friends when, after all, there's going to be an Atlantic Ocean between us and we have almost nothing in common and I've never understood you in the first place."

Roberts noticed the sudden flush of cruelty on her cheek, a blush of red. The smoke from her cigarette rose to the ceiling and hovered there like an angel of doom. "I feel so old tonight," she continued. "I feel as though I'll never have sex with a man again. I'd join a convent if I thought it would do any good. Damn you anyway."

Roberts surveyed the room, a sailor seeking his longitude. The ceilings were molded in the old Victorian style, and there were books in every cranny and nook, shelves of books, old hunting prints, a gently frayed woven rug done in pearl and blue. Now the windows hummed with rain.

"Not a convent, please," he said.

"I mean it."

"I'll be in Miami tomorrow afternoon," he said stupidly. It was another nonsequiter, called for in the script. This was a badly acted scene, no drama, no climax. "I'll write," he said, just for spite.

Amanda wiped her eyes. They were tearless as yet, but she always wanted insurance. He had told her so many times.

"It isn't like the movies, is it?" she asked him.

"I don't know. Not really, I suppose."

"You say tomayto and I say tomawto. You say potayto and I say potawto. Let's call the whole thing off. But they don't call it off. They swoon before a moonlit ocean, then there's a crescendo, and together they waltz across the deck arm in arm."

"Try not to worry," he said. "I can't think of a single thing we agree about, from poetry to politics. Not a solitary shred of existence charms us mutually. We have no instance of a shared moral stance."

"You're joking, you ass, am I right?"

"Of course I am," he said. "I feel like a shit and I don't know what to say. This is your home and it isn't mine. You have your London life and I have my American life, and as you say, there's an ocean between. We're middle-aged and nothing fits, and because we've worn everything we own for so long, it has become comfortable as hell. A person gets used to his old shoes, even if they're ugly. Your pants fit and another pair doesn't."

Amanda pretended to think. A bus roared downhill on the Park Road.

"Balls," she said. "I'm grumpy and I'm tired." She poured herself a shot of neat whiskey from a bottle of Bell's. With both her elbows on the teak coffee table, she drank it in a single gulp, choked slightly, then set down the glass. "You'll take care, won't you? Do you know what you'll do?"

"Go back to Colorado eventually," he said.

"I'm sorry, you know."

"So am I," he said honestly.

"Do you want to go out tonight? Are you hungry? We could go round to the pub for some supper."

"Not tonight," he told her.

"It would be gruesome, wouldn't it?"

"Pretty much so," he admitted.

Amanda batted her eyes at him, self-consciously though, an old trick put through the wringer. "I do think you're a lovely man, you know," she said.

Until that moment, Roberts had felt lucid and well. His sixth sense told him that now an eruption of irrationality was just around the corner, that they would suddenly veer into that realm of pity or remonstrance that had always been a prelude to their most brutal arguments, ugly storms of rage and protest.

"I'm just going to go downstairs tonight and pack," he said.

Amanda poured another whiskey. The rain brushed the windows like silk.

"This is going to sound richly exploitative," she said, "but God, I'd like to fuck you once more before you go."

3

*m*itch Roberts," read the ticket agent from her screen. She was a young Irish woman with proverbially red cheeks and a lush smile. "Destination Miami, Flight 1045. You're confirmed, sir. Checking the luggage and fishing poles?"

The preliminary check-in counter at Heathrow was noisy, an international din of conflicting languages, voices, dissonant ethnic music.

"Fishing rods," Roberts corrected her. "They're called rods, not poles. Sorry."

"I see," the woman said.

The Sunday airport crowds were pushy, organized by hidden authority into walled phalanxes, like Greek helots on the move. Roberts stood on queue for twenty minutes before arriving at the first check-in counter, and he was becoming impatient to go.

Before, precisely at nine o'clock, the radio taxi had come down Kensington Park Road to pick him up, a brilliantly metallic blue Ford Cortina driven by a turbaned Pakistani about fifty years old. Roberts relaxed in the back while they cruised through elegantly lacquered Edwardian realms of the West End, London calmly receding through concentric circles of suburb and square, industrial waste, sudden traces of countryside where red-brick houses alternated with open fields, small garden plots, the occasional inn. Then came the remnants of villages hanging onto their individuality.

Later, they made the motorways, traffic clogged end to end, bumper to bumper, even on Sunday morning.

The Pakistani was polite, an eternal emigrant. He wore his black hair in a net under a turban, and he smelled faintly of curry and peach chutney, of long winters in rooms full of children and coal fire. The interior of the taxi was just as immaculate as the exterior, vacuumed and brushed until the carpet nap stood highlighted in electric splendor. Are you an American, sir? Of course. No, not rich, not on holiday, just on the way home. The questions wearied Roberts for no good reason, and he felt angry with himself for allowing his frustration to grate against the cheerful cabman who was, after all, an innocent, a poor man from Karachi who now lived across the river in Brixton with his eight kids in three rooms. The Pakistani explained that the taxi had been vandalized once by neighborhood thugs, that he was still afraid it might be the target of children throwing rocks. Somebody had painted slogans on the sidewalk outside his flat. The least Roberts should have been able to be was pleasant.

At the airport, Roberts received his ticket back from the agent, stamped and approved, the woman telling him he was ready to proceed through Security. There, he was asked the standard questions and his passport was examined and stamped. He stood in line for another thirty minutes, then passed through a metal detector and walked into the international departure lounge. He sat in an ersatz pub drinking Guinness Stout, smoking a small black cheroot. He walked down a corridor and purchased more cigars at a tobacconist. The lounge was decorated in timeless and impersonal beige, flooded by fluorescence, the late twentieth-century cultural garb of postmodern capitalism that had finally reduced every event to a quantum of information, as empty and drab as evening telly.

His flight was called and he watched while "passengers who needed assistance" were wheeled and led through the tunnel. When he himself finally boarded, he was delighted to discover that his seat was in a row just behind the bulkhead, and on an aisle to boot. For twenty or thirty minutes, he sat in air-conditioned anonymity until, at last, a perky flight attendant wearing a smart blue blouse and skirt, red-and-white silk scarf, unfolded her own bulkhead seat and eased down just in front of him.

He stared at her legs, rudely. For some time, he studied her face, noting the warmly tanned texture of her skin, the full and succulent lips, the upper one like a rose petal. He marveled at the golden throb of her sun-bleached blond hair, her green come-hither eyes. She could have been an Orange Juice poster, or Miss Florida in waiting. No wedding ring, long tapered fingernails perfectly manicured, hands with petal-shaped propensities.

"Please keep me in vodka," Roberts said. "I'm not one of those unruly drunks."

The flight attendant smiled ruefully. Above the seats, a safety film was being shown, instructions for a crash landing, the nearest emergency exit, musings on water ditches, oxygen use, fire. Escape, head down, ditch, burning fuel. It all passed over Roberts in a rush. The passenger next to him was an elderly woman who looked like a professor of art history. She snored peacefully into her big breasts.

"Tough week?" the attendant asked.

"Tough three years," Roberts replied.

They were not rolling yet. The attendant unbuckled her seat belt and disappeared around the bulkhead for a moment. When she returned, she handed Roberts three miniature bottles of Smirnoff. Roberts was so grateful he felt like sobbing.

"Be discreet," she said, buckling up again.

Her nameplate read: Rosemary.

"Rosemary is a beautiful name," Roberts said.

"Are you flirting with me?" she asked coyly. A smile revealed two rows of impeccable white teeth. Perfect in every way.

Roberts nodded imperceptibly, the way he had seen George Sanders do in old movies. Neither an explicit yes, nor an implicit no. An implicit yes, nevertheless.

"Heading to Miami?" she asked.

"Ultimately southern Colorado is home," Roberts told her. "I thought I might go down to the Keys and do some fishing first. I seem to have been cold for three years and I could use some time in the sun. I want to get a tan and catch a bonefish."

"I'm based in Miami," Rosemary said. "Ever been down to the Keys?"

"Once or twice," Roberts acknowledged.

The big jet bucked forward onto tarmac.

"You might keep that vodka to yourself," Rosemary said.

The engines roared. Outside, rain spit against the already streaked Plexiglas windows.

"Oh, I'm a quiet drunk, believe me."

"You'll get wine with dinner, then liqueurs. I could presume to be generous with both."

"I'd be grateful, and quiet."

"What's your business?" Rosemary asked him. "Not that it's any business of *mine*."

They were rolling smoothly now, forcing out into fog and wind.

"I'm a private detective," Roberts said. "I raise and train horses, too."

Rosemary seemed to ponder this reply. On the intercom, the captain was making his welcoming remarks, time of flight, altitude and course, assuring the customers. They seemed to move more quickly through miles of interchanges, runways, crosspoints. Interminable waits then. It seemed impossible to Roberts that man could manipulate this kind of maze in a massive machine powered by jet engines. Why didn't they crash against something and burst into immediate hellfire? What net of ultramodern technology supported this web?

"My last name is Collins," Rosemary said. "I'm in Coconut Grove. You wouldn't have any trouble contacting me in Miami, and I'm off this weekend. Starting tomorrow."

"I must be dreaming," Roberts said.

"Please buckle up, Mr. Roberts," Rosemary said.

They lifted off, suddenly airborne. Roberts uncapped a bottle of vodka and poured fire down his throat.

4

---

*t*he jumbo jet banked right, revealing to Roberts the ribbon of a turquoise Gulf Stream, its pulse tinged by gray. He could see the outline of Florida now, a hazy green thumb of land in the low sun, sand-fringed, with the Everglades lying flat and pale in the heat glaze. They had flown after the sun for eight hours against strong headwinds. Roberts had his own headwind consisting of four vodkas, two glasses of red wine, three strong shots of Drambuie.

Why did his musings feature Bobby Hilliard? Was it the alcohol?

Roberts thought back twenty years to rookie camp in Georgia, where he had heard stories about Bobby. Roberts had been shagging balls for one of the coaches when he overheard some of the players telling how one unlucky day Bobby Hilliard had been struck by lightning near second base, where he stood fielding grounders. It was a dark, cloudy day with the smell of ozone in the air, and all at once there erupted a hideous electrical crack hard and low over Bobby's head. In a whorl of blue smoke, Bobby was thrown twenty yards onto the outfield grass while hail poured down from a bruised and yellow cloud. When they got to him, they thought he was dead, his eyebrows singed to red skin, one of his baseball shoes knocked clean off the field and out into the parking lot, the other onto the pitcher's mound, where it was found by a coach. One of the players swore that he had found a metal cleat from Bobby's shoe half a mile down the road at a liquor store where the team bought beer for long bus rides.

First on the scene was a seventeen-year-old pitcher with a juglike Adam's apple, all arms and legs and knuckle joints, who rushed to where Bobby lay quietly, being pelted by hail. Bobby opened his eyes and said, "If that don't beat all," and dropped dead again.

The doctor said Bobby's heart had stopped for a minute or two that day. The trainer who hurried over found no pulse. It was probably true, then, what they said, that Bobby Hilliard died that day, that he had expired for all intents and purposes, while a phantasmagoric hailstorm pounded his body with balls of ice the size of half-dollars. Rocks of Georgia ice pelted down as the trainer frantically tried to locate life in Bobby Hilliard and failed. Pumping at Bobby's chest, the trainer located a nonexistent heartbeat and almost gave up hope. And then Bobby opened his eyes and said, "Elmer, get the fuck off me, will you?"

First thing into camp, they told Bobby stories. How after lying in that hailstorm, he began to paint his body with daubs of white, making the hailstorm his talisman. They said that Bobby was different after he'd come back from the dead, meaner, if that was possible, harder to read. Whatever happened to him, it was scary. He could be heard after games in the locker room talking to himself in mumbo jumbo. At first base, he engaged opposing players in helter-skelter conversation. He threatened them with violence, he stepped on their feet with his cleats, threw dirt on their uniforms from behind, spit on their heads, allowed the pitcher's toss to first to strike them on their arms and legs and skulls, just for fun, or for ugliness, or because he was knocked off his pins by lightning. And Bobby took to giving his teammates nicknames. He played practical jokes on them until he became a common nuisance in the clubhouse. One pint-sized player he called Turbo. He chummed up to Turbo and then he sewed Turbo's wallet inside his dress trousers. He snipped a tiny hole in Turbo's pockets so that all his change would dribble onto the floor. Others he called Jelly Bean, Jet Head, Stumpy, and Tar Baby. This last nickname caused a fistfight with a black player from Tallahassee who knocked Bobby down and had to be held back by a dozen others.

Being struck by lightning was the beginning of the end for Bobby

Hilliard and his career in baseball. It wasn't the practical jokes—
Bobby uncapping the salt shaker at team supper, guffawing as
mounds of salt poured over mashed potatoes, Bobby throwing pats
of butter onto the ceiling where they stuck, falling later on an un-
suspecting head as the room heated up in the late afternoon. It
wasn't the mumbling to himself on the field or the fights with opposing players that did Bobby in, but something else. It was something profound, even mystical. But it was weird, whatever it was.

The weirdest was what happened at a beer bar in Gulfport, where
Bobby had gone with some of his teammates to drink beer and eat
shrimp after a rookie-league game that first season. One big catcher
from another team was there, and they said that the catcher had
stepped on Bobby's foot after rounding first base that afternoon,
but who knows? When Bobby came into the biker bar, he leaned
on the bar rail with one elbow and observed the bikers and the
biker chicks and the pipe fitters and the roustabouts, and when he
saw the big catcher, he went into a pure daze. He walked over to
where the catcher was nursing his beer at the bar and without saying
a word, he picked up a bottle of Dixie and slammed it down hard
on the big catcher's left hand.

Roberts hadn't been there, but they told him it took over one
hundred stitches to close up that catcher's left hand, a wound that
severed tendons and revealed white bone and damn near cut off
two fingers. The big catcher was gone from the game, unable to
play after that, and Bobby himself was out of the game several weeks
later, just a few weeks after Roberts joined the team.

Roberts remembered seeing Bobby for the first time one hot,
dusty June day in Amarillo. Tall and angular with red hair and a
freckled face, he was taking throws at first, tossing laconic grounders
to the infielders for practice. He looked younger than his twenty
years, lost in the eyes, half-baked. Because Roberts was new to the
club, they assigned him Bobby as a roommate.

Roberts would hear him talking in his sleep. One night after a
game, he watched Bobby break a mirror in the clubhouse with his
right hand. He watched Bobby pace their shabby motel room muttering about his sister who had been killed in a car crash outside

Valdosta, Georgia, one stormy night. One evening after a double-header in Amarillo, Bobby Hilliard spent twenty minutes decorating his body with painted hailstones and proceeded to stroll down the middle of town, stark naked. "Courting that lightning," he told the police, who trapped him like a possum and put him in jail. It was Roberts who bailed him out next morning and took him back to their motel. It was Roberts who'd watched Bobby pack his duffel bag, and it was Roberts who took him to the bus station for the long ride back to Georgia and home.

Some time later, one of the boys told him that Bobby Hilliard had gone down to Miami during the "Gold Rush" and had done really good. Really, really good.

The way the world was going, Roberts could believe it.

5

Waiting in the jetway to exit, Roberts broke a hard sweat. Even so, he felt cold as the closeted air seeped around him, processed molecules that smelled faintly of diesel fuel, sea salt, and baked coral. The line moved, hovered, moved again, and finally he found himself in a brightly painted art-deco corridor dense with recorded salsa music, a polyglot crowd of Caribbeans and South Americans on shopping holiday, rich Latins toting Louis Vuitton luggage, bright-eyed kids with backpacks on their shoulders heading for the Ecuadorian outback, grandpas and grandmas on ecotours. He hiked for fifteen minutes through the harsh phosphorescent glare until he made it to immigration, where he presented his passport and was passed on toward customs. By that time, his inappropriate flannel shirt was soaked through.

He stood in line again while Spanish was spoken all around him. He could hear the roar of jet engines far away. In the vast hall where he stood, there were no windows and the walls were a uniform gray corkboard punctuated by convivial travel posters featuring happy tourists on their way to Curaçao, London, and Munich. He let his weariness exploit these riches of modern travel, a visceral tearing of time zones. To pass the time in line, Roberts watched slim-hipped attendants pull their carry-ons by. When finally he reached the head of the customs line, he was confronted by a blond brute with wide shoulders and a sardonic expression in his steel-blue eyes. The man's

blue uniform looked just laundered and pressed. He took Roberts'
passport and studied it for an inordinately long time.

"You've traveled outside England?" he asked.

Roberts was being pushed from behind by an Indian dervish
about ten years old, male, copiloting a plastic facsimile of Batman
along Roberts' back.

"Africa. Ireland."

"You were in England how long?"

"Three years. Just under."

On either side, streams of people were passed through customs.
Roberts was carrying his luggage and his rod case. He set them
down in frustration. The atmosphere was ultra air-conditioned, as
cold as a meat case in the supermarket. Across the way, coming
toward Roberts, a male customs official was being dragged by a
black Doberman. A woman with brick-red hair followed the dog.
They came up from behind Roberts, and the dog began to growl at
him ferociously. The blond customs agent behind the counter
snapped shut the passport as though he were killing flies. He cupped
it in both hands.

"Would you mind following these officers?" he asked.

"What's the problem?" Robert inquired. He was too tired to be
angry, but he was mystified.

"There are some questions," the customs agent said. The Doberman sat looking at Roberts as though the two might engage in
conversation. "It won't take long, sir," the blond man said politely.

Roberts felt himself being towed by an elbow, his luggage taken
by the woman. At his heels, the dog lumbered gaily, a taffy-pull
jaunt in its step. A mountainside of eyes followed Roberts as he
walked. He caught a fleeting glimpse of Rosemary Collins and her
flight crew, the woman looking fresh and alert in her blue flight suit
and red scarf. She looked as crisp as ice cold lettuce, and Roberts
wondered how she managed.

He felt a hand on his back, gently shoving him inside a nonde-
script, windowless gray room, light-blue carpet, a circle of chairs
around a metal table littered with customs forms, charts, a pair of
handcuffs.

"Just sit down please, sir," the redheaded woman told him. She lifted his bag onto the table.

"What's going on?" Roberts asked.

"You fit a profile," the woman agent said. She seemed to gnash her buck teeth like a rutting mule deer. "Do you mind?" she continued, gesturing at Roberts' luggage. He shrugged. He knew it was only a matter of time before they found the gun. "It's routine," the woman said.

"This is ridiculous," Roberts commented.

The woman said, "Don't give me an attitude."

"I don't have an attitude," Roberts told her testily. "I have constitutional rights."

"Not here you don't," she said.

"I have rights everywhere I go," Roberts replied.

The dog sat propped on its rump, observing Roberts. It was useless to resist, so Roberts produced the key.

"You're in a customs zone," the woman said. "Right to search anytime, anywhere, for any reason."

The male agent had found the weapon and was unwrapping it from its black plastic and newsprint. He studied the parts with all the concentration of a nuclear physicist. It was the barrel of a gun, pure and simple. In less than a minute, the guard had discovered every piece of the Glock and had placed the parts in a rough symmetry. "It's a Glock," he said. "Nice weapon, actually. Ammunition is probably in the lining."

"Come on," Roberts pleaded.

"Tear it open," the woman instructed.

"Don't bother," Roberts said. "Look, I have a permit for the weapon, issued in my home state. It isn't illegal to transport it broken down in my luggage. I'm sure of that. It isn't dangerous. I checked the bag through. It's done all the time."

The male agent gleefully ripped open the lining. Roberts took his permit out of his wallet and dropped in on the table. Behind him, he heard the crackle of a walkie-talkie as the redhead reported in. Roberts could hear her call for the FBI on-site team. The lining of his leather suitcase was ragged, the side pockets stripped clean.

"I want a lawyer," Roberts said, half-jokingly.

An FBI agent arrived in ten minutes. He wore a rumpled seer-sucker suit and a red bow tie, a straw hat with a sweat-stained crown, black shoes that were scuffed and unpolished. His face was red-flushed with the heat, as though he'd been outside drinking gin gimlets for hours. Roberts was impressed by the blasé cruelty in his expression.

"So, you want a lawyer?" he asked Roberts.

"That's right."

"You don't get one in an international customs zone," the FBI agent said.

"Don't make me laugh," Roberts said.

"Do I look humorous to you?"

"In an egg-sucking kind of way," Roberts admitted.

"Oh, that's good," the agent said. "Let's strip-search this funny man and see what's up his ass."

6

the agent told Roberts his name was Lawrence Littrow, "ou" as in ouch. For starters, he wanted Roberts to know that he'd been assigned to both Atlanta and Dallas, and that he'd been through all the big ones, the aftermath of presidential assassinations, child murders, all the conspiracy theories in the world, and from what he knew of the men who toiled in the Agency, they were hardworking guys with families who had the good of the American people, blah, blah. "Guys like you can't understand guys like them," Littrow concluded, escorting Roberts into a drab room that looked like a gas chamber where they put puppies to death at a suburban vet clinic. Littrow took off his seersucker suit coat, revealing his automatic handgun holstered just above his right hip. Roberts sat and listened to canned salsa drip from speakers outside the door, a reminder of rum, sun, girls, freedom on the high seas during a blue island day. Barefoot pagans danced in grass skirts under a sliver of silver moon. Again, there was the jumble of walkie-talkie noise and police-speak.

"Let's strip him down," Littrow said to another agent.

Roberts swallowed hard and took off his flannel shirt, his chinos, his boots, standing in the cool air in his socks and his underwear. The temperature in the room had to be around sixty, and goose bumps appeared on Roberts's skin. When the door opened, a man about sixty-five with a balding head and rheumy, penetrating eyes stepped inside. Wearing yellow latex gloves and a blue smock, he looked like the executioner of those unwanted suburban puppies.

"Bend over," the man said.

"Call me up on the computer," Roberts said. "You'll see I'm clean. And I want my gun back. It's legal."

"I hope you're right," Littrow said. "Just bend over and drop them."

Roberts leaned forward on the table, his head just touching it.

"He's a profile?" the bald-headed man asked.

"Don't hurry," Littrow answered.

The two men laughed, sharing a joke, a pleasant experience at Roberts's expense. Roberts felt the doctor probing around inside him, pondering his cavity. When it was finished, Roberts pulled up his shorts.

"Too bad," Littrow said as the doctor shook his head.

The bald-headed man left and Roberts was alone with Littrow and his sidekick.

"I could have you x-rayed," Littrow said.

"Go ahead," Roberts told him.

"All right, asshole," Littrow said. "Get out of here. Go on, get out of here."

When Littrow had left, Roberts put on his clothes and stood quietly and alone for a while, allowing his anger to ebb. Outside, the redhead escorted him back to the customs area, where he repacked his torn suitcase. He assembled the Glock and made sure every section was accounted for. Then he rewrapped each section in newspaper and hid the pieces back in his bag. He strapped the bag and heard the Doberman growl behind him.

"Have a nice day," the redhead said. She flipped at the dog's chain and the Doberman sat.

Roberts walked out into the lounge area. He went down two separate corridors bustling with life, across rampways, up and down escalators, through beige tunnels howling with chattering cruise-ship passengers snapping photographs of everything in sight. He merged into a cavernous hall, disoriented and tired.

"I wondered what happened to you," someone said.

Roberts caught a whiff of delicious perfume. A foot or two behind him, Rosemary Collins stood streaming good American values, her dimples puckered at the corners of her mouth, a Miss Florida smile at four hundred watts.

"I fit the drug-courier profile," Roberts said.

Rosemary Collins was pulling a portable carrier, and together they moved slowly through the milling throngs. She was taller than Roberts had imagined her from the airplane, though her movements were as natural as wave power on a deserted beach.

"There's a lot of smuggling here," Rosemary said. "The flight crews are always being searched, planes delayed, all sorts of fiddle-dee-dee. I've had to wait hours onboard a craft while they dismantled every piece of cargo."

"They stripped me down," Roberts said.

"Oh, that's different, of course." She pouted politely.

"It's all right," Roberts said, beginning again. "I was overdue for a prostate exam anyway." He was glad to see her laugh warmly.

"Still going to the Keys?" she asked.

"I'm supposed to have a rental car ready for me."

"You're not renting a compact, I hope. They're not safe in this traffic."

"Believe it or not, I've got a good-sized Buick. I'm going first-class for now."

Rosemary Collins actually bit her tongue for Roberts, then showed him an itsy-bitsy twinkle.

"I know a place for drinks," she said. "If you feel at loose ends, you could relax there."

Roberts put down his bag and rod case. "I could use a drink," he lied. "Maybe I couldn't, but it sounds fine."

"Perhaps we could meet?"

"I'd like that," Roberts said.

"Let me go home and freshen up," Rosemary Collins said. "I could come and meet you at a place called the Tropical Lounge, just off LeJeune near the golf course. It's only about five minutes away. Do you think you can find it?"

"I can find it," Roberts told her.

"Just wait for me in the parking lot, okay? I don't like to walk into bars alone. I'll be along. I hope you've got express check-in."

Roberts told her the name of the car-rental agency and said he'd hurry along the process. Rosemary said she'd slip down to Coral Gables and put on a skirt.

Roberts watched her wiggle across the polished floor of the Miami-Dade International Airport, her rear end in surrealistic rhythm with the high-tech salsa grinding the air.

7

*I*t took the better part of forty-five minutes, but Roberts got the luxury car of his dreams: black, streamlined, green switches, knobs, dials, and meters. Automatic windows, headrest, and seats. Antennae. He paid with his credit card and walked out of the airport down a ramp to the pickup-and-loading zone, where dozens of airport buses, taxis, private and public limousines whooshed by in a blue haze of diesel smoke and blowing dust. The air outside was thick with humidity, and all the palm trees seemed wilted by pollution.

Roberts waited for his car to be delivered, and totaled up his worldly goods. One thousand one hundred dollars in cash, all in hundreds, a credit card, some credit at a feed store in Trinidad, Colorado, and an abused line of credit at a small-town bank near San Luis.

As he waited for his dream Buick, he observed a string of wilted palms lining a mile or so of chain-link fence, in the near distance some pastel warehouses and hangars, a bud of cumulus cloud building up to the east where the ocean ought to be. For all the traffic and humidity, the air was breathable, barely. Finally, a young man in a Power-Ranger T-shirt drove the Buick up, and Roberts turned out of the airport toward LeJeune through slow traffic in the gathering twilight. He had given the young man a five-dollar tip and was told that the Tropical Lounge was not more than five minutes straight down the canal. It was rush hour, and it took more like thirty minutes of stop-and-go crunching, and he had to pay a toll. While he drove, Roberts rolled down the windows and listened to merengue from a Latin station in Delray Beach.

All at once, he felt happy and relaxed, as though he hadn't a care in the world. He listened to "Tia Maria," a salsa number featuring dozens of horns and a loud electric piano. Now big thunderheads in the east were shaded purple and gold, the bottoms tinted by a setting sun, the air laced by the scent of hibiscus and salt water. To his right, the Tamiami Canal cut gray-blue straight through the heart of Miami itself, white egrets poking in sewage for a meal. The evening wind had commenced, and it was knocking the palm fronds into a frenzy. Outside the airport, Roberts caught LeJeune at a stop-light and went south past the municipal golf course, where old men in Bermuda shorts were still plunking the white ball a few yards at a time. From under an expressway, he caught sight of the Tropical Lounge on the corner of a busy intersection. Its walls were pink-and-green stucco. Its roof was green italianate tile. It had porthole windows and the statue of a Tiki idol out front beside a covered walkway.

Roberts cut across two lanes of busy traffic and darted his Buick into the parking lot. Flowering hibiscus and a dense oleander hedge surrounded about sixty spaces. There were exactly four cars in the lot, two fancy German sedans, a pickup truck, one silver Mercedes. Roberts stopped in the back of the lot, away from traffic, where he thought he could hear the music on the radio better. He lit a cigar and adjusted the headrest and sat smoking with one arm over the door. He thought he was about to fall asleep, when he felt something cold on the back of his neck.

"Take it easy," a voice said. "Nice and gentle."

Roberts fought his fear and tried to snatch a look at the source of the voice in his side-view mirror. Blue ski mask with holes for the nose, ears, and mouth, dark bushy eyebrows, black leather jacket, and tan pants. Something expensive and well-pressed about the guy, not like the usual mugger at all. He was holding a chrome-plated .357 Magnum. Roberts thought the guy might have a beard and be darkly complected. He caught sight of a mole on the lower lobe of the man's left ear.

"You're the boss," Roberts said quietly.

"Get out of the car slow. Don't turn around."

Roberts opened the door and got out. He felt himself being guided by the gun barrel, his wallet being lifted.

"That's all there is," Roberts said.

"Walk down the hedge," the man said. "Don't turn around. Don't fuck this up."

For a moment, Roberts considered going for it. Quick turn, kick, grab, punch. He did take a sidelong glance in the mirror again and then moved down the line of hedge. His stomach was squeezed tight against itself, into an existential ball about the size of an isotope of strontium 90. At any moment, he expected to hear the whizzing-fly buzz of a bullet entering his brain, then quiet. He expected to see the searing light of nothingness ahead, all quiet on the Western Front. He continued to walk slowly until he heard the car door slam and the sound of an automobile engine. He turned long enough to see his Buick disappearing into the heavy evening traffic on LeJeune.

Roberts took a deep breath in order to stop shaking. He walked over to the Tropical Lounge, went inside, and was immersed in a Polynesian atmosphere. Rattan chairs and tables, rattan bar with rattan stools, Tiki-themed murals on the walls above luxury booths trimmed in imitation leather. He took a seat at the end of the bar and waited until the bartender had finished serving a tanned male twosome dressed in matching green-khaki survival gear. Probably belonged to the silver Mercedes, he decided.

"What'll it be?" the bartender asked. He was a stocky kid in his twenties, bearing a resemblance to Bob Crosby.

"I need to use the phone," Roberts said. "I just got mugged in your parking lot and I lost my cash, credit card, and car. My luggage and fishing gear are in the trunk."

"No shit?" the bartender said.

"No shit," Roberts answered.

"Hey, too bad. Okay then." The bartender walked to the end of the counter and came back with a cell phone. Roberts dialed in 911 and told his tale.

The bartender watched. "It'll be hours," he said.

"What do you mean, hours?"

"Hours, you know. Hours before the cops come. Hey, it's Miami, crime capital USA."

"That's just great," Roberts said.

"Hey, are you gay?" the bartender asked.

"No, I'm not gay."

"Well, this is a gay bar."

Roberts thought this over. "You have a phone book?" he asked finally.

The bartender brought over the book. Roberts spent a few minutes trying to find Rosemary Collins in Coral Gables, but came up blank. He punched information on the cell phone, but there was no listing, and nothing unlisted either.

"I'll spot you a brew," the bartender said.

"I'll just wait outside," Roberts told him.

"Suit yourself, cowboy," the bartender laughed.

8

above the steady pulse of hot salsa music and the din of recorded flight messages, warnings, announcements, Roberts could barely think, let alone hear. He was facing a nervous car-rental agent who kept eyeing him as he tied up the business phone.

Roberts could barely follow the connivings of a nameless bureaucrat on the other end: "I'm sorry, Mr. Roberts, we can't reissue that card until reapplication. You must confirm new employment and address. Besides, another couldn't be issued for several days in any case."

"I'm stuck in Miami. I have no money."

"I understand. I'm sorry."

"I don't have any cash, don't you hear? My money and my rental car were both stolen. I have no clothes."

"Your card has been inactive for years."

"I just used it to rent the car."

"Our mistake."

"Your mistake?"

"Those are the rules."

"What rules?"

"Inactive cards must be updated. This card should have been canceled, but it wasn't. It was overlooked. Now, you'll have to reapply for another card."

Roberts had been having this argument for ten minutes. The

restless car agent reached for the phone. Roberts backed off, still trying to get a card.

During the evening, he had waited under the awning of the Tropical Lounge. Two hours later, a Miami cop named Martinez had pulled into the parking lot and offered to make a report. The two men sat in sweltering heat, listening to the sound of steady traffic along LeJeune. Martinez had explained to Roberts that upward of fifty cars a day were stolen in Dade. Sometimes more. Lots more in the Metro. Besides, it was just a rental, wasn't it? Roberts had sat in the back of the cruiser listening to the police radio, filling out a written questionnaire. He'd thought about mentioning Rosemary Collins to the cop, but he'd realized he might be paranoid, or that it would be futile in any case. Eventually, Martinez had dropped him off at the car-rental agency at Miami-Dade International.

While Roberts argued his case with the credit-card voice, he kept having sensations of metal against his neck, a man in a dark ski mask behind the barrel, black leather, and heavy-duty adrenaline. Then there was the mole on this guy's lower left earlobe.

"You don't get the fucking picture!" Roberts shouted into the mouthpiece.

"Oh, I sympathize," said the voice. "I trust there is someone you can wire for cash. Perhaps you have friends in Miami."

The car agent grabbed for the phone again. Roberts hung up and leafed through the phone directory until he found a listing for B. F. Hilliard Enterprises, an address in Bay Harbor.

Roberts wrote down the number and address on a pad and thought back to Amarillo, twenty years earlier, Bobby Hilliard standing in a shabby motel room packing his duffel bag, ready to go home to Georgia. Roberts had driven Hilliard over to the downtown bus station and had waited with him in the departure lounge until the bus was ready to load. He could see Bobby Hilliard in his mind's eye, angularly tall, snake muscles in his forearms, beaklike nose, unruly red hair with a cowlick in front like a fan. Roberts remembered seeing him in jail, his body covered with white dabs of paint, the mythical hailstone mementos of his encounter with

God. He remembered Bobby Hilliard sticking his head through the bars and cursing the police who'd trapped him in an alley and arrested him. They heard the bus called and Hilliard got on. He took a seat and opened a sliding window. Looking out at Roberts, he had said, "I'm making the big leagues." He had a southern drawl, something tight as wire in his voice. "Hey," he said, "I won't forget you for this." Roberts could think of nothing special he'd done. Driven a guy to the bus station. He'd walked over to the bus and shaken Hilliard's outstretched hand. As the bus backed slowly out of its stall, he'd offered Hilliard two thumbs-up, a last gesture before good-bye.

Roberts took back the business phone while the car agent wasn't looking. He punched in the number for Hilliard Enterprises, but got a recorded message and an emergency number. He touched in the emergency number and breathed deeply.

"Hilliard," a voice on the other end said. "Speak to me."

"Bobby Hilliard?"

"Who wants to know?"

"I don't know if you remember me," Roberts began, "but my name is Mitch Roberts. Third base in Amarillo."

A brief silence made Roberts uneasy. "Sure, I remember you. You in Miami?"

"I just flew in from London. Some asshole stole my rental car, my fishing rods, my luggage, all my cash, and my credit card. I'm kind of stuck."

"Welcome to Miami," Hilliard said.

"That's what everybody says," Roberts replied. He waited two beats. When nothing came back, he said, "Anyway, I wondered if you could help me out. I'm in a big jam and I know it's Sunday night and I know it sounds like bullshit coming from somebody you haven't seen for twenty years, but I'd like to borrow a hundred bucks. I've got a plane ticket to Denver, but I could use the cash to buy some clothes. I could take a bus home from Denver even. I'll wire you the money when I get to Colorado."

"Wow, a hundred bucks," Hilliard said calmly. "You at the airport? Grab a cab and come over."

"I mean it. I don't have a dime. Maybe fifty cents. I haven't looked in my shoe yet."

"That's pretty bad," Hilliard said. "I tell you what. Grab a cab, come on over, and I'll pick up the taxi fare. We can talk."

"Why don't I just hop the next flight? I don't want to get in your face on a Sunday night." Roberts hated to put the touch on Hilliard, but he wanted out of Miami. "I was planning on going down to the Keys for a couple of weeks of fishing, but that washed out in the parking lot of the Tropical Lounge."

"That's a fag joint," Hilliard said.

"It's a long story, Bobby."

"You're not a fag, are you?"

"I've got references if you want," Roberts said.

"That's good," Hilliard said. "Grab that cab." Then he mentioned a home address on Bay Harbor Street, across the Broad Causeway in Bay Islands. "After all, I owe you something for Amarillo. You'll have to buzz your way in the gate. I'll be waiting for you."

Roberts said his thank-you's and hung up. He walked out the main concourse and hailed a taxi. On the long ride away from the airport, he tried to calculate his need. Maybe with a hundred, he could buy some underwear and a bus ticket down to Pueblo. With two hundred, he could buy some jeans, socks, and a clean shirt. This time it would be crazy Bobby Hilliard putting Roberts on a bus for home. It was a wild world all right, a world full of clichés.

Roberts opened the taxi window and breathed in hot night air.

9

*t*he moon had risen and was bathing a cumulus bank with its tinny glow. On an elevated path of the 36 Expressway, Roberts could see downtown Miami and its fiery blocks of glass and steel. For miles, the taxi seemed to cruise amid low stucco houses painted pink, blue, green. They drove up an overpass and Roberts suddenly could see the ocean spread out like a great slab of sheet metal, a dark-gray dance in cold moonlight. At Highway 1, they turned north, heading through the suburbs of Little River, Miami Shores, past Biscayne Park with its evening strollers, and then turned back west across the Broad Causeway to Bal Harbor with its collection of yachts. Roberts smoked a cigar as they went, letting the smoke curl away and the hot wind stroke his face. He considered the salt smells and the gaudy necklace of neon around Miami Beach and the steady stream of Rolls Royce and Mercedes Benz automobiles pouring out of the fancy hotels and discos, this richly fabricated fairy world for the sleek and the beautiful.

When they got there finally, Bay Harbor was surrealistically quiet, almost sedate, with its ornamental hedges and shaded stands of Norfolk pine, towering palms, stucco walls that hid unknown palaces of pleasure and light. The Jamaican taxi driver cruised the streets, muttering that he couldn't see any addresses.

"This be it, man," he said at last.

He stopped the taxi on a drive lined by oleander and flowering hibiscus. A wrought-iron gate faced them, a security camera affixed, its one red eye agog. Roberts stepped out of the taxi and matched his address with the gold-tinged brick address beside the gate. He rang the security buzzer and told an answering voice who he was. The gate clicked open, Roberts got back in the taxi, and they eased through, the gate whisking shut behind them. It was impossible to say how much green lawn confronted them, an acre or two at least, a profusion of royal palms, a macadam drive with potted plants in the median. At the end of the drive was a two-story, Spanish-style stucco mansion, red-tiled roof, raised flagstone porch, gun-turret windows, wrought-iron railings around balconies from an opera fantasy. Roberts asked the driver to wait while he went up the steps and rang a bell.

Crazy Bobby opened the door. Dressed in white cotton pants, an island-print silk shirt, huaraches, he seemed taller to Roberts, though the rest of him was the same. The eye was cold, the muscles in his arms like tortured snakes. Hilliard had grown a wispy red beard.

"Time flies," Hilliard said.

Roberts smiled. They shook hands and Roberts could feel the steel grip he remembered. Bobby Hilliard would have made a good first baseman if he hadn't been so crazy. Isn't that what everybody had said?

"Hey, I know this is short notice," Roberts said.

"Go pay the Haitian," Hilliard told him. He held out a rumpled twenty-dollar bill.

"He's Jamaican," Roberts said.

Hilliard cocked his head, robin-style. Roberts took the twenty and walked to the taxi. The Jamaican took the money and then backed his taxi slowly down the drive, turned around and went through the open gate. Roberts stood still, watching the Jamaican go, feeling the ocean breeze cool him. He didn't know where, but he knew Biscayne Bay was out there someplace. He could smell it, clean and fresh as a newly laundered sheet.

Roberts almost stumbled into the brilliantly lit house. In one corner of the main room was a baby grand piano. Persian throw rugs had been scattered designer-style, and there were mounds of ersatz colonial furniture. Potted palms, begonias in clay pots. Every square inch of the walls were decorated with Haitian art. Both the north and south sides of the house opened onto vast patios. Hilliard was standing in front of a Haitian primitive, a pyramid of red apples. Roberts sat down across the way.

"How long has it been?" Hilliard asked. "You want a drink or something?"

"Orange juice would be good," Roberts said.

Hilliard went into the kitchen and came back with a tumbler full of ice, fresh juice, a dash of grenadine. "It's been twenty years," he said.

"You have a great place here," Roberts commented.

"Most people like it," Hilliard said. He poured Roberts some orange juice and handed it over. "You said you had fishing plans."

"Not anymore," Roberts said. "If you could lend me some traveling cash, I'll catch the morning flight to Denver. Then I catch a bus, and I'm home."

"You been overseas?"

"London. Three years."

"Doing what?"

"Investigative work," Roberts said, cheating on the truth. Odd jobs. Living in basements. Sucking the breath out of faith, hope, and charity.

"Investigative work," Hilliard said.

"What about you?" Roberts asked. He spread his arms, indicating the expanse of house, its comfort. The paintings and expensive rugs and cut-glass decanter. "Where'd it all come from?"

"Hilliard Enterprises," Bobby Hilliard said. "I opened myself to the world's possibilities."

"I guess the world is full of them."

"If you know where to look," Hilliard said. He had begun to pace, six steps up, six back. "How long did you play ball?"

"Two years," Roberts said. "No-hit, bad arm, lousy field. Other than that, I was pretty good. I loved the game, but love is never enough." He sipped his juice. It was fresh from the tree, with tiny bits of pulp and seed. It had been a long day and night and he was bone-tired. "I got into the detective business by accident. Working for someone else on a lark. Then I stayed with it, doing insurance claims, fraud, some part-time security. I got tired of it and moved to Colorado to train and stable horses." Roberts saw the moon through some of the Norfolk pines. It moved him the way the moon always moved him. "So this," he continued. "Where'd it come from?"

"This?" Hilliard said. He did a pirouette, three hundred and sixty degrees through his domain. "Things blow hot and cold on the Gold Coast. Whatever is hot, that's what I'm into." He turned to face Roberts. "There's a shack out back," he said. "You can crash there. We'll see what happens in the morning. Maybe we can work something out."

Roberts thought for a while, but drew a blank. He didn't want to stay, but he needed sleep. He wanted to leave, but he didn't have any cash.

"All right," he said finally.

"Hey, I owe you, right?" Hilliard asked.

*h*e woke completely refreshed. For a long time he lay in the pale blue light listening to breezes in the pines, the sighing of palm fronds.

When he sat up, he saw someone staring at him through a screened door. She was tall, dressed in a pleated crepe dress of brilliant turquoise and deep cerulean blue, a short-sleeved, molded cotton blouse patterned with beaded orange trees and gilded jaguars. Her dark skin seemed almost luminous to Roberts, as plausible as a dream. She wore her hair at shoulder length, hair that shaped and sculpted every angle of her face, each nuance of bone. Roberts blinked, trying to convince himself that he was dreaming, but she remained fixed in his gaze, an insouciant, fully customized woman, built exclusively for speed.

He had been led down to the "guest house," a miniature version of the mansion, something Hilliard referred to as the "shack." Its tile floors were ocher and gray, and there was a small bar in one corner of the room, a vast leather couch and Spanish leather chairs, a chest of drawers, and a small bathroom with shower.

Roberts sat back on one elbow, wondering exactly what time it was and when the dream would end. Through the open screen of the door, an onshore breeze ruffled the woman's crepe dress. Reflexively, Roberts looked at her ankles.

"I'm not really snooping," the woman said.

Roberts was naked under his sheet. He pushed a pillow against the stucco wall and rested. The woman inched open the screen and worked a leg inside. "Bobby is gone," she said. "I'm Dolores. Dolores Vega."

Roberts told her his name. "Excuse me for not getting up," he said.

"I hope you don't mind me coming down here like this," she said. "I'm in business with Bobby."

"Where is Bobby?" Roberts asked. "What time is it?"

"It's after eight," Dolores said. "Bobby gives you his best regards. He's out doing business. He'll be back later in the day."

"You're his emissary?"

"You could say that. I manage his galleries."

"Bobby has galleries? He didn't say."

"He's not very talkative with strangers."

"That's what Hilliard Enterprises does?"

Dolores Vega laughed. She let the screen squeeze shut behind her. "I don't know about Hilliard Enterprises," she said. "There may be more fingers in more pies."

"What kind of galleries are we talking about?"

"Latin art. Haitian primitives mostly. But he deals in Dominican and Central American work as well. Bobby imports art and sells it to rich people in Florida and New York. You'd be surprised at the markup."

"I guess I would," Roberts said.

He stretched his tired muscles. The warmth of the day was coming over him now, although it had been chilly during the night. His sleep had been plagued by a number of persistent dreams, none of which he could remember. Now, though, he thought he could smell orange blossoms and the aroma of fresh-brewed coffee. Dolores Vega studied him with her dark-brown eyes. Roberts caught her gaze and blinked.

"Actually," Dolores said, "I'm more a baby-sitter than an emissary. I'm supposed to look after you this morning."

"I could use some looking after," Roberts said.

Dolores took two steps forward and balanced back on the edge of a leather couch. She placed her hands on her hips, come-hither style.

"Bobby said you got mugged last night," she said.

"Parking lot of the Tropical Lounge."

"I know the place. Over by the airport."

Roberts sat up against the wall, trying to find a comfortable spot. He was embarrassed for himself, for what was happening under the sheet.

"I know the rest," Roberts said. "It's a gay bar, but I'm not gay. I've never been to Miami. It seemed like a good place for a drink. There was no sex-preference sign out front. Besides, I didn't even make it inside."

She laughed and shook out her hair. "You're lucky," she said. "Some of our tourists never make it home. People get targeted at the airport. Rental cars, straw hats. It all makes them attractive to muggers. Sometimes they get shot."

"It could have happened that way," Roberts said.

"Are you hungry?"

"Famished. I forgot I hadn't eaten."

"Bobby has breakfast made up. Did you just come out here and go to sleep?"

"Took about a minute to fall asleep. I was too tired to worry about food. I came in here to lie down and the next thing I knew, there was a vision haunting me."

"That was quite a speech," Dolores said. "No wonder you're hungry, with an imagination working overtime like that. When did you eat last?"

"Sunday, on the plane."

"Bobby said you came over from London."

"Late-afternoon flight. Hopped off the plane and got mugged."

"Maybe you *should* eat."

"I'd like to take a shower. My clothes are dirty, but I'll manage if you don't mind."

Dolores backed out through the screen. The door was double-wide with pink flamingos in wrought-iron on either panel.

"You'll find T-shirts and underwear in the dresser," she said. "Come on up to the north patio when you've had a wash. Lilly, the housekeeper, will set the table for us. The galleries are closed on Monday, so maybe we'll buy you some clothes to wear. I'll show you the town."

"You and Bobby," Roberts said. "It's none of my business."

Dolores touched her bright-red lips to the screen. Roberts envied the iron flamingos.

"I manage Bobby's gallery in Coconut Grove. Nothing else."

"Sorry," he said. "I'm just curious naturally. I like to see a map before I go on a trip."

Dolores shook a hip at him.

11

a smallish Venezuelan woman they called Lilly served French toast topped with powered sugar and maple syrup, freshly squeezed orange juice, pale pink sliced mangoes and decorative slabs of pineapple. Roberts had showered, but he was wearing his old chinos and hiking boots. Before going to bed, he had rinsed out his socks and underwear, but he still felt dirty.

They sat at the back of the house, and from the flagstone porch Roberts could see wide green lawns, a few pieces of statuary, a tall brick wall painted white. The sky lay still above them like a silk drape, and the air was blue and hot. When he got a good look at Dolores in daylight, he decided she was the most beautifully perfect woman he had ever seen, almost too good to be true.

Dolores poured black coffee into white china cups. Patterned cornflowers ran along the top edges of the cups. Lilly had placed red gladiolas in a bowl on the table. Although the air was hot already, it seemed somehow bearable because of the fresh breeze off the bay.

"Feel better now?" Dolores asked.

"Lilly is a miracle," Roberts told her.

"I did the coffee," Dolores protested. "But Lilly is a real gem. You have to wonder where she learned to make French toast like this. The oranges come from the grounds here. They're good, aren't they?"

Roberts detected a dot of juice on Dolores's upper lip. He agreed with her about the oranges, but he was thinking about something else entirely.

"I didn't know there was this kind of money in art galleries," he said.

"I didn't think you were that naive."

Roberts relaxed with his mango and coffee. Off to the west he could see a complex weave of tile roofs spreading toward the horizon, royal palms, stucco walls painted white, ocher, and beige. Not having eaten for most of a day, the caffeine in the coffee was going to his head. He was quiet, trying to imagine the path that had taken Bobby Hilliard from the dusty streets and jail of Amarillo to the scented exclusivity of Bay Harbor. Surely Hilliard hadn't hopped down from his eastbound bus to land in a mansion. When Roberts ended his reflection, he found himself pondering a magenta-polished fingernail.

"How did you know Bobby?" Dolores asked.

"We played baseball together. A rookie league down south. That was twenty years ago. I joined a team in the middle of a season and they put me in as Bobby's roommate. He played first and I played third. Not long after I joined the team, Bobby left. I put him on a bus for Georgia. Somebody told me later that he had struck it rich in Miami, but I didn't half believe them. I didn't give him much thought until I landed in the parking lot of the Tropical Lounge with a gun pointed at the back of my neck."

"You didn't think Bobby would make it good?"

"I didn't think much about it. I don't know Bobby that well."

"And what about you? What have you been doing all these years?"

Roberts took her through the routine, drifting and fishing, years of private investigation, his recent attempts to raise and train horses.

"And how is your business now?"

"It isn't easy," Roberts said. "Everything is expensive in the horse business, but the income isn't much. Feed, tack, rent, vet bills, interest on the loan. Not many people in my part of the world can afford to board their horses, or to have them trained by outsiders.

So they don't. Most people break and train their own stock. In my part of Colorado, putting food on the table is an all-day job."

Dolores listened intently. She finished her coffee and French toast, then lit a cigarette.

"What about you?" Roberts asked.

"I'm from Santo Domingo," Dolores said. "The great Dominican Republic, you know. I grew up there, went to Catholic University in the city. I knew a lot about Caribbean art, so I came to Miami looking for work. I wanted off the island and into the glamorous life, and just by luck, I ran into Bobby Hilliard when he was looking for someone to manage his first gallery in Coconut Grove. I was cheap, so he hired me. That was almost eight years ago now. He's planning to open another gallery in Lauderdale, on Las Olas. It was supposed to be opened two months ago, but our first shipment of Haitian art was either stolen in Port au Prince or hijacked out of customs here. Bobby thinks our art scout might have stolen both the money and the art. It's a shame. The building has been leased, painted, and all the fixtures are in place. There's been a new cooling and humidity-control system installed for a long time. It cost Bobby a fortune to set it up, and now there aren't any Haitian works to display. Bobby hit the roof when the shipment was lost, but what can we do?"

"You answered an ad and got a job?"

Dolores tapped her cigarette on a cut-glass ashtray.

"I knew some people," she said, "who knew some people who knew some other people. Those people knew there was a gallery being planned for Coconut Grove. I got on the Dominican grapevine and swung it all the way to Bobby. And I was lucky. Miami is a hustler's paradise and we Dominicans are natural hustlers. Not in a bad way, mind you."

"I think I understand," Roberts said.

"So, what *exactly* did you do in London for three years? Bobby told me you'd just come back from there."

"I hustled," Roberts said. "Only there isn't any American grapevine in London. I didn't come up with much to sustain me. If I'm going to starve, I'd rather do it in the Rockies."

"I know what you mean. I think about Santo Domingo all the time."

"Your family?"

"My mother mostly," Dolores said. "She's a housekeeper. She works hard. My father left us when I was little."

"You go back much?"

"All the time now," Dolores said. "I do some art junkets for Bobby. Airfare is cheap. I have some time."

Roberts pushed away his plate. After the food, he seemed gently weary again, as though he could sleep another few hours. So many time zones having their revenge. He pictured himself lying on the green Bermuda lawn, Dolores scratching his neck with her magenta fingernails.

"You never really answered me," Roberts said.

"About what?"

"Is there this much money in art galleries?"

"Maybe you should ask Bobby," Dolores said. She flicked a wrist to one side and Roberts could see Bobby Hilliard standing in the open French door to the patio, black banlon shirt, dark wraparound sunglasses, tan trousers, beige silk socks. From his left ear dangled a thick leather thong, at the end of the thong a sea-green emerald suspended, funky-scary style.

12

Why do you think they call this the Gold Coast?" Hilliard asked. "You find what's hot and go with it, right?"

The sun had come up over the trees, and Roberts had broken a sweat. The breeze had died, and the pines and palms were still.

Roberts flashed back twenty years. The team had been playing in Gulfport, a grubby waterfront town and they were staying in a cheap court motel north of town, four dirty walls and two dirty single beds and enough cockroaches in the bathroom to fill a bushel basket. Sheets that stank of Lysol, cans of bug spray instead of packets of chocolate hearts.

One night they had taken the team bus to a minor-league stadium where several hundred redneck fans had been anticipating the evening by drinking whiskey and chasing it with beer. Roberts was new to the team, and so he sat in the dugout and watched the game. It was his first taste of many nights like that, motels on back roads, meals of grits and fried eggs, the long curve toward failure revealing itself slowly. He remembered the night vividly, the air hot and dank, and a powder of gray moths overhead like a dust storm on the high prairie, insects that peppered the players like snow and got in their eyes, while out over the ocean, huge dark cumulus clouds unleashed their sheet lightning as storms moved and circulated. That night, Bobby Hilliard was playing first base, the Bobby Hilliard that Roberts had just begun to hear about, Crazy Bobby H, an insane guy who was subject to sudden fits of violence and muttered to himself and got into fights. Roberts had watched Hilliard warming up by tossing looped throws to his infielders, Bobby moving lithe as a panther around the bag, scooping balls out of the dirt and darting hard throws toward home. Hilliard sometimes had looked a little awkward, but he had a certain grace as well, an implicit power.

In the third inning that night, Hilliard got into a shoving match with a stocky Gulfport outfielder who had reached first on a chopper. Roberts marveled as Hilliard leaned against the guy, shoving him off balance, stepping on the instep of his foot with a cleat. Roberts watched while the pitcher whirled and threw to first, just as Hilliard blocked the runner into the ball, grinning as it whacked into the guy's back, knocking him down. In a way, you had to admire Bobby for doing it, a dirty fighter, a dirty ballplayer, a dirty politician, all evoking the kind of long-distance charm peculiar to dirty men at work. But it seemed so personal to Roberts, so useless, so utterly unenjoyable. That night, Roberts had wondered what was going on inside Hilliard's head. He wondered the same thing now.

"You look hot," Hilliard said. He sat down at the table and nodded to Dolores.

"London this isn't," Roberts said. "I'm used to cool and rainy and dark."

"Mr. Roberts slept until almost eight," Dolores said.

"I thought it was later," Roberts said. "This light is entirely different from England's."

"Lilly fixed breakfast," said Dolores.

"I appreciate it, Bobby," Roberts said. He tried not to stare at the emerald dangling from Bobby's left ear. "You live here alone? You married? Catch me up."

"Just me and Jimmy Glide," Hilliard said.

"Jimmy is Bobby's alter ego," Dolores said.

"Whatever the fuck that means," Hilliard said sharply. "Jimmy is cool. Don't bother Jimmy and he don't bother you. Ain't that right, Dolores?"

"Just a joke, Bobby," Dolores said.

"Jimmy ain't no joke," Bobby Hilliard said.

"I could have said worse," Dolores said.

Roberts shifted his weight uneasily.

"Yeah, like what?" Hilliard asked the woman.

"I could have said Jimmy Glide is the bat who sleeps upside down on the second floor."

"Jimmy has qualities," Hilliard said.

"What qualities?" Dolores asked him.

"He's stand-up, that's what," Hilliard replied.

"So, bring me up to date," Roberts said.

Hilliard turned his face to the sun. His skin seemed paper-thin in the direct light. Roberts could tell that wheels were turning in his head, well-oiled wheels that moved without any squeaks. The sun was glinting off his sunglasses, movie-star style.

"Yeah, the long years," Hilliard said. "I got on that bus and went home to Valdosta. Then I got on a bus to Miami. The rest is history, ain't it?" He began to drum his fingers on the table. "You treated all right here? Anything you want?"

"Just fine," Roberts said. "If I could get a couple of hundred, I'd ride over to the airport and catch the next jet to Denver."

"So, you catch *me* up," Hilliard said. "On the long years. As they say."

Roberts tried to run Hilliard through twenty years of history as fast as possible. Drifting through odd jobs after baseball, a stint in the California fast lane, watching drunken husbands hanker after pink-skinned blondes. "I was down to my last eleven hundred, Bobby," Roberts told him. "Then some guy took it away from me in the parking lot, like I told you."

"Sad, ain't it?" Hilliard said. His face was pointed to the rising sun. "You got your big city and you got your innocent victims." He reached into his pants pockets and extracted a huge roll of bills wadded together with a rubber band. He slipped out three hundreds and gave them to Dolores. "Hey, Dolores, take this guy up to Las Olas and buy him some fucking clothes. You got the day off, am I right?"

Dolores sneaked an embarrassed smile at Roberts.

"Not necessary," Roberts said.

"Oh, necessary," Hilliard replied.

Roberts noticed a dark-complected, heavy-set man standing just behind the French doors. Dark beard, black bushy eyebrows, wraparound sunglasses, and a weight-lifter T-shirt revealing hugely muscled shoulders and arms. Designer jeans, alligator belt, black deck shoes. Roberts got a clear view at the black mole on the lower edge of his left earlobe.

"Jimmy, hey," Hilliard said. "This is Mitch Roberts. Me and him used to play ball together."

Jimmy Glide nodded imperceptibly. "Phone, Bobby," he said.

Roberts was empty of thought. His mind blank like a placid ocean, miles from land. How many guys in Miami had a mole on their earlobe? Five thousand, maybe more? Hilliard rapped the breakfast table loudly with a hard-knuckled hand, then left without saying a word.

13

*d*olores took Roberts to a men's store in Surfside, just down the street from Bay Harbor. When they returned to the house, he was the proud owner of a canary-yellow cotton shirt with orange and blue peacocks woven into the fabric, light blue cotton pants, and a pair of expensive Oscar de la Renta sandals. "He's Dominican, you know," Dolores had told him, holding up the shoes in a prideful pose. They picked up two packages of inexpensive boxer shorts, two pairs of tropical-weave lounge pants, some T-shirts, one gray with a Marlins logo on the front, one dark burnt-orange with a dolphin jumping through hoops, an incongruous alligator-skin belt.

Dolores waited in the mansion while Roberts changed in the guest house into one of the tropical-weave slacks, iron-gray, his Marlins T-shirt, Reeboks purchased at a surfshop on the beach, worn without socks. He came out of the bungalow and walked around to the north patio but couldn't find Dolores, so he circled the house and saw her in the front drive, sitting calmly in her silver Beamer convertible with light gray leather interior, phone, fax, maximum-noise CD player, and an instrument panel that could have come from the space shuttle. She opened the door and he got into the Beamer and they were off in a crunch of gravel.

They drove straight north on A1A toward Sunny Isles. Along the beach, the day was high blue and glazed white with hurricane-season clouds, a hard wind blowing off the ocean, wind that filled the air with bits of blowing sand. Dolores told Roberts that it was typical hurricane-season weather and that several big storms had already formed off the coast of South America, had headed north, then had curved away just in time to miss South Florida. Some had slipped into the Gulf, but had petered out before making it to Texas. Roberts listened to her talk, admiring the calm of her attitude, the way she would tear through traffic, the ocean off to their right, her shoulder hunched as she grasped the wheel like a life jacket.

Dolores reached under the seat and came up with a pair of expensive sunglasses, a pink ribbon around one lens.

"These are from me," she said.

"You shouldn't have," Roberts said stupidly. "You spent way more than three hundred."

"Not way more," Dolores laughed.

She reached in the backseat and came up with a plastic bag. When Roberts opened it, he found a pair of swim trunks, satanic black trimmed in gold. He held the trunks up and examined them, Dolores still smiling, still driving through heavy oceanside traffic. Wind had caught her crepe dress, throwing the pleats up between her legs. Roberts couldn't help but admire the shape of them, legs structured for aerodynamic speed, legs chronically maddening. He put on his sunglasses and modeled them for her. Her own sunglasses were wildly and torturously large, orange frames and smoky-black lenses. Her earrings were carved pineapples, lacquered and hand-painted.

"What's all this?" Roberts asked. "Where are we going?"

"You like to swim, don't you?"

"Sure I like to swim."

"Well, this is my day off. I'm not going to waste it buying clothes for someone without an ounce of fashion sense. I thought we'd have some fun."

"No fashion sense?" Roberts said. "You watch me."

"I have," Dolores said playfully.

Dolores turned on the CD. Along with the roar of the Beamer engine and the sound of the surf, they got heavy merengue, horns, piano, lots of drums. They made their way north, through the forest of white-towered high-rises built along the oceanfront, long panels of dark glass that caught the sun and reflected it back. Everything seemed white to Roberts, white sand, white concrete baking in the heat, the dark-green ocean topped with whitecaps.

While they drove, Dolores told him about her mother, who had cleaned and prepped rooms at the Santo Domingo Hilton for thirty years, seven in the morning until ten at night, five, six days a week, sometimes through Saturday evening, coming home tired with twenty dollars in cash for the day. She had made beds, scoured toilets, emptied trash baskets, done the dirty work of tourism that nobody ever notices. When Dolores had gone to Catholic University in the city, it had been a family tragedy, her mother and older sisters expecting her to snag some rich gentleman from among the elite of Dominican society—because she was beautiful and light-skinned. She was destined, or so they thought, to raise a family and keep her mouth shut when her husband philandered. "Too much Catholic weight for me," Dolores explained to Roberts. They were stopped at a traffic light in the beach town of Dania when Dolores asked Roberts if he'd ever been to the Dominican Republic.

"You should go," she said.

"I'd like to."

"Wonderful people. So much poverty, but so much life. And the riddles and games and proverbs you hear. I could tell you one!"

"I'd like you to!" Roberts said.

"Okay." Dolores laughed. She popped the clutch and they lurched forward. "One day a professor was traveling across a river on a boat with a young boy. The professor asked the boy if he knew how to read and the boy was ashamed and told him no. 'Too bad,' the professor said. 'You've lost your whole life.' After a while, there was a storm over the river, and the boat was caught in a wave and began to sink. The boy asked the professor if he could swim and the professor was afraid and said no. 'What a pity,' the boy said. 'You are about to lose your whole life.' "

"It's a good story," Roberts said.

"Maybe it's a story about Bobby," Dolores said.

"He's the boy?"

"Maybe."

"He can swim in rough water," Roberts said. "And is he crazy?"
"Crazy? Yes, maybe."

The beach on their right was lined with tourist motels and camping spots. Bars, three-story seasonal condos. All the way through Dania, they talked about life in the Dominican Republic, Haitian art, the culture of South Dade.

"There's a state park just north of here," Dolores said. "It's very beautiful and not many people go there during the week. We should enjoy it, no?"

Roberts agreed. He tried to focus on what was happening at the moment, but his mind kept drifting back to Bobby Hilliard. They passed half a mile of antique shops, motels, the huge pale-pastel jai-alai fronton with its neon seahorses and fantastic stucco moldings, a seashell by Dali. Dolores pulled the Beamer off the Federal Highway and drove down a palm-lined lane between two irrigation canals, paid three dollars to a guard in a cypress-plank shelter, and parked near some changing booths. Roberts went to one of the booths, put on his new swim trunks and met Dolores back at the Beamer, where she got some flip-flops out of the trunk and some towels from the backseat. She was carrying a small wicker basket, and wearing her bathing suit. Together they waded a shallow mangrove lagoon and found a shady spot on the sand at the high-water mark. The heavy September wind was raising a surf, throwing up salt spray. The sea looked turquoise, and there were plastic jugs and a reef of refuse about half a mile out. The horizon was like cake frosting, it was that white.

Roberts settled down in the sand. "So, what is it with Jimmy Glide then?" he asked.

"Oh, him," Dolores said. "He's a union guy from Brooklyn. He was a big man in the Baggage Handlers' Union at JFK. My policy on Jimmy Glide is don't ask, don't tell."

Dolores had brought lunch in the wicker basket. Mango-and-crab salad with tiny shrimps embedded in mayonnaise. Crusty French bread, strawberries, white wine on ice. They swam for an hour and ate some lunch. They slept in the shade for Roberts didn't know how long.

14

*I*t was evening when Dolores Vega dropped him off at the Bay Harbor mansion. A badly sunburned Roberts stood on the macadam drive and watched the silver Beamer disappear down the shade-striped lane, green and gold trees barely moving in a slight onshore breeze. The cumulus clouds out over the Gulf Stream had turned coral in color, and hundreds of gulls were circling the inland cypress and mangrove stands. Roberts listened to the sounds of mockingbirds in the trees and then he walked around to the side of the house, carrying a plastic bag with his wet swim trunks. He was tired, but the swim and the sun and the long nap under the palm trees had refreshed his spirits. When he turned the corner of a big hibiscus, he saw Bobby Hilliard sitting alone in a white wrought-iron lawn chair. Bobby seemed hardly conscious, lost in thought, occasionally sipping iced tea.

"Hey, Bobby," Roberts said.

Hilliard tapped another chair with his toe, and Roberts sat down across from the man, both of them in deep shade. The sky was brilliantly backlit by the sunset's kaleidoscopic array of pastels. Grackles had joined the mockingbirds, and the air reverberated with their squawkings. The breeze was picking up as the sun set, ticking through the royal palms.

"You and Dolores have a good time?" Hilliard asked.

"Sure. Thanks for the clothes. I'll pay you back." Roberts's sunburn was hurting him. "I think it's time for me to move on down the road, Bobby."

"How much did you say you lost in the robbery?" Hilliard asked. It was as though he hadn't heard a thing Roberts had said.

"Eleven hundred cash. A credit card."

"You said something about fishing rods."

"Two rods. My good fly reel. I was headed to the Keys. I'll be back another time."

"You come to my town, you shouldn't hurt so bad," Hilliard said. Again, he produced a wad of bills from his pocket and peeled off eleven hundreds. Crisp bills, green as the emerald suspended by a leather thong from his left ear. He spread out the bills on the table near them. "Pay me back when you can," he said.

"I appreciate the gesture, Bobby," Roberts said, "but I don't need the eleven hundred. It's my problem."

"Cops won't help you, man," Hilliard said.

"I don't expect that."

"Take it." One of the bills had blown off the table and Roberts was forced to pick it up. "You like this place?" Hilliard asked. Roberts let the money stay on the table.

"Sure I like it, Bobby," Roberts told him. "It's a terrific place."

"It isn't like on late-night TV," Hilliard said mysteriously. "You ever been up late at night? I can't sleep, so I watch this shit they put on late-night TV. They got ads where a bunch of square-heads are sitting in an audience while some bald guy with a checked suit on tells them how to get rich quick. Borrow money, no collateral, buy buildings with no money down, that kind of shit. Guy says he owns twenty-five apartments in downtown Chicago, got them all with no money down. All the square-heads in the audience are eating it up like dog food. They baa like sheep. Only you don't ever hear the punch line, not right off anyway. Which is that the bald fuck in the checked suit is selling a packet to get you started. The packet costs three hundred bucks cash. No checks, you dig? Money-back guarantee if you ain't rich in six months. The square-heads can't wait to line up and hand over their three hundred. Hey, you think that's how people get rich? You think that's how I got this house in Bay Harbor, down by Biscayne Bay?"

The evening air had turned blue, as if bonfires had been lit somewhere far away and were burning slowly. Once or twice Roberts had noticed Hilliard touch his emerald.

"I don't know how you got this house, Bobby," Roberts said.

"You know how I got rich?"

"I don't know how people get rich, Bobby," Roberts said. "I never wanted money that bad."

"It shows, bro," Hilliard said. He was quiet, sipping his iced tea while mockingbirds quarreled in the royal palms overhead. Finally he said, "Come on. You can't be serious."

"I'm serious, Bobby," Roberts said. "There aren't enough days in the year, hours in the day, minutes in the hour as it is. I don't want to work that hard making money."

Hilliard laughed grimly. "You think it takes hard work, don't you?"

"That's how it looks to me."

"Hey, most assholes get rich by getting lucky. They inherit the dough. They marry it. That's the same as stealing it, isn't it? So, why not steal it up front?"

Roberts bought time by rubbing some sand from his eyes and hair. His burned skin was cooling and beginning to itch. He wanted to go down to the bungalow and take a shower and have another nap and take a cab to the airport or to a motel and get away from Bobby Hilliard. He wanted to breathe mountain air and listen to the pines rattle in a strong downhill wind. He wanted to touch horse flesh and ride through a meadow of mown hay where there were hundreds of yellow butterflies at play. Down deep, he knew he might stay. He might stay because of Rosemary Collins and the guy with the mole on his left earlobe. There wouldn't be any other reason to stay.

"So, how *did* you get rich, Bobby?" Roberts asked at last.

"I fucking stole it," Hilliard laughed. "But hey, that's another story." He turned to face Roberts. "You said you wanted to go fishing?"

"Bonefishing. It's a dream of mine."

"Why fuck things up?" Hilliard asked. He searched his pocket and produced a set of car keys that he placed on the stack of hundreds. "I got a place down in the Ten Thousand Islands. It's a cabin on Dismal Key. You hump down 1 to Islamadora and you'll see a sign by the highway for a turnoff to Jakob's Landing, a fishing outfitter, and a dumpy bait store. Old guy there named Jakob can run you over to my place. He takes care of it when I'm not there, which is most of the time. Puts up the hurricane shutters during a storm. He'll skiff you over."

"Thanks, Bobby, but I couldn't."

"Why not? What you got better to do?"

Roberts didn't answer, not right away. Then he said, "I haven't got any equipment."

"You got eleven hundred bucks, don't you?" Hilliard said. "The keys belong to a tan Bronco out in the garage. It's rusted out but it runs good. Drive it down there and have some fun. I might come down and spend a day. You could show me your stuff. We could hoist a beer. Besides, you wanted to go fishing, didn't you?"

Roberts wanted to fish, only he didn't want to do it with Bobby Hilliard.

"I suppose I could go for a few days," he said.

"Bronco is in the garage," Hilliard said.

"All right, Bobby, I appreciate it."

"Dolores treat you okay?" Hilliard asked.

"She treated me fine," Roberts replied.

Suddenly Hilliard got up, tapped the table, and left. Roberts watched him walk hurriedly around the house, then he went down to the bungalow, where there was a plate of cold cuts, fresh bread, some conch fritters, and a bottle of orange juice laid out for him on a sideboard. He showered and ate alone, sitting outside in the gathering dark, surrounded by fireflies. The sun went down and the moon came up and everything was bathed in silver.

Only later did he go back and pick up the money.

15

*r*oberts was headed south on the Federal Highway well before rush hour. He woke at dawn and left the bungalow, hoping to avoid Hilliard. Dressing in the nearly opalescent morning, he'd stood outside on the small flagstone patio and gazed again at the ornate, Spanish-style mansion, its tile just beginning to catch the first light of the sun, the vast royal palms gently rustling in the morning breeze, while the sky expressed itself in shades of purple and turquoise.

In Coral Gables, he found a family-style café and ate a big breakfast of bacon and fried eggs. He spent some time browsing through a local telephone directory, looking for the number of Rosemary Collins, finding nothing remotely like the flight attendant who'd led him toward a rendezvous in the parking lot of the Tropical Lounge. He finished his coffee, fixing once and for all the picture he had in his head of the mugger: stocky, muscular build, black leather jacket, dark mole on the left earlobe. He strained to connect Jimmy Glide with the picture his memory was producing, trying to clear out the haze hanging between the past and some kind of realization, recognition, any shred of evidence to connect Jimmy Glide to the gun the mugger had pressed to his flesh. Over and over in his mind, Roberts asked himself what a baggage handler from JFK was doing in Miami. He finished his coffee, left a couple of dollars for a tip, and went outside.

The mid-morning sky was already hazed over and hot. Another

humid, hurricane-season day. By ten o'clock, he was in Florida City
shopping for fishing clothes at a rundown mini-mall about a mile
from the highway. He bought several pairs of khaki four-pocket
fishing shorts, wading boots, thermal socks and more underwear,
three long-sleeved work shirts, heavy gloves, and yellow-tinted
glasses for mornings out on the shallow water, where there would
be heavy sea glare. He bought a straw hat for evenings of lazing
around, and a long-billed fishing hat for trolling from a skiff. In a
pile of dollar-sale items, he found some yellow flip-flops, sunscreen,
mosquito repellant, things he knew he could use in Ten Thousand
Island country.

By the time he made it back to the highway, it was nearly eleven
and the traffic had thinned to a reasonably dense crawl across the
long white bridge over Barnes Sound. The water in the bay was
blue, ruffled by a strong late-morning wind from the ocean. He
drove with the windows down and merengue blaring from a station
in Homestead. For the first time in a year, he felt himself unwind.
He felt free. He felt like a man who'd lost everything and who had
nothing more to lose.

Passing Key Largo, he stopped for a limeade. By one o'clock, he
had made it into Islamadora, and it took only a few minutes to
spot the turnoff to Jakob's Landing. The road was of gravel and
crushed coral winding between cypress stands, Key pines, and ragged melaleuca waste. At the end of the road, he found the building,
a cypress-and-cedar shed that had weathered to earth tones and
chipped paint. In front was a shallow-water marina dredged out of
coral. The marina was sumplike and full of diesel fuel and floating
garbage. There was a gas pump onshore and two piers jutting into
the water. The front porch of the bait store faced the sea, looking
out toward Florida Bay, a wide expanse of brackish water dotted by
cays and shoals. Roberts parked in a glen of Key pines and sat in
the car for a while, noticing the quiet. The breeze hummed through
the small palms and he could smell the aroma of bait fish and diesel.

He got out of the Bronco and walked through soft dust to the
side of the building, where he discovered an old man sitting in an
Adirondack chair enjoying the shade. The old man was skinny and

dirty and was smoking a clay pipe. His legs were splayed, and Roberts watched while he rubbed his white beard once or twice. He had jug ears, a red complexion, creased and lined skin, a man who'd spent his life in the outdoors under a hot sun. Roberts kicked up some dust, just to make noise.

"I'm looking for Jakob," he said.

"You've found him," the old man said.

"I've come down to use Bobby Hilliard's place on Dismal Key. I've got permission from Bobby, and he told me you could take me over and show me around. I don't plan to stay long and I won't be any bother. I just want to catch a bonefish and get some serious sleep. Then I'll be on down the road."

"You a friend of Hilliard?"

"I wouldn't say that," Roberts told him.

The old man sucked on his pipe. Roberts squatted down in the dust. He looked at the boats moored to marina pilings. Three old outboards and one rotting cabin cruiser.

"I'm Jakob Liamsson" the old man said, extending his hand. "You'd be?"

"Mitch Roberts." They shook hands. "I thought I'd buy some fishing equipment from you. Or I could rent it if you prefer. My rods were stolen in Miami. Never been bonefishing. Thought about it my whole life. Caught a lot of rainbows, though."

"Rainbow's a good fish," Liamsson said. "Nothing like a bonefish, you ask me." He swiveled in his chair to look at Roberts. "You no friend of Bobby Hilliard, then how'd you come onto this place?"

"I knew him twenty years ago. Haven't seen him in that long. I just happened through Miami and called him when I lost my car and my cash. He offered the place and I took him up on it."

Liamsson got out of his chair with difficulty. He stood looking out at the bay, both hands on his hips. He was slightly stooped, but wiry, and his grip was strong. "I don't mind taking you across," he said. "Dismal Key is thirteen miles or so over yonder." He gestured to the north. "If you don't mind the loneliness and the sand fleas, you'll do fine. The Key is about six hundred yards long, maybe two hundred wide. Most of it is mangrove. The cabin isn't much to look at, but she'll do. Got a wood stove for boiling water and lanterns for light. There's a gas cooker if you're inclined to live dangerously. No electricity. You got to pack over ice and water in coolers. You'll need fruit and rice and plenty of beer. You get scared, you can walk back. Water's only knee-deep. Might not take you more than three or four days."

"Sounds like what I came down for," Roberts said.

"Now that's just flat sad," Liamsson laughed.

16

She was a shallow-drafted ten-footer that had seen better days. On the stern was an ancient twenty-five-horse Evinrude that Liamsson had overhauled a "dozen times," perhaps more if memory served him. Roberts had slept the night in a hammock in back of the bait shop, and he rode now in a fishing chair bolted to the bow. Dawn came up like a vermilion forest fire, chains of red and azure lifting out of the low clouds and staining the sky pink. There was a light offshore breeze and small waves lapped over the gunwale of the skiff, wetting Roberts's tennis shoes. Once they got a mile out, the water turned glassy and soft. It was like moving over the surface of a mirror.

The afternoon before, Roberts and Liamsson had gone to a small supermarket in Islamadora for supplies. Roberts bought five boxes of food, mostly rice, tuna fish, cans of orange and grapefruit juice, two cases of beer, a box of bad cigars, pasta, fresh fruit and vegetables, cans of soup, dried beans, peas, and lentils. Liamsson supervised the loading and he gave Roberts three coolers filled with shaved and block ice, bottles of water, six T-bone steaks, and some hamburger. That night they sat out under the stars and drank beer and watched the ocean turn inside out with color. Roberts slept in the hammock like a monk and woke up as lucid as a little boy.

They shoved off under a tremendous halo of blue light. After an hour on the water, bruised cumulus clouds had built up over the bay. The clouds had purple bottoms and looked like onion bulbs.

Somewhere in the clouds there was a brief display of lightning, then the clouds drifted away and the sun came down hot as hellfire. They passed mangrove cays, shallow pools of sandy water, shoals of yellow-gray sand baking in the mid-morning heat. The colors were dreamingly vivid.

Liamsson sat in back. He was wearing a pair of tattered cotton pants that came down only to his shin bones, a plaid work shirt, flip-flops. Roberts lit two cigars and passed one back to the old man, who clenched it between his bluish lips.

"You know Bobby Hilliard much?" Roberts called back.

Some pelicans began to follow them, lurching up and down on the sea breeze.

"Not much," Liamsson said. Liamsson was a quiet man, and they hadn't talked long the night before. They had played a game of chess and swapped a few fishing stories. Roberts watched the water for signs of fish. He thought he saw several marbled shadows fleeing the boat. Maybe amberjack or bonito.

"You like him?" Roberts asked.

"Not much," Liamsson said. "It ain't no secret."

"He come down here often?"

"Not often."

"He like to fish?"

"He ain't no fisherman," Liamsson said.

"Where'd he get his money?"

"Don't know. Don't care." Liamsson shaded his eyes against the sun. The sky was white now, like a sheet of glass with a lightbulb behind it. "You keep a secret?" Liamsson asked finally.

Roberts told the old man he reckoned he could keep a secret up to a point. Liamsson throttled back and they ran slow over shallow, sandy water.

"That guy ain't much good," Liamsson said. "I ought not to say this seeing as how he's paying me to watch his place. I go over once in a while, mostly when I'm out guiding or fishing on my own account. Check the hurricane shutters, see to it nobody's squatting out there. Which they wouldn't be less they was crazy. Anyhow, Dismal is as far out as you can get and be anywhere. But I've hauled that Hilliard and his kind over there maybe once every few months and I see how they leave the place. Liquor bottles and garbage in the water. Folks get it in their head that the bay is a dump. That's how they treat it. I don't like that trashy kind of behavior."

"He comes down with people?"

"Him and a fellow from Miami."

"Jimmy Glide?"

"I wouldn't know the name. Fellow don't say nothing. Big, dark hair and black beard." Liamsson smoked his cigar and looked at the water. Waves spanked the boat and rocked it as they proceeded.

Liamsson was forced to skirt a shoal, pulling the skiff around to the east for a time. The sunlight lay on the water like gasoline about to burn, and a dozen ragged pelicans swooped in for a look-see. Out of sight of land, they were alone with the Ten Thousand Island country and Roberts couldn't help but feel its power, its absolute dignity.

"They tell me Hilliard owns art galleries," Roberts said. "He doesn't seem very aesthetic to me."

"Drug dealer more like," Liamsson said. He took a long drag from the cigar. "Me and my mouth," he continued. "I shouldn't have said that. Forget it."

"Okay, no problem," Roberts said.

To their starboard, a narrow key of sand and coral rose from the water, covered with nothing more than a fringe of sea grape and mangrove.

"How long has Hilliard had the place?" Roberts asked.

"Three years, more or less," Liamsson said. "Came down to the marina one day and said he'd bought it from some timber outfit that used to own it. Wanted me to take him out. Bought the damn thing sight unseen. Had some woman with him. Nice-looking gal, too."

"Dolores?"

"Didn't get the name. To Bobby Hilliard, I might as well be a cigar-store Indian. Blonde though. Good-looking as heck."

Liamsson throttled up some.

"Am I going to get a bone?" Roberts asked.

"You say you never fished for bone?"

"Just trout. Rockies. Caught some yellowfin down in Old Mexico."

"You got to use steel leader for bone," Liamsson said. "I've brought you down a box of saltwater flies. I'll show you some spots here and there and we can do some practicing this afternoon. After that, you're on your own. Bones get down in the shallows and chase whatever moves. They're hungry bastards and you can catch a few if you know what you're doing. If not, you won't touch one. They like to eat and they're good at what they do, and when you hook one, you'll know you've been in a fight."

"Sounds terrific," Roberts said. "Want to stay the night? Do some fishing? I'd pay you a guide fee."

"Damn it all," Liamsson said. "If I'd have known you were going to ask, I'd have brought some rum."

They shared a laugh and then got quiet for a long time, both of them watching the water and the pelicans and the dots and dashes of sand shoals. After half an hour, Dismal Key appeared straight ahead of them, a green fringe of mangrove, a few ragged palms, some palmetto dunes, and a shallow estuary leading inland. Liamsson toured Roberts around the Key, showing him the best spots for bone, barracuda, a few little bonito one could eat for lunch. He told Roberts that he'd scare up a ray or two walking the shallows, but they weren't dangerous.

It was well after noon when they unloaded the last of the supplies and stacked them on the porch of the cabin. In the noonday heat, they sat in the shade and smoked two more cigars.

"How'd you get all the way down to the Keys?" Roberts asked the old man.

"I was a boy in Norway during the war," Liamsson said. "The Nazis took over and my parents sent me to America." He savored his cigar. A hot wind rippled the water. "These days, there are Nazis everywhere. Flat sad, isn't it?"

17

*t*he cabin on Dismal Key stood elevated on six concrete pillars that had been driven into the hard-packed coral earth. Its dark-cypress planking had been hand-hewn and was so weathered that it had turned the color of rust and was shedding flakes of cypress bark. Fifteen feet square, it had four large windows equipped with hurricane shutters, and the single room inside had been partitioned into a sleeping quarter and a small kitchenette with an icebox, wood stove, and gas cooker. In the common room there was a double bed, a cot, two Adirondack chairs, some old sea trunks, a dining table, and a reading desk. "No toilet, mind you," Liamsson told Roberts again. They had spent half an hour unloading the supplies and had stocked the icebox with fruit and perishable vegetables. They had organized the water and the fishing tackle, and Roberts had unpacked his clothes. "You'll sleep with the sand fleas and wake up with the pelicans," Liamsson laughed as they surveyed their work. "Otherwise, you'll be alone." He had brought up a final crate of soup and crackers and dropped it on the worn pine table. "That is," he said, "unless smugglers come through here at night."

They made some tuna sandwiches, and Liamsson spent time showing Roberts how to light the lanterns, operate the gas cooker, and rig a bonefish line. He opened the hurricane shutters, and the cabin was flooded with afternoon light. Roberts poured some water in a porcelain pitcher and commenced to wash his hands and face, his neck and arms, trying to take the sting out of his new sunburn.

He brushed his teeth and went out to the porch to join Liamsson, who was sitting on the upper step smoking a cigar. From the porch, they had a clear view of the vast southern horizon and the bay, its blue water rippling in the light breeze, a few shoals and cays, the weather as it built up to an afternoon storm somewhere over the Keys. The cabin's roof was made of tin and you could hear it tick in the steady heat of the afternoon. Sand made a spackling noise as it banged against the cabin. Now that the sun was going in and out of clouds, the heat of the day was easing back and the roof began to groan with its cooling-down. Roberts walked over to the estuary and looked at the palmetto dunes. When he came back, Liamsson had finished his sandwich and was rigging a rod.

"You have family here?"

"Never did," Liamsson said. Roberts wondered if he'd detected a wistfulness in the old man's tone.

"My parents sent me off to America. I went to school in upstate New York, where my folks knew a family they'd met in the diplomatic corps. I learned English pretty fast and then I heard my folks had died. After the war, I came down here to work building a bridge and I just stayed on. I learned to fish and became a guide. I guess I've been too busy to get married. Not many women down here then. Kind of an isolated place, you know. I have brothers and sisters in Norway, but we've mostly lost touch. You know how it is. They live in a little town in the north and they go to church. Me, I live way out here on open water." Liamsson began to tie a silver streamer on Robert's line. "You alone?" he asked.

"Pretty much," Roberts admitted. "I've had my chances but they've slid by."

"You came down here when?" he asked Liamsson. He squatted in the sand in the bottom of the stairs.

"Forty-three," Liamsson said. "Wasn't doodly down here then. I was just a boy and it seemed to me that sometimes the sky got so dark with seabirds it was just like night. In those days, there were thousands of snail kites with V wings, bald eagles so big they looked like bombers, woodstorks, woodpeckers, snowy egrets that would make you cry they were so beautiful. You'd look out at the horizon and you'd swear a storm was coming, but it would be those damn birds looking for fish, all in a flock, swooping down, their necks pumping and wings flapping, and they'd go over in a whoosh so loud you'd swear they'd break your eardrums. That's what it was like then. And the fish, too. Now you've got your melaleuca bush some damn fool brought over from Brazil and it's choking the mangrove where all the birds used to live. You got your Miami parking lots and your condo developments and your tomato growers pouring poison into the water, and you got your sugarcane farmers up north chopping the land into squares and fouling the canals, salting the water up so's its no good. And it isn't only me remembers things that way." Liamsson lit a cigar and sat for a while. "I'm sorry I'm so talkative like that. I don't usually speak up that much."

"You want to come fishing tomorrow?"

"Yes, I do," Liamsson said.

"What about the bait shop?"

Liamsson smiled wryly. "I guess it won't be open, will it?"

Roberts laughed and went inside the cabin and poured them some soda on ice and brought the two glasses back outside. He had found the glasses in a hand-hewn cabinet on the wall where there were dozens more glasses, plates, utensils, plastic jars for food storage. When Roberts brought back the sodas, Liamsson had finished rigging a rod.

"I got to get back," Liamsson told him. "Got to shut things down and run some errands."

"You coming back over early?" Roberts asked.

"Not real early," he said. "Bones eat all day."

"I'll be ready," Roberts said.

Liamsson handed him the rod, a nine-footer rigged with steel leader, heavy-gauge line, a box of saltwater flies.

"Here now," Liamsson said, finishing the knot. "See how that works for you."

Roberts walked thirty yards down coral-packed beach to the water's edge. He was wearing fishing shorts, and the splash of the water on his legs angered his sunburn. The sun was low in the west, and an edge of moon was just peeking over the eastern horizon. He touched the silver streamer and unhooked it from the cork handle of the rod and sent the lure soaring into the afternoon air. The lure landed softly and rode the water for a moment, Roberts popping and dipping it to simulate a bait fish. He hauled in and cast three more times, Liamsson sitting on the porch, smoking his cigar and watching. The old man got up and walked down to the beach and stood behind Roberts.

"You've got a fair toss," he said.

"It's a fine rig," Roberts told him.

"She's been called a sea of grass," Liamsson said. "The Everglades, I mean."

"I've heard that," Roberts answered.

"Used to be, too," Liamsson said. "Grass moving in water all the way to Okeechobee. Two hundred miles or more of moving grass in a river of fresh water. Alligator, crocodile, manatee, too many birds to name them. I'd like to kill the man who changed it." He knelt down in the sand, took some of it and sifted it through his fingers. "But hell, it wasn't just one man, was it?"

"It's still beautiful," Roberts said.

"I guess it is," Liamsson agreed.

"But I know what you mean," Roberts said.

"Old men are flat sad, aren't they?" Liamsson replied.

18

*r*oberts discovered the dead Haitians on day ten. He didn't know they were Haitians, but he found out later.

He had slept late that day and had eaten a breakfast of sliced apples and canned mango juice, some crusty rolls that were going stale. About eleven o'clock, he grabbed his rod and a box of streamers and wandered east to the end of Dismal Key, across dunes and palmetto waste, under a blazing sun, and began to work the flats that stretched out three or four hundred yards to another cay much smaller than Dismal. High pressure had settled over the Ten Thousand Islands and the wind was running strong from the east, making it difficult to cast during the day. The shallows were ragged with whitecaps, even in the inlets and estuaries. For an hour, he chased the ghostly bonefish through mangroves, across the light-dappled dunes of underwater sand. He was wearing yellow-tinted sunglasses and he could see the bones darting across the bottoms. Once or twice he spotted some barracuda, their needle noses hard against the surface, slipping craftily through sea grass. He circled a shoal, searching for more bone, the tell-tale shadows and spins of water where one or two would break the surface, then dive and resurface.

In ten days, Roberts had caught dozens of bonefish. He had chased them through the shallow water until he thought he was beginning to understand some of their patterns and habits, their fighting spirit, their predatory awareness, and their evolutionary toughness. He had taught himself to stalk the fish, to stay in a zigzag course across the muck, through razorlike sea nettles, scaring up a winged manta here and there, working the bone for a few minutes, for a few hours. Out here, time stood still under the relentless sun.

He was two hundred yards off Dismal, working a dark brown shoal in water no more than sixteen inches deep. The water was blue-green, and where it was backed by rippled sand, it caught the sun and split each ray into a million shards. On his left, the cay was ragged with dune and sea grape. Roberts trudged fifty yards around the head of the cay to where a stunted mangrove lay low to the northeast, and he saw the bodies piled like rag and bone where wind had washed them up on the beach. A few spindly arms, a leg. The barracuda must have been at the flesh for a long time, because there was almost nothing human left.

Roberts stood ten feet out in the sun, shading his eyes and trying to see. When he splashed closer, he saw the rags as men, their clothes bleached by water and sun. There was a foot wearing a tennis shoe. Another foot wearing strapped sandals. The faces had been erased by feeding barracuda, tips of fingers missing, toes, noses, all gone, the bodies bloated by days in seawater. Roberts knelt for a few moments and tried to think, to quiet his heart. It was nearing noon now, and the wind was dropping as the day became humid and still. He splashed back to Dismal, washed the salt off his body, then made himself a cold soda with the last of the shaved ice and sat on the porch, watching pelicans fly over in a storm of ragged brown wings, feathers, and squawks.

He sat that way for hours. He thought of Jimmy Glide and he thought about Rosemary Collins, and pretty soon he smoked a cigar and thought about the emerald Bobby Hilliard wore on a leather thong from his left ear. Thinking back, he remembered the white daubs of paint on Bobby Hilliard's body those many years before.

Just as it was getting dark and the mosquitoes were coming out, he ate some canned stew and stale bread for dinner. Once the sun had set and the stars had appeared, he walked down to the water's edge and fired off green flares, four of them at ten-minute intervals, then others at half-hour intervals for another three hours. He went back into the cabin and washed again as best he could in his remaining water, changed his clothes, and sat on the porch in his cotton pants, a print shirt, some tennis shoes. He had combed his hair and rubbed coconut oil into his purple skin, which had been burned and burned again.

It was just after ten o'clock when he thought he heard the sound of the skiff. Under the wind, a putt-putt, maybe Liamsson coming over. The moon was high in the sky now, and light bubbled the water with halos and auras. In time, Roberts could see the old man coming into view. Roberts walked down to the water and caught the bowline.

Liamsson hopped out and splashed ashore.

"What's all the fuss?" he asked.

"I found two dead bodies," Roberts replied.

Liamsson rubbed his beard. "I see," he said.

"They've been out here for weeks, it looks like. They're bloated and eaten up bad. They look like young men."

"You find their boat?"

"I didn't see any boat. It could have floated off."

"I don't know about that," Liamsson said. "Not much current out here in the shallows."

"Refugees?" Roberts asked.

"Son, the refugees wash up in Miami."

"You mean?"

"Never mind."

"What do we do?"

"Depends," Liamsson said, rubbing at his beard again. "I could go over tonight and call the Coast Guard up in Key Largo. And they'd tell me to sit tight and they'd be down sometime tomorrow. Or we could forget it for now and do some fishing and I'll run over in the morning and tell them then. I guess we could sit up tonight and drink some rum and talk about the old days. You're the one who should decide." He waded out into the water and dragged his skiff onto dry land. It was dark and there was a heavenful of stars overhead.

"I'm not callous," Roberts said, "but we can't do those guys any good tonight."

"We can't, that's a fact." Liamsson reached back into the skiff and pulled out a double-layered plastic bag full of ice and stone crab. In a paper sack he had a bottle of Barbados dark rum, one-hundred-sixty proof. "You like stone crab and dark rum?" he asked.

"I could get to," Roberts said.

They walked to the cabin porch and sat under its tin awning. Roberts got two glasses and Liamsson poured them each two inches of the dark rum. It had a heady molasses odor. Liamsson reached into the plastic bag and pulled out two claws of crab. Roberts could smell that it had been marinated in lime-and-lemon juice, maybe with a dash of garlic and pepper.

"You said refugees wash up in Miami," Roberts said.

"Yep," Liamsson replied.

"Then what about those guys out there?"

Liamsson drank a inch of rum.

"You'd have to think drugs, wouldn't you?" he said.

"That's flat sad," Roberts said.

19

a Coast Guard launch came to Dismal the next afternoon around three o'clock.

Roberts and Liamsson had drunk dark rum and eaten stone crab until midnight. They sat on the porch steps under the stars and worked over the remains of a sliced bonito Roberts had marinated in lime juice, eating the slices one by one, taking drinks of rum, devouring crab claws on hunks of stale French bread. They smoked cigars, and after the breeze picked up and blew away the mosquitoes, they walked around the perimeter of the Key, talking about horses and fishing.

They had rounded the northeast edge of Dismal and were looking across fifty miles of bay. Liamsson had told Roberts about the big saltwater turtles he used to see before it all went to hell.

They slept until nine, Liamsson taking the cot, snoring like a train all night. After he left in the skiff, Roberts went fishing again, walking off his hangover in the day's heat, then taking a long nap in the shade of the porch. When he woke, he played some chess on a battered traveling set he had picked up in Coconut Grove. Then, about three o'clock as he sat out on the porch, he saw three tiny specks on the horizon: three boats—a launch, a skiff, and a smaller rowboat being towed. When the specks got close, he could see two Coast Guard officers on the deck of the launch, Jakob behind them in a skiff towing the rowboat. As he watched, a third man came from the lower deck of the launch, an INS officer in a green uniform. Roberts went down to the beach and steadied the skiff while Jakob poled the three men into shore. They were introduced around, and then Roberts took all the men three hundred yards east of Dismal to the shallow mangrove where the Haitians were lying dead in a jumble, half in and half out of the mangrove, partially buried in sand. Roberts and Liamsson sat in palmetto shade while the officers dug out the bodies.

Thirty minutes later, a lieutenant came over and knelt down in front of them. He was as clean-cut as a peach, a short fringe of blond hair, bright baby-blue eyes. He seemed barely to have broken a sweat in his short sleeves and duck pants.

"You found them?" Roberts asked him. Roberts had already told them his story. There was nothing more to say.

"How long have you been on the Key?" the officer asked. He was a graduate of the academy, name of Ridley. He shaded his eyes and gazed across the shallows to the cabin.

"Eleven days now," Roberts said.

"See or hear anything at all?"

"Nothing. I haven't seen anybody but Jakob. No boats have been by, no fishermen. Nothing. I haven't heard anything that even sounded like a motor. Those guys look like they've been there a long time."

"You have a weapon here?" the officer asked.

Roberts thought for a moment. The young officer looked away. Roberts could hear the other two men busy bagging bodies, making a search of the beach.

"There aren't any weapons on Dismal," Roberts said.

"Nothing for sharks. Like that?"

"Nothing," Roberts said.

"Mind if we look in the cabin?" he asked.

"It isn't mine," Roberts said.

The officer shrugged. "Two males, it looks like," he said. The glare came hard off the sand, like a white-coral laser. "I'd say at least one was shot in the back of the head. We won't know until an autopsy comes down from Key Largo. You didn't hear any gunshots?"

Roberts told him again. He'd heard nothing, saw nothing. He was fishing for bones, trying to sleep ten hours a day and keep quiet.

"Nobody knows much about you," the officer said.

Roberts had told Jakob a great deal about himself, rum talk under the stars. It was obvious the old man had been discreet to the Coast Guard.

"I know the owner of the cabin, just barely," Roberts said. "I was passing through Miami on my way home to Colorado. I looked him up, and when he found out I was a bone fisherman, he offered the place. I came out here for two weeks. That's about up and I'm leaving."

"You from Colorado?"

"San Luis Valley."

"You got ID?"

Roberts told the officer about his mugging. He said he'd ordered a new driver's license and credit cards, but they hadn't arrived. He had a temporary license that had been faxed to him from Denver.

"We'll be running your name," Ridley said. "It's just procedure."

"No problem. Don't worry about it."

"You say the owner is Robert Hilliard?"

"I didn't say," Roberts told him. "But that's right."

"We'll talk to him," the officer said.

The other men had piled the two bodies in bags along the beach. They were in black plastic.

"No boat," one of the men called over.

"Haitians," Ridley told Roberts.

"You think so?" Roberts asked.

"Looks that way," Ridley said. "Found some letters in a wallet. Map of Port au Prince. Say, you didn't take anything off those guys, did you?"

Roberts said he hadn't. He'd seen them, knelt down for a few minutes, gone back to the cabin and flared for Jakob. Ridley listened and rubbed his face, then splashed back toward the bodies. Jakob squatted down next to Roberts.

"I didn't tell them anything," he said.

"It doesn't matter," Roberts said. "Those Haitians have been dead for weeks. Besides, why would I kill some Haitians and call the Coast Guard?"

"That's right," Liamsson said. "They're going off to look for their boat."

"I've got a hangover," Roberts said.

"You going to let them search the cabin?" Liamsson asked.

"I suppose I will," Roberts said. He hated to do it, but he didn't want a hassle.

"Your hangover is going to get worse," Liamsson said. "Hilliard telephoned the bait shop to say he'd be coming down tonight. I think he wants to party. I'm supposed to skiff him over. Probably having himself a big Saturday and Sunday."

"Well, shit," Roberts said.

"It's flat sad all right," Liamsson laughed.

*r*oberts spent late afternoon on the flats. He caught and released five bonefish, fighters that would clutch and run in the shallow water, raise their tails and go crazy trying to hide in sea grass. Just before sunset, he washed off and changed his clothes, then sat on the porch nursing a glass of slightly chilled mango juice.

About seven o'clock, as twilight was changing the sky from hazed gray to vermilion, he heard motors across the vacant distances of cloud and horizon, a thin high-wire whine like electricity in a line. An evening breeze carried the whine and it sifted down to him, its modulations against the faint sound of thunder from faraway storms. When he saw them finally, he was surprised that there were two boats, Liamsson in the lead, Jimmy Glide standing in the stern of a bass boat behind. Glide turned and made for the estuary and when he did, Roberts caught sight of Dolores Vega sitting in the bow in a white halter top, white short-shorts, a red ribbon around her auburn hair, and big gaudy sunglasses that reflected the sunset and sent it back at Roberts. Hilliard was in the skiff with Liamsson, and Roberts gave a halfhearted wave as both boats came up the estuary. He went down and caught the bowlines.

Bobby Hilliard was in white: deck shoes, cotton pants, white cotton shirt setting off the emerald dangling from his left ear. His sunglasses were wire-rimmed and had turquoise lenses that contrasted with his pink skin and red, wispy beard. Liamsson hopped into the shallow water and together he and Roberts dragged both boats toward the beach. Glide said nothing, just watched as the boats neared shore. Roberts helped Dolores Vega into the shallow water and she splashed happily through it in fancy flip-flops. Glide ran some paper sacks up to the cabin and sat on the porch. Dolores grinned at Roberts and spattered him with wet sand playfully.

"Hello, bro," Hilliard said, coming through the water. His voice was husky with alcohol.

Roberts said hello and glanced at Liamsson. Dolores gave Roberts a friendly hug. As usual, big cumulus clouds had built over the southern horizon and in the sunset, the water was a violent shade of green, coral-pink, hummingbird metallic red. With Roberts's help, Liamsson pulled the boats halfway out of the water.

"I'm heading back quick," Liamsson told Roberts. He asked Hilliard when he wanted a ride home.

"Noon or so," Hilliard said. He was standing on the beach, hands on hips. "We'll be ready to go by then."

Dolores hooked her arm around Roberts's waist. Hilliard turned and began to walk up the beach toward the cabin and they followed him, three or four paces behind.

"I love the place, Bobby," Roberts said.

Hilliard only nodded. Roberts could see Glide sitting on a porch step, motionless as Buddha except for smoking a filter cigarette and tapping the ashes off with quick flicks of his hand.

"I'm glad to see you," Dolores whispered to Roberts.

Roberts winked at her.

"Dolores, she wanted to come down bad," Hilliard said. "I think she's got a case of the hots for you."

"Shut up, Bobby," Dolores snapped.

Hilliard laughed harshly. Glide went into the cabin and came back with a bottle of beer.

"Party time, bro," Hilliard said. "You really doing some fishing down here?"

As though it mattered, Roberts recapped for Hilliard his eleven days of fishing. Bonito, a rooster fish or two, one or two small shark that got away. No redfish though, a species that was being overfished and killed off.

Down on the beach, Liamsson was waving at Roberts. He was in his skiff, paddling back into the shallow estuary. When he was off about ten yards, he gunned the outboard to life and began to make for open water. Roberts turned and waved as a flock of pelicans cruised overhead. He could smell the sweet aroma of marijuana coming from the porch as Jimmy Glide smoked a number in the near dark.

"Hey, Dolores honey," Hilliard called back. "Take these paper sacks inside like a good girl and make us some sandwiches. I want to talk to the man here."

Dolores started to say something, then looked at Roberts. She went up the steps of the cabin and gathered two paper sacks into her arms and went inside, leaving the three men alone. Glide continued to smoke the joint, inhaling and holding his breath for a long time, heading into the solitude of his mind. Roberts watched Liamsson going out into the bay and wished he were with him, anywhere but here. A wild, windy night was coming up. You could tell it by the colors in the clouds.

Hilliard crouched down on the porch steps. "Coast Guard called me," he said. "Wanted to know all about you."

"I figured they would," Roberts said.

"Too bad about the Haitians. But that shit happens."

"That's what everybody says."

"You kind of like it here?"

"It's good. But I'm leaving in a couple of days. I'll send you your money when I get home. Maybe in a week."

"I'm not worried, am I, Jimmy?" Hilliard said. Glide blinked and said nothing. "But I thought you might want to do some work for me. More a favor, actually. Help yourself while you're at it."

"I want to go home," Roberts said. "I haven't been home in three years."

"He wants to go home, Jimmy," Hilliard said, taking the last of the joint from Glide and hitting at it. "Hear me out," he said, smoke leaking from his mouth. "I want you to run over to the beautiful island of Hispaniola for me. Right now, I'm fresh out of people I can trust to do it. You'd be perfect. Gone maybe two weeks at the most. I'd pay you good, too. You could use extra money, couldn't you?" Hilliard finished the roach. "Couldn't he use the money, Jimmy?"

Glide smiled and said nothing.

"I'm tired, Bobby," Roberts said. "I want to sleep in my own bed."

Jimmy Glide was wearing cutoff jeans and a muscle shirt, dark sunglasses. He drained his beer and threw the bottle onto the beach.

"It's worth two grand to me," Hilliard said. "Plus expenses. You couldn't use two grand? You look like a guy could use two grand, don't he, Jimmy?"

"What's this about, Bobby?" Roberts asked.

"Business, my brother," Hilliard told him. He took a joint from his shirt pocket and lit it with a match. He smoked for a few minutes while it got dark. "Want a hit, brother?"

Roberts said he didn't. He smoked cigars, that was it.

"Make it three grand then," Hilliard said. "Dolores can tell you the whole deal. It's her problem, anyway."

Hilliard tapped Jimmy Glide on the shoulder and they walked up the beach together drinking beer. Roberts sat on the porch until Dolores came out with the sandwiches.

*d*uring his wanderings on the north side of Dismal, Roberts had discovered a thriving mangrove rookery of snowy egrets. The grove lay in a quiet lee from the wind, and every evening you could hear the birds returning to nest. Roberts had gotten into the habit of taking his instant coffee there in the morning, and a cold beer there in the evening, watching the great birds rise from nests, or swoop back from a long day feeding in the shallows, and it had given him great satisfaction. It had become his place of peace, his palace of ultimate solitude. That evening he showed it to Dolores Vega.

They took a couple of sandwiches and two sodas and walked there together in the gathering twilight. From the cabin, they could hear loud salsa on a jambox Jimmy Glide had brought out to the porch. It seemed a shame to ruin the evening with loud music, but that's what Hilliard and Glide were doing, sitting on the porch, smoking pot, throwing beer cans onto the white sand beach. Dolores had taken off her sandals and was walking barefoot, kicking through the hard-packed coral. She had taken off her gaudy sunglasses, too, and had hooked them onto the bodice of her halter top. About two hundred yards from the cabin, they paused in a cove backed by cypress drift, away from the water, a place where Roberts sometimes went in the heat of the afternoon to read. Across a hundred yards of shallow water was the mangrove. Roberts opened the sodas and handed one to Dolores, who took it and sipped easily. She sat on a drift log, digging into the sand with her toes.

"I'd like to know what's going down, Dolores," Roberts told her. He didn't want a fight, but he needed to know.

"Please don't be hostile," she said.

"Why are you here? What are they doing here?"

"I'm here because I want to be."

"They make me tense, Dolores," Roberts said. "They're getting wasted, and Hilliard made me some kind of crazy offer to do some kind of errand."

"Are you sorry I came?"

Roberts thought for a moment. The egrets were coming back, dozens of them now, like white angels drifting to earth from their heavenly abodes.

"Not sorry exactly," Roberts said. "No, I'm not sorry. But I'm confused and upset."

"Please tell me I don't make you tense, too," she said. "I'm not playing games here. When I heard Bobby was coming down, I asked him if I could come. I wanted to see you."

Roberts sat down on the drift next to her. He could see the fine hairs on her skin, light brown against darker brown, a composition in two shades.

"You don't make me tense," Roberts said. "But I'd like an explanation about what Bobby said."

"He does need somebody to go to Hispaniola," Dolores said.

"So, explain." Roberts sipped his soda, watching the stars come out one by one. They powdered the sky with points. "I don't pretend to like Bobby. Jimmy either, for that matter. I'd like to know if you've ever been down here before."

"Never been here in my life," Dolores said, crossing her heart. "Look, I told you Bobby has two art galleries. I'm just a manager he hired on the cheap. It's a good job. I like it. I take some crap from Bobby from time to time, but that's all I take. The gallery I manage now is in Coconut Grove, very posh, very swishy, with a clientele that couldn't tell the difference between Andy Warhol and Claude Monet. It handles mostly South American art, which is popular. We do some Haitian primitive works, and that's probably the hottest stuff on the market. People come into the gallery to spend money furnishing their homes. They want to make an impression, so they pay top dollar for new and emerging painters. I deal with them all the time, and they see art as big dollar signs on their walls. Not many have taste. Some do, some don't. But like collectors everywhere, they spend money on objects other people value. My gallery is called Escape. Believe it or not, it makes money. Bobby takes very little interest in it. Sometimes he has an accountant check the books. I let him call me "girl." I let him insult me here and there. But I like my job and I don't want to lose it."

Roberts nodded. "Fair enough, Dolores," he said. "But what does Bobby want from me?"

"About six weeks ago, Bobby sent an art scout to Haiti to collect new work. Bobby buys cheap and sells dear, but the artists are poor and need the exposure. They have no market at home, and the American market is one of their only hopes for recognition. The agent Bobby sent out is named Raymond Cobo. He's a Cuban who lives in Miami. He speaks fluent Spanish of course, and some French and pretty good English. Bobby gave him two hundred thousand in a letter of credit and sent him packing to buy over there. I gave Cobo a list of artists and galleries and made up an itinerary for him based on what Bobby wanted done. Bobby decided that if he spent around two thousand for every painting, he could get about two hundred works, enough to set up the new gallery's Haitian section. Less expenses, Cobo's fees, and customs and shipping, there would be a nice profit."

"Where'd Bobby dig up Raymond Cobo?"

"I don't really know," Dolores said. "He's been around the immigrant community for a while. A regular on Calle Ocho."

"What about him? Does he know art?"

"Nothing. That's the point. I gave him a few lessons in Haitian primitivism. I made a list of up-and-coming artists and how to find them. Raymond Cobo only had to buy the works and ship them back through customs."

"What happened, Dolores?"

"The works never made it back. Bobby told me that they were evidently purchased on account. But the artists were never paid and the shipment didn't show up at Miami customs. The pieces either disappeared in Port au Prince or Miami, and the money was never paid over to the artists as promised, though the letter of credit has been cashed out. Raymond Cobo never made it back to Miami. He might be in Honduras right now, spending Bobby's money. I feel bad because we're supposed to pay the artists a twenty-five-percent royalty on each sale as well as the initial payment of two thousand. So these poor men are really being hurt. I suppose everybody lost except Raymond Cobo. And where he is, we don't know."

"What about insurance?"

"Insurance on what? You can insure the shipment, but not the transaction."

"Was the stuff shipped?"

"You'd have to ask Bobby. I don't know."

"He call the police?"

"I think he did. I don't really know. That isn't up to me."

"So, what am I supposed to do?"

"Do what Raymond Cobo was supposed to do. The itinerary is already made up. Visit studios and buy art. Make sure it's packed, crated, and shipped. Clear customs."

Roberts looked at the mangrove. It was white with birds, hundreds now, settling in for the night.

"Bobby must be short on friends," he said.

"Bobby doesn't have friends," Dolores told him. "He has associates."

"And Jimmy Glide? Why doesn't he go?"

"You ever talk to Jimmy?"

"Not at all. He doesn't talk."

"Jimmy Glide is too scary to send around buying art," Dolores said. She slipped off the drift log and sat in the sand with her arm on Roberts's knee. "I could help you with the project. It might be fun. Tell you about the artists and the art. Connect you with people in Port au Prince. Maybe come over for a weekend. We could swim or something."

Roberts regarded the woman for a while, her auburn hair shining in the evening moonglow. "Why not you?" Roberts asked. "After all, it's your field. The art is for your new studio?"

"The art is for Las Olas, sure," Dolores said. "You'd have to ask Bobby. I told him I wanted to go. He said it was too dangerous. The political situation is volatile there now. You have to deal with dangerous people. You have to carry cash. I get the impression he thinks it's too much for a woman."

"Well, that's Bobby," Roberts said.

"Maybe," Dolores answered. "It's true that Haiti is going through troubles now. But I could bring you up to speed on the art in no time. You'd be gone for two weeks, at the most."

"If I didn't get killed."

"We don't know that Raymond Cobo was killed. Let's not talk like that. I think he stole Bobby's money."

"Okay," Roberts said. "We won't talk like that."

Hilliard and Glide were listening to the soulless racket of Jimmy Buffet on their jambox. Roberts suggested to Dolores that he walk to the cabin and get two sleeping bags and some rattan mats. He said they could build a fire and sit on the beach and talk. He didn't want to join the party, or whatever it was going on down at the cabin.

*t*he two of them were walking down Las Olas in Lauderdale when a brief and violent thunderstorm broke.

Roberts had stayed on Dismal for another day. He'd cleaned the cabin as best he could, packed his gear, burned the garbage he could burn and buried the rest. He stacked the old beer cans left over from Hilliard's so-called party. He had found a cheap motel on the Federal Highway near Dania Beach, just south of the jai alai fronton. Monday morning had dawned gray and windlessly hot. Dolores Vega had picked him up in her Beamer convertible and they'd driven up to Las Olas. The thunderstorm caught them strolling down the posh shopping street where all the men had white poodles with rhinestone collars and all the women were wearing flesh-colored spandex.

When the rain hit, they were five blocks from the beach. They scurried into a boutique café and ordered a plate of black-and-white cookies, some cappuccino, six bucks a pop. It rained for a few minutes, a machine-gun storm that peppered down, and then it stopped, leaving the streets steaming and puddled. It felt to Roberts as though the temperature might rise twenty degrees. Dolores was wearing red for the day: red cotton-jumper pants, red vest with sequins, bright red lipstick. She had painted her nails—toe and finger—a matching crimson.

"Have you decided to go?" she asked Roberts when they got their cookies and coffee.

"Three thousand dollars," Roberts said, shrugging. "Money talks." He hated to admit it, but it did. "I have a place in a nice valley. The motor on my water well is shot. Fence is down. I'm behind on my personal property taxes. The money makes a big difference." He frowned into his expensive coffee.

"That a *but*?" Dolores asked.

"There's always a but," he told her.

"You feel like talking it over?"

"Bobby and Jimmy give me the creeps. It's that simple." Roberts smiled and shrugged again. It wasn't simple, but it was a place to begin.

"Bobby is good for the money," Dolores said. "He'll pick up your expenses. I don't think you have to worry about that."

"It isn't the payment," Roberts said truthfully. "I don't know about you, but I get vibes from people. It isn't a science. It isn't based on anything but emotion. Just feelings. And hey, Bobby rescued me when I needed rescuing. I appreciate that. But both of them give me the creeps. And right now I don't need any hassles. I told you, it's been a rough three years."

"I've never had trouble with Bobby," Dolores said. "He lets me buy art and he pays on time. I know what you mean about them, but without Bobby, I'd be cleaning toilets and waiting tables at some hotel on Miami Beach."

"I don't think so," Roberts said.

"I'll take that as a compliment," Dolores said.

"It was meant that way," Roberts told her. "What I meant was that a woman with your intelligence, style, wit, charm, and ability could make it anywhere, anytime."

"Why, thank you, sir," Dolores said. She sipped her cappuccino and took a page of notepaper from her purse, unfolded it and spread it out on the wicker table. "Here's a sample itinerary for Haiti. I've listed four artists and three galleries. It's the same itinerary I gave to Raymond Cobo. The artists have studios or they work from their homes. Sometimes they move around, so you might have to search them out. They aren't well-known yet, and they do good work."

"I told you I know nothing about Haitian art."

"And I'm telling you it can be learned. You have the name of the artist and the location of the studio or gallery. You must bring back authentic works, but if you bring back a couple of clunkers, we'll sell them, too. Bobby has a high markup anyway. Besides, there is always the bozo from New Jersey with no taste, right? Or somebody who will take the artist's work no matter how hastily or clumsily made it is. Sometimes collectors have fetishes about these things."

"All right," Roberts said. "It might work."

"There's a daily flight to Port au Prince. Either American or Air France. Take your pick."

"And the letter of credit?"

"Bobby does that part. He'll draw it on a bank in Port au Prince and when you get there, the money will be in an account. Nothing could be simpler." Dolores nibbled at a cookie and put it down. "I told you I might come over. I guess I could show you around at the beginning of the trip and then come home. We could visit the Centre d'Art and the Iron Market, the Marche au Fer. When you've seen those two places, you'll know the good from the bad."

"I guess it's lucky the mugger didn't get my passport," Roberts said.

He drank his tricked-up coffee and watched the men and women swish down Las Olas. The storm had passed and now the day was hazed over and stifling.

"Bobby gives me the creeps, too," Dolores said. "You shouldn't feel so all alone."

Roberts paid the fifteen-dollar tab.

"Let's not worry about Bobby now," he said. "But I've seen Bobby in action. I've heard stories. They say he was dead and then he came back to life."

"Like a zombie," Dolores said.

Roberts left three ones for the waitress.

"So, you get vibes from people?" Dolores asked him.

Roberts told her he did. Didn't everybody?

"What vibes do you get from me?" she asked.

"Pleasant ones," Roberts said.

"I've got a house in the Grove," Dolores said. "It's quiet and cool there, and there's a patio out back in the shade. I think I have a bottle of white wine in the refrigerator. We could go over and talk or something."

"Whatever comes to mind?"

"Something like that."

The leather seats of the Beamer were wet. Roberts dried them with a beach towel and they headed south along the ocean.

23

While the letter of credit was being processed at a French bank in Miami Roberts took a week off to fish and do some reading on Haitian art.

On an early Thursday morning he drove the tan Bronco down to Islamadora and spent two nights sleeping behind the bait shop in a hammock, showering in the old man's trailer across the main highway. The two of them would hoist a rum punch for lunch, then go off fishing up and down the outer Keys, packing themselves a snack of bonito sandwiches, cans of fruit cocktail, iced tea and lemon. Just for the hell of it, Jakob closed his shop for two days and they skiffed around Coot Bay near Flamingo, stopping beside any likely looking mangrove, where they fished for bone, bonito, and barracuda. They scouted the deeper water for dolphin and rooster fish, but had no luck. Roberts hooked two roosters, but they threw his lure and escaped into the distance. Liamsson talked a lot about his days as a guide, when he would lead groups into the Everglades and fish for bass. He explained to Roberts how the northern water had been dammed and channeled and diverted until the red algae bloomed when the days got hot in summer, killing the fish, choking off the tide until the mangrove turned gray, and the nesting habitat for all the ocean birds was destroyed.

More than once they spotted shifting beds of orange algae, huge expanses of dead sea grass, miles of rotting water lilies, carcasses of egrets, mangroves burning in the shallow, salty water. Liamsson con-

jectured that even the northern pine barrens up by Coot Bay were
dying, suffering from drought and bad water and insecticide runoff.
Now that fresh water no longer flowed from the Kissimmee River
south into the heart of the grasslands, down through Lake Okeechobee, filtering into the swamps and keeping them from turning
brackish, the Ten Thousand Island country was drowning in salt.
Its normal balance had been lost, and with it went the wildlife. All
the birds and fish were being killed off by greed and economics,
which were the same thing according to Jakob. At sundown, they
would run the skiff out into the shallows between islands and watch
from binoculars as the heady red sun sank into the west. Everywhere, they saw melaleuca crowding out mangrove, dead fish belly-
up, red patches of algae floating in hot water.

On the following Thursday, Roberts drove back to Bay Harbor.
He parked the Bronco in the garage and walked to the south patio
of the mansion. He wanted to drop off the keys and catch a cab to
his motel, but Hilliard happened to be there, drinking a Greenie
with Glide. Glide saw him coming and ducked inside the house.

"It's my Brother Mitch," Hilliard said. He had on a black ball
cap, bill backward gang-style, turquoise-lensed shades, a light blue
tank top, and black-cotton slacks. "You ready to head 'em up?"

Roberts sat down at the patio table opposite Hilliard. Afternoon
sun slanted through the pines. He was still sunburned, maybe worse
than ever. "Tomorrow or the next day," he told Hilliard. "Probably
tomorrow."

"Dolores give you the rundown?"

"I'm ready," Roberts said. "I've got the itinerary. Contacts in Port
au Prince. Do's and don'ts of art buying and the directions to the
shipping agent. She says the letter of credit will be drawn on a
French bank in Port au Prince." For a moment, Roberts thought
Hilliard was going to speak, but he didn't. "I pick up the art and
ship it through Port au Prince."

"My shipping agent is Champagne Lambert," Hilliard said. "Those
Haitians and their names, huh? He's got an office near the port. You
can't miss him. He's a mulatto and speaks good English."

"What about Raymond Cobo?"

"Leave Raymond Cobo to me."

"You after him now?"

"I think he stole my money. Wouldn't I be after him?"

"You have insurance?

"I insure myself," Hilliard said.

"Just curious," Roberts told him.

"Hey, just stick to business. We'll both make out."

"Seems strange. You trusting Raymond Cobo with two hundred grand. He ever run errands for you before?"

"Some," Hilliard said. Sweat ran down the bottle of Heineken and made a puddle on the tabletop. "I made some inquiries down on the Calle Ocho. Maybe I'm still looking. Don't trouble yourself too much about Raymond. I can handle him."

"Suppose I run into Cobo?" Roberts asked. "Suppose I find him hanging out on a beach down in Haiti with a wad of your money in his fist?"

"You won't," Hilliard snarled.

"You sound pretty sure about that."

Roberts could see the jaw muscles working in Hilliard's face. For some reason, Roberts recalled the sound of lightning striking, a sharp, dreadful crack that sounded like the door to Hell creaking open.

"I protect my own interests," Hilliard said after some effort of thought.

A breeze off the ocean ruffled the pines, making a soft, sighing sound at odds with everything Roberts was thinking at the moment. Hilliard was staring at the middle distance, and Roberts couldn't see his eyes behind the turquoise shades. It was like having a conversation with a tape recording.

"What if I find Cobo?" Roberts asked flatly. He was going to hammer away at Hilliard come what may.

Hilliard swiveled slightly, stared at Roberts instead of nothing. "I get it," he said at last, taking a sip of beer and wiping his mouth with a bare palm. "You want a finder's fee. That's it, isn't it?"

"Five percent if I find Cobo," Roberts said. "Twenty-five percent if I get your money back."

"The fuck didn't you say so," Hilliard said, grinning like a malevolent cobra. "Have at it."

Roberts thought to himself: Fifty thousand dollars out there somewhere, maybe nowhere. When he managed to shut off his mind, he felt stifled by the South Florida heat. Rivulets of sweat were running down his neck, his shoulders, and his hands and arms were slick with sweat as well. He was sunburned and exhausted from fishing, and his neck muscles ached from hours of searching shallow water for bonefish, their faint tailing shadows slipping furtively through pillowed ripples. First Hilliard, then bonefish, now Cobo. Predators one could only catch glimpses of, almost by accident.

"Good then," Roberts said, ready to leave. "We've got a deal. Fifty thousand dollars if I get your money back. Ten thousand if I find Cobo for you."

Hilliard only nodded.

"I'll keep my eyes open for you," Roberts said. "You have a photo of Raymond?"

Hilliard paused, then laughed. "You must be joking."

"Humor me, Bobby."

"All right, my brother," Hilliard said. "Raymond, he's a big, square guy. Two fifty or sixty after a shower, but a lot of that is fat. Big brown eyes. Looks like a bear."

"He just never came back from Haiti?"

"He just never came back."

"Just like that, Bobby?"

"Just like that. He never came back."

Hilliard peeled ten hundreds from his wad and gave them to Roberts. "Expenses up front," he said.

Roberts picked up the bills. He had put his scruples about cash behind him. "What about Jimmy Glide?" he asked. "How does he earn his keep around here?"

"Never mind about Jimmy," Hilliard said.

Roberts drove back to his motel and spent some wind-down time studying the colors over the ocean. The wind had turned offshore, cooling things. He sat out by the motel pool and thought about Raymond Cobo. In his plan, he saw himself taking two weeks to do the job, then returning to Islamadora for another few days of fishing with Jakob Liamsson. After that, he would fly home to the San Luis Valley and catch up on his ranch. He hated even to call it a ranch. It was just a shack and a mile of fence, some outbuildings, and a hot spring where you could take a bath while it snowed. That was something Bobby Hilliard probably wouldn't understand.

24

*r*oberts shouldn't have done it. And when he did it, it went against his better judgment, but he did it anyway.

He looked up the fifteen Cobo listings in the Miami directory and began making calls. Then on call six—bingo—he got a woman named Lillith who said she was Raymond's sister and didn't want to talk. There was a long silence on the line as Roberts kept at her. He soothed her, told her he wanted to help find her brother, until finally the woman agreed to meet him in Bryan Park, southwest Miami. Did he know where Bryan Park was?

Roberts lied to her and told her yes, he'd find it easily. He studied a map before taking the Bronco out to Calle Ocho, then across Highway 41 to 23rd Street. He found himself in a neighborhood of rundown stucco bungalows with louvered "Florida" windows, dusty palms in grassless yards, chain-link fences and yapping dogs and baby strollers. Broken glass was scattered menacingly in the streets, and young kids played soccer and basketball in the empty lots and alleyways. Roberts cruised Bryan Park looking for someplace to put the Bronco and finally found a spot two blocks away. He walked over to the park and sat on a bench alone. It was a forlorn little patch of inner-city grass, brown Bermuda that hadn't been trimmed in weeks, one swing set, a walkway that toured empty flower beds, a drinking fountain on the fritz. Two or three groups of gang kids stopped to look, then moved on, seeing nothing to steal.

Roberts had just about given up when he saw her shuffling down the sidewalk, a slightly stooped figure in a black shawl, a gray skirt, a light blue blouse washed to within an inch of its life. Her black hair was swept back into a bun, and when she neared Roberts, he could see the pouches under her eyes and a hangdog stare usually seen on combat soldiers. She might have been forty and she might have been fifty, but she was probably twenty-five. As she got closer to the park, she slowed almost to a crawl. Then she looked at Roberts and gathered herself, as if she were looking for the courage to throw herself off a high bridge into icy water but couldn't quite muster it. There were no other people in the park, and the late-afternoon sun was hot, slanting through a fog of engine exhaust and windblown dust. Roberts thought that if he sat in the park long enough, he would be buried in pollutants. He stood and flashed a welcoming smile. He introduced himself and offered her a seat.

"You know my brother Raymond?" she asked. Her voice seemed to quiver like an arrow stuck in wood. "You have information about my brother, please?"

Roberts admitted he didn't know her brother. He wanted to prolong the conversation, and it was obvious that the woman was hanging onto a hopeless hope. Something slender was keeping her from utter despair. "I'm going to Haiti tomorrow," Roberts told her. "I thought perhaps you might give me information that might help me locate your brother." A city bus blundered by on Calle Ocho. Black exhaust billowed into the heat-glazed sky.

"You seeking for my brother?" she asked. She sat stiffly on the park bench, staring at something far away.

"I could look for him," Roberts said.

"Who are you? What you want?"

"I'm an agent for the art gallery your brother worked for. I'm going on the same kind of job."

"Why you care about Raymond?"

"I have an interest."

The woman lifted her eyes as if to pray. "Raymond went to Haiti. Seven weeks now, maybe more." She told Roberts she'd come to Miami by way of Bogota, escaping Cuba. She went south, then she went north. Her mother and father were still in Santiago. Raymond had come direct to Miami during Mariel. And now he was gone.

"What do you think happened to Raymond?" Roberts asked her.

"I have not news of him," she said. "Does you work for this Mr. Hilliard?"

"Indirectly," Roberts lied. "I work for the Las Olas Gallery in Fort Lauderdale."

"What they do to Raymond?" she asked. Now she turned to face Roberts, a trace of anger in her expression. "Why you want to make trouble for me? I have done nothing to you."

"I don't want to make trouble for you. I want to help find Raymond."

"You want to kill him, no?" she asked without emotion.

Roberts was stunned momentarily. "Why would I want to do such a thing?" he asked.

"They come to my house," she said. "A man, someone else waiting in a car outside." The woman gathered her hands in an attitude of prayer. "This man, he forced his way inside."

"I'm not using force," Roberts said.

"No," the woman said quietly.

"Who was the man who forced his way into your house?"

"I don't know him, some man."

"What did he look like?"

"Why should I tell you this?"

"What did he come for?"

There were tears in the woman's eyes.

"When Raymond does not return from Haiti," she said, "I go to the police. I say I am wanting to find my brother. He does not return, I tell them. I tell the police who he is working for, that he does not come home."

"Did they help you?"

"No, nothing was done. Then the man comes to my house, forces his way in. He says the police could not help me. He tells me Raymond stole money and disappeared. He warns me not to go to the police again. And then he gives me two hundred dollars."

"Did this man have a dark beard? Did he have black hair?"

"He threatened me," the woman said.

"That's the man?"

"He was strong. He had a black beard and black hair. He wore sunglasses. He makes me afraid to go to the police. Who is this man? Who are you?" The woman lapsed into a torrent of Spanish. When she was finished, Roberts told her his name again. She was beginning to cry now, her shoulders shaking with the effort.

"How did Raymond explain his job in Haiti?" Roberts asked at last.

"Like you, he was working for the gallery. He says he goes for only two weeks. Nothing more. I plead with him not to go. It is a dangerous place. Raymond tells me he is doing it for the money and when he returns, we will have much money." The woman looked down at a patch of brown dust at her feet. Another gang of street kids, perhaps fourteen or fifteen years old, wandered by, kids in ball caps, sneakers, denim jeans. "Money is hard since we come from Cuba," she went on. "But where now is Raymond? We are in need, and where is my brother? Why does this man come to my house and threaten me not to go to the police? Raymond did not steal his money. I know he didn't."

"How did Raymond earn a living in Miami?"

"He takes odd jobs. He is good with his hands. Our father taught him to make cabinets."

"Has the man with the beard bothered you again?"

"Never," the woman said.

Roberts thanked her for coming. He told her he would look for Raymond in Haiti. He told her that he would try to find her brother and that if he did, she would know right away. As quickly as that, the woman scuttled crablike down the sidewalk, leaving Roberts alone on a park bench in southwest Miami, temperature about ninety, humidity just under seventy percent, a storm of particulates raining down, an ocher veneer of chemicals and dust.

25

*t*he *Miami Herald* headlines—KKK RALLY SPLITS COMMU-
NITY; BIKER RIOT!—told Roberts all he needed to know to buy
a gun. Davie was the Nazi skinheads' capital of South Florida, and
after sitting for a while in Bryan Park thinking about Raymond
Cobo, he hit I-95 in heavy rush-hour traffic. Creeping and crawling,
then speeding and careening on a four-lane, crash-test speedway, he
reached Lauderdale in forty minutes and turned west on 81 toward
the Glades.

There was a cracker bar on the state road and he sat in its cool
and dark for a time, drinking a rum-and-Coke, perusing the local
telephone directory in search of gun dealers, finding three in Davie
that looked like they might suit his need to avoid waiting periods,
federal identity checks, background exams. He looked at a map of
Broward County and oriented himself before taking off into the
wastes of gigantic malls, palmetto dunes, trailer courts, the whole
chain-link mélange of watchdogs and motorcycles that was the western county.

He finally found the first dealer, located in a stucco pawn shop
converted from a failed Quick-Trip, now an emporium catering to
gun freaks and their personal paranoia bags, military buffs with
closet sadistic tendencies, bikers, and genuine right-wing fanatics.
Outside the shop there flew a suitably huge American flag, and
several Hogs were parked willy-nilly in the gravel lot. An old-

fashioned cigarette machine sat near the front door. On it was a hand-lettered sign inviting kids under eighteen to have a smoke.

Roberts went inside, emerging twenty minutes later with an unregistered and unlicensed .25 automatic Colt that had set him back five hundred dollars. What was the gun worth, he wondered, looking it over as the long-haired biker clerk watched. Two hundred, tops?

He stayed in a motel in Dania, closer to the southern end of town, near the Lauderdale airport. He took a taxi to Miami-Dade and made a call to Dolores Vega, getting her machine. He tried the gallery in Coconut Grove, but she was away from her desk with a client, so he left another message. Over two hours early for the flight, Roberts checked his baggage through to Port au Prince, got his boarding pass, and started wandering around the glass-and-steel airport. He had broken down the gun and wrapped each piece in aluminum foil and newsprint, tying them with twine. He wasn't sure what he was going to do at Haitian customs, but he had a copy of his Colorado gun permit and his private detective's license, and he thought he could bluff his way out of any situation with those documents, along with some green persuaders.

Roberts ate an expensive roast-beef sandwich at a stand-up bar in the departure lounge, then walked to airline customer service at the end of the gate. A young man in a blue uniform looked up and smiled alertly.

"I'm trying to locate one of your flight attendants," Roberts explained seriously. "I lost a small diamond pinkie ring on a London flight and I think she can help me locate it." He smiled warmly, establishing contact, trying to make up for the weakness of his story. "I've forgotten what part of the plane I was in. You know, big plane, too much wine."

"Let's see what we can do," the counter clerk said. "Which flight was it?"

"Well, if you could just put me in touch with Rosemary Collins, that would be great."

"I'm sorry, sir," the clerk said. "I can't do that. It's entirely against company policy and regulations. I'm sure you can understand."

"Look, this is important," Roberts persisted. "The ring belonged to my grandmother."

"I'm certain we can help," the clerk said. "Just give me the flight number and the date. We'll call you up on the computer and punch in the missing item. I'll see that our cleaning crews are alerted and every effort is made to find the ring. Our passengers frequently lose things onboard. We'll find your ring if it's humanly possible."

"I certainly hope so," Roberts said.

"Your name? Flight number?"

"Can't you tell me how to contact Rosemary Collins? I'm sure she'd remember the situation. We talked about the ring."

"You've made a report already? Or what?"

"Not yet," Roberts admitted.

"Well, then," the clerk said, "let's just have you fill out an official lost-and-found report. These clean-up crews are meticulous. They'll have a record of your seat number and we'll search extra-specially hard."

The clerk pushed a form across to Roberts. "I'll just take this back to the lounge," Roberts said, "and fill it out there."

"You were incoming to Miami when you lost the ring?"

"That's right," Roberts said. "Hey, I'd like to talk to Rosemary Collins, huh?"

"You gotta name, pal?" the clerk asked, abandoning his smile. He crossed his arms and stood eunuch-like.

"It's important," Roberts said pleadingly.

"Take a hike, Jack," the clerk said. "Before I call Security."

Roberts hurried away, losing the battle. He walked back to the international departure lounge at the end of two long corridors and through a tunnel. The air inside the lounge was refrigerated to cadaver level. Through tinted windows he could see acres of tarmac, miles of crisscrossed runways and intersections, rows of monstrous hangars, jetways, warehouses. Every seat in the lounge was occupied by departing passengers, so Roberts stood against a pillar and watched the people come and go. Most of the passengers were black or mulatto, men and women in worn suits and dresses, carrying bundles of clothes in plastic shopping bags, boxes full of electronics, baby food, miscellany in all shapes and sizes. He found a seat finally, beside a skinny young black man in a shiny black suit, worn at the elbows and knees. Across the way were three women who looked like sisters, dressed in vivid purples and blues, carrying hand luggage and several woven baskets full of clothes.

Roberts nodded at the skinny man and said hello.

"Honneur! Respet!" the young man said in a shout. He introduced himself rather formally to Roberts as Paul-Pierre Pierre and said he was going home to Port au Prince, where he hoped to find his mother and father, his cousins, and his beloved half brother, all of them alive and well. He hoped to bring at least some of them back to Miami, where they would be safe from the political violence sweeping the nation. "Is no blancs coming to Haiti now," Paul-Pierre said. "So, why you coming to Haiti now?" He produced a gap-toothed grin.

Roberts made an offhanded friendly reply, something about collecting Haitian art. Just then an attendant announced the first boarding call. Roberts would be sitting forward in the plane, so he was in no hurry to board. Paul-Pierre stood jauntily, revealing the front of his badly frayed white shirt, the missing buttons on his suit coat. Roberts could see newspaper stuffed into the bottom of his shoes, headlines acting as a sole.

Paul-Pierre smiled at Roberts again. "Satan, ale!" he shouted, crossing himself.

Satan, be gone!

Part 2

Terror consists mostly of useless cruelties perpetrated by frightened people in order to reassure themselves.

—Friedrich Engels, letter to Karl Marx,
4 September 1870

26

*r*oberts fell asleep listening to a Mozart divertimento. He dreamed of a terrifying car crash, glass blizzards, severed heads, a litany of horrors.

Someone next to him was saying, "Mes-z-amis, awake! Mes-z-amis, it is Haiti!"

They descended through layers of hurricane-weather cumulus, bumping down in mist. Far below lay Hispaniola, its red mountains wrinkled like dried prunes, rivulets of land jutting directly into a deep-blue Caribbean sea. Roberts could see the folds and declivities of the mountains, gray hills devoid of vegetation, cooking under a yellow sun. He could see the harbor of Port au Prince, a vague horseshoe shaping miles of barren coastline into a yawning U, the low city sprawling up and down gutted canyons and flatlands. Beside him, Paul-Pierre was rubbing his hands together in obvious excitement, leaning over Roberts's right shoulder trying to catch a glimpse of his country through the narrow porthole.

"Eh, Blanc," Paul-Pierre exclaimed happily. "You know Mr. Columbus tell the queen that this place look like a crumpled piece of paper when she ask."

The airplane banked and Roberts saw mountains again, steep red cliffs and washed-out patches of scrub plain, then banana and pine groves.

"It's certainly rumpled," he said.

"Gade sa! Gade!" Paul-Pierre said.

They passed directly over Port au Prince, heading to the airport north of town. Roberts was amazed at the vastness of this Caribbean city, its pastel jungles of shacks and shanties and low concrete buildings baking in dead heat. There were endless eternities of slums, rusted tankers in the harbor, and pasteboard-and-tin structures extending from the center of the city almost to the edge of the water. Plumes of smoke leaked into the air, smoke rising from cook fires and charcoal braziers, mounds of garbage smoldering. Open sewers ran like rivers from the hills to the ocean. The jet was so low now that Roberts could see children playing in the streets, and all sorts of animals being led—pigs, donkeys, chickens, goats. A thick pall hung over the city like a shroud, soot and dust and diesel exhaust collecting in the nearly breezeless valley.

Paul-Pierre had moved close to Roberts now, straining to see. They flew over the slums north of the city, a former swamp.

"Gade sa," Paul-Pierre said. "C'est les terraines vagues." He leaned across Roberts and put his hand on the Plexiglas window, palm down. He crossed himself and smiled sadly at Roberts.

"Vague terrain?" Roberts echoed.

"Have you any French?" Paul-Pierre asked.

"Only a little," Roberts said. "Un peu."

"Be careful, Blanc," Paul-Pierre said. "They is a bad time in Haiti now. The Tontons, they fight back. The Frap, they making murders all the time in towns and villages. They say they going to stop Aristide. Me, I don't know. But you be careful, Blanc."

The pilot had air-braked for final approach. Roberts heard the landing gear going down. Attendants were circulating, checking seat belts, giving final instructions. Paul-Pierre's face seemed to shine in anticipation.

"You think Aristide will return?" Roberts asked.

"God only knows this, Blanc," he said.

"What's this about Frap?" Roberts asked.

"Oh, that," Paul-Pierre said, waving a hand. "Old Papa Doc's men dressed up in new clothes. They take the Tontons and they call them attachés. Frap is the same old party of Duvalier. But the police, they behind Frap and they kill anyone who make the support for

Aristide." An attendant behind Pierre was trying to make him sit down and buckle up. Finally he seated himself across the aisle and buckled his belt. "Koupe tèt, boule kay," Paul-Pierre said. Over another intercom announcement, he said it again: "Koupe tèt, boule kay."

"I don't understand," Roberts called over.

"You don't talk Creole, huh, Blanc?"

Roberts admitted he didn't speak Creole.

"Cut off his hand, burn house," Paul-Pierre said. "That's what the Frap say they do to Aristide men. The Americans say Aristide come home, but Frap say no."

The airplane was low now, grazing the shanties of the waterfront.

"You ever hear of somebody named Champagne Lambert?" Roberts asked.

"Pas conné," Paul-Pierre said. "Not him." The man crossed himself again and closed his eyes. When he opened them, he said, "Hey, Blanc! You need a ti-moune in Haiti?"

"I don't understand," Roberts told him.

"A little servant," Paul-Pierre said. "My half brother. He be your ti-moune. He speaks English good, Blanc. He is very intelligent. He can write and read. He knows the whole city like, how you say, the back of his hand."

"Maybe I could use a guide," Roberts said.

"My brother is a good boy," Paul-Pierre said. "He clean your clothes. Shine your shoes. He make your breakfast if you want."

"I just need a guide," Roberts said. "I'm at the Holiday Inn, at least for a while."

They dropped through a smoky glaze into Port au Prince airport. The sky and the mountains disappeared and the jet skidded suddenly on the tarmac, a short concrete runway skirted by banana trees, circled by shacks and shanties, more open sewers, rutted tracks leading away to the barren hills, where people shuffled under a dense tropical heat. Paul-Pierre had closed his eyes and was muttering a prayer.

"Papa Legba, ouvri porte ou," Paul-Pierre chanted. "Papa Legba, ouvri porte ou." Over and over, Paul-Pierre intoned his prayer.

They had hit tarmac with a hard smack. An airport tower jutted out of the smoky distance.

Roberts finally puzzled out the Creole with his schoolboy French: God Legba, open the door!

27

*r*oberts walked down the ramp and stood on the hot tarmac, breathing diesel fumes. He was sweating heavily and his shirt was soaked through to the skin. The sky was like a fiery kiln of clay glaze, smelling of sulfur and charcoal smoke. He looked at the low airport complex, sets of concrete buildings with tin roofs, a long hedge of cactus separating the runways from miles of confused, jumbled slums. In the west, high brown mountains rose into crabbed valleys and wrinkled ridges, then a slash of green. All around him the Haitian passengers were lugging their packages and bundles toward a tin customs shed located at the far end of a concrete building with several broken windows and an air conditioner leaking water. Soldiers in green fatigues lounged at the corners of buildings where they had some shade, smoking cigarettes, regarding the passengers. Roberts noticed a few men in blue jeans and denim shirts or ragged shorts and T-shirts who seemed to be carrying pistols, old shotguns, a few machetes. Their dark sunglasses held the light so that it did not escape.

Paul-Pierre worked his way to Roberts through the dense crowd. "Don't look at no Tonton in the eye," he told Roberts. Paul-Pierre was carrying a white sheet tied off at one end. It had his belongings, gifts for his family, a few sticks and stones that would become heirlooms in the future. "They think you give them the evil eye and it go bad for you," he continued.

Soon the passengers divided into two lines, Haitian citizens and others, both waiting in the heat for customs inspections and immigration checks. In the background there was terrific noise, traffic, metal against metal, horns tooting and honking, animals. Roberts had an overnight bag with his spare shorts, socks, fresh underwear, a change or two of shirts and pants. And the gun.

A soldier approached Roberts and regarded him quietly. He wore a green beret, black sunglasses, and baggy green fatigues. He balanced an automatic rifle in the crook of his arm and fingered the trigger.

"Ap vini blanc!" the soldier called. "Alé, ap vini blanc!" The soldier stared at Roberts as though seeing a Martian.

Paul-Pierre leaned to Roberts. "They calling out that the white man comes. They not used to blancs."

Roberts was one of the three white people in line. He stood behind an elderly couple who looked as though they might have just come from Salt Lake City, missionaries on a mission. In his line there were several foreigners, diplomat types, a salesman, by the look of his gear. They waited in the hot sun while the line failed to move. Roberts could see a soldier at the head of the line drinking rum from a dirty bottle. The man swigged at the colorless liquid, some of it dribbling down his shirtfront, then wiped his hand across his mouth and eyed the line unsteadily. Thirty minutes later, the line had moved inside the shed, a colorless square of concrete that seemed on fire with the heat. The walls were light green and dark blue in alternating stripes of peeling paint. On the walls, too, were several portraits of severe Army types in sunglasses, dark green uniforms, rows of colorful ribbons catching the flash of the camera. Across the way, some soldiers were pestering the Haitian group, swatting at them with sticks as if they were cattle, poking and swinging their machetes and howling Creole. A Haitian had reached the head of the line and was abruptly shoved into a corner, where his plastic bag was opened, its contents dumped on a bare table. The soldiers rifled through the mess.

"Hey, Blanc, c'est, la," a soldier called to Roberts.

Roberts moved up to a table where the soldier was sitting on a metal chair. Green fatigues, automatic weapon, dark sunglasses.

"Parle Français?" the soldier asked.

Roberts regarded the soldiers, two more of them leaning against a wall.

"Un peu," he said.

"English?"

"American," Roberts told him.

"Huh," the soldier grunted.

Another soldier appeared from an inner room, as well as a Tonton in blue jeans and denim shirt, a red bandanna. "Passporte," the soldier said. Roberts handed over his passport and watched while it was studied by the soldier and the Tonton.

"Ap vini blanc," the Tonton said to someone in the inner room. "Blanc American." The Tonton held a thick club in his right hand and tapped it against his leg.

"Ouvre baggage," the soldier said.

From across the room, Paul-Pierre caught Roberts's eye. There was fear exchanged and Roberts felt tense with the expectancy of violence.

"Aristide man?" the soldier asked. Roberts smiled at the Tonton, impassive behind dark glasses. "Vous Aristide man?" the soldier said, louder now.

"No politics," Roberts said, without French. "Pas politique."

"Ouvre baggage," the soldier commanded.

Across the room, a soldier was struggling with one young black man over the contents of a plastic sack. At the door in the inner room, a large man in a white suit appeared and watched the proceedings. The Tonton eased away, making room.

"Hey, Blanc, you Aristide man?" the soldier asked again.

Roberts unzipped his overnight bag. The soldier was smiling at him, tapping a truncheon on the table. The man in white spoke quickly to the soldier.

"Hey, Blanc," the soldier said. "Es necessaire, impôts de passage, no?"

"Pas conné," Roberts said, remembering this Creole phrase from his conversation with Paul-Pierre. "Pas conné impôts de passage."

"Pas conné!" the soldier laughed. The Tonton moved closer, arms folded now, a brief smile creasing his lips. They exchanged a quick phrase or two in Creole. "D'argant blanc," the soldier said. He made a motion as if to spit on the floor.

"Money," Roberts said. "D'argent."

The man in the white suit entered the room. He was clean-shaven with a shaved bald head, immaculately manicured nails, polished shoes. His eyes were the gray of flint and there was a dust of gray hair on the backs of his hands. He looked to be about fifty years old and held himself stiffly erect. Standing behind the soldier, he looked at Roberts and smiled.

"Bonjou msye," the man said in Creole. "Ban-m nouvel-ou?"

"Je ne comprens pas," Roberts replied.

His overnight bag stayed on the table, unexamined.

"Bonjour," the man said in French. "Como sa va?"

"Bonjour," Roberts said. "Bien merci."

"So, you don't speak Creole," the man said.

"So, you speak English."

"A little. Enough. We don't see many whites here now. Tourists have gone. These are strange times in Haiti. Perhaps you have come to see the sights."

"I'm on business, actually."

"I thought as much," the man said. He extended a hand across the table. "My name is Champagne Lambert. Welcome to Haiti."

Roberts shook his hand. He noticed Lambert's tie pin in the shape of a question mark.

28

*L*ambert spoke to the soldier in Creole. For a moment, the soldier regarded Roberts with disgust, then stamped the passport and zipped the overnight bag and passed it across the metal table. Nearby, the Tonton adjusted his dark glasses and tapped his truncheon against the concrete wall.

"The formalities are complete," Lambert said.

They walked down a corridor that smelled of urine and human sweat. The walls were painted institutional green, and many of the louvered windows were broken out. Shards of glass lay in the hallway, along with bits of newspaper. Roberts was carrying his overnight bag under his arm, thinking about the gun. He was two steps behind Lambert.

"You knew about my arrival?" Roberts asked him.

"Ah, that," Lambert sighed. "Let us say I was informed by Radio Thirty-two."

"Radio Thirty-two?"

"But of course," Lambert said. "In Creole, it is called the telejiol."

"Word of mouth," Roberts said. He was sweating heavily, wondering how Lambert and the soldiers managed to stay crisp in their layers of clothing. "It's odd how word of mouth gets around so quickly, isn't it?"

"The chattering of thirty-two teeth," Lambert said. "It is magie noire, n'est pas?"

"To be sure," Roberts said.

He caught up to Lambert in an entryway. It was a glass foyer full of bright sunlight, a few dead potted plants near the doors, while outside, a parking lot baked. There were only a few military vehicles parked in it. Out on the main road, Roberts could see what he imagined were hundreds of taxis, public buses, tap-taps painted rainbow-shaded colors of blue, green, yellow, red. Dozens of beggars shoved at the barricades police had erected just at the entrance to the airport. Men and women were sleeping in the shade, bundled in rags.

"Where do you stay?" Lambert asked.

"The Holiday Inn, Rue Capois."

"A good choice," Lambert said.

Roberts watched as children played soccer near the barricades. They were skinny black kids, some with the reddish hair of kwashiorkor, serious malnutrition. Many of the beggars were missing limbs, legs, arms, their teeth, too. Most were bald or nearly so from lack of nutrition. He saw men sleeping standing up; those he would later learn were called "domi kanape." They dozed leaning against abutments, columns, parked cars. Roberts passed through the glass doors and stood in air scented by charcoal smoke, rotten fruit, burning garbage. There was no breeze and the sun bore down mercilessly.

"This upsets you, Blanc, eh?" Lambert asked. "Our titis, our domi kanapes?"

"It would upset anybody," Roberts said.

"You will understand soon," Lambert told him mysteriously.

Roberts had to cough, his throat irritated by the thick, toxic air. Up in the hills, the shacks and shanties of the wretched seemed to stretch for miles. Along the flats of the harbor there were more slums, and he could see their myriad shapes, rectangles, pyramids, squares, all constructed haphazardly from tin and plywood and used rubber tires, recycled pasteboard, clapboard, sticks of driftwood, plastic sheeting, all manner of refuse. Every square foot of slum was occupied by a human being, many of them children, babies.

"I'll need a taxi," Roberts said.

"But allow me," Lambert offered.

As they walked across the hot concrete, it seemed to Roberts that all of the men and women on the other side of the barricade were directing comments, remarks, salutations, and exhortations to him. "Honneur, respet! Blanc, fè foto m, fè foto m. Pagen kòb! San maman, Blanc, San maman! Pagen kòb!" In the middle of his walk, Roberts slowed and watched the people, the many crippled and deformed, some lying on the hot concrete trying to sleep, clutching a few articles of clothes, some rags, a single shoe composing their entire personal belongings. Roberts fought his feeling of disgust, pity, an overwhelming desire to flee.

They reached a silver Audi with dark-tinted windows. Lambert leaned on its roof, his arms askew, and looked at Roberts, who dropped his overnight bag near the passenger door.

"What are they saying?" he asked Lambert.

"The old men are honoring you, Blanc," he said. "They think blancs have special power. The titis are begging for money of course, telling you they have no mothers. Some of the titis are asking you to take their photographs. They want to earn some dollars from the blanc."

Lambert got into the Audi and started the engine. Roberts sat down in the passenger seat and was immediately grateful for the air-conditioning, a chance to get away from all the heat and din. He wondered if one could wind up hating all the poverty-stricken people instead of sympathizing with them.

"Hilliard told you I was arriving?" Roberts asked.

"But of course," Lambert answered.

They drove down a potholed asphalt road between rows of dusty palms. The breeze blew red dust in whorls and the car windows were caked with it.

"And did you pick up Raymond Cobo at the airport?" Roberts asked.

Lambert smiled knowingly. His teeth were very white and a gold star was imbedded in each of the two front ones. They reached a manned barrier and Lambert waved to the soldiers. One of the soldiers stared at Roberts through the tinted passenger window. To the south was Port au Prince, a few glass buildings in the yellow haze, a vast sea of concrete bunkers, one pink cathedral shining under the tropical sun. Patches of green graced the hills, and far up in the mountains behind the city was more deep green space that seemed to hang suspended in the sun-splashed distance. The mountains themselves were astonishingly red where all the trees had been cut down. To the west, the sea was deeply blue and capped with white. In the ditches beside the road, cactus grew in profusion. Garbage was piled up on every corner, some of it burning. Lambert closed his window with an electronic whoosh.

"What was it you said, Monsieur?" Lambert asked.

"Did you pick up Raymond Cobo at the airport?"

Lambert sucked his teeth. His skin was iron-gray in color, wrinkleless.

"Mr. Cobo is a thief, no?"

"Which hotel did he stay at?"

The road was two-laned, now beginning to crowd with people and their animals. Lambert drove recklessly fast.

"I believe the Holiday Inn, n'est pas? Like all the blancs when they come to Haiti."

*t*he closer they came to Port au Prince, the more clogged and congested the highway became. Everywhere Roberts looked, there were people and animals: donkeys, goats, chickens, stray dogs. Women led their goats and donkeys on tethers made of palm fronds, carrying huge bundles on their heads: bananas, coconuts, fruit of all kinds. Beside the road were temporary shelters, homes made of reeds or mud and plywood. The color and confusion were extraordinary, like a hallucination, as dazzling as a drug-induced paranoia. From the hillsides ran streams of untreated sewage, human and animal waste gushing toward the harbor. Young children were bathing in the sewage traces.

"Hilliard told me you are a shipper," Roberts said. Lambert stared straight ahead at the road, honking at times when an animal blocked their path. "Now I see you're a kind of customs official."

"I have a connection to the customs," Lambert said.

"You appeared quite official back there," Roberts pressed. "How long have you and Hilliard been in business?"

"We are not in business, as you say," Lambert snapped. "I do the shipping, that is all. You have many questions."

"I'm a curious fellow," Roberts said. "You handled the shipping details for Raymond Cobo?"

"It is customary," Lambert said. He turned his gaze on Roberts for a moment. His sunglasses were black-lensed, and Roberts wondered how he could see anything at all through them. "There are many bureaucracies in Haiti," Lambert continued. "M'ser Hilliard understands the value of doing business with a person who, shall we say, realizes the importance of proper connections."

Now the outskirts of Port au Prince appeared, rough two-story, cinder-block bunkers painted white, blue, green, and red, multicolored shades smudged by charcoal smoke. Windows broken. Beggars and idlers on every veranda. Roberts was overwhelmed by the sheer number of people either walking, on bicycles, or riding tiny motor scooters that shot sprays of exhaust into the already overheated air. Tires screeched, buses lurched from corner to corner in a dangerous avalanche of wheels and people. Corner vendors hawked trinkets, chewing gum, small captured birds, barbecued slices of pork and chicken, oranges, mangoes. Here and there, police in dark uniform wandered through the crowds, automatic pistols at their sides.

"But did you handle the Cobo shipment?" Roberts asked again.

There was a silence from Lambert. Roberts could see the cathedral now, off in the distance, its spires pink in the blazing sun, a gold cross on each of its two cupolas. A plume of choking red dust scoured the streets.

"What did M'ser Hilliard tell you?" Lambert asked.

"He told me Cobo disappeared with his money and the paintings."

"And what else?"

"Nothing else," Roberts said. "I'd like to know if Cobo delivered his shipment to you. Or if it disappeared before that."

"We have made inquiries for Mr. Cobo."

"Do you think he left the country?"

"It is possible."

"And did you inventory his paintings?"

Lambert pushed the Audi down Rue Courte, just up the street from the main cathedral. The glass-and-steel Teleco building gleamed in the sun, its windows catching the rays and breaking them into a million bits. Everywhere, the city seemed to glow with red and reverberated with the constant banging of pots and pans, the braying of donkeys.

"This is not necessary," Lambert said.

"What isn't necessary?"

"Your inquiries, Monsieur. You have a job, no? And it has nothing to do with this Raymond Cobo."

"I think Mr. Hilliard would be delighted if I found Raymond Cobo. There is a great deal of money at stake."

"I remember, Blanc," Lambert said.

They drove up a side street beneath mimosa and ceiba trees. Roberts could see the back wall of the Holiday Inn, a clutch of palm trees, and an iron gate to the parking lot. Lambert turned a corner and suddenly they were in front of the hotel.

"This is the Holiday Inn, Blanc," he told Roberts.

Roberts put the overnight bag on his lap. He thanked Lambert for the ride.

"Be careful, Blanc," Lambert said menacingly. "We have a saying in Creole. 'Peyi-a ap fè bak.' You know what that means?"

"I don't speak Creole."

"It means . . . 'The country is going backward.' " Lambert smiled again, showing Roberts his gold stars. He ran a hand over the instrument panel. "It is like you, Blanc. If you keep looking for this thief Raymond Cobo, you would be going backward. You should always look ahead, Blanc. That way, you can see where you are going and you don't trip and fall. Ha, blanc tombé. The blanc is falling. If you ever hear that—blanc tombé—you will know what has happened. And it would be very dangerous to fall in this country, Haiti. Who knows, you might wind up like Raymond Cobo. Remember, blanc tombé!" Lambert gave a mirthful laugh. "A friendly warning, Monsieur Roberts. Haiti is a sinister place. Do not become political. Do not become curious. Do not go backward."

Roberts got out and stood on the sidewalk. He watched Lambert guide the Audi down a shaded lane and turn left into a side street. Where he stood, in the shelter of some tamarinds and palms, it was cooler. A breeze had blown up from the sea and the air seemed fresher. A thin-boned black man approached.

"Mes-z-amis!" the man said happily. "I am Virgil Dieudonné!"

"Excuse me?" Roberts said, puzzled.

"Virgil Dieudonné," the man said. "You know me! I am the half brother of Paul-Pierre Pierre. Surely he told you I am to be your ti-moune!"

30

*r*oberts stripped off his sweat-soaked clothes and took a tepid shower. His room was on the third floor of the hotel, a saggy double bed, teak dresser, rattan furniture, walls papered in brown-and-ocher jungle scenes. Standing in the sliding-glass doorway of the patio, a towel around his waist, he could see a shimmering blue rectangle of swimming pool below, rows of chaise lounges, trellises of hibiscus and blooming bougainvillia, banana trees with tiny pods of green fruit suspended. A few swimmers were doing laps in the pool, and waiters were serving drinks at the Happy Hour. One or two Army officers were drinking at the bar, and there were some journalists talking and smoking, eating hors d'oeuvres at wicker tables. Roberts lit a cigar and smoked it, letting the offshore breeze cool him.

He dressed and walked down to the lobby and changed some dollars to gourds, the official currency. He had placed his gun in a leather carrying case and asked the clerk to lock it in a safe. The lobby was quiet, lined by huge philodendrons, the carpet smelling faintly of dust and mildew. Roberts walked through the lobby and found Virgil Dieudonné waiting on the hotel steps, the man dressed in black worn slacks and a frayed white shirt. He was rail-thin and his ears were tiny, almost preternaturally so. One hand seemed slightly withered.

"Mes-z-amis!" Dieudonné said with a grin.

"We need to talk, Virgil," Roberts told him.

"Come, come!" the young man said.

They strolled up Rue Capois beneath dusty pepper trees. Dieu-donné was wearing flip-flops that made swishing sounds on the dry, fallen leaves of the trees. Smoke from thousands of braziers lay heavily on the city, like a woolen blanket of air. The sound of music drifted faintly from bars and shops, from the upper floors of concrete buildings. Every now and then, a beggar would approach and say, "Muven pagen kòb, Blanc." Virgil Dieudonné would look at him with pity, then look at Roberts, who would hand over a gourd or two. "Sitiyasyonan ki di ampil, pauvre," Virgil would say.

Roberts bought a paper sack full of grilled peanuts from a street vendor. They walked and ate peanuts while the darkness commenced to roll across the flatlands. Roberts caught a glimpse of Boutilliers, the highest mountain above the city.

"Virgil," Roberts said, "where did you learn your English?"

"Saint Jean Bosco School," he said. He gestured to the east, toward Grand Rue. "It is the church of Aristide. You know Aristide?"

"Of course. Everybody has heard of Aristide."

"He will come back from America, no?"

"People say he will."

"You want me for your ti-moune?" Virgil looked at Roberts hopefully. They had stopped under a pepper tree, letting several old women pass with their burdens. Another woman lay in the street. The passersby let her lie there.

"I don't know what to say," Roberts replied.

"I speak good English," Dieudonné told him. "I know the city. If you need to travel, I can guide you outside the city. I am a very helpful ti-moune. I make your breakfast and I shine your shoes and I wake you in the mornings for coffee."

"I don't need a servant," Roberts said.

"You need a ti-moune," Virgil said.

Down on Grand Rue, there were many police. On every corner stood a man in a blue uniform with a weapon. A gang of street beggars approached and Virgil spoke to them in Creole.

"Maybe you could help me," Roberts said at last. "But I can't get you to America, if that's what you're thinking. I've spoken to

Paul-Pierre and I know that's what you're hoping to do. But I'm leaving in two weeks and I won't be coming back. That's the end of it."

Virgil looked away. Roberts had the impression that a great emotion was breaking into his heart.

"Pas problem, sir," Virgil said. "You pay me what you think I am worth. I will show you the city. I will show you Haiti. Perhaps I can be of some service."

"I'll be renting a car soon," Roberts said. "We'll be traveling down to Jacmel and up to Cap Haitien."

"I know these places. The roads."

"All right. You're my ti-moune."

They walked down dark streets where the concrete-bunkered houses were dirty and bare. Roberts supposed the electricity had gone out, the only light coming from candles and battery-powered lamps in the windows. In the near distance he could see a Catholic church, a crowd standing in the street near its entrance, many in the crowd blowing into conch shells, banging pots and pans with machetes, singing Creole songs. Down an alley stood a line of soldiers carrying automatic weapons. Two carloads of Tontons were parked in the shadows of a market on one corner.

"What's going on, Virgil?" Roberts asked, once they had gotten to within a block of the church.

"Saint Jean Bosco," Virgil said. "The people are making a tenèb. A political protest."

In the street lay a body beneath blue-plastic sheeting. Several women knelt beside it, shrieking and crying. Roberts could see the soldiers moving, ghostlike figures in the near dark. The church was white in the rising moon, its cross gold.

"There's a dead man," Roberts said.

"Oui," Virgil agreed. "They have mutilated one of the Aristide men. They leave him in front of the church as a lesson to the people."

"Who did it? Frap?"

"Tontons. The Frap. Who knows? They wish to frighten the people. They wish to stop Aristide from returning."

Roberts felt fear for the first time. "You brought me here for a reason, didn't you, Virgil?"

"We must go now, Monsieur," Virgil said. "There will be trouble. Besides, there is an informal curfew. When it is dark, the streets belong to the Tontons. They will cause us grief, surely."

The soldiers had seen them. Three of them had crossed the street and seemed to be following along. One of them called out to a Tonton, who looked at Roberts with dark sunglassed eyes.

They made it back to the Holiday Inn in half an hour, just before full dark. Roberts told Virgil good night on the steps of the hotel and gave him cab fare back to his house in one of the neighborhoods north of the city. Then he walked into the lobby and leaned across the front desk, waiting to catch the attention of a young clerk. He asked the clerk if a man named Raymond Cobo had checked into the hotel seven weeks ago on a Friday night, a big, square man going to fat, with slick black hair, weighing seventy-five kilos. Maybe less, maybe more.

"Of course," the clerk said. "He stayed a few days and then he checked out."

"He was alone?"

"For a time," the clerk said. "And then a woman came and they departed together." The clerk turned to answer a room call.

Roberts had a late drink in the hotel bar. He listened to Dominican merengue for a while. Then he went to bed and tried to sleep on soggy sheets.

31

*b*ad dreams and sporadic gunfire woke Roberts in the early morning. He had lain in bed for hours, tossing and turning in a sweat, and then he had tried to read until the electricity went off and there was no light. When he finally got out of bed, he was as tired as if he hadn't slept at all, and he took a swim to try to unwind. He ate a breakfast by the pool: sliced mango and papaya, fresh orange juice, strong black Haitian coffee from large white jugs that had blue-patterned herons on the handles. He interrupted his breakfast twice by trying to telephone Dolores Vega in Miami, hoping to convince her not to come to Haiti during the political violence, unrest, confusion, and murder. She wasn't at her home in Coconut Grove, nor at the Escape Gallery, so he left a message on her machine.

A harried waiter brought him a copy of the *Nouvilliste,* a widely circulated newspaper in Port au Prince. Roberts couldn't read much of it with his bad French, but the parts he could read told him that during the night three Tontons had been trapped by an angry crowd of slum dwellers near St. Jean Bosco. The Tontons had been dragged into the middle of the street, necklaced, mutilated, their bodies displayed as part of the "dechoukaj," an uprooting of evil, revenge of the people. Much of the newspaper was filled with political musings about the possible return of Aristide, a Catholic priest who had been duly elected president of the republic, then exiled after a coup. Much of the agitation in Haiti seemed to Roberts both democratic and popular, a true people's movement, spontaneous and unre-hearsed. Elements of the ruling mulatto class were deathly afraid of the impoverished blacks, an underclass of poverty-stricken prole-tariat. There was talk of open class warfare in the city. Tontons had attacked the Cite Soleil, Port au Prince's largest slum, and had burned two dwellings of suspected Aristide supporters in retaliation for the killings. Many Aristide supporters were in hiding, fearful for their lives, and for the lives of their families.

Roberts had finished his first pot of coffee when he spotted Virgil Dieudonné striding jauntily through the hotel lobby, still in his shiny black pants and ragged white shirt, worn flip-flops. He was smiling hugely, strutting as though he had just scored a winning touchdown for Notre Dame. Roberts waved and invited him to sit down and share some coffee and breakfast. He ordered more orange juice, a boiled egg, and some crusty rolls. It was too early for swim-mers as yet, and the two men were alone by the pool. A morning breeze was gently ruffling the palms and the pepper trees, and it was not yet hot. Even now, the sun had not risen over Boutilliers, and they were in deep shade.

"So, you had a good sleep then, M'ser?" Virgil asked.

Roberts told him about the gunfire. "Except for that, I slept fine."

Dieudonné grabbed some mango like a man possessed and wolfed it down. He finished three slices, then drank some orange juice quickly.

"It is a dangerous time for Haiti," he said. "In Creole, we say what means in English that "when you cannot pay your rent, feed your children, and dress them, life looks like hell." He smiled sadly and said, "Please forgive me for swearing, sir."

"Virgil, I'm curious. What do you do for money?"

"I am the letter writer," he replied. "I prepare documents. I write protests and translate. In another life, I might have been a notary."

"You've had a good education, haven't you?"

"Very good, sir, up to a point."

"Does it bring much in?"

"Money, you mean?" he laughed. "As the saying goes, M'ser."

"I take it, no," Roberts said.

Dieudonné only drank a sip of his coffee.

"There are many problems in my country," he said. "We are a slave country. There is the race problem. The problem of the military. Superstition, illness, disease. Too many mouths to feed. We have cut down all the trees. Larger countries have abused us."

"You mean the United States."

"Not only that, sir. Others."

"And how is Paul-Pierre getting along?"

"He is with his mother and father."

"And you, where do you stay?"

"Let us say that I do not live in Martissant!" he laughed. Martissant was the rich enclave high in the mountains above Port au Prince. "Until the situation with the military and the Tontons is clarified, we will all be in hiding."

"Metaphorically?"

"Yes, of course."

"And your real father, what about him?"

"He is long dead, M'ser."

"I'm sorry, Virgil," Roberts said.

The waiter brought a boiled egg and Virgil devoured it like a vulture. "It is part of life," he said.

Roberts had ordered more coffee, and the waiter brought it, too, in a white jug. There were some slices of French bread on a plate.

"And the generals? They are part of life?"

"Oui," Virgil said, his mouth full. "Namphy and Cedras. They fight over the scraps of customs receipts and drug money."

"The newspaper says Aristide is coming back."

"It is rumored," Virgil said. "The telejiol is always active."

"How did you get to the hotel so quickly yesterday?" Roberts asked.

"I was at the airport to meet Paul-Pierre!" Virgil said gaily. "He gave me money for a taxi."

The sun peeked over Boutilliers and it began to get hot again. Roberts already dreaded daylight, its yellow smog of diesel smoke, burning charcoal, garbage. He explained to Virgil that he needed a jeep and that he needed to make a trip to the Iron Market before the day was out. He knew of a rental agency near the Teleco building in Pascot, and Virgil told him they could walk there if no protests were scheduled.

Roberts paid the check with dollars. He gave Virgil some bills as an emergency fund, and together they walked out into the lobby, which was being cleaned by a cadre of old women. Its carpets were bright yellow-and-brown weaves, now badly worn, and there were huge green philodendrons in clay pots scattered about. The two men stood beside the windows looking out at the residential streets, already alive with people and animals.

"I'm looking for a man," Roberts told Virgil. "His name is Raymond Cobo. He came here to buy art, just like I've come here to buy art, and he came here at the direction of the same man who directed me here. But he disappeared. Perhaps seven weeks ago. He stayed in this hotel, and a woman came to visit him."

"This man, he is American?"

"Cuban, living in Miami. Can you take me to the police? I want to make an inquiry."

Virgil looked worried. "You would need to speak to the chef de section at Reserches Criminelles."

"Can you take me there?"

"I can, but it would do little good, M'ser."

"Certainly someone must know of this man."

"I will take you to Reserches Criminelles. But I must make myself, how you say, invisible."

"No problem," Roberts said. "You think the police are so unreliable as this?"

"We have a saying," Virgil said. " 'Rat ki gen ke pa janbe dife.' "

"What does it mean?"

" 'Rats with tails don't cross fire,' " Virgil told him.

*b*eggars hounded them for blocks. As they walked along the dust-choked residential streets of Port au Prince, Roberts could hear the Creole pleas echoing in the alleyways. Three limbless men on small four-wheeled carts pushed themselves behind him, beseeching him for anything—money, gum, trinkets, food. Young children clambered to have their photos taken, anything to make a gourd or three. "Dekous," they shouted in unison. "Two kous, M'ser," they would howl happily. Everywhere they went, Roberts saw the deformed, men, women and children alike, malnourished and suffering from measles, rickets, kwashiorkor, children with huge heads and hollow stares, tiny hands outstretched in supplication. Donkeys were beaten through the streets, loaded down with bananas, charcoal, coconuts, small bundles of firewood, barely enough scraps of sticks with which to cook a piece of goat meat, a bit of chicken, some cornmeal mush. The wood had been scrounged from the hillsides, which were already barren, and a small bundle might bring a family enough gourds to buy a meal of beans or rice, a slice of bread. Roberts gave out his gourds and then there was nothing left, and all he could do was to keep walking.

They skirted the white Presidential Palace and walked across the Place des Heroes in the dusty shade of pepper trees, then down Rue Jean Marie Guilloux in bright, suffocating sunshine, the mountains above them as red as Mars, glowing in a yellow glaze of heat. The breeze had died and Roberts was sweating heavily again despite his swim, despite the light cotton clothing he was wearing, despite trying to keep in the shade of the many verandas.

The office of the chef de section was in a two-story concrete bunker about three blocks from the Presidential Palace. It had once been painted bright green, but the paint had chipped and flaked, leaving spots of bare gray. Many evening fires had been built on the sidewalk in front, and blackened patches were clearly visible. A bright red-and-green Haitian flag had been wrapped around a pillar beneath the veranda of the office.

Dieudonné tapped Roberts on the shoulder.

"Frap has taken over the office," he whispered. "You should be very careful what you say."

Roberts saw two Tontons on the steps ahead, each in identical black sunglasses and denim jeans and shirts, bright-red bandannas around their necks. One of the Tontons was muscular and had a rope of gold chains around his neck. The other, anemic and dirty. Roberts told Dieudonné to cross the street and wait in a stationery store. He watched Virgil go, chewing some gum as he walked, then disappearing inside the shop.

Roberts eased his way around the Tontons and into the office. It smelled of curry powder, and on the wall was a photograph of Papa Doc Duvalier in his peaked cap, dark sunglasses, the pockmarked face of a smug voodoo priest. A police officer in blue sat behind a marred metal desk, smoking a cigarette. Roberts asked in French to speak to the chef de section. The officer eyed him curiously and then left, returning to escort him into the office of the chief. He was a short, fat little man, sweating profusely, dressed in a white guyabara and gray polyester slacks. The chef de section looked at Roberts through porcine eyes and frowned.

"You are American?" he asked.

Roberts flashed his passport and sat down without being asked. The chief studied the document carefully, like a man who couldn't read.

"You have a problem?" he asked.

"I'm looking for a man," Roberts said. "This man disappeared in Haiti about seven weeks ago."

"Another American?"

"Yes," Roberts said. "He lived in Miami. He traveled with an American passport, although he was Cuban. His name is Raymond Cobo."

"What is your connection to this man?"

"He was here to purchase art, just as I am here to purchase art. He has not been seen since coming here."

"Buying art," the chief said. "I have heard of no such case. In this office, we have no report of a missing American."

"Would you check your records?" Roberts asked.

"Where do you stay?"

"The Holiday Inn."

The chief touched his thinning hair. It was black and slicked back over a bald spot. He pretended to make a note in his ring-binder notebook.

"And what is your interest in this man?" he asked finally.

"He is a colleague," Roberts said.

"You are here to buy art? That is all?"

"For two weeks."

"If you will wait outside, I will call the central office."

Roberts walked to the veranda and sat down on a wooden bench in the shade. The two Tontons seemed to regard him from behind their dark glasses. He found it remarkable that there were no beggars or children around the office. Once he and Dieudonné had gotten to within a block of the place, these people seemed to disappear.

After a few minutes, the chef de section called out to Roberts from the inner office. He held a ring binder and had donned a black beret. He had put on sunglasses and was smoking a cigarette.

"I have made an inquiry," the chief said.

"There has been a report of the missing man?"

"You will be contacted," the chief told him.

"This American could have been murdered," Roberts said.

"You have information?"

"He has disappeared. Do you think he could be living happily in the hills?"

"Perhaps so," said the chief.

"You have information?" Roberts mocked.

The chief smoked and thought this over. "We have a saying in Creole," he said. " 'Pavèt pa gen rezon bèk poul.' "

"I don't speak Creole," Roberts said.

"This means 'The cockroach has no case against the hen's beak.' "

"Raymond Cobo bit off more than he could chew?"

"I do not understand the phrase."

Roberts offered to shake hands, but the chief stood without extending his own. "You will be contacted," he said.

Roberts went outside and had to ease his way around the Tontons. He had no doubt that he would be contacted again. No doubt at all.

*t*hey walked north along Rue Courte, keeping under the many verandas for shade. At midday, the streets were packed with human beings, animals, donkey carts, taxis, tap-taps roaring in billows of black exhaust, motorbikes making a thin whine. They had walked for fifteen minutes when Roberts thought he noticed two Tontons following them on the opposite side of the street. They were the two from Reserches Criminelles, the muscular Tonton in the lead, trying to stay hidden in the crowd.

"You've seen the Tontons?" Roberts asked Virgil.

"They are following us," he said.

They halted outside a variety store and Roberts bought several slices of fresh pineapple from a street vendor. Standing in the shade, they ate the sweet meat of the fruit. A brightly colored tap-tap painted in gold and red stopped across the street, letting off a swarm of people. Roberts noticed the name of the tap-tap: Scooby Doo. The Tonton with the gold chains was holding a truncheon, what Virgil called his "coca macaque." The Tonton leaned against a pillar, tapping his thigh with the weapon.

"I guess I shouldn't be surprised," Roberts said. "They look rather sinister, though."

"Tonton means 'uncle,'" Virgil explained. "From the name of Baron Samedi, who reigns over Saturday night when Jesus is sleeping in his tomb."

"And macoute?" Roberts asked. He sucked the cool pineapple, its juice as sweet as candy.

"The macoute is a knapsack," Virgil said. "Samedi carries the macoute with him when he walks the night. In it, he places the souls he captures."

"The Tontons pretend to be Baron Samedi?"

"In a way," Virgil said. "They wish to frighten the people by appearing as vestiges of the Baron."

"Voodoo politics," Roberts muttered. He finished the pineapple and waited while Virgil ate the last of his own. Nearby, an herb doctor, or "docteur feuilles," pitched the sale of his wares: chicken legs, goat heads, frogs, fish, the bodies of pickled snakes, bottles of potions.

"I wonder what they're after," Roberts said of the Tontons.

"It can be no good," Virgil told him. "You must be wary of the police and Tontons. We should keep moving, M'ser."

At Rue de Fronts Forts, they turned west and walked toward the ocean. Roberts could see the waterfront and its quays, a mass of low concrete abutments, tin sheds, piers, with a few rusted container ships anchored in the harbor. They had gone downhill and were on the hot flats of the city, the hills and mountains far behind them, doused in hurricane-season clouds. Yellow dust blew through the streets and dogs howled everywhere.

Near Rue Corbe, they reached the monumental arched entrance to the Iron Market. When they went inside, Roberts found it almost impossible to move through the dense crowds, a press of beggars, salesmen, hawkers, and hustlers. In front of the many stalls lay piles of rice and potatoes, sacks of nuts, and fruit of all kinds—mango, orange, lemon, banana—plastic sacks jammed with secondhand shoes, shirts, and suits the people called "pepe kenedi," named after the shipments of used clothing sent by the Kennedy Administration in the early 1960s. Roberts studied the piles of furniture, handmade rattan, wrought iron, used CDs and tapes, mounds of carved wooden objects.

He found a selection of paintings and hunted through them.

There were hundreds of oil works done on plywood, board, occasionally real canvas. Effigies in tin hung from rafters, along with musical instruments, bird cages, gloves and hats. Roberts was staggered by the number of limbless beggars, speechless beggars, children covered by flies, heaps of rotting fruit and garbage. In time, he purchased some cotton pants and a new white shirt for Virgil, along with some knockoff Reeboks and white socks. When they finally emerged from the Iron Market, they were not far from the port warehouses and the Cite Soleil. Somehow, the Tontons had managed to follow them. Quickly, Roberts hailed a taxi, and they headed back to the Holiday Inn.

They drove south, then back east, Roberts riding with the window down. "The police chief cited me a Creole proverb," he told Virgil. " 'The cockroach has no case against the hen's beak.' "

"Yes, it is a common saying."

"I can only guess what he meant."

"You were asking about M'ser Cobo?"

"I made an inquiry. He didn't seem anxious to give me any information."

"And this is what he said, this proverb?"

"He said he'd check with his superiors."

"I think he means that Cobo is dead, M'ser."

They went past the vast Presidential Palace with its white marble facade, its many windows and perfectly manicured lawns. They rounded a corner and were in the Place des Heroes, which Roberts had heard called the Place des Zeroes, a mock honor to the Duvalier years. In truth, all the heroes had disappeared and Tontons ruled the streets.

Roberts ate lunch beside the hotel pool and read a book about Haitian art, given him by Dolores Vega. He napped and then went to his room and changed into a swim suit and took a fifteen-minute dip. Walking back through the lobby, he was called over by the clerk.

"You have a message, M'ser," the clerk said.

Roberts picked up the message and asked the clerk for his leather pouch.

"A woman has checked into the hotel," the clerk said. "She wishes to see you when you return. She has written down her room number."

Roberts thanked the clerk and tipped him a dollar. He was handed the leather pouch containing his weapon. He took an elevator to the third floor.

*t*hey made love to the rhythm of a violent rainstorm that lashed Port au Prince as darkness fell.

Roberts had gone to his room and called her and she came to him in a thin, cream-colored chemise. As thunder crashed, they tortured each other with passion, and then they lay still, listening to the rain in the trees outside. She was bread to a starving man. She would lick his neck and bite his face, and the thunder would burst and they would lie still for a long time again as the minutes ticked away. Finally, when the storm had passed, they talked for an hour as the city filled with smoke and the smell of charcoal. Strangely, another storm broke about midnight. With lightning and strong wind, it seemed to pass in minutes and they watched it from their bed, languid as two hibernating bears, while the neighborhood dogs barked.

When they woke from sleep, it was hot in the room. Roberts had turned off the air-conditioning unit and had opened the patio doors, but with the passing of the storms, the night had become still and humid. He lay sweating as the uproar of the city drifted around them. She was beside him, tangled in a sheet.

In the morning, they agreed to meet for breakfast beside the pool. When Roberts arrived, he found Dolores and Virgil chatting over coffee.

"You've met, I see," Roberts said, taking a seat at the table.

Some swimmers were doing laps in the pool. It was Sunday

morning, and the city was doused by the sound of bells. Virgil told Roberts that the waiter was bringing eggs, French bread, and mugs of coffee. The waiter arrived and offered melon from a serving tray. Roberts took some of the fruit and began to butter his bread.

"There is a Creole riddle," Virgil told them. "What is the melon?"

"I'll bite," Roberts said.

"In Creole, dio kouche."

"And that means?" Dolores asked. She looked wonderful to Roberts, her white cotton dress, her auburn hair, a perfect picture.

"Water lying down," Virgil laughed.

Roberts caught a glance at the front page of the *Nouvilliste*. He could barely understand the French, but it seemed to be a report of political violence all over the country.

"There was much trouble in the city," Virgil said. "Last night another Tonton was killed near Saint Jean Bosco. There were demonstrations against the curfew. There was a march against Cedras. And one of the Aristide men was badly beaten. Now we must all be careful. The city is tense. One false look at a Tonton can be disaster. And I'm worried about these Tontons who were following you yesterday."

"Tontons following you?" Dolores asked. "What's this all about?"

"Don't worry," Roberts told her. He had decided to wear his long chino fishing pants. They allowed him to carry a gun. Over breakfast, they agreed to let Virgil take them on a tour of the city. They would see the Cathedral de la Sainte Trinite, one of the centers of Haitian cultural life. They would visit some galleries and a local art shop or two. After that, they would take in the museum of Haitian art and have a good lunch up in Petionville, where it would be cool and green.

After breakfast, they hired a taxi for the day. Roberts and Dolores rode in back with the windows down, while Virgil took the front seat, lecturing them on Haitian history and culture as they drove. On Rue Jean Marie Guilloux, soldiers had cordoned off the Presidential Palace and stood at attention in the sun, their automatic rifles slung over their shoulders. On every street corner were two or three Tontons. The tension was palpable, and as they drove north toward the cathedral, the sound of tenèb became more and more apparent, a rattle of machetes, a clang of pots and pans banged together, a steady trill of conch horns being blown. They stopped at the corner of Rue Pauvée, and Roberts told the driver to wait.

Services in the cathedral had ended and a large crowd was milling about outside, people dressed in their finest clothes, straw hats, brilliant print shawls. The church grounds occupied most of a square city block, the gleaming pink cathedral with its twin towers, cupolas, naves. Virgil led them through the crowd and inside the church, where it was cool and dark. Dolores showed Roberts the huge primitive murals that covered most of two walls, "The Last Supper" by Philome Obine, with its black Christ and black apostles and gaudy colors, and "The Marriage of Cana" by Wilson Biguad, a surreal rendering of the famous biblical story.

They were near the altar when the explosion hit. Roberts was on a step, trying to see some of the details of "The Last Supper." Dolores and Virgil had wandered up an aisle toward one of the naves. Roberts felt the concussion before he heard the sound, an echo inside his head, a flash of reddish stars. In that instant, a tiny fish of pain swam to the top of his head and lingered, then disappeared as dust pattered down from the high ceiling of the church. He heard screams from outside as more wisps of dust filtered through the huge mahogany doors. Then everything went oddly silent.

Virgil found a side door and led them through a small garden toward a Catholic elementary school. Down the street reverberated the sound of sirens. When they emerged on Rue Pauvée, they saw bodies in the street, broken glass, bloody rags. A few stray dogs were sniffing the dead and wounded. Roberts walked over to one of the bodies and knelt down. It was a child, a little girl in white taffeta and sandals. Her head had been severely gashed by shrapnel or debris. Virgil came and touched Roberts on the shoulder.

"We must go," he said.

"Shouldn't we try to help?"

"The ambulances will come."

Roberts stood and looked at the litter in the street, already women beginning to cry.

"But there are wounded."

"We must take Dolores away from here. There may be more explosions. The Tontons may come."

By some miracle, their taxi was waiting.

35

---

*t*hey were stopped twice at police roadblocks on the way to Le Perchoir. Each time, Virgil was forced into long conversations with armed men, all speaking in heated Creole that Roberts couldn't understand. It was the first time Roberts had seen the police with real revolvers drawn, at the ready, and he wondered if the three of them were safe. Even the taxi driver sat in horrified silence as Virgil negotiated their passage.

The restaurant seemed suspended in a green jungle. They were led to a patio on the side of a steep hill from where they could see the city spread out below, miles of vague terrain, slums, the gleaming Teleco building reflecting tropical sunlight. The pepper trees were alive with birdsong, and big cumulus clouds hovered in the mountains. They ordered pumpkin soup, griots, grilled whitefish, and cold beer. A guitarist sat under a flowering orchid, strumming his instrument and singing in lilting Creole:

> Dodo titit manman-li
> Do titit manman-li
> Si tititi-la pa vle dodo
> Krab non kalalou va manje-li

Roberts sat quietly, thinking about the explosion, the mangled bodies of children, listening to this Creole lullaby so at odds with his inner visions. Dappled sunlight spread over them, drifting down the rough pepper trees. Virgil was quiet, too, sipping his sweet Secola Orange, while Dolores explored the pumpkin soup without tasting a single drop.

"I want you to go home today," Roberts told Dolores.

"Yes," Virgil added. "The politics is very dangerous. You should go home now, I think. Perhaps it is none of my business."

"I'll go home," Dolores said, "when my plane leaves. I have two more days. Let's make the best of them."

Virgil shrugged. "As they say in Creole, 'Jodi-a se jou malè.' It means that 'Today is an accursed day.' The people, they have risen up against the Tontons and the Army, who have oppressed them for many years. And now there are explosions on Sunday morning in front of the church. It is a very evil day, Mademoiselle."

"Why the church?" Roberts asked.

"Ah, so evil," Virgil said. "Many of the Aristide people are devout followers. So the Tontons, they attack where the terror is great. And that means they must terrorize the faith of those who support Aristide. In these days and times, it has been the Aristide church that has supported the poor in their efforts to have a scrap of food, to have a roof. In all these years of Papa Doc, the country has been robbed and robbed until there is nothing left. The rich, they play in their shaded villas and they ride polo horses on their green fields and they drink Scotch and pretend they are living in Paris. And meanwhile, there are the citizens of Cité Soleil, Canapé Vert, all the other slums, who must live on garbage, drink sewer water, scour the gutters for bits of bread or a piece of meat that has dropped from the mouth of a dog. 'Peyi-a ap fè bak,' they say in Creole. Which means, 'The country is going backward.' "

Roberts took Dolores by the hand. "I still want you out of here now. Let me take you to the airport today."

"I'll leave when my ticket says I'll leave."

"But be reasonable," Roberts pleaded.

"I want to be with you," she said. "I want you to see the Centre d'Art and the Musée d'Art Haitian du Collège Saint Pierre, and maybe the Musée Defly on the Champs de Mars. I want us to go swimming at Ibo Beach, and I want you to see the Musée National. After all, they have the jawbone of Henri Christophe inside there!" Dolores smiled knowingly. "You need your introduction to Haitian primitive art. It's why I came over here, isn't it?"

"That's why you came over?"

"Well, part of it anyway."

Roberts had no appetite, but he tried to eat the soup. When the griots and fish came, he tried to nibble at them, but he kept thinking of the little girl in taffeta, her face all bloodied. He kept seeing dogs roaming through the carnage, sniffing blood.

"Can we be ready to travel on Tuesday?" Roberts asked Virgil. "I want to take Dolores to the airport that morning, then start making our visits to artists. I think it's important we get this over as quickly as possible."

"I'll be ready, M'ser," Virgil said.

"Until then, I want you to stay with us. You'll have to get us through police checkpoints. I know it's a great strain."

"I can do the dèbroillard," Virgil said. "I am the best hustler you know!"

Virgil looked very smart in his new guayabara and gray cotton slacks, his brilliantly white Reebok knockoffs. He had rolled up the cuffs of his pants so that everybody could see his new shoes.

The singer wandered over to the table and Roberts gave him a handful of gourds. Maybe it was the quiet and the shade and the coolness in the air that distracted him, but he failed to see the look of fear that crossed the singer's face. Below, a black Chevrolet had parked in the lot and two Tontons were walking up the stairs to the restaurant. Both were wearing blue jeans and denim shirts, red bandannas, black sunglasses. Roberts recognized the muscular one from the police station. Both carried coco macaques, tapping them on their hips as they walked.

The muscular Tonton licked his lips and looked at Roberts. "Bon jou, tout moun alawonnbade," he said sarcastically.

"Bonjour," Roberts said.

Virgil blinked and broke a sweat.

"Hey, Blanc," the Tonton said. "Ale, you come."

Virgil spoke quickly in English. "The chef de section wishes to speak with you," he told Roberts.

"Tell them I'll come down myself. Fifteen minutes."

"They say they will drive you."

Roberts decided he'd better go. He didn't want to make trouble at the restaurant lest Dolores or Virgil be hurt. If there was trouble, he would encounter it alone. His heart was pounding and he could feel a tremor in his hands.

"Let's go," he said. "I'll see you back at the hotel in an hour," he told Dolores.

"Be careful, please," she said.

36

*t*hey put Roberts in the backseat, where he could be seen. He rode that way while the skinny Tonton drove and the muscular one eyed him in the rearview mirror. Through miles of plywood shacks, they drove down into the heart of the city, where the crowds had thinned as the day's heat increased. The skinny Tonton careened recklessly, probably trying to frighten Roberts. Once into town, they parked on the south side of the Place des Heroes, just a block from the police station, and Roberts walked in front of the Tontons around a circular garden of hibiscus and oleander and big mapous trees that created pools of shade on the statues of Haitian military heroes. The Tontons made sure that Roberts went into the Reserches Criminelles, then waited on the veranda outside. Roberts found the chef de section smoking a cigarette at his desk. Roberts took out a small cigar and lit it, waiting for the chief to look up.

"Asseyez," the chief told him.

Roberts took a seat. "Eh votre name?" he asked.

"Zacharie Filo," the chief replied. He was dressed in green polyester. On the collar of his shirt was a rhinestone pin in the shape of a question mark. "You must forgive me for requesting your presence on a Sunday," he said.

"I was having lunch," Roberts told him.

"You have been to church?"

"I was at the cathedral," Roberts admitted.

"Then you know of the explosion."

"I was there. It seems to me that many innocent people were killed or wounded."

"It is a trick of the Aristides," the chief said.

"They kill their own women and children?"

"For propaganda purposes."

"I was looking at the murals," Roberts said.

"You found them interesting?"

"The explosion intervened. I find it hard to believe that the Aristides would kill their own people just to make some propaganda gains."

"We have a saying in Creole," Filo said. " 'Jesus bon, mais Damballa puissant.' " He crushed out his cigarette and ran one hand through his thinning hair. His skin was mottled with white patches. "Does this saying please you?"

"If you could translate."

" 'Jesus is good, but Damballa is strong.' "

"Damballa is a voodoo god?"

"One of them," Filo said.

"And Damballa caused the explosion?"

"You have put words into my mouth."

"I'm told that Aristide will return."

"It is a fantasy of the Americans."

"Surely as a policeman, you hold yourself aloof from politics?"

"Nobody is free from politics. It is when you think you are free of politics that you are most unfree. Were not the German Jews free from politics?"

"Perhaps you have a point," Roberts said.

"You yourself should be free from politics in Haiti," said Filo.

"I'm always very careful," Roberts told him. He began to worry that he would be searched, the gun found in his pocket. He imagined himself in the Casserness Dessalines down by the port, perhaps tortured. It was in the Casserness that many of the political foes of Papa Doc had been tortured, then killed, their bodies dumped in the bay for shark food. It was said that Tontons rounded them up at night, cut off their hands, burned them, shocked them. It was the source of a legend surrounding Baron Samedi, the God of Saturday night, who puts your soul into a wicker sack. The creator of zombies. The annihilator of innocence. Samedi, the implacable foe of Jesus. "Why did you bring me here?" Roberts asked finally.

"Perhaps you should be more careful," Filo said.

"I still have work to do."

"Yes, you are an art collector," Filo said.

Roberts continued to smoke his cigar. The street outside the police station was deserted at late afternoon. "And exactly why did you ask me here?" Roberts asked. "I thought perhaps it was about my colleague, Raymond Cobo."

"Ah yes," Filo said. He took a manila folder from the desk and managed to give the appearance of reading it. Flies circled the room and there was a lizard on one wall, climbing for a barred window. "We do have information on M'ser Cobo. It seems he entered the country quite legally and there is no report of any crime on his dossier. It seems that he left Haiti. He was free to go, and he did go. He was not officially involved in any way."

"That's very interesting," Roberts said.

"I can assure you," Filo said, smiling. "Perhaps we should allow Monsieur Cobo to rest in peace."

The lizard skittered out the window. It stopped on the sill and turned to stare at Roberts, its eyes on stalks. "Did you happen to meet with Raymond Cobo?" Roberts asked.

"I suggest you forget this Cobo," Filo said. "Do your work and leave Haiti."

"That's all I ever intended to do," Roberts said. "And I'm curious about the pin on your collar. It is very unusual."

"Eh, dramatic, no?" Filo said.

"It has a meaning?"

"It provokes," Filo replied.

"What does it provoke?"

"Fear, perhaps," Filo said.

"I suppose an ignorant man could be easily provoked."

Filo waved a hand in annoyance. "I assure you," he said, "that there is no Raymond Cobo in Haiti. I have made the inquiry you requested." Filo stood, indicating that the interview had ended. "Forgive me, but I have work to do," he said.

Roberts went out to the street. The Tontons had disappeared and he didn't see their Chevrolet parked at the Place des Heroes. A brightly painted tap-tap named "Je Sui Q'il Vit" roared by in a plume of diesel exhaust and dust. Roberts walked the mile back to the Holiday Inn in a bright, glazed heat. He had the feeling that he was being followed, but he was too hot and tired to care.

*t*he dead chicken had been doused in blue paint. Its throat had been cut, and splattered blood made a kind of horrible bow tie on its neck.

Roberts had walked down to the Holiday Inn, past the Place des Heroes, and then down the Rue Capois in a city made silent by the eerie force of airborne tension. He bought some peanuts from a street vendor and ate them as he walked. When he got back to his room, he found the dead chicken on his bed, its neck slashed, its feathers sticky with blue paint. He left the chicken on the bed, took a shower, and put in a call to Dolores.

When he got to her room, she had showered and was wearing a terry-cloth bathrobe. Her hair was wet and she looked beautiful but worried. She had bought a bottle of good rum, and it was standing open on her bureau, along with a bowl of half-melted ice. Roberts kissed her hello, then poured them each a small glass of the rum.

"I imagined you not coming back," Dolores told him.

They went out to the shaded patio and stood drinking their rum, looking down at the swimming pool, deserted in the heat. The sky was yellow with soot, and a breeze was blowing dust through the streets.

"The chef de section wanted to talk," Roberts said.

"I was frightened."

"He told me Cobo had left the country."

"It's possible, I suppose," Dolores said.

"He's lying, of course," Roberts told her.

"You think so?"

"I'd bank on it."

"Virgil is downstairs in the restaurant. He's been drinking one orangeade after another, worried to death about you."

"He's a great fellow," Roberts said. "He's essentially an orphan. A family took him in and raised him. Imagine what that means for someone poor. To take on an extra mouth to feed. They must be wonderful people."

"He's a very good boy," Dolores said. "Those Tontons at the restaurant frightened him out of his wits. But he stood up to them nonetheless."

"Did you know that Cobo stayed here?"

"No, how would I know that?"

"I suppose you wouldn't," Roberts said. "He saw Champagne Lambert at the airport. A woman visited him in this hotel. You wouldn't know who the woman might be?"

"Of course not," Dolores said. "Are you cross-examining me?"

"Not exactly," Roberts answered. "It's a curious thing, though. I feel like Cobo's shadow, following along in his footsteps."

"Please," Dolores said. "Let's not talk about Raymond Cobo."

Roberts sipped his rum. "I found a dead chicken in my room," he told her. "Somebody left it on my bed. It was covered with blue paint. Its throat cut."

Dolores closed her eyes for a moment. "I'm afraid I don't understand any of this," she said. "Do you think those Tontons could have done it?"

"They were gone when I left the police station. I don't imagine it would be hard for them to get into my room."

Dolores put down her drink and hugged him. "Come back to Miami with me," she said.

"What does the chicken mean?" Roberts asked.

"It is a silly voodoo curse," she said.

"Meaning?"

"Just a curse, magie noire. It is a token of bad luck, an ill omen.

For those who believe, it is a symbol that they will sicken and die, they will shrivel. The superstitious are always using these curses."

"I'm going downstairs," Roberts said. "I've got to make a plan with Virgil about the rental car."

"Let's just leave Haiti," Dolores urged.

"And do what? Go where?"

"At least let's leave this hotel. We could go to the Olaffson. Perhaps they will leave you alone now."

"I have to go to the bank tomorrow," Roberts said. "I have to rent a jeep. You have to show me the museums and galleries. Let me have the value of your expertise."

Dolores kissed him hard. "You've already had the value of my expertise," she said.

Roberts put his hand beneath the robe, feeling her body. He slid his hand down her long leg. Then he finished his rum and went downstairs to find Virgil. The young man was sitting at a booth in the restaurant, forlornly sipping at a sweet drink.

"I am so glad to see you, M'ser," Virgil said.

Roberts ordered another rum. In a high breeze, the banana trees outside were making a racket. For now, there was air-conditioning, but soon the electricity would be shut off, and it would be hot, at least until the generators were turned on. Virgil listened intently while Roberts told him about his visit with Filo, the long walk to the hotel, the dead chicken on his bed.

"But this is terrible," Virgil said.

"Dolores tells me it is a curse."

"It is no laughing matter," Virgil assured him.

"Don't tell me you believe these things?"

"I do not believe, but neither do I laugh."

Virgil finished his orange drink. "I'm not exactly laughing," Roberts said.

"We have a Creole saying," Virgil said. " 'Sa Bondye sere pou-ou lavalas pa janm bwote-l ale.' "

"And this means?"

"It means 'What God holds for, no flood can wash away.' "

"You're telling me not to tempt fate."

"The person who curses you has a strong belief. Some people say that a strong belief can defeat any disbelief."

"Tomorrow we rent a jeep," Roberts said. "That's one thing I'm sure of. We need to meet here early in the morning."

"I will be here, M'ser."

"By eight o'clock," Roberts said. "We leave on Tuesday."

"There will be many roadblocks, M'ser," Virgil said. "Have you read the newspapers?"

"What about them?"

"Namphy and Cedras quarrel over the bones."

"Let them quarrel," Roberts said.

"There are factions. It only increases the tension."

Roberts paid his bill and they went outside to the pool. Up in Boutilliers, black clouds had gathered and Roberts could hear the sound of distant thunder. He walked around to the lobby and checked at the front desk to inform the clerk that there was a dead chicken on his bed. The clerk seemed startled, almost in shock. He told Roberts that the same thing had happened to Raymond Cobo. Then Monsieur Cobo had gone to another hotel.

*h*e was awakened at six o'clock by the sound of bats. In his dream state, he thought that the electricity had failed again, and he lay in the dark, propped on an arm, until he saw the shapes of the bats outside the patio window, huge numbers of them streaking toward the mountains, velvet marks on a gray background.

He got up and walked to the sliding-glass door and opened it, allowing in the humid morning air. Bats dove uphill, scouting the pines and banana trees for insects, heading for the pepper trees of Boutilliers, Kenscoff, Petionville, rich suburbs where the elite lived in leafy suburbs, huge enclaves surrounded by brick walls, electrified fences, broken-glass barriers. On the grounds roamed Dobermans and armed guards. Perhaps the voodoo tales were correct and bats were lost souls searching for their homes, flying off into a nether wilderness, half-dead, half-alive. He watched the bats for fifteen minutes and then went back to bed.

He slept for another hour, showered, and went to the pool for an early breakfast alone. The sun was just behind the mountains, and already the city was sending off an urban howl of noise. Dogs barked, chickens crowed, small motorbikes beyond the hotel compound roared and hooted through the suburban streets. The sky had turned yellow with soot, and there was thick laterite dust aloft. Roberts was finishing his second cup of coffee when he saw Virgil striding purposefully through the lobby. He raised his hand in greeting and Virgil smiled. His new pants were caked with dust and his shoes had lost their angelic whiteness. Virgil sat down and Roberts poured him a cup of coffee.

"There has been a coup," Virgil said.

"I didn't hear a thing."

"It was bloodless, so they say."

"I saw bats, that's all," Roberts told him.

"The bats were old generals going to the hills."

"And the new generals?"

"Cedras alone. No more junta. He has vowed that Aristide will never return. He will defy the Americans."

Roberts was eating bread and jam. The waiter brought along a plate of mangoes and papaya, Virgil eating happily while he talked.

"The streets look normal," Roberts said.

"Under the Army, everything is normal. That is precisely the problem, M'ser."

"And the roadblocks?"

"I have not heard. Where is Mademoiselle Dolores?"

"I let her sleep. She had a difficult day yesterday. I told her that this morning we'd run our errands. This afternoon we're going to Ibo Beach and the museums. You think we can drive to the beach?"

"We will see, no?" Virgil said. "Cedras has promised elections."

"You have a saying in Creole, no doubt?"

Virgil clapped his hands gleefully. "In Creole, we say 'Bilten se papye, bayonet se fe.' "

Roberts puzzled over the words. " 'Ballots are paper. Bullets are iron'?"

"Very good, Monsieur," Virgil said. "In my country, ballots are only paper."

"In my country, ballots are meaningless as well. They are purchased with millions of dollars on TV."

"But the Americans have a choice," Virgil said.

"It makes no difference now," Roberts told him. "The truth is not influential in my country."

"We have no sayings in Creole about truth," Virgil said. "There are some things too desperate for a homily." He drank some coffee and ate a slice of bread. He seemed caught by a fleeting mood, folding his hands in his lap. "Mes-z-amis," he said at last. "This matter of the Tontons and the chef de section is most serious. You must be very careful."

"I'll be careful," Roberts said. "We see our artists in the city. We drive to Jacmel and we drive to Cap Haitien. I deliver the goods to Champagne Lambert and then I'm off for home. You'll be well paid."

"It isn't the money, M'ser," Virgil said. "There are monsters roaming this country."

"I have a job," Roberts said. "I appreciate your concern. Tell me, how is Paul-Pierre?"

"He makes like the débrouillard."

"And what about the father and mother? His other brother?"

"They are safe for now. He is trying to obtain a visa for them, but it is very hard."

"And what about the explosion? Who is responsible?"

"The chief of police, Michel François, theorizes that the Aristide supporters are themselves responsible."

"Filo told me the same thing."

"It is a common theme," Virgil said. "They believe we are trying to create martyrs. But there are already enough martyrs in Haiti."

After breakfast, they took a taxi to the rental agency on Rue Carbone, just near Place St. Anne. On Monday morning, the streets were jammed with beggars, vendors, men and women going to market with bundles on their heads, donkeys being driven behind carts. Twice the taxi was forced to stop as huge herds of cochons noire, the skinny black Haitian pigs, were driven through crossroads. Hustlers followed the taxi for blocks, shouting at the blanc for money. At the agency, Roberts arranged to pick up his jeep the next morning by ten o'clock. Virgil led him over to the French bank near Teleco, on Grand Rue. It took forty minutes to see the manager, open his account, and deposit the letter of credit. When he left, Roberts had obtained a drawing right and a small set of desk checks. The bank manager remembered Raymond Cobo, but was not at liberty to say more.

39

*t*hey checked out of the Holiday Inn at noon. The day had become stiflingly hot, with scattered hurricane-weather mist blown to the tips of the mountains, where it lingered and dissipated.

In the streets, there were no signs of the coup. People said that the soldiers were staying out of sight in order to give Cedras a good start. Sunday's explosion had killed two and injured fourteen, most of them women and children who had just come from Mass. Headlines stated the obvious. The chief of police blamed Aristide. After all, hadn't an American senator accused Aristide of insanity? And wasn't it a topsy-turvy world just as Virgil said it was, where truth was a lie and lies were the truth, a grand truth, civilians accused of war crimes while the generals banked millions?

After Roberts rented his jeep and did his banking, he and Dolores walked toward the Musée d'Art. Roberts had the feeling he was being followed again, this time by three Tontons who hid in the market crowds. But when he made a conscious effort to spot them, they seemed to disappear. Dolores was beautiful, but lost in thought. She was wearing gray chiffon pants, a red halter top, and sandals. She had tied her hair behind her head and wore a broad-brimmed straw hat to keep off the sun. She was carrying a large straw basket for her things—sunglasses, creams, lotions, small bottles of soda water they would share as they walked. They strolled through the crowds, but said almost nothing to one another.

They bought griots and fried bread from a street vendor and

nibbled them as they went through the market stalls. Later, they spent two hours in the museums. She showed him the work of Wilson Bigaud and Philome Obine, two painters who single-handedly had created the primitive modernist style of Haitian oil, along with Castera Bazile and dozens of other Haitian geniuses who painted in a colorful, crazed manner. She tried to teach him the good from the bad, the elements and categories of brush stroke, the metaphorical musings of these masters. At the Iron Market, she showed him the artificial and dull, contrasting them with the original and spontaneous. She lectured him on the fine points. She was distant. They hardly touched.

When they wearied, they took a taxi to the Foret des Pins above Port au Prince and ate a late lunch in a fancy restaurant. It was almost three o'clock and the sun had passed over the mountains and was dropping in the west, red and flat over the blue Caribbean. Dolores ordered grilled shrimp and salad with fruit. Roberts was having lobster, though to him, it seemed criminal to eat so well fifteen hundred meters above the abject misery of so many millions. He could see the slums down by the port, slag piles of human life, men and women and children living in shanties amid garbage and squalor. It seemed to stretch for mile after endless mile to the sea, north toward the airport.

A waiter brought them bottled water, and orchids in a tiny dish of cut glass. He placed the orchids on the table and smiled. They were on a shady patio and Debussy was playing over outdoor speakers. While they ate, clouds gathered on Boutilliers, threatening rain.

"I haven't been much company," Dolores said. "We'll have a nice night together at the Olaffson. I promise."

"Don't worry," Roberts told her honestly.

"I keep seeing that little girl at the church," Dolores said. "The blue chicken you told me about. It frightens me. All of it."

"You've been very brave," Roberts said. "In the newspapers, the little girl was listed as only severely wounded. She is going to live."

Dolores sighed and poked at her salad. The Debussy was soothing, a counterpoint to everything else.

"Somebody followed us today," she said.

"I saw them. It's the Tontons."

"What about the beach? Still want to try swimming?"

Roberts said he'd love to go swimming. It seemed foolish to both of them. There had been a coup. There were roadblocks and Tontons and nervous soldiers in the countryside. Even so, they agreed that they'd pick up their bags at the Holiday Inn, check into the Olaffson, then drive up to Ibo. They could be there in an hour, swim for a while, then return to the city before dark. Nobody was certain if Cedras would impose a curfew, but there was always the informal curfew to worry about.

When they finished lunch, they taxied to the hotel, finding that Virgil had stacked their luggage on the steps and had arranged for a taxi to Ibo Beach. They threw their bags in a battered Plymouth, stopped by the Olaffson, and then headed to Ibo over rough, pot-holed roads. When they got to the beach, they found it dirty and garbage-strewn, forlorn, and almost empty except for a few dispirited hawkers and food vendors. There was only a little shade, and the hawkers seemed to congregate under the ragged palms, displaying their strings of barbecued crabs, offering tepid Orange Secola. Roberts paid the taxi man to wait, but they went back to the city after only twenty minutes.

The Olaffson sat just above the Presidential Palace on a little hill where there were still some pepper trees and a few big mahoganies that hadn't been cut down. Its three stories of gingerbread Victoriana had seen better days. Its verandas sagged, paint peeling, the pool full of leaves and dirt. Even so, it had a kind of imperial majesty as well as a fantastical aspect that appealed to Roberts immediately. There was a bar buried in a crush of huge philodendrons and potted hibiscus. There was flowered wallpaper and rattan and wicker furniture and a few dozen lizards sunning themselves in the hallways.

Once they had checked in, Dolores went to her room to take a nap and Roberts wandered down to the bar. A brilliant sunset washed the western horizon in purple and gold. Roberts ordered a rum punch and walked with it to the edge of the pool and sat down in a white rattan chair.

It wasn't long before a dapper Englishman came out and sat down across from Roberts. He wore bottle glasses and had thinning sandy hair. His hands and face were mottled with freckles, and the veins around his nose had broken down.

"Basil Davis," the man said cheerfully. They shook hands and Roberts mentioned his own name.

"Welcome to the Olaffson," Davis said. "I'm the temporary substitute interim manager, just so you'll know to mind your *p*'s and *q*'s." Davis was drinking neat rum from a footed tumbler. He looked at the amber liquor through a prism of sunshine. "You're an American, what?"

"It's pretty obvious, I guess," Roberts said.

"Excellent punch, isn't it?"

"Very good indeed."

"Olaffson's famous for it," Davis said. "May I ask what you're doing in Haiti now? The hotel is nearly empty. Been a bloody coup."

"I'm buying Haitian art for a gallery in Miami."

Davis thought that over. He sipped his rum like a man inured to the experience.

"You're the second like that we've had," he said.

"You don't say," Roberts said.

"Another chap last month. Perhaps longer ago. Fat fellow, large gut, Hispanic. Can't think of his name."

"Raymond Cobo?"

"That's it exactly," Davis said.

"He's a colleague."

"Came and went rather quickly," Davis said.

"How's that?"

"He checked out in a hurry," Davis told him. "Left in a huff, complaining about voodoo and the Tontons. Nonsense. Probably drinking too much. Happens when one gets stuck here."

40

*t*he *Nouvelliste* reported Americans on the way. The telejiol murmured that Americans were coming, and Radio 32 chattered the imminent arrival of the Americans, planes and shiploads of them. Cedras threatened to close the airport and impose a dusk-to-dawn curfew, ban political demonstrations, close the churches. Two Tontons had been necklaced in a village near Gonaive, and a dozen slum shacks had been torched in Canape Vert, near Port au Prince.

Roberts and Virgil were sitting amidst the confusion of the airport, watching Dolores Vega walk across the tarmac toward her jet.

"I'm glad she's going, M'ser," Virgil said. "Only because of the danger. Only because the airport may not be open much longer."

Roberts had to agree. He watched her trudge up the jetway steps and disappear inside the airplane. Virgil had bought them two cups of coco frio, cold coconut juice, and they were sipping it through straws. The air-conditioning had failed in the lounge and the building was humid and airless. Soldiers had taken the place of police at the checkpoints. Rumor had it that American Airlines would suspend daily flights to Port au Prince.

When her plane had gone, they went up to Furcy, above the city. Roberts drove the jeep and Virgil navigated the tortuously crowded streets, passing roadblocks manned by nervous soldiers, up through the environs of the rich, Petionville and Kenscoff. Behind them lay the sprawling, overheated city, drowning in yellow haze, untouched by the ocean breezes and the pine smells of the mountains. Once they got into the countryside, Roberts flew down narrow lanes lined by sugarcane, banana trees, hedges of flowering oleander. Off in the distance he could see a coffee plantation, and farther away in a clouded haze, red laterite gullies that marked the limit of cultivation. Higher up were the eroded valleys of central Hispaniola, the cactus deserts and burning plains. Virgil directed him down a grassy lane to the habitation of Gerard Delva, the first artist on Roberts' itinerary.

The bohío was built of simple lime and mud, painted alternating white and dark-red bands. A small yard in front of the house was of pounded dirt, chickens roaming, a charcoal brazier guttering under a palm. Delva came out into the yard, a tiny, handsome man with hands like spiders, grizzled gray hair, maybe half his teeth. He moved like a fly might move, sudden spontaneous motion, more a flick than a walk. He greeted them warmly and took them into the house, where there was only one room, two benches, one broken-armed easy chair, a homemade cupboard containing a few cooking pots and pans, utensils, cracked plates. An easel had been set up in one corner near a window, and one wall was hung with dozens of paintings. Delva's work was a stunning inventory of hallucinatory green, bright blood-red, twisted tornadoes of color and excitement, village scenes, ascending saints, purple serpents with twisted tongues, all suffused by bright orange sunlight.

Delva spoke softly, his voice raspy. "You are interested in my work?" he asked.

Virgil squatted in the doorway. Roberts sat on a bench, looking at the splendid art. Wind rippled in the cane fields not far away, rattled the banana palms.

Delva spoke in a mix of Creole, bad French, English. At times, Virgil would interpret from his doorway perch.

"It's quite beautiful," Roberts said. "You are a very great painter."

Delva smiled, showing his few teeth. "You wish to buy?" he asked shyly.

"Very much indeed," Roberts said.

"You are an American?"

"Yes. I have money to buy."

"It is interesting," Delva said. "The French come here to admire my work. The English come to drink and tell me I am a genius. Only the Americans come to buy. And in these days and times, there are not many of those. One last month, and none for many months before that."

"A large Hispanic man?"

"He called himself Raymond," Delva said. "He was not American. But he said he had American money."

Roberts asked to look at the paintings. Delva showed him through a collection that leaned against one wall of the bohío. Roberts found them stunning, awesome, purposefully surreal. Snakes, burning villages, generals with velveteen wings, flying rabbits, organized cadres of devils and angels, zombies, great golden-headed chickens with burning cockroaches in their beaks.

There were fifteen paintings. "I'll take them all," Roberts said.

Delva covered his mouth. "At what price?" he asked.

"Two thousand American dollars each," Roberts told him.

"This other American did not pay cash," Delva said.

"I'll pay you cash," Roberts told him. "I have checks that can be drawn against the French bank."

"Are you sure?" Delva asked in French. "This other man offered to buy my paintings, too. I let him take ten away on a promise to pay me. I have not seen him since. Nor have I been paid."

"This is cash. We'll drive you to the bank in Kenscoff. And there will be a commission of twenty-five percent when the paintings are sold in Miami. You have my promise."

Delva almost laughed. "I will be famous," he shouted in his raspy voice. "Brigitte Bardot will come and make love to me. I will live in a château on the Loire!"

"Let us take you to Kenscoff," Roberts said. "I'll open an account for you and see that the money is paid over on the spot."

"You Americans are so direct," Delva said. "But there is such great hypocrisy at work with your government, isn't there? For years, you support Batista and Trujillo, who murder and steal from the people. Let a Castro appear and he is boycotted."

"This has nothing to do with me," Roberts said.

"It has to do with each of us," Delva told him. "But I am being ungenerous. I am grateful to you, M'ser."

Roberts could see a dirty child in the front yard, chasing a chicken.

"You'll be famous," Roberts joked. "Brigitte Bardot will bear your children."

"All right, Mr. American," Delva said. "But this other man, this Raymond, he cheated me. You will not be privileged to do the same. You will take me to Kenscoff and open this account. And I want a writing telling me the details of this gallery in Miami."

Delva smiled at Roberts, almost apologetically, then shrugged and began to wrap his precious paintings in burlap and twine. Roberts told him there was a written letter of agreement he'd brought with him. He couldn't blame anyone for mistrusting the Americans. After all, they'd given Papa Doc plenty of guns, hadn't they?

*r*oberts had been in Haiti for seven days when Champagne Lambert paid him a visit at the Olaffson.

Roberts had been touring the studios, buying a painting here and a painting there, and he had visited four more artists who lived in the hills around Port au Prince. During those days, he had spent perhaps half of his stipend and he looked forward to another week on the road, then going home, maybe fishing with Jakob and heading to Colorado. There had been major political demonstrations in some of the provincial capitals, and many tenèbs in Port au Prince, but no major upheavals. Every night there were one or two deaths reported, sometimes a Tonton in the provinces, a village mayor, an operative of Frap, or a slum activist. Rumors circulated that werewolves were invading the city, hairy beasts that roamed the streets at night stealing babies from their cribs, eating young girls. One or two alleged werewolves had been hunted down by combites, work groups that lived in rural areas and cut cane. Cedras had imposed an ineffective curfew, then rescinded it, then imposed it again, all to no avail. Roberts went to sleep to the sounds of tenèb, and sometimes awakened to the sound of bats. He did not see a werewolf, but Basil Davis at the Olaffson told him it would be only a matter of time and several bottles of rum before one would come down from the mountain and take a swim in the pool.

That afternoon Roberts was sitting at the bar drinking his third rum punch when Lambert's blue Audi pulled into the lot just down the hill from the pool. The sun, low on the horizon, made the Caribbean waters ripple and pop with color. There were big banks of cumulus out over the southern ocean, and occasional lightning scarred the clouds. Lambert came up the steep steps to the bar, wearing white duck pants and a dark-blue cotton dress shirt. His face was bathed in sweat, beads of it on his forehead.

"Good day, Mes-z-amis," Lambert said jauntily. He took a seat at the bar next to Roberts, where he was eyed curiously by Davis. "I see you decided to try the justly famous Olaffson," he said.

"They have wonderful rum punch," Roberts replied.

"You have purchased some art?"

"Quite a bit," Roberts told him.

"Your lovely lady friend, she flies back to America, no?"

"You know about her, do you?"

"Ah," Lambert laughed. "The telejiol transmits all."

Behind them, a trellis of flowering bougainvillia separated the pool area from the bar. To Roberts' right was a bowl of mangoes, a bowl of limes to his left. Lambert had not worn a tie, nor his question-mark tie pin. He ordered rum punch, another for Roberts. The evening was muggy and still, an offshore breeze just beginning on the flats down by the harbor. Roberts sipped his drink and waited.

"Your other friend, Dieudonné, he is absent?" Lambert asked.

"You know about Virgil, too?"

"Of course," Lambert said offhandedly. "It is possible this Dieudonné is a subversive, you know."

"Because he is black?" Roberts asked.

Lambert spread his hands on the bar. "You misunderstand me, Mes-z-amis," he said. He drank some of his rum punch as Roberts observed his large, spatulate fingers, the two diamond pinkie rings. Roberts drank his punch quickly, as the ice in the drink melted fast. Once the ice melted, the punch became watery and stale. It was another thing about Haiti that Davis had noted. Melting ice equals quick drinking.

Lambert said, "We no longer have the politics of color here.

Monsieur Duvalier destroyed the so-called doublare. We are all equal in Haiti now."

"Is that why Duvalier lightened his skin?" Roberts asked.

"It is a lie," Lambert retorted.

"So, there is no mulatto elite?" Roberts asked.

They sat together in the evening heat as the smell of charcoal drifted up from the city. In the sunset, it looked as though the whole town had burst into flame and was incinerating slowly. Through the haze, the sun burned an orange hole. Roberts thought he might be coming down with a slight fever. For two days, his nose had been running, and there had been a steady ringing in his ears.

"American propaganda," Lambert said finally. He waved his massive right hand in the air dismissively. "It is the Dominicans who are the true racists on this island," he said. "And besides, you Americans have no race problem?"

"Race is always a problem," Roberts said.

"Enough," Lambert said. "We did not wish to talk politics, did we?"

"What did we wish to talk?"

"You've purchased paintings, no?"

"Thirty or so," Roberts told him. "There are a few miniatures and some tin sculpture as well."

"And I've had a wire from Monsieur Hilliard."

"I'm surprised," Roberts said.

"He wishes to know of your progress," Lambert continued. "If you have paintings, he wants you to place them in bond at the warehouse."

"He must not trust me," Roberts said. He motioned for the waiter to come with a platter of roasted pistachios, peanuts, some grilled goat. "Did he want anything else?"

"Just to know that you are well."

"May I see the message?"

"Oh, I'm sorry, M'ser," Lambert said. "It has been destroyed." Lambert finished his rum. "Perhaps it is the case of Monsieur Cobo that prompts Monsieur Hilliard's caution."

Roberts ate some peanuts when they came. "I'm curious," he said to Lambert.

"May I be of service?"

"Why don't you tell me about Raymond Cobo?" Roberts asked. "I seem to be in his shadow wherever I go. He stayed here, you know."

"Perhaps you should inquire of the police," Lambert said.

"Let's not spar, it bores me," Roberts said.

Lambert shrugged knowingly. "I agree." His blue shirt was soaked through with sweat. "I saw Monsieur Cobo at the customs warehouse. He deposited a few paintings and left. That is all I know."

"How many paintings did he warehouse?"

"There were only a few," Lambert said. "He must have stolen away with the rest. Did not Monsieur Hilliard tell you of his theft?"

"He mentioned it," Roberts said.

Lambert tossed gourds on the bar, an utterly worthless currency. He must have known Davis would have no use for them. He asked Roberts to follow him down the hillside to where the Audi was parked, just inside a barrier to the drive. When they got there, Lambert opened the Audi trunk and produced a rattan cage. Inside the cage was a brilliantly green anolis lizard.

"A gift for you, Mes-z-amis," Lambert said.

Davis was wandering the verandas, lighting kerosene lamps.

Roberts held the cage while Lambert got into the car and backed down the hill. Roberts watched him go and then he trudged back uphill to the bar and ordered another rum to stanch his fever. It came as no surprise when Davis walked over and took a seat beside him.

"Pays in bloody gourds," he said angrily.

"He's not a friend of mine," Roberts said.

"I didn't suppose," Davis laughed. "Where'd you come by the voodoo curse?" he asked.

Roberts looked at the cage, the lizard sleeping.

"Voodoo curse?" he asked.

"Lizard in a cage," Davis said. "Supposed to be a captured soul. Baron Samedi carries them around to scare the natives."

42

*t*hey skirted the Massif de la Selle, driving for miles through green fields of cane. In the distance, mountains rose up into great bundles of lush foliage, cloud-rimmed and magnificent. In time, the cane fields ended and they cut into country dotted by cactus and dry savanna, stretches of chalky gray soil, red laterite, and blowing dust. There were only thatch-and-wattle shacks then, a few adobe buildings where one could buy a liter of gasoline, some jars of honey, a bottle of warm beer. Above them, the sky burned like napalm, and every once in a while they would stop the jeep and rest in the shade of a lone mimosa, sip coco frio or mango juice, suck the occasional orange.

Roberts drove, while Virgil kept watch for potholes and boulders, deep ditches in the road, rocks that could puncture a tire or kick up into the radiator and put them out of business. At times, they came to streams down which they would have to run in four-wheel drive, going slowly through gorges of erosion runoff, barren ground that had been flooded, salted, then flooded again. They had finally run out of the cane-and-grass country and there were no more ceiba trees, and they had finished with lianas, gum, tamarind, pepper, and were in a country of ashen hills.

Early that day, Roberts had supervised the packing and crating of sixty-five paintings, iron sculptures, and miniatures. Virgil rounded up several of his "secret political friends," and together they spread out the paintings on the veranda of the Olaffson and went about the job of cataloging, rewrapping, and crating them in boxes. Roberts made his mark on each piece of work, noted the artist's name, the price paid, the date purchased, and entered the information in a notebook. He found a print shop and made copies of all the contracts he'd signed for royalties. When they had done with the packing, he treated his "crew" to lobster, fried grouper, rice, beans, eggplant laced with nutmeg and mace. They drank beer for hours and listened to merengue and told stories. Late in the day, he delivered the paintings in two shipments to Champagne Lambert at his custom's warehouse just north of the airport.

After breakfast the next day, Roberts and Virgil drove through the terraines vagues on the outskirts of northern Port au Prince, miles of daub-and-wattle shacks, lean-tos built of used plywood crates, discarded tires, bits of rag, bottles, dented hubcaps. Driving through such wastelands, Roberts felt haunted by the specter of Raymond Cobo, that shadow of himself. Against the weight of his fever, he kept seeing the question-mark tie pin worn by Lambert, by Filo, the torn visage of a little girl outside the cathedral in her taffeta dress, the blood that had soaked through her bodice.

What was it that Lambert once called himself? "Un blanc noire," he had told Roberts as they drove into the Holiday Inn that first day. "A black white, a mulatto." Roberts remembered Lambert glaring at Virgil with contempt as he and his friends unloaded the crated paintings. Was it hatred? Or only suspicion?

After driving all day, they were stopped by a police roadblock about six kilometers from Jacmel, on the south coast. Roberts had driven between some cactus hedge and he saw the police, three of them drinking raw tafia, the unclarified rum of the rural villages. As he slowed for the roadblock, he could hear the police muttering to themselves in drunken Creole. They had staked their position on the edge of a dry streambed. As they talked, they passed the bottle of tafia among themselves.

"We must arrive at Jacmel before dark," Virgil said to Roberts. "These police are very drunk, M'ser."

The mosquitoes were out, and a breeze was kicking up red dust.

"Bon soir," Roberts called to the police.

"Let me talk Creole," Virgil said. "French will make them angry."

The police lined up like hungry rats, automatic weapons on their shoulders. Roberts halted the jeep at the edge of the dry stream and Virgil began speaking hurried Creole. Two of the soldiers laughed hysterically and circled the jeep. Roberts had been driving with the windows down to conserve fuel by not using the air conditioner. In the map pouch between his knees, he had his weapon.

"I have told them your business," Virgil whispered. "They want us to get out of the car."

"Tell them we don't have time," Roberts said.

Virgil gulped. He spoke again in Creole, this time to a soldier who stood beside the driver's window and seemed to be in charge.

"They are insistent," Virgil said, after the soldier had made a speech.

Roberts reached in the backseat and got a bottle of four-star Barbancourt. He unwrapped it from its paper cocoon and took a long swig, then passed it to the soldier, who eyed the bottle and drank about two inches off. One of the soldiers who had been inspecting the jeep lit a kerosene lamp and placed it on an empty orange crate. It made a pool of yellow light at his feet. Roberts gestured to the soldier that he should pass the rum around. He said to Virgil, "Tell them I'm ready to pay an impôt de passage."

At these words, the head soldier stood tautly. He listened while Virgil spoke in Creole.

"He is interested," Virgil whispered. "But he is drunk and confused."

Roberts produced a ten-dollar bill and handed it to the soldier. The soldier focused on the bill and staggered a bit. He said something to his compatriots and they all shared a good laugh.

"They think there is more," Virgil said.

"Tell them we're returning this way tomorrow," Roberts said. "Perhaps there will be another impôt de passage."

Virgil grimaced. He said, "Si ou gen youn sous kap ba-w dlo, ou pa koupe pye-bwe kate-l."

The soldiers clapped each other heartily and laughed. One of them rounded the jeep and stood drunkenly pounding his hand on the hood as if it were a donkey. Roberts pushed the jeep forward slowly, testing the soldiers.

The head man said, "Sot ki bay enbesil ki pa pran!"

Roberts descended into the dry streambed and accelerated up its other side. He watched the soldiers as each swigged rum, the three of them dim in the rearview mirror. They wound through cactus hedge for ten minutes, surrounded by barren hillsides. A slice of moon rose to the east, and they could smell the ocean somewhere nearby.

"What did you say to the head man?" Roberts asked finally.

"I told him the Creole saying: 'If you have a nice stream, don't cut the trees around it.'"

"And what did he say back?"

"He said, 'It is a fool who gives, and an imbecile who doesn't take!'"

There were a few bohìos on the road to Jacmel. The electricity was off, and it was utterly dark.

43

─────────────────────────────────

after traveling another three kilometers in the dark, they began to smell the fires. There were the shapes and shadows of people against hillsides, figures running here and there amid burning piles of trash and tires. On the outskirts of Jacmel, they met a line of somber mourners carrying a coffin toward the cemetery, men and women in tattered clothes singing Creole dirges. A young boy threw a rock at the jeep, but it missed. The only light in town was from charcoal braziers and a few tallow candles in windows, the occasional kerosene lamp kept by a bar owner or shopkeeper. Roberts could hear the sound of drums, ethereal and frenzied, down by the ocean.

"We should have arrived before dark," Virgil said, frightened. "This artist Compere Duffault we seek, he is reported to be a houngan."

"A voodoo priest?" Roberts asked.

"I'm afraid so, Mes-z-amis," Virgil replied.

Just then, a crowd of men blocked the jeep. Roberts and Virgil were stopped in the middle of a potholed lane, surrounded on each side by low concrete shops, a few hovels, some adobe bohìos. Growing on either corner were groves of banana trees and a few gums. Above the drums, there was singing, insistent as the buzzing of a bee.

A man naked to the waist emerged from the crowd waving a machete. He was shouting in Creole.

"They have killed a loupgarou," Virgil said.

"A werewolf? They've killed a werewolf?"

"C'est dommage," Virgil whispered.

"What do we do?" Roberts asked.

The crowd hovered but did not move. Someone in front was holding a burning torch, and the street was cast in moving shadows.

"Drive ahead slowly," Virgil said. "They'll see you are a blanc."

Roberts put the jeep in gear and advanced into the crowd of perhaps twenty men and boys. Virgil leaned out the window and inquired in Creole about the man Compere Duffault. When Roberts was near enough to see, he could discern the form of a man with a tire chain around his neck, wax plugged into his nostrils. He was carrying a wicker basket containing rice that he was sprinkling on the ground as he walked.

"One kilometer toward the beach," Virgil said. "Compere Duffault is straight ahead, then left along the sand."

Roberts pulled through Jacmel, leaving the crowd behind. Now there were a few two-story buildings, made of concrete, windows shuttered. In the suburbs were Victorian gingerbread mansions, a few brick public buildings. Perhaps the city had once been beautiful. Everywhere there were burning tires and small piles of smoldering garbage.

"What's going on here?" Roberts asked. They were two blocks from the beach. Waves lapped gently to shore.

"It is Saturday night," Virgil answered. "The Baron has come to town and there is a loupgarou."

"There was a man with his nose plugged by wax."

"On Saturday night, one must take precautions," Virgil told him. "There is a cemetery here and the people are afraid of bokors and zombies. These are old stories, M'ser. One should not take them lightly. The wax protects him from the spirits coming in. Rice prevents the Baron from following."

"A bokor?" Roberts asked.

"A witch, the servant of Samedi."

"What about this loupgarou?"

"I think they have killed a Tonton," Virgil said. "He has been dismembered and will be burned. It is the only way to kill a werewolf. You see, the people believe the Tontons are bokors, werewolves, zombies. The Tontons revel in this belief. It gives them strength. But now the people are making the dechoukaj. They pretend they are killing a loupgarou. It gives them the courage to kill a Tonton."

Roberts drove down a ditch full of reeds and reached the beach, where the surf was merely a whisper. On their left was the cemetery, a necropolis of tombs, half-slabs tilted at odd angles, decrepit mausoleums. Hundreds of candles in the cemetery cast an eerie glow.

"They say Duffault leads a Champwel," Virgil said. "The secret society meets tonight. We should be respectful of their service."

Roberts saw a grass hut surrounded by banana trees. It was a large, circular structure with a doorway covered by a blanket.

"This is the hounfor," Virgil whispered. He crossed himself quickly twice. "Just stop and we will wait."

Roberts and Virgil left the jeep and waited, standing in the sand near the hood of the vehicle. From the darkness a toothless old man approached them, staggering slightly and dressed in a ratty T-shirt and ragged shorts, no shoes. He extended a bottle of tafia to Roberts, who accepted it and drank, choking down the fiery liquid. In the other hand, the old man held a rooster. As Roberts watched, the old man held the rooster aloft and spit rum into its face. The rooster struggled briefly, then was quiet. They followed the old man to the door of the grass hut and stopped. Inside, twenty or more people were dancing and chanting. A few noticed Roberts and said, "Ap vini blanc! Ap vini blanc!" Roberts caught a glimpse of a priest near a small fire in the center of the room. He had on a white robe and was scattering rice on the dirt floor of the hut.

Virgil tugged at Roberts' shirtsleeves. "Let us go to the beach and wait," he said. "It would be more respectful."

They returned to the jeep, where Roberts fetched a bottle of rum from his bags. They sat down in the sand and waited for the old man to come and sit down beside them. Roberts offered the old man some rum and he drank it happily. He began to chatter uncontrollably.

"What's he talking about?" Roberts asked Virgil.

"Many things," Virgil said. "He thinks you are bringing Aristide home. Because you are an American. He talks about the loupgarou. He has seen many white men, but none for months. He thinks you are either very brave or very foolish." Virgil laughed with the old man. "He says he thanks you for the rum."

The old man continued to talk and spit rum at his rooster. Loud singing came from the grass hut.

Roberts felt sick with fever, exhausted by the long drive down from Port au Prince. He was hungry, and he was thirsty for cold water. Instead, he had rum to drink and sand to sleep on. He wondered if Raymond Cobo had felt this bad upon his arrival in Jacmel.

*r*oberts fell into a half-drunk, feverish sleep on the beach. He un-
furled a tarp and tried to doze in the sand, listening first to the
sound of the voodoo ceremony and then to the sound of the surf,
and finally to the sound of the old man singing plaintive Creole
songs as he drained the good rum. At three o'clock, mosquitoes
drove them into the jeep, where it was hot and airless, too hot and
airless to sleep. Virgil sat in front and tried to rest with his head
against the window glass, while Roberts crawled in the back and
stretched his legs. Even inside the jeep, they could hear the sounds
of chanting and singing from the hounfor. For a long time, they
listened to the ceremony, and finally they were so tired they must
have slept.

Toward dawn, Roberts was awake, watching a line of men and
women snaking toward the cemetery along a crushed-coral path
built on a sandy ridge above the beach. Many of them carried small,
hand-carved caskets. In the lead was the houngan, Compere Duffault, dressed in a white robe. Roberts was exhausted from his fever,
but he wanted to follow the procession and so he left the jeep and
trailed behind by about fifty yards. Staying on the ridge, he watched
the group walk silently to the cemetery gate, where there were hundreds of concrete stones marking the perimeter of the grounds, a
few mausoleums, some wooden statuary. Most of the candles he
had seen at night had guttered out. The air was salty and gray in
the morning light.

For a moment, the marchers stopped and knelt on the ground, their heads bowed, while the houngan sprinkled the sand around them with rum and particles of rice. Duffault then lit a candle and placed it on one of the larger concrete mausoleums. Roberts watched for a long time while the priest walked among his followers, knelt, drew intricate designs in the sand, and sprinkled each person with rum and rice. Roberts sat with his back to a palm tree, too tired to move as the marchers and chanters melted away into the foliage behind the cemetery. Finally, only Duffault was left. He raised a hand in greeting and began to walk toward Roberts.

"Hello, Blanc," Duffault said.

Duffault slipped the robe from his shoulders. In the waxing daylight, the robe was less impressive. It had been patched and laundered and repatched. Duffault himself was a thin man with taut, ropy muscles and a huge, bobbing Adam's apple. His hair was a mess of dreadlocks and he was wearing cutoff shorts and a white undershirt beneath his robe.

"Good morning," Roberts said wearily.

"I speak some bad English," Duffault said. He knelt beside Roberts in the sand. There was no breeze as yet, and the hot morning lay heavily on Roberts. "They said the Americans were coming," Duffault continued, "and now I see it is only another of these art thieves."

Duffault smiled at his own joke. He began to make complex drawings in the sand, undecipherable letterings. Roberts watched him create a maze in about ten minutes.

"It is said you are a fine painter," he said.

"I paint," Duffault said.

"I came to purchase some of your work, not to steal it."

"We have a saying in Creole," Duffault laughed. " 'Lawouze fe banda touttan soley pa leve.' " He erased the drawings that had taken him so much effort.

"I don't understand Creole," Roberts told him.

Duffault sat down and crossed his legs. "This means, 'The dew gleams until the sun shines.' " He smiled again, broadly, enjoying his own humor. "I suppose you would say that talk is cheap."

"You are wise as well as talented," Roberts said. "May I ask the purpose of your ceremony?"

"Saturday is very evil," Duffault said. "The Baron rules the dead. Those coffins you saw are full of rice and they allow the Baron no rest. For my followers, it is a test of faith, if you will. For them, a cemetery is a very frightening place, especially on a Saturday night. Many of them have relatives and loved ones buried here. And sometimes even a strong tomb will not keep the Baron at bay. Their motivation to come to the cemetery is very strong. They wish to keep their loved ones safe from the Baron's embrace."

"They say a loupgarou was killed here last night," Roberts said.

"I've heard this, Blanc," Duffault said.

"Do you think these stories are true?"

"Perhaps."

"You said I was another art thief," Roberts began.

"Ah, yes," Duffault said, raising a bony hand. "He, too, came to purchase my work. I let him have ten of them on a promise to pay. I have never been paid, nor have I seen my paintings again."

"A large Hispanic man?"

"Raymond Cobo was his name," Duffault spat. "Do you know this man?"

"I know of him. How was he going to pay you?"

"Something about a letter of credit in Port au Prince. I'm afraid I let my vanity overwhelm my common sense."

"Where was he going from here? Do you know?"

"To Cap Haitien," Duffault replied. "And then, that night in Jacmel, he became very frightened. He was drinking too much rum, I'm afraid. There had been some violence in the rural areas near here and he believed he was being followed. He sat in my bohío that night and began to shiver with fear. He asked me about the work of the painter Morriseau in Cap Haitien."

Roberts tensed at the name. He would be going to visit Jules Morriseau in Cap Haitien.

"He left with your paintings?"

"I helped him wrap them in burlap."

Roberts closed his eyes and imagined a stream in the Colorado Rockies. An evening sun, a cool meadow of mown hay.

"Do you feel ill, Blanc?" Duffault asked.

"I have a fever," Roberts admitted.

"You and this other come to breakfast," Duffault said, gesturing toward the jeep, where Virgil was asleep. He took Roberts by the arm and helped him up. Roberts was surprised at the strength of the small man. "There is some coffee and a little rice. What I have is yours."

The sun climbed through a break in the palms. Roberts could see a dusty track leading through a collection of shacks toward the town of Jacmel, a low melange of concrete huts, shops, and stores. He felt too sick to eat, but he knew he should try anyway.

45

*d*uffault offered them chairs at a battered Formica table on a patio behind the hounfor. The sand had been swept away to bare dirt, a recessed area bounded by potted cactus, flowering hibiscus and orchids. Virgil sat half-dazed, trying to straighten out the wrinkles in his new white shirt, while a tiny skin-and-bones woman with a complexion the color of polished mahogany brought a small pot of freshly brewed coffee and four white cups. On a pottery plate she spread out a few slices of mango, orange, and some freshly shaved coconut, along with a bowl of white rice laced with goat milk and sugar. Duffault introduced the woman as his wife, but before Roberts could say a word in acknowledgment, she skittered back inside the grass hounfor, which served as Duffault's bohio by day. Roberts could hear her inside, humming as she went about her chores.

"I have many children," Duffault said proudly. "They are privileged to eat at church school on Sunday morning. Perhaps you will meet them later."

"How many do you have?" Roberts asked.

"There are six of them now. Two died."

"I'm sorry," Roberts said. He drank some coffee, finding it aromatic but weak.

"This is why you must not cheat me again," Duffault said. "On account of my children."

Flies were bothering them, and Roberts had to brush them away from the fruit time and time again. His fever seemed easier, but he still felt uncomfortable. On a hillside above the patio there was a hedge of cactus. Beyond that, a few orange and tamarind trees. They were getting a slight breeze off the ocean, but it was going to be a hot day nonetheless.

"You will not be cheated," Roberts said. "And I don't think it was Raymond Cobo who cheated you."

"How could that be?"

"I think someone stole the paintings from Cobo."

"And who is to say they will not be stolen from you?"

Roberts pondered the question. He ate a slice of orange and said, "Whether the paintings are stolen from me or not, you will be paid in cash. An account will be opened for you in Jacmel and the money will be deposited. Tomorrow we'll go into town and I'll write a check that the bank manager will deposit in your name. That will give me time to examine your work. Besides, there are some galleries and shops in town, no?"

"Of course," Duffault said. He fixed Roberts with his impressively passionate eyes. "La Salubria is a fine gallery. There are others on Rue Commerce and Grand Rue. They exhibit my work, but there are few buyers now that Haiti is so troubled." He tapped a small clay pipe and filled it with shards of tobacco. He lit the pipe and began to make marks in the sand with a curved stick. It was as though his compulsion to paint was working itself out of his every pore. Looking up at Roberts, he said, "I am consulting Erzulie, the goddess of love and human emotion." He smiled playfully and continued to construct a phantasmagoria of designs in the dirt. Roberts had almost begun to understand the game, its rules having originated someplace in West Africa, translated now through the experience of slavery and colonialism, the enormous cruelty of exile.

"Perhaps you can consult Erzulie for me," Roberts said. "Back in Port au Prince, I found a blue chicken on my bed at the hotel."

Duffault expressed surprise. "You believe in this curse, Blanc?" he asked.

"Not in the least," Roberts told him honestly. "But later I was given a present by one of the custom's agents in the city. A green lizard in a cage."

"The captured soul," Duffault remarked. "What you say is interesting, M'ser. Raymond Cobo was cursed as well. When he arrived here, he was clearly in a state of limbo."

"In what way?"

"He was feverish. Sometimes he made no sense."

"Perhaps he was drinking rum, as you say."

"I believe experiences were overwhelming him."

Virgil said, "M'ser, perhaps we should find a hotel."

"The Manoir Alexandre is good," Duffault told them.

Virgil had devoured some rice, a little mango. Roberts was on his second cup of coffee. What he really wanted was some porridge and a good sleep.

"Would you like to see my work?" Duffault asked.

After breakfast, he led them up a narrow path to a small wooden shed buried in a ceiba grove. The studio itself was no more than ten feet square, but it was crammed with easels, and canvases in every stage of preparation were visible. Roberts spent a long time wandering through the many works, examining their composition and detail, their intricate blocks of color, the schemes and designs and bizarre metaphorical allusions. There were paintings of flaming ladders leading to a heaven billowing with purple serpents, village scenes out of Hieronymus Bosch, murals that mixed politics, voodoo, and slave revolts. Roberts had been looking for thirty minutes or more when he stopped before an easel that held a large painting in progress. The work depicted a single pile of rotting apples in the shape of a pyramid. On each apple was the face of a mulatto general of the ancien régime. The apples had been piled into a wheelbarrow that was being pushed by a Haitian peasant with wings on his feet.

When Roberts was finished, the three men sat alone in the dust of the studio.

"This is is beautiful work," Roberts told Duffault.

"Thank you, Blanc," Duffault said.

"What do you call the apple painting?"

"It is called 'By Their Fruit.' "

"That's a wonderful title," Roberts said. "But I've seen this painting, or something like it, before."

"That is not possible," Duffault said. "This is the second time I have done this work. It is a replica of one of the paintings that Raymond Cobo took away from here last month. It was one of the paintings that he stole from me. Naturally, I must try to render it all over again."

"But I've seen it before," Roberts persisted. "It was hanging on the wall of a home in Miami. The man who had it was named Bobby Hilliard."

"Are you certain of this, Mes-z-amis?"

"Absolutely certain."

"What does this man Hilliard do?"

"He says he owns galleries in Miami."

"Perhaps he bought this painting on the black market."

"Perhaps," Roberts said. "When do you think you will finish the new version?"

"It could be finished in two days."

"Or one, if you hurry?"

Duffault smiled. "We have not discussed price."

"I'm sure I can make you happy."

Before the morning was over, Roberts had selected fifteen of the paintings. They agreed that an account would be opened at the French bank in Jacmel the very next day. Roberts and Virgil walked down to the hounfor in late morning, where they found half a dozen sleeping dogs beneath banana trees. The water was flat and gray-blue in the heat, and there were a few children cooling themselves in the shallow surf. There were no clouds in the sky, and fierce heat was only two hours away. Duffault's wife, toothless and bent with arthritis, waved happily at them from her doorway.

a young boy brought Roberts news of the beating. He was a scrawny child with a heavy, hairless head, thin arms and legs, wearing tattered shorts and a torn T-shirt. Roberts could hear him below, shouting, "Ti-moune tombe! Ti-moune tombe! Avant, Blanc!" When the boy reached the foot of the stairs, Roberts got up and went to look down at him, the boy still shouting, "Ti-moune tombe!" as the patrons at the hotel began to notice. The waiter came over and told Roberts that the boy was saying in Creole that the little servant had been beaten near Frap headquarters and that Roberts should come quick.

Roberts had been on the upper veranda of the Manoir Alexandre, just finishing his lunch of djon-djon, tossin, and pain patate. He had checked into the hotel and then sent Virgil off to see if any of the gallery owners would be open on Sunday. He was drinking a cup of coffee and gazing south at the blue horseshoe bay of Jacmel, its surf lapping against the dirty black beach littered with tiny rocks, bits of garbage, dunes that were deposited by a hurricane that had destroyed the waterfront nearly a decade before. Down on Rue Seymour Pradel, Sunday strollers paraded in their best outfits, just out of church and wanting to be seen. Roberts had been watching the waterfront and the wharf, noticing the few sailboats gliding through the water. There were two yachts anchored just offshore.

After breakfast, he and Virgil had driven into town. Jacmel was an old coffee port scattered over three hills. Once it had been the

second-largest town in Haiti, full of mansions of exporters, gingerbread concoctions of true Victorian oddity. Now the exporters and
planters were gone and the mansions had become ragged with dis-
use. Virgil had directed Roberts up into the hills so he could see
some of the old splendor, gabled magnificence and iron fretwork
and scrolled wood and gargoyles carved into cupolas and turrets
and porches that seemed to go on forever through a series of curl-
icues and flowing escarpments of grillwork. Most of the mansions
once had been painted in brilliant blues, pinks, and oranges, but
were now faded and weather-beaten. Behind the homes were hills
choked by gum trees, mimosas, peppers, and tamarinds, and everywhere Roberts looked, there were huge poincianas and bougainvil-
leas in bloom, the green of the hills soaked by buckets of blazing
flowers. The sky above the hills was powdery blue and flaked by
hurricane-season clouds.

Roberts paid the waiter and hurried down to Rue Pradel, where
the tiny barefooted boy was hopping up and down from one foot
to the other in excitement. Roberts calmed him down and then led
him to the jeep, parked down the block. They drove down to the
waterfront and then north along Rue Commerce. They went
through an area of decrepit warehouses until, on their left, Roberts
saw the old fortress and prison. Nearby, a concrete bunker flew the
flag of Frap, black and green and white. A few soldiers and police
were congregated outside to smoke cigarettes and drink clarin in
the bright sunshine. As Roberts drove around the corner and
headed due north, the boy ducked down in the front seat and hid
from the soldiers and police. The boy told him to continue up into
the hills on a rutted street where there were single-story houses with
tin roofs.

Roberts found Virgil in one of the houses at the top of the hill.
He was in the back one of two rooms in the house, being tended
to by frightened teenagers. Roberts thanked them in French and
they went out to the front porch.

"Mes-z-amis," Virgil managed to mutter.

His right eye was blackened and closed, rivulets of yellow pus
oozing from it. A huge blue gash had been opened on his forehead

just above the eye, and Roberts could see white bone in the wound. One black bruise ran from his left ear and down his neck, almost to the shoulder blade. Roberts knelt on the plank floor and began to examine the damage.

"What happened, Virgil?" he asked. The teenagers had cleaned him up and given him water. "Who did this to you?"

"I was walking up Rue Commerce," Virgil said. "I could see the prison and when I came around the corner, I was surprised to see a Frap headquarters and all the soldiers and the Tontons standing in front. I tried to hide myself, but they had already seen me and it was too late."

"What happened then?"

"Do you remember those soldiers at the roadblock on the way to Jacmel?"

"The ones we bribed?"

"One of them was there. He was very drunk already."

"Which one?"

"The superior. The one who shouted to us and took your American dollars and the rum."

"Do you know his name?"

"They were calling him Albert. Three of them came down for me and surrounded me in the street. This Albert, he accused me of being one of Aristide's men and they began to call me names, and then the superior one hit me with his coca macaque on the eye and I fell to the ground. I tried to cover myself, but the superior kicked me and hit me on the neck with his stick. I was afraid they would kill me. They were drunk and they took out their machetes but by then, there was a crowd of people and the Frap soldiers became concerned and they left me alone. I lay in a ball until two young men brought me here to their house. Please, Mes-z-amis, you must help me leave here before this family has trouble, too. They have done enough."

Roberts helped Virgil to his feet. On the way out of the house, he left a twenty-dollar bill on a table and thanked the two teenagers who were on the porch. He got Virgil into the backseat of the jeep and made him lie down. On the way to town, he stopped at a small market and bought some iodine and bandages, then drove Virgil up to Manoir Alexandre and made him lie down on the bed while he went for some ice. Virgil slept most of the day, Roberts coming and going to check the eye and the gash, which he thought would have to be stitched. Late in the day, Roberts found a doctor who came to the Alexandre and put eighteen stitches in Virgil's forehead. By that time, it was almost night again and Virgil had gone back to sleep.

In early evening, Roberts went down to the hotel bar and drank rum and listened to the sound of rara music played through loud-speakers suspended from pillars in the corner of the bar. The mos-quitoes were bad, and at about eight o'clock, the electricity went out, plunging the city into utter darkness again.

*d*uffault looked as though he felt out of place in the veranda bar of Maison Alexandre. He sat in a tattered suit, sipping coffee and gazing distractedly down at the harbor and the wharves. The emerald bay, curving through early morning light, looked as though it might combust at any moment, its pink and coral tendrils snaking out toward the horizon, its water burning with an inner fire. Below, the Rue Commerce was jammed with market women carrying all manner of goods—chickens for the butcher, bags of rice, wicker sacks of clothes, shoes, merchandise. Roberts had decided to buy fifteen paintings and they had been neatly wrapped in burlap and twine by Duffault and his children. Now they were all eating a self-conscious breakfast high above Rue Pradel at the Manoir.

Duffault would sip his coffee and exchange pleasantries with Virgil in Creole while the waiters buzzed around them affectionately. He would spread his small hands on the white tablecloth and examine his skin, and his fingers would begin to move over the textured damask, drawing invisible scenes. The morning light filtered down through the green hillsides above the hotel, and Duffault's bright orange polyester shirt seemed like some huge bloom. Even Virgil looked almost presentable. Roberts had been up most of the night packing Virgil's eye with ice, checking the sutured wound on his forehead. The doctor had no antibiotics, and Roberts was deathly afraid of infection.

"The bank will open at ten," Roberts told Duffault.

"The money is of great consequence," Duffault said.

"I hope it secures your future," Roberts told him.

"For my children, perhaps," Duffault said reflectively. "But for me, my future is here."

"You couldn't leave Haiti with the money?"

"Leave Haiti?" Duffault laughed. "I have religious duties. The people, they rely on me."

"But the country is dangerous," Roberts said.

"There is a saying in Creole."

"I thought there might be," Roberts said.

" 'Bouch manje tout manje men li pa pale tout pawol.' "

"Which means?"

" 'The mouth eats all food, but it doesn't speak all words.' "

"So," Roberts said, "money isn't everything."

"Precisely," Duffault said. "Besides, there is my work and my wife. I am too old to leave Haiti, M'ser Roberts. My time here is already short."

"You will send your children abroad?"

"Not in the sense you mean, M'ser," Duffault said. "The elite send their children to Paris. My children will be educated in Haiti. Perhaps they will travel when they become older."

"After what I've seen, it's hard to understand."

"Haiti is upside down, M'ser," Duffault said. "Someday perhaps it will be rightside up. I wish to participate. Have I said this correctly? My English confuses me."

"You do wonderfully well," Roberts told him.

Duffault had brought with him a large package wrapped in brown paper. He'd placed it on the floor beside him, and now he handed it to Roberts across the breakfast table. "This is for you, M'ser," he said.

When Roberts unwrapped the package, he discovered the apple painting, complete, stunning, utterly alive.

"You cannot do this, please," Roberts said.

"But I can!" Duffault laughed. "Perhaps you will remember us in Jacmel when you return to America. You know, Wilson Bigaud painted the "Earthly Paradise." It is a scene from the rural parts of

Haiti. It hangs in Port au Prince. And truly, my country was once an earthly paradise, now gone forever. This lost innocence is the theme of every life, isn't it? In my country, this lost innocence is paid for in terror. I live for the day this terror ends for us."

Roberts told Duffault that he'd seen terror on three continents, including his own. "Perhaps Haitians don't own the patent on terror. But I hope you live to see it end."

"Perhaps we in Haiti have developed a special type of terror, that's all."

After breakfast, they went to the French bank on Rue Commerce, where Roberts opened an account for Duffault and deposited thirty thousand dollars for the fifteen paintings he had purchased. Duffault could hardly believe what was happening, and he kept chattering to Virgil about the school he would build, the public bath, the grove of banana trees for his children to cultivate. Roberts drove Duffault back to the beach and the two men shook hands. Duffault gave Virgil a gentle hug and then they departed, Duffault riding his donkey down the Rue Pradel toward his bohìo, Roberts watching him go.

Before noon, Roberts bought some blankets at a dry-goods store on Rue Commerce. He put down the seats in the jeep and made a pallet of the blankets. Virgil was able to hobble down from the Mansion Alexandre to the jeep, and Roberts helped him lie down on the bedding in back. Virgil's eye was deeply purple, tinged with yellow, but it was no longer oozing pus. Roberts was angry at himself for placing Virgil in such a dangerous situation, but he knew the danger was endemic, something he could never quite avoid. He paid the hotel bill and they drove north along the road toward Port au Prince, up into green hills where there were still patches of rain forest. They drove in shade and across fields of overcultivated land, through groves of banana trees and oranges. Virgil was awake in the back, humming softly to himself, easing around his pain.

Just after one o'clock, Roberts saw the roadblock. Now there were only two soldiers manning it, each standing on the opposite side of the dry creekbed. They were passing a bottle of clarin between them, and the superior called Albert, who had beaten Virgil, was smoking a cigarette. Roberts saw the one other one stiffen and smile at the sight of the oncoming jeep, touching his trigger guard. Roberts had daubed the license plate with mud, and the gun was again in a pouch between his legs.

"Aha, Blanc," cried the superior as Roberts drove up. He stopped the jeep at the edge of the dry creekbed and clambered over.

"Bon jour," Roberts said.

The superior scowled angrily. "Bonjou, msye. Ban-ma nouvel-ou?" He had red eyes and moved haltingly. It was likely that he had been drinking all morning. His compatriot crossed the creekbed and sat on the hood of the jeep, eyeing Roberts contemptuously. The superior crossed to the driver's side and leaned his head inside the jeep. "M vin tire bef m pa vin konte vo," he hissed.

Virgil whispered, "He says he comes to milk the cow, not to count the calves."

Roberts struck the soldier hard in the face with the point of his elbow. The superior howled and blood spurted from his nose as Roberts jacked the jeep into first gear and plunged down into the ravine of the dry creekbed, sending the second soldier sprawling over the hood, then tumbling off into the ditch. Roberts gunned the jeep up a rocky incline and onto the potholed roadbed. In the rearview mirror, he could see the superior sprawled on the dusty ground, holding his face. The second soldier had tumbled into the creekbed and was lying still.

"What have you done, sir?" Virgil asked.

"Lie back and rest," Roberts told him. "It's called payback. We have a saying in my country."

"You have a saying?"

"What goes around, comes around," Roberts said.

Virgil moaned and closed his eyes.

48

they made the trip from Jacmel to Port au Prince in six hours. They passed through five roadblocks and Roberts was forced to pay bribes at each. He passed out drinks from a bottle of Barbancourt, the soldiers bored and fractious in the heat, Virgil having long conversations in Creole from his backseat pallet. More than once, attachés and Tontons threatened to search the car and deprive Roberts of his paintings and money, but each time, at the last moment, they relented, perhaps fearing that Roberts was a diplomat, a missionary, an aid worker who would make trouble with the embassy, or cause them difficulties if and when the Americans came. On the road, Virgil tried to sleep, but the constant bouncing through potholes, numerous drives down into ditches to avoid boulders or fallen trees, jarred him awake. Finally he stopped trying to sleep and entertained Roberts with Creole jokes, riddles, and songs.

Near dark, they made it to the home of Paul-Pierre in the suburbs on the St. Marc road, about six kilometers from the city center. It was a neighborhood of wooden houses painted blue or green or yellow, and an equal number of newer concrete-block bunkers, where families of ten or more lived in a single room without electricity. Roberts parked the jeep in an alley beside a concrete market shop, and it was immediately surrounded by dozens of curious black children who clapped gaily as the blanc climbed out. As night fell, it seemed that hundreds of neighborhood dogs began to bark, just as the air was suffused with rara music.

Roberts could see Paul-Pierre making his way slowly through the throng of children.

"Mes-z-amis!" he shouted happily. "Honneur!"

"Respet!" Roberts shouted back.

Two women watched them from a doorway of their bunker. The sky was absolutely black, starless, and saturated with the smell of charcoal smoke.

"Blanc v'le café pote," Paul-Pierre said to the two women. Bring the coffee.

"No, please," Roberts said. "Virgil has been beaten up by soldiers in Jacmel. Help me get him inside."

Roberts opened the hatch of the jeep and let Paul-Pierre see his half brother. Virgil looked frail and tired. Paul-Pierre gasped and touched him on the shoulder.

"I'm sorry for this," Roberts said.

"It's not your fault," Paul-Pierre said.

They moved Virgil to a concrete bunker, where the two women put him on a cot in one corner. A single lightbulb hung from an electric wire in the center of the room, but it had been a long time since there was electricity. In the tremulous kerosene-lantern light, Roberts could see dozens of faces straining to watch through the open door of the bunker, some of children, some of old men and women. A teenage girl dressed in rags brought Virgil a small demitasse of weak coffee.

Virgil put his feet on the dirt floor.

"You've got to lie down," Roberts told him.

"I will be all right, M'ser," Virgil said.

Paul-Pierre moved the kerosene lantern near to Virgil and began to examine the head wounds.

"Thank you for bringing him," he said. "We will take care of him."

"I'm going to pay Virgil now," Roberts said. "The situation is too dangerous for him to continue with me."

Virgil looked agitated and began to squirm.

"We are not finished," he said.

"You are. You've earned your pay."

"But you must go to Cap Haitien, no?" Virgil said.

Paul-Pierre tried to make his half brother lie back and drink some coffee, but Virgil resisted.

"Take it easy, Virgil," Roberts said. "I can make it to Cap Haitien alone."

"You cannot find the road," Virgil protested. "I am your timoune. You cannot abandon me."

Paul-Pierre and Virgil spoke for a long time in Creole. Roberts could pick out only a few French or English words, the rest a blur. Some of the children who had been standing outside now crowded into the small room. They stood quietly, respectful, watching the blanc on his knees.

"Please give us a few minutes alone," Paul-Pierre said.

Roberts made his way through the children and stood outside, near the jeep. A few children had stayed behind to admire the shiny vehicle, its chrome wheel covers, the black panels. They ran their tiny hands across and around the tires and caressed the bumpers. To Roberts, the children seemed tragically tiny, stick arms and stick legs and the enlarged bellies of undernourishment. In the road were mounds of uncollected garbage, rotting fruit of all sorts, coffee grounds, human waste. A few mangy dogs picked their way through the garbage, in tandem with old men and women carrying wicker baskets. Above them, in Boutilliers, a clutch of lights twinkled in the distance. Somewhere up there were the homes of the elite, their mansions and high walls and cool green swimming pools guarded by cameras and Dobermans. Roberts drank his coffee and watched the children watch him, some of them breaking big smiles.

In time, Paul-Pierre came out and stood beside Roberts in the half-light.

"Virgil is very committed to the trip," Paul-Pierre said. "He believes he has let you down and you will abandon him."

"That isn't it. I'm afraid for him."

"We are all afraid, Mes-z-amis."

"What do you think?" Roberts asked.

"It isn't the money, M'ser," Paul-Pierre said. "It is the mission itself."

"All right," Roberts said. "Tell Virgil I'll come and get him first thing in the morning. Tell him to take heart."

"I am so glad," Paul-Pierre said. "It is not good for a man to live in fear."

"No," Roberts said. "It is the worst thing."

49

*b*asil Davis told Roberts that Zacharie Filo was waiting by the pool. When Roberts went down from his room, he saw that the pool had been drained of its murky water and that lizards trapped on the bottom were frantically trying to slither up the sides. Twenty or thirty of the creatures were dead already, their toasted bodies shriveled on the bottom of the pool, cooked by the noonday sun that blazed straight down on the white surface.

Filo was sitting, watching the struggles of the lizards. He was wearing a dark blue suit and a blue beret. As Roberts approached, he adjusted his sunglasses and slicked back his thinning hair to cover a bald spot. A few couples had gathered on the veranda for afternoon drinks and to watch the lizards. It seemed like a sport, watching the lizards. In another few hours, it would be time for the bats to come out for their evening meal. For now, a slight onshore breeze moved through the palms, and Roberts could smell the beginning of charcoal smoke. Filo kicked a dead palm frond down to the bottom of the pool, where it clattered serely.

Roberts had found some penicillin for Virgil at the local Peace Corps office. He had seen to it that the paintings were safely delivered to the hotel manager, who agreed to keep them locked in a back storage room. In between making his rounds to the bank and the pharmacist, he had managed about four hours of fitful sleep. The fever seemed about to break, but he was tired, and suffered from occasional stomach cramps. He was bored with the heat and the flies and the evening mosquitoes.

Filo neither rose, smiled, nor offered to shake hands with Roberts. Roberts sat down and watched some of the lizards struggle toward the rim of the pool, only to slide back down to the bottom.

"Bon soir," Roberts said.

Filo flinched when he heard the French. He turned and told Roberts his name again. Roberts said he remembered the chef de section. How could one forget the chief of criminal investigations?

"I have good news," Filo said. He spoke fractured French, escaping Creole only by inches. "I am certain that you will be pleased."

"Would you like a drink?" Roberts asked. "The rum punch at Olaffson is very good."

"A beer, perhaps," Filo said.

Filo bore a faint resemblance to the Dominican dictator Trujillo, whose portraits Roberts had often seen, stout, overbearing, the vanity of the slicked-back black hair, pig eyes sunk into a cruel face. Roberts signaled a waiter for two beers and went back to watching the lizards. When the waiter came with the beer, Roberts lit a small black cigar, and the two men sat in white rattan chairs beneath a poinciana in bloom, smoking quietly. There had been reports in *Nouvelliste* of a hurricane forming in the Caribbean basin beyond Puerto Rico. One could sense a change in the weather.

Filo crossed his legs and took a long draught of his beer. A lizard peeked over the edge of the pool, climbed to the concrete surface and scurried into the underbrush not far away.

"A survivor," Filo remarked.

"He will forever enrich the gene pool," Robert joked.

Filo seemed to ignore the remark. "We have located the records of Raymond Cobo," he said.

"Excellent, sir," Roberts said. "I'm surprised you've gone to all the trouble."

"It is no problem," Filo said. "Pas de problem." He held up the glass of beer, subjecting it to the scrutiny of his gaze. "It seems that Raymond Cobo flew to Miami. There is a record with immigration of his departure. You have no reason to be concerned for his safety in Haiti." Filo drank some of the beer, leaving a slight frothy mustache on his lip.

"I wonder why there is no trace of him in Miami," Roberts said. "His sister has reported him missing."

Filo shrugged his shoulders. "With this, I cannot be concerned."

"And the paintings he purchased in Haiti have disappeared," Roberts continued.

Filo drained his beer and stood, walking to the edge of the pool. He looked down at the bottom, contemplating the trapped lizards. He returned to his chair and stood over Roberts. There was silence between the men. Up on the hotel veranda, Davis was making his rounds, lighting kerosene lanterns. In time, Davis would start the hotel generators, but for now, he was content with kerosene.

"We have a report from Jacmel," Filo said at last. "A blanc in a jeep attacked two soldiers. One of the soldiers has a broken nose and the other has a fractured wrist."

"This concerns me?" Roberts asked.

"You must be more careful, Blanc," Filo said. "For now, you are being protected. But you must finish your business quietly."

"Who's protecting me?"

"Perhaps it is just luck," Filo said. "Finish your business in Cap Haitien and then go home."

"How did you know I had business in Cap?"

Filo paused and set down his beer bottle on the ground. He kicked it and the bottle rolled to the edge of the empty pool, then over, crashing to the bottom. Some of the hotel guests looked over the veranda to see what had caused the sound of shattering glass.

"Good-bye and good luck," Filo said. "By the way, have you read the newspaper today?"

"Not all of it," Roberts said.

"A boatload of American and Canadian soldiers was turned away from Haiti today. The people would not let it land."

Roberts watched Filo leave by a gate to the pool area. He sat quietly with his beer until Basil Davis came down from the veranda and joined him.

"I'm impressed," Davis said. He had brought Roberts another beer, a neat rum for himself. "The chef de section."

"He was being polite by threatening me gently."

"I am doubly impressed," Davis said.

"He knew things he couldn't possibly know," Roberts said.

"It's the bloody drums," Davis laughed.

Part 3

Yon jou Tantafè ale lakay Papa Bondye. Lè li rive li mande: "Papa Bondye, konbyen yon milyon anne ye pou ou?" Papa Bondye reponn: "Yon ti moman." Apesa Tantafè di: "Konbyen yon milyon dola ye pou ou?" Bondye reponn: "Senk kòb." Alo Tantafè di: "Papa Bondye, tanpri ban-m senk kob." Bondye reponn: "Ak gran plezi petit-mwen, tann yon ti moman."

One day Tantafè went to God's home. When he arrived, he asked: "Good God, how much is one million years to you?" God replied: "Only a moment." Then Tantafè said: "How much is one million dollars to you?" God answered: "Just five cents." Hence, Tantafè said: "Dear God, please just give me five cents." God replied: "With great pleasure, my son. Just wait a moment."

—Haitian Proverb

*r*oberts made Virgil remain in the jeep with the air-conditioning running and the doors locked. After three days of rest, Virgil had begun to look and feel better, the eye less swollen, the big bruise on his neck now a stringy trail of blue where the coca macaque had struck home. In the steamy heat, Band-Aids refused to stick to the gash on his forehead, so he walked about with a jagged row of stitches showing. When Roberts had locked the door of the jeep, he tapped on the window and smiled. Virgil smiled back and nodded happily.

The Lambert warehouse was built on a coral shelf that jutted into the harbor, just beyond the main wharves and jetties of the port. In front of the metal building was parked a blue Audi, its tinted windows dark, the finish perfectly polished to a sheen, despite the dust that blew constantly through the city. Roberts had sent the paintings ahead with a courier service run by two French homosexuals, and he had received word that the boxes had been delivered just after lunch. The afternoon sky was cloudless, and waves of stench rolled in from the water. It was so hot that the green hills behind the city seemed sere from a distance, faded photos of themselves.

When he went into the warehouse, Roberts was eyed by two black men in blue dungarees, white T-shirts with red bananas, sunglasses. Men like this had taken to calling themselves attachés now, but they were Tontons in all but name. These two, leaning against several packing crates, were smoking cigarettes. They carried neither coca macaques nor machetes. After searching Roberts, they leaned back and looked bored. Roberts could see Lambert inside a glassed-in office, inspecting some papers. He was surrounded by file cabinets, a few stacked boxes, a watercooler. The black-mahogany desk over which he was working was scarred by cigarette burns and knife marks. As usual, he was wearing a white suit. In the half-light of the office, his skin seemed to match the color of his Audi, a luminous shade of gray-blue. As Roberts approached, Lambert looked up from his work and smiled enigmatically.

"Mes-z-amis, honneur," he said.

"Good afternoon," Roberts replied, standing just inside the glass door of the office.

"You have done well," Lambert said. "How many is it now?"

"There are eighty," Roberts replied. "You've got a detailed invoice, and each piece is marked by me. There are a lot of works by Delva and Duffault. There are some others I purchased in shops and galleries."

"Eighty is correct," Lambert said.

"You have prepared my receipt?"

Lambert produced a yellow invoice written in French. Roberts looked it over. He didn't think it mattered much what the form said, but he folded it and put it in his shirt pocket anyway.

"You are at the end of your task now?" Lambert asked.

"One last trip."

"Cap Haitien, yes?"

"Jules Morriseau is on my list," Roberts said. "Will you be shipping the canvases you have?"

"A very good idea," Lambert said.

"And I have had a visit from Zacharie Filo."

"The chef de section!" Lambert barked.

"He told me he'd found a record that indicated Raymond Cobo flew out of Haiti."

"I told you as much," Lambert said.

"I had the impression something happened to Cobo. His sister in Miami hasn't seen him since he came to Haiti. You'd think he'd be back in Miami if that's where he headed when he left here. I presume you saw him here when he brought back some paintings from Cap Haitien."

"Of course. He was in good spirits."

"Funny," Roberts said. "Monsieur Duffault said he was frightened. Not at all happy. Almost frantic."

"I assure you not," Lambert said. "Perhaps it was the idea of returning home that made him anxious. After all, he was planning a theft, no?"

"And you shipped some of his purchases from here?"

"That is correct, M'ser."

"Do you mind telling me the shipper?"

Lambert stood and spent some time smoothing down a wrinkle in his suit pants.

"I am the shipper," he said.

"The carrier, then."

"Of course," Lambert said. "Pan-Carib."

Roberts had heard of the line, a small branch of the Haitian commercial operation. It held to an erratic schedule, but flew mostly to destinations around the Caribbean—Miami, Kingston, Caracas, Panama City.

"Very good then," Roberts said. "I suppose Cobo stole the two hundred thousand dollars and the paintings and disappeared?"

"So it would appear," Lambert said.

"And some of the paintings were hijacked in Miami."

"I have no information. I have the bill of lading, that is all."

"And how did Cobo manage to smuggle the other paintings out of the country?"

"He had American money, no?" Lambert walked Roberts to the warehouse door. "You have heard the news?" he asked.

"The news? I'm not sure."

"The Americans and Canadians have been turned away."

"Perhaps it is only temporary."

"You think they will try again?"

"I wouldn't know. I should think so."

"Perhaps they are afraid to land?"

"I don't think so," Roberts said.

"You are very confident."

"Not confident. It is only a prediction."

Lambert extended his hand and Roberts shook it.

"Have a safe journey," Lambert said.

"I'll be back in two days with twenty more works."

"Of course you will," Lambert said, smiling. He was wearing the question-mark pin on his lapel. He fingered it once or twice.

"Good-bye," Roberts said.

"Your Haitian friend? How is he? I heard he had an accident in Jacmel."

"Where did you hear that?"

"Oh, Mes-z-amis, the telejiol is very loud."

"Radio Thirty-two?"

"Yes, the chattering teeth. They make a tremendous noise in Haiti. You can hear them everywhere. In the wind, in the trees, in the sound of the waves."

"Can you hear the agony of the people?" Roberts asked.

Lambert laughed. "You are too serious, my friend!"

*r*oberts drove north along the Boulevard Dessalines, through the slums of the waterfront, then back east along Rue des Ramparts. For blocks, he looked at the concrete and breeze-block bunkers and pitiful handmade shacks of the poor. Everything seemed to shimmer in the heat, the hills above the city rippling, waves of dry heat rising and settling and disturbing the green in the mountains. When he reached the end of the road to the airport, the cutoff for Cap Haitien, he continued up into the neighborhood where Paul-Pierre lived with his family.

"You have missed your turn, sir," Virgil said. The young man sat mussed in the back of the jeep amid all their gear: shovels for digging them out of sand and mud along the roads, sleeping bags, bottles of water, a case of good rum for the soldiers and attachés at roadblocks, chocolate for children they would meet in villages. "We must go to Cap Haitien on the airport road."

"You're not going to Cap Haitien," Roberts said. "I'm sorry, Virgil."

"But, sir, I'm your ti-moune," Virgil said. Roberts could see the stricken look on his face. "I must go. It is necessary."

"It's too dangerous," Roberts told him.

"It is always dangerous in Haiti. We have discussed this matter before, sir. Please."

"You'll be paid your fee, Virgil," Roberts said. "Don't worry. It isn't about money. It's about your personal safety."

From the backseat, Virgil placed a hand on Roberts's shoulder. Roberts cruised slowly through a steady parade of women with their children and goats, donkeys led by ragged children, small handcarts towed by tinkers, merchants, old men in cast-off clothes. As always, children began to follow them, smiling and shouting and touching the metallic surface of the jeep. Piles of garbage smoldered in the alleys, a stark contrast to the gaily painted facades of the commercial buildings, their vibrant pinks and blues and otherworldly oranges. A tap-tap passed them going downhill fast, its engines belching diesel smoke, loud rara music blasting from jamboxes. People were hanging onto the sides of the bus for dear life, standing on the running boards, clinging to the roof.

Roberts found a tiny lane that led uphill to Paul-Pierre's house. There were a few trees shading it, dusty peppers that had survived the onslaught for charcoal and for wood to make lean-tos. Paving stones had been dug from the street and haphazardly piled, weapons for the people in their battle with the Tontons and the Army.

"But, please," Virgil said pleadingly. "I am your guide."

Roberts parked about a block from the hovel where Paul-Pierre lived with how many others—who knew? The sun burned down through a cloudless sky.

Roberts shut off the motor and eased down the electric windows. A terrible heat rushed inside the vehicle. There was only a little breeze and he was sweating profusely.

"They're going to kill me," Roberts said to Virgil.

Virgil blinked twice. The two men were silent.

"You know this?" Virgil asked him after a while.

"I'm pretty certain."

"But, sir, how do you know?"

"I purchase art for a gallery in Miami. The previous agent collected art for the same people. I am convinced he came to Haiti, was given the same instructions as I was, and was murdered in Cap Haitien, just at the end of his journey."

"But why?" Virgil asked.

Roberts thought for a moment. A dozen or more children were

clamboring after the jeep, climbing onto the hood of the car, laughing and shouting in Creole.

"He was set up," Roberts said.

"I don't understand this word," Virgil said. "Set up," he repeated.

"He was deceived. The art was stolen from him. It was stolen in Port au Prince, but disappeared in transit to Miami. One of the pieces even got to Miami. When Raymond Cobo purchased these paintings, he made promises to the artists to pay them. The money was deposited in a bank in Port au Prince. But the art was never paid for and Raymond Cobo disappeared in Cap Haitien."

"But why would they kill him?"

"With Raymond Cobo dead, there would be no witnesses to the theft. He would be blamed for stealing the art, and the money, too."

"This is what they plan for you?"

"I think so, Virgil."

"Do you have proof of this?"

"I've seen one of the paintings that was stolen. It was a painting of apples. It was hanging on a wall in a house in Miami."

Virgil put his head on the window ledge and seemed to think for a long time. Roberts watched him sitting there in the backseat with all his traveling gear, a young man in old clothes that were new— polyester pants, white guayabara streaked with sweat and dust, the Reebok knockoffs soiled with mud. His eye was a tiny slit now that the swelling had subsided, and the bruise on his neck was barely visible under the collar of his shirt.

"Is it Lambert?" Virgil asked.

"Lambert, Filo, the Tontons, any or all of them. Who knows?"

Virgil placed his hands together in an attitude of Christian piety. "I want to go with you to Cap Haitien," he said solemnly.

"No way," Roberts said. "I'm paying you some money. I want you to try to go to America with Paul-Pierre. You deserve a new start, a good life. Perhaps your half brother can do something about getting you a visa."

"I am not his half brother," Virgil said quietly. The children were looking through the front windows at them, grinning furiously. "He tells people that I am his brother. He treats me as his brother, and for this, I am grateful. But I am an orphan. When I was a tiny child, his parents rescued me from the streets and raised me as their own. I have no chance to come to America with Paul-Pierre, his family. I am not documented, as they say."

"Perhaps there is a way," Roberts said.

"It matters little," Virgil said. "Haiti is a nation of orphans, is it not?"

"Still, I'm going to give you five thousand dollars," Roberts said. "Imagine it. Imagine what you can do with that kind of money. You deserve it. Perhaps you can go to France."

"You are very kind," Virgil said. "It is too much money. I have not earned it."

"It isn't my money. You've earned it."

"Still, my fate is here." Virgil turned and looked at Roberts with pain in his expression. "I am your ti-moune. We must stay together. Besides, you need my help now more than ever."

"You can't help me," Roberts lied.

"I can guide you to Cap Haitien," Virgil said. "You've said you're staying in the Hotel Christophe?

"Yes, of course."

"This is the itinerary they've given you?"

Roberts shrugged his assent. "By the people in Miami, yes."

"It is near the Frap office," Virgil said flatly.

Roberts hadn't known, but he wasn't surprised.

From the hill where they were parked, he could see down to the city and the port, a view of the yellow-baked Casserness Dessalines, where so many Haitian citizens had been imprisoned, tortured, fed to the sharks. He looked at the prison for a long time.

"It's too dangerous," Roberts said finally.

"You told Paul-Pierre that living in fear was the worst thing for a man. Do you remember this?"

Roberts admitted he remembered.

"It is bad for me as well, sir."

In that way, Roberts was obliged to take Virgil to Cap Haitien.

*a*fter passing through the first roadblock, about two kilometers north of the airport on the Cap Haitien highway, they stopped for lunch at a take-out eatery. The soldiers manning the roadblock had been bored and surly in the sultry noonday heat, but they were not drunk. Roberts had offered them long swigs of good rum, and he'd offered to take their photographs, which pleased them as it pleased the tiny children who always followed them. Now, parked beside the road in available shade, they ate two platters of grilled goat, some roasted peanuts, slices of pink mango. Roberts drank a cold Haitian beer.

The dusty hills on either side of the road were rutted and overgrown with cactus, fine brown dust blowing down from the heights. They began to drive again after lunch, skirting the Cahos Mountains, which were as gray and bare as the flanks of an elephant. Not long afterward, they came to the town of Cabaret, which had once been named Duvalierville after the president, a rotted hole of muddy, postmodern structures, wide potholed roads in which chickens and goats wandered freely, piles of moldering garbage and burning tires under a fierce sun.

When they left Cabaret, they were halted again, this time by soldiers who examined their documents and allowed them to pass without trouble or confusion. For two more hours, they drove the narrow asphalt highway between shallow canals of brackish water, steaming rice paddies, small stands of wilted sugarcane. The land lay flat for miles ahead of them, and in the distance, puffy cumulus clouds rode a hazed horizon. In the shallow rice paddies, gangs of coumbite workers toiled sowing rice, stirring up the hot muck. At Pont Sonde, they crossed the Artibonite River, which ran slack and brown with silt, no more than a hundred yards wide. In its inlets, hundreds of men, women, and children were splashing and bathing, washing themselves, defecating, cooling their animals. For a time, Roberts thought that they were being followed by an old Chevrolet full of attachés wearing sunglasses and denim shirts, but he lost sight of them somewhere in the salt pans outside Gonaives. There they stopped beside a roadside fruit stand in the shade of a pepper tree on the dusty outskirts of an industrial and warehouse area of the town, and Roberts made Virgil drink a Secola Orange to ward off the heat. They both suffered from headaches, from the heat and dust, and for a time, Roberts reconsidered his decision to allow Virgil to come. He thought he might stop and force the man onto a public bus back to the capital, but Virgil seemed so serenely content, so happy to be free and driving north on an important mission, that Roberts gave up the idea entirely.

An hour later, they began to climb away from the dismal salt plains along the coast and into the Chaine de Belance, where they encountered their first pines and banana trees, a few clumps of tall grasses. Coconuts were sold at stands along the road and children were herding goats, and women walked their chickens to market. Men were riding bicycles piled with all manner of goods: pots and pans, sacks of mangoes. At Limbe, on top of the mountain, they stopped to take a look at the valley behind them, and Roberts bought some fresh orange juice. He took a walk down a narrow incline and gazed at the valley, shimmering and burning in the inferno of the afternoon. Then they drove again along the spine of the mountains and finally they caught a glimpse of the arc of L'Acul Bay, the outline of Cap Haitien, and the miles of green coastline where the city met the Atlantic Ocean. Down in the city were the spires of the pink cathedral, the patchwork quilt of the port. They were meeting truck traffic now, and an increasing stream of bicycles and handcarts. There were motorcycles and motorbikes and hundreds of people on foot.

After their mountain stop, Virgil had climbed into the front seat and was leaning out the window, catching breaths of fresh air coming off the ocean.

"Morriseau has his gallery in the Ateliers Taggart on Rue Cinque," Roberts told Virgil.

"It is near the main boulevard," Virgil said. "In the commercial district. You must follow the highway to the port. There are many galleries in the area."

"Guide me there," Roberts said.

"You must not stay the night at Hôtel Christophe," Virgil warned.

"What do you suggest?"

"At the Cormier Plage. There are guest homes. You will not be in the center of the city."

"What good will it do?"

Virgil smiled haltingly. "The telejiol is slower. That is all."

"I'm sending you home by bus tomorrow."

"I would rather return with you, sir," Virgil said.

Virgil guided them through the warrens and unmarked streets of the city. Just at dark, the electricity failed and they were in deep shadows. It was said in the street that the electricity would return before midnight. It was an article of faith that the electricity would return before midnight in order to ward off the loupgarous. The sun had not quite set, and in the panting duskiness of evening, the city seemed to breathe in a way Roberts had not experienced in Port au Prince. The green of the hills lent a freshness to the air, making the smell of charcoal seem less dense. The town slipped gently down toward the commercial district and the wharves. There were neighborhoods of gingerbread Victorian houses, tracks of breeze-block shops, slums as bad as any in the capital.

Virgil had Roberts park where the tap-taps and commercial buses parked during the day. There were no tourists at the market and the streets were almost deserted. The market itself was a low wooden building divided into many stalls, an open area in the center where food was served, cafeteria-style. Even in the evening, many crafts-men were at work on leather goods, wicker, wood carvings, oil paintings.

The artist named Jules Morriseau stood near the front of the market, speaking in Creole with an old woman stooped from ar-thritis. Behind, an herb doctor was closing up shop. He was a small, thin man with only one arm, dressed in an outdated powder-blue pants suit, white shoes. When he finished speaking to the old woman, he returned to his stall and sat before an easel. Roberts came up behind him and he turned, revealing a long scar running down the left side of his face from ear to chin. To Roberts, the artist's thinness seemed unnatural, almost frailty. He could not have weighed more than one hundred pounds. He had limpid brown eyes and short, frazzled, gray hair. The bones in his hands and face were discernible through the skin, and the dark black skin around his mouth had stretched itself to cadaverlike tautness.

"Your paintings are very beautiful," Roberts said.

Virgil repeated this in Creole.

"Bonyou msye," Morriseau replied in a squeaky tone. "Meci, thank you."

On the canvas, he was painting a feathery blue chicken against a field of surrealistic orange. It reminded Roberts of Chagall gone stark mad. Roberts pulled up a wicker chair and watched the one-armed man paint. He sent Virgil for a bottle of rum from the jeep, and when Virgil returned, Roberts offered some of the rum to Mor-riseau. The three of them sat for a long time without saying a word, drinking occasional swigs of rum from the bottle. The sun set, and dull motes of dust fell through the rafters of the ceiling, obscuring the color.

"They say the electricity will be on at midnight," Roberts said finally.

The artist shrugged without turning. He touched a brush to the fantastic chicken, the last wisp of a beard of white paint as dark-ness fell.

53

No, M'ser," Morriseau said in his quiet rasp. "Raymond Cobo did not return to me. He wrapped ten of my paintings and took them to his hotel. In the morning, I was to meet him at the French bank, but he did not come. There were rumors on the telejiol that a blanc had been killed, but nothing was in the newspapers. It remained a rumor, nothing more. There was great turmoil in the city then, and in those days, the dechoukaj had just commenced. There were killings by the score. Who knew how many killings there had been, or how many were to be? Many days and nights passed without electricity, and attachés roamed the city. You must understand that the blanc may have fled. It would not have been unreasonable."

They were sitting in wooden deck chairs just above the beach. Morriseau had closed his studio and they had driven across the nearly deserted city and Roberts had checked into the guest house. He had taken two bungalows at either end of a long, covered walkway overlooking the water. Each bungalow was furnished with teak and mahogany furniture, open to the air by wooden-louvered windows, with rattan mats on the floor and batik wall hangings. Below the terrace, miles of white sand beach spread like wings on either side of the hotel.

At night, a steady wind cascaded through the blooming hibiscus, sand willowing in from the beach. There was no moon and the ocean was jet black. Perhaps, thought Roberts, the Tonton will arrive in the dark. It would be typical of Baron Samedi to collect his souls in the darkness. Then another nameless blanc would disappear and become the subject of rumor.

Roberts asked, "The blanc you talk about, did he tell you of his future plans for the paintings?"

Virgil wiped his face with a handkerchief. "Morriseau says that Cobo was driving a rented car. He told Morriseau that he would return to Port au Prince and then go home. He says there are many sharks in the bay, but they do not consume automobiles."

"Meaning?" Roberts asked Virgil.

"Meaning he thinks that Cobo disappeared but that somebody must have stolen his vehicle."

He had ordered rum punch from the bar. A waiter brought them a tray of glasses, small bottles of rum, a dish of sliced limes. There was no ice because the electricity had been off for hours. Marcellin, clad in his blue pants suit, opened a bottle of Barbancourt and poured a glass of the rum neat, then squeezed lime into it. He drank and watched the nothingness of the ocean. He would speak in Creole, Virgil would translate, back and forth that way in the dark as the ocean circulated against the flat sand of the beach. It must be beautiful in the moonlight, Roberts thought, soft sand glistening and water laced by pale silver spears. But now, in the dark, it was sinister. Down the terrace, the staff had lit citronella candles to provide light and to fight the mosquitoes. Still, the insects were bad.

Roberts poured a rum, admiring the artist's humor. The artist would grasp a tiny bottle of Barbancourt with his hand and swing it under his stump, uncap the rum, set down the bottle, pour a shot, the motion repeated on and on, over and over. Roberts remembered what Basil Davis had told him. The lack of ice made for great drinking. Could this be true?

The silence annoyed Roberts. In Port au Prince he had grown accustomed to the blare of merengue from jamboxes, the din of radios and the roar of tap-taps and buses, the horsey nervousness of urban life. Here, life seemed to hover on the edge of the world, suspended in a spiderweb stretched tight.

At the market, Roberts had chosen ten of Morriseau's paintings for purchase. Some young men from the square had carefully packed the paintings in straw and brown paper, then loaded them into small paper-box crates. All ten had been hefted into the back of the jeep, now parked in a guarded yard near the hotel lobby. A boy from the neighborhood was guarding the jeep personally, too.

"I will pay you in cash," Roberts said.

Virgil translated, Morriseau nodded, sipping his rum in the dark. Roberts knew it was stupid to carry cash on him, but he had done it anyway. It was the last of Hilliard's money, and he wanted it in the hands of the artist as soon as possible. He had already opened an account for Virgil at the bank in Port au Prince. Five thousand U.S. dollars.

Virgil said, "He thanks you profusely."

Roberts could not help staring at Morriseau's stump, at the long scar on his face.

"May I inquire how you received your injuries?" he asked. "I hope it is not impolite." He handed Virgil a manila envelope with the cash payment. Virgil placed it on the bamboo table between them, where it remained. "I do not wish to invade your privacy, but I am curious."

"One has to paint," Morriseau said in broken English. He squeezed lime into a fresh glass of rum and continued to speak, using broken English, Creole, and French. "I was young when Papa Doc came to power. At first we had much hope for the future of our country. After all, he was one of us, a black man, the first to become president. But it was not long before things turned, as they will. And in those days, my father was a fisherman. He had his own boat and he managed to make a living for my mother and my brothers and sisters. It is a simple story, isn't it? One day my father took me to the port. Sometimes I went out with him on the boat. My father began to drink rum with his friends, and then a political argument grew up between groups. One group was for Papa Doc, while the other group was embittered. There was a scuffle and ma-chetes were used during the fight. It was during this fight that I was injured. I was nine years old at the time."

"And your father?" Roberts asked.

"He was unhurt," Morriseau replied, "but in time, he lost his boat. It was said that my father had used witchcraft to make another fisherman ill. The police came and confiscated his boat and gave it to another man, one who supported Papa Doc and the Tontons. My father was disappointed. He became depressed and disoriented. Then he became a vagabond and cane cutter. Finally he disappeared entirely, and my mother never saw him again. In my country, it is not an uncommon story."

"I'm very sorry," Roberts said. "How will you use your money?"

"I have no use for the money," the artist said.

"It is a great deal of money."

"I have what I need."

"You must deposit the money in a bank."

"Surely," Morriseau said.

"Perhaps you could leave Haiti," Roberts suggested.

"I would never leave Haiti," Morriseau said in Creole. "I am in the middle of my age. I could never adjust to another kind of life." He juggled the bottle to his stump, under the armpit, uncapping it with his hand, pouring the rum into an empty glass. "You will leave tomorrow?" he asked Roberts. "Like Raymond Cobo?"

"Not like Raymond Cobo," Roberts said. "I'm not leaving like Raymond Cobo."

Virgil engaged the artist in conversation for several minutes while Roberts fell silent and watched the bats swoop after insects.

"He says you should be careful," Virgil said to Roberts. "He thinks a Chevrolet followed us from the market."

Roberts asked Virgil to drive Morriseau to his home in the suburbs of Cap. He told them to take the back roads and avoid the police. He would go to his room and wait.

*h*e sat quietly in the timeless dark. The louvered jalousies he had opened caught a breeze and threw it into the nearly airless room, but it did little good. In Port au Prince, there had been a morning and evening breeze, though Roberts did not know the reason, whether geographical or seasonal. He wished for a good wind, something to blow away the dust and the stillness, something to cool him while he cleaned his weapon. But there was no wind and the slight breeze only stirred the heat, reminding him of the mosquitoes that buzzed around his head. He could hear the sound of the ocean licking the sand along the beach, and he could see the citronella candles flickering out one by one on the terrace. When the last candle had gone out, there was not even the promise of light.

In his hand, the small automatic felt as insubstantial as a butterfly. Daubing oil on a rag, he ran the cloth up and down the barrel, cleaning the inside of it with the rag folded around the tip of a pencil, unloading the clip and holding each bullet in his hand, one at a time, feeling its weight. While he worked, he thought back to the beach at Dania, where he'd been dozing next to Dolores Vega. He remembered waking suddenly to find his head propped against the skin of her thigh, and he could remember seeing the blond, downy hair on her leg like whirlwinds of sand on the complexity of her body. He remembered thinking to himself that he wanted to lick the skin, touch his forehead to it, how sparks seemed to dart from his body to hers. She had stirred, asked him if he was awake, and he remembered being fondled like a baby, touched by the inordinate wizardry of desire.

Carefully, he reloaded the clip and slipped it into its cradle. A wilderness of sound assaulted his ears, although it was nearly quiet. Crickets exploded in the outer dark along the saw grass, an orchestra of insect legs shirring ceaselessly. There was a sudden passage of bats, like drapery being drawn in some musty theater of a room, their wings replacing the nonexistent wind. A million piston-engined mosquitoes roared in his head.

The clip snapped in its chamber. He thought he heard the far-away sound of an automobile engine coming slowly, then a steady purr of its idle, the sound of a slamming door. He rose from the bed where he had been sitting on its rumpled coverlet and placed a chair cushion on it, which he covered with a sheet. He walked to the farthest corner of the room and sat down in the now-cushionless chair. He closed his eyes and imagined the many-watered meadows where he would walk in Colorado, about four miles from his ranch in the valley. A spring gurgled through his mind and he rollicked in fields of bunchgrass and jimson, hoarding to himself the gray sage with its yellow flowers where bees gathered to such sweet juice. He pondered the blue daisies and the red paintbrush flowers sheltering in the lee of ditches, all manner of redwinged blackbirds wheeling in the convected air. He listened to the conversation of the bees and the sound of the wind in the junipers, felt the aroma of good dirt in his nose.

It was the muscular Tonton from Port au Prince who opened the door a crack, slowly, then partway. There were no shadows to fix, and the Tonton stood in nearly pitch blackness, unaligned to light, each man sheltered from the other by the fathomless depth of night. The Tonton raised a machete in his right hand, and Roberts turned his head slightly to see better in the dark, an old trick. He thought it remarkable how clearheaded he had become, how calm he felt, as though he'd suddenly been bathed in mounds of ice. He covered the barrel of the automatic with a pillow.

The Tonton gave a short sigh and dashed the machete against the bed cushion. There was a dull thud, then another as the man ripped his blade against an empty bed.

"Blanc tombe," the Tonton whispered.

Roberts aimed and fired once. The pillow muffled the crack of the gun and there was only a mild pop. The Tonton fell to his knees slowly and dropped the machete. On his knees, he waited for death, then slumped his head against the bed and sagged to the floor. Roberts rose from the chair and walked over to the prone Tonton and turned him face-up. Even in the dark, the Tonton was wearing his sunglasses, giving him the appearance of a huge cockroach, a zombie, the nerveless servant of Samedi.

Roberts rose and left the bungalow, shutting the door behind him. Toward the beach, the terrace was deserted. Walking down to the parking lot, he found the Chevrolet parked about two hundred yards from the lobby. The car was empty, its doors locked.

It took Roberts fifteen minutes of hard work to drag the dead Tonton up the beach and into a copse of sea grape and mangrove. He laid the dead man down and sat looking into his face for a few moments, then hurled the machete into the water, maybe twenty-five yards out. When he returned to the hotel, he went to Virgil's bungalow and tapped at the door, whispered his own name, then tapped again, this time louder.

Virgil opened the door.

"We have to leave now," Roberts told him.

"What is wrong, M'ser?" Virgil asked.

"Pack quickly. We have no time left."

"But there is an unofficial curfew," Virgil protested. "What has happened? If we leave, we will brave the curfew. It is perhaps not wise."

"I've killed the Tonton," Roberts said.

Virgil stepped back from the door as though he'd been struck a sharp blow. He crossed himself and began to mumble in Creole.

"I didn't want this to happen," Roberts said. Inside the room, Virgil began packing his small bag. He had his clothes, a few toiletries, an extra pair of flip-flops he wore to save his knockoff Reeboks. "I'm sorry I've put you in this danger, but it can't be helped now."

"They killed M'ser Cobo, no?" Virgil said. He tied off the end of his plastic traveling bag and began to put on his new clothes. "Why would they do such a terrible thing?"

"Mr. Cobo was made to appear a thief," Roberts said. "He was sent here with money. He purchased paintings and then he was killed. They called him a thief, and nobody would defend Mr. Cobo, would they? If I were killed in the same way, who would miss me? I am the perfect person for their mission. No father, no wife, no children. I am a man about whom nobody would ask a question."

Virgil finished packing and they hurried to the jeep. It was only ten o'clock, but with no electricity, there were few guests at the hotel, no patrons at the bar, nobody eating at the outdoor restaurant. It was likely that the management had little gasoline and did not want to waste what they did have, especially with so few paying guests. The only thing to do in Cap Haitien was to drink rum in the dark or go to sleep.

Roberts backed the jeep downhill.

"What shall we do?" Virgil asked.

"Take me to Morriseau," Roberts replied. "I'm sending you back to Port au Prince by bus. I'm going over to the Dominican Republic, try to catch a plane to Miami. Anything to get out of this country as soon as possible. I'm sorry I've involved you in this situation, Virgil. I didn't know it would be this way."

"You must not be sorry, M'ser," Virgil said.

"Even so."

They bumped along a rutted road toward town. Only a few bicyclists had braved the dark and the informal curfew, the possibility of police roadblocks.

"I do not want to say good-bye," Virgil said.

"We'll say adieu."

They were at the edge of the city, unspeakable slums of cardboard, tin, discarded tires, plywood.

"I want you to remember this," Roberts said. "I've opened an account for you at the French bank in Port au Prince. There are about five thousand dollars in the account. When I reach Miami, I have some things to do. I'll try to return when I can. I'll try to take you out of here."

"It is not necessary," Virgil said. "Neither the money nor the trip. You must keep yourself safe."

"But it is necessary," Roberts said. "It is the only necessary thing I know."

55

*m*orriseau lived in a weathered Victorian about five blocks from the central cathedral. Virgil knew the back streets, so as they drove, they encountered no roadblocks or police checks. By all accounts, the police were as afraid of the people as the people were afraid of the police. So far as Virgil knew, the confusion of coups in the Army had kept most units firmly fixed to their bases around Port au Prince. As he drove, Roberts cradled the gun in his lap, willing to use it on the slightest pretext. There was no way he would be arrested in Haiti, imprisoned in Casserness Dessalines, thrown to the sharks.

The artist answered the door wearing cutoff dungarees and a sweat-encrusted T-shirt. He leaned against the doorjamb, his weight on his arm stump. He looked up and down the street, then let them in the house, a dilapidated shingle-and-board structure with a roof that looked as though it might crumble and fall at any moment. Every square inch of the walls was covered with the man's astounding work, a vibrant cacophony of color and motion.

"What is wrong?" Morriseau asked. "Is something wrong?"

Roberts stood quietly amid the trash and strewn refuse of paint tubes, discarded easels, stiff rags. It seemed likely to him that the artist lived alone. He could hear no sounds of children. Only a few pieces of wicker furniture were scattered about the room, one table piled high with painting supplies, brushes, mixing vials, books. He took a seat when asked, as Morriseau lit a small candle, illuminating the three men in its faint glow.

"Something is badly wrong," Roberts said. "I've had to kill a Tonton."

Morriseau listened impassively as Virgil translated into Creole. His stump appeared in the candlelight as a purple cauliflower.

"He came to my room at the Plage and was going to kill me with his machete. I shot him in the side and he is dead. I dragged his body up the beach and put him in a mangrove-and-saw-grass swamp, partly covered by sand and water. His body might be found tomorrow, or it might not be found for weeks. Whoever sent him to kill me will miss him in a few days, maybe less."

Morriseau raised an eyebrow. "Do you want some rum?" he asked. The artist seemed utterly unperturbed by what he'd heard. "I have a bottle of Barbancourt," he continued. "It is the first purchase in celebration of my new wealth and fame." He grinned, revealing his deformed teeth, the missing gaps in front. With one hand, he sliced a lime and squeezed some of the juice in three paper cups. Roberts took his cup and drank the rum. Morriseau raised his cup to the ceiling and said, "To the death of more Tontons."

The rum was like pale fire. "I thought you should know the truth," Roberts said.

"But why would a Tonton want to kill you?" he asked.

"It is complicated," Roberts told him. "The man who sent me here is a thief. He is also a murderer. It is he who is to blame. The same thing was done to Raymond Cobo."

Morriseau reflected for a long time. He sipped his rum and stared at the cup, as though seeing images in it. Roberts was soaked by sweat. The room in the old house was airless and confined.

"You have come here for a reason," the artist said flatly.

"I'm afraid so," Roberts admitted. "I have no right."

"That is not the question," Morriseau said in French. "If I can help you, I will. There is not a single citizen in Haiti who has not suffered under the Tontons. They have fouled our atmosphere for decades. Tell me what it is you want."

"I want you to hide Virgil for the night," Roberts said. "I realize there is great danger. I will return to the hotel and Virgil will travel to Port au Prince tomorrow on a bus."

Virgil hesitated in his translation, then completed it with a frown. He looked at Roberts and said, "But, M'ser, there is no need. I will stay at the hotel and drive the jeep back to the capital tomorrow."

"You wouldn't make it," Roberts said.

"If there is trouble, I can deal with it directly."

Morriseau said, "Please, please. Your friend is welcome here tonight. The Cap is a tolerant city, no? Even Frap has made little headway here."

"Then I'll leave Virgil with you," Roberts said. "With my thanks."

"But, my friend," the artist said, "what will you do?"

"Tomorrow I'll try to make it to the Dominican border. I will cross however I can."

Morriseau refilled his own cup. Roberts sipped at his rum. His headache was quaking. "You have no chance," Morriseau said. "A blanc is very noticeable here."

"I'll have to take my chances."

"But the Tonton will be found."

"Perhaps not," Roberts said.

"Ah no, M'ser," the artist sighed. "Haiti is very crowded. Children play at the beach. People bathe in the water. On every square inch there is a man or woman making love. You should have put the body in the water for sharks."

"There was no time," Roberts said, thinking back to his fear, making excuses. "And there was a danger that someone would see me taking the body out into the surf." He sipped at his rum again, feeding his fatigue.

"I know a better way," Morriseau said dramatically, lifting his cup ceilingward.

"You must not involve yourself."

"But we are already involved," he said, gesturing with his arm at Virgil, the door, everything outside the room that had symbolized a conspiracy. "In a time of terror, men of goodwill are brothers, true?"

"But your family," Roberts protested.

"I have no family," Morriseau said. "My wife and my children are dead. I am alone. It is another reason I have no place to go. Do you understand this? Do you know what I am saying?"

"I think so," Roberts said. "I too am alone."

"It is settled then," the artist said emphatically. He drained his rum with a flourish and snapped the cup down on the table. "My cousin is a fisherman. He owns a small boat with a motor. In it he can take you along the coast toward the Dominican Republic. The Siete Cayos at Monte Cristi lie a few miles beyond the beach. You can wade to the islands, and in the morning, you can take a ferry to Monte Cristi. The Dominicans will welcome your dollars. You can take a bus to Puerto Plata, and from there, you can fly to Miami." Morriseau smiled his gap-toothed smile. "Of course, immigration is a problem. But not so bad a problem as the Tonton macoute."

"Your cousin has a family?" Roberts asked.

"Several families," Morriseau laughed. "He hates the Tonton. Suppose my cousin takes this Tonton out into the bay and throws him to the sharks as well? Huh? How would that be? It is dark, imagine the darkness. My cousin is a good fisherman but he is crazy, too. He would laugh to throw a Tonton to the sharks. It would give him nothing but pleasure. He will tell his many grandchildren how he fed a Tonton to the sharks of Cap Haitien. You will be doing him a great favor, my friend."

Morriseau drank from the bottle of Barbancourt. Roberts nodded to Virgil, who returned his nod. They decided that Virgil would leave the jeep in Cap and take the first bus to Port au Prince in the morning.

Morriseau raised the bottle. "To the sharks," he said.

*r*oberts went to the Dominican Republic with Morriseau's cousin who told him he wasn't afraid of the Tontons. "After all," he'd said in a raspy monotone, "I am nearly seventy years old. What can they do to me that they haven't done already?"

First, they went up the beach and gathered in the Tonton, who lay partly covered by sand, and they put the body in the boat and covered it with an old quilt. Then the old man had rowed them out beyond the slow breaking of the surf. Roberts sat in the boat with his legs straddling the Tonton and watched the old man tug on the starter rope of the decrepit fifteen-horse engine, which choked to life after three pulls. About two miles out, they dumped the Tonton as the old man cackled to himself.

At Los Cayos, Roberts waded ashore as dawn broke. He was carrying an overnight bag, his field glasses, some spare tennis shoes on a string around his neck. He planned to explain if questioned that he was a birdwatcher who'd missed the last ferry to the main-land, but none of the fishermen or children who spotted him even bothered to ask. There were no cafés on the tiny island, so he drank some coffee with a fisherman and tried his rusty high-school Span-ish for about two hours. Around ten o'clock, on a cloudless, baking morning, the first ferry unloaded some children, fishermen, a few snorkelers, and Roberts took the boat back to Monte Cristi. That day he rented a room in the only commercial hotel in the dusty town center and slept. That night he ate dinner, comida criolla—

rice, beans, and grilled meat—and sat outside at an umbrellaed table as the deserted town filled up with darkness and insects. He watched pied crows pick through garbage. He counted the flies on a Coca-Cola sign.

The next day he caught a bus into Puerto Plata and bought an airline ticket to New York from the local agent. At immigration, he was barely noticed in the horde of tourists and businessmen getting onto the flight, nor was he bothered when he landed in New York. Somewhere off the coast of Haiti, he had dropped the small Colt automatic in sixty feet of blue water.

In New York, he spent the best half of an afternoon sitting on a hard-backed plastic chair in the departure lounge of an airline terminal. He read the *New York Times* and did the crossword puzzle, then dozed as best he could in a sitting position, his sleep broken into shards by terrible car-crash ensembles, snowy blizzards, voices calling to him from inner darkness. On the 737 to Lauderdale, he managed to sleep cramped between a businessman and a tourist, and the episodic nightmares concluded. In Florida, he found the weather grainy and picturesque, colored up, as sailors might say.

At a motel in Dania Beach, Roberts managed about six hours of good sleep. It was Saturday night and the crowds at the jai-alai fronton were noisy, traffic not letting up on the Federal Highway until almost two o'clock in the morning. Once or twice he woke and went out onto the balcony and watched the whores ply their trade on the street, then went back to sleep. Crowds of high-school kids roamed the pavement, drinking beer, smoking joints, having a grand time at the expense of everybody else's peace and quiet. When he woke on Sunday morning, the beach was littered with discarded plastic cups, paper sacks, garbage from ships beyond the limit. After a shower and shave, he dressed in chinos and a dark, short-sleeved shirt, sunglasses, and a straw hat. He drove his newly rented black Buick down to Coconut Grove and parked across the street from the small condominium that Dolores Vega was buying on time, just away from Calle Ocho and five blocks from the gallery. He sat quietly, smoking a small cigar, then went down to a pay phone at the corner of Calle Ocho and telephoned her.

She answered on the third ring, her voice sleepy. "Be quiet," Roberts said quickly. "It's me, Mitch. Are you alone?"

"Madre de Dio," Dolores said.

"Too loud," Roberts told her hastily. "Are you alone?"

"Yes, please, where are you?"

"Open the door for me. One minute."

Roberts hung up and hurried across the vacant street. It was a shaded avenue overhung by palms and live oaks, and the sun coming through the clouds had plunged it into contrasts of light and dark. The sky looked as though it had been stained by ox blood, and flocks of pigeons and pelicans fluttered south toward the water of the bay. Sand was ticking through the streets, tiny dunes of it gathering in the empty doorways of the closed bars and restaurants, wings of sand powdering the plate-glass windows and peppering the leaves of the oaks.

He knocked on the door and Dolores Vega opened it. The condo was on the first-floor rear, sheltered from the street by a covered flagstone walkway, plantings of hibiscus, oleander, and bamboo, a huge beige-stucco wall with an iron gate that swung open without a key. Dolores wore a dark green-satin robe, and her auburn hair was mussed from bed. In an instant, she was in his arms, kissing his face.

"I thought you were dead," she said.

"Why would you think that?" he asked.

"Bobby said you were missing in Haiti."

"When did he tell you that?"

"For God's sake, come inside."

They went through the kitchen and out the sliding-glass doors to the patio, a square of flagstone and terra-cotta covered by a cantilevered tile roof. Dolores had planted pots of orchids, and some of them were blooming, tiny insectlike blossoms of purple and red, huge grapefruit-sized flowers of purest white. She brought out two cups of strong coffee and they sat at a wrought-iron table while the wild wind blew up clouds of sand and coral dust around them. Streaks of red buffed the sky, and it looked as though it might storm at any moment.

"Tell me what Bobby said," Roberts asked.

"He just said you were gone," she told him. "This was about five or six days ago. Then nothing. I asked him what he meant, what had happened, but he just smiled at me. He said you'd dropped out of sight near Cap Haitien."

"He was right about that, anyway," Roberts said.

"Can you tell me what's happening?"

Roberts looked at her, a beautiful, sleepy princess. He wondered if he should trust her.

"I wonder about you," he said.

"I wish you wouldn't."

"I don't know what to do."

"Whatever you need, you can rely on me."

"Perhaps that's why I've come."

Dolores put down her coffee cup and sat on his lap. She held his head and stroked his hair. Roberts could smell sleep on her, an aroma of washed sheets, perfume, a rich coffee taste in her mouth when she leaned down and kissed him.

"There's a storm out in the Caribbean," she said. "It's been a bad hurricane season."

*r*oberts caught Jimmy Glide on Bay Harbor, just near the post office and city hall.

It was a gusty day with high, gray clouds and a stiff east wind that had blown all night. The dull heat was making him itch inside his clothes, and the headache he'd gotten in Haiti still pounded his temples. He had slept at the motel on Dania Beach, had breakfasted at a little café in South Lauderdale, then headed down I-95 after morning traffic had eased. He'd parked the rented Buick about half a block from the Hilliard mansion, then followed Glide when he came out of the driveway in a black Corvette.

Roberts watched Glide enter the post office and come back out of the building carrying two brown-paper parcels. Glide wore black-cotton pants, a gray T-shirt with a Dolphins logo on the front, his standard-issue turquoise sunglasses with aviator frames. He had trimmed his heavy black beard, and he was wearing a baseball cap, bill turned backward. Roberts watched him get into the Corvette, which he'd parked in a red zone outside the post office.

Roberts stayed a steady half block behind, all the way across Broad Causeway in light traffic. On Biscayne Bay, whitecaps danced between buoys to the south, and the city of Miami towered into a jagged pile of shiny glass skyscrapers and granite cones. The air-conditioning in the Buick poured out cold air and Roberts listened to Schubert on a classical station from Broward. Glide caught I-95 going south, then turned back west toward the airport road. Roberts followed him to a short-term parking lot and stayed behind as Glide got out and walked to the terminal area.

It was late Monday morning and the normal hordes of people hustled to catch their rides to New York. It would be another month or two before cruise passengers began to pour into Miami.

Roberts managed to catch up to Glide in the international waiting area. He watched the man buy a coffee at Starbucks, a bagel from a stand in the lounge. He wandered from newsstand to newsstand, past coffee bars, wearing his new straw hat and sunglasses, a pair of anonymous chinos, a blue sports shirt patterned with sailfish and dolphin. The loudspeakers in the lounge blared a succession of messages, and Muzak fuzzed the silence.

Roberts had been watching Glide sit outside one of the arrival gates for about fifteen minutes when Rosemary Collins walked down the ramp. She was wearing her blue stewardess uniform, a bright-red silk scarf, and professional in her starched clothes, she guided a wheeled luggage carrier. They kissed happily and Glide took the carrier. Roberts noted the flight number and point of departure—Flight 1095, London to Miami.

Roberts phoned Dolores from a booth near the short-term lot. He could barely hear her voice over the roar of jet engines and canned salsa music. They made a date to meet for lunch at a café near the condo on Calle Ocho. Then he bought a newspaper at a kiosk and waited for noon. He drove over to the café and parked in a lot, four seventy-five an hour, six-hour maximum.

They sat in the back of the café under a whirling ceiling fan. The owner had jerry-built a garden atmosphere, a tiny fishpond with goldfish doing laps, wilted philodendrons, a pair of awkward sculptures in bronze. Roberts ordered a Cubano sandwich, and Dolores the house salad, a glass of white wine.

She dabbled at her salad when it came. "I wish you'd talk to me," she said finally.

"Everybody needs to trust someone," Roberts said. "For me, that someone would be you."

"You think you're taking a chance, don't you?"

"It occurred to me," he said. "I'm sorry."

Dolores sat over her salad, the tiny shrimp and the white clams, a dribble of red cabbage. She sipped some of the white wine and watched the traffic on Calle Ocho, far up front. Wind was rattling the plate-glass windows.

"You trust me or you don't, it's up to you," she said. "But I wish you would. It makes a difference to things."

"All right," he said. "I trust you. As far as Hilliard and Glide are concerned, I want to stay dead for now. Let them think I disappeared in Haiti. They may not believe I'm dead, but with every day that passes, they'll think it more and more."

"What happened to Raymond Cobo?"

"He's not pretending," Roberts told her. "He's really dead."

"You know this for certain?"

"I haven't seen the body, if that's what you mean." Roberts toyed with his Cubano, too much sandwich piled with pork and cheese. "The Tontons probably fed him to the sharks up in Cap Haitien. I'd bet on it."

"But why? What did he do?"

"It's simple," Roberts told her. "Hilliard sent Cobo out to buy art. Hilliard has contacts in the Haitian military and customs. People who can get things done in the shipping and export business. People who work with Tontons. Cobo landed in Haiti and his every move was shadowed. They even played on his fears, sent him curses to make him fearful, to make him crazy and careless. Then when he'd collected all the art, they murdered him and dumped his body in Cap Bay. Somebody withdrew the two hundred thousand he'd brought with him, and the paintings disappeared. Cobo gets the blame."

"But the paintings aren't in Miami," Dolores said.

"One of them is," Roberts told her. "One of them is hanging on Hilliard's wall in Bay Harbor."

Dolores thought for a time and then said, "But what does Bobby do with the other paintings?"

"He sells them in New York, I don't know. He finds buyers on the black market. You told me yourself the trade isn't too scrupulous."

"I suppose it's possible," she said. "But what about the Las Olas gallery?"

"He doesn't care about it, Dolores," Roberts said. "He doesn't make his money from art. Have you ever really looked at his accounts? Have you compared the accounts with the mansion he lives in? He probably tried to open the Las Olas gallery to continue to look like a big art dealer. It's a front."

"Then how does he make his money?" she asked. She looked as though she might cry, already knowing the answer.

"Whatever is hot in South Florida, isn't that what he said? You tell me what's hot in South Florida."

Dolores watched the goldfish swim in circles. They made bubbles that rose to the surface and escaped. Neither Roberts nor Dolores had touched their food for a long time.

"It's a cliché, isn't it?" Dolores asked. "Drugs and guns."

"I guess it is," Roberts said.

58

Weather reports placed two tropical storms six hundred miles out in the convergence of the Atlantic and Caribbean, just off the shoulder of Puerto Rico, each storm steaming northwest, though nobody on the face of the planet could explain how they worked, or where they might end up.

Roberts had slept ten hours and he had taken a long swim in the surf off Dania Beach, plowing through waves capped by white water, tugging himself out three hundred yards beyond the undertow, turning on his back to float under the gray sky, allowing his mind to clear as leathery sunlight filtered down later. After about forty minutes of swimming, floating, swimming again, he dragged himself back to the beach, toweled off, and had a continental breakfast on the deck while he listened to the weather news. He went downstairs and sat on a lounger by the empty pool, studying the South Florida aviation reports, trying to get a fix on Pan-Carib Airways' flights for the past two or three weeks.

Pan-Carib was a small carrier registered in Panama, with several offices listed throughout the Caribbean basin. Most of its flying was done on an irregular basis, some of it bare charter, with only two regular flights at Miami each month, one departing during to Panama City through Trinidad and Tobago and on to Panama, the other arriving out of Panama, through Port au Prince, on to Miami. Another flight, Roberts noticed, flew from Panama through Vera Cruz and on to Mexico City, sometimes stopping in New Orleans to pick up cargo. From what he could gather, even these flights were sometimes disrupted, canceled, delayed, depending on cargo availability, crews, maintenance problems.

After his breakfast of rolls and coffee, Roberts drove out to Miami International and found Northwest Seventh just opposite the Blue Lagoon, where the Baggage Handlers' Union had a small office. He parked in a weedy gravel lot and walked into the small stucco building. The front windows had been tinted gray to cut down on the western evening glare, and for a time, Roberts stood in the stuffy lobby looking across the shallow lagoon to the airport tarmacs and runways, the concrete decks and asphalt roads sending up drafts of heat that wrinkled the morning air, giving it the unhealthy sheen of a sick cat.

The office itself was a rectangle of corkboard and linoleum, bisected by a chest-high counter with a glass top. Behind the counter sat a desk with a typewriter on it, some filing cabinets against a wall, a small old-fashioned dial telephone. Roberts tapped a bell and from the back room emerged a sprightly man in gray slacks and black Ban-Lon shirt, simultaneously smiling and zipping his fly. He had jug ears and a hearty face and stood about five and a half feet tall, about a hundred and twenty pounds dripping wet. He leaned over the counter and grinned at Roberts.

"What's up, bub?" he asked.

Roberts leaned on the counter and introduced himself, shaking hands.

"I'm Warren," the man said. "Doughty."

"I'm trying to get some information," Roberts said cheerfully.

"Yeah?" Doughty said.

"I just got out of the Air Force," Roberts lied. "I'm looking to fly through my retirement, you know. Double-dip kind of thing. About all I've come up with is Pan-Carib. I can't find out much about them."

"You don't say?" Doughty replied. "I'm not surprised."

"You know anything?"

"I know everything."

"Would you mind?" Roberts asked respectfully.

Doughty poured himself a cup of stale coffee from an electric pot. He offered a cup to Roberts, but Roberts had already drunk his limit.

"Pan-Carib, huh?" Doughty said, musing.

"What do they fly?"

"They'll fly 707's, I guess," Doughty said. "But you're looking at old tubs nobody will touch. If you want the word on maintenance and safety, you can check the FAA. That's your best bet, anyway."

"What's their cargo?"

"Now there I can tell you something," Doughty said. "A lot of times they'll fly in manufactured ticky-tacky out of Panama and Haiti. Shoes, baseballs, goofy stuff. Out of South Florida they do mostly electronics, heavy-construction equipment, cats, bulldozers, cranes."

"If it's heavy stuff, who loads it?"

"We do," Doughty said. "My men. Good jobs, too. If you're worried about out-loading, my guys are the best."

"They unload it, too?"

"Sure, right out here, sometimes up to Opa Locka if they're out of New Orleans."

"I know a guy named Jimmy Glide," Roberts said.

"Oh, sure," Doughty said, interrupting. "Guy's got steel balls, that the guy?" He finished his cold coffee. "You know that guy?"

"Sure, I've met him a couple of times."

"Black heavy beard?"

"That's the one."

"Yeah . . . well, Jimmy, he's a big shot. He supervises the Miami-Dade crews."

"I can't get a line on who owns Pan-Carib."

"You can check with FAA, but Pan-Carib runs out of Port au Prince. I don't know where they're registered. Like I say, we load and unload, that's about all."

"I just wanted to see if the off-loaders were good."

"Best in the business," Doughty said. "But if you ask me, Pan-Carib is a bunch of morons. Be careful."

"Jimmy Glide knows his business, huh? I mean, loading and un-loading can make a big difference to safety."

"I told you," Doughty said. "He supervises the loading and un-loading. You ain't never heard of Pan-Carib going down in a fireball because some dozer punched a hole in the firewall, have you?"

Roberts extended his hand again. "Thanks," he said.

He was out the door, standing on the crushed-gravel parking lot, then heading toward the black Buick, which was parked in direct hot sun. Big jets were landing at Dade International, a tremendous morning noise.

Roberts drove toward downtown Miami, listening to the news on talk-radio. Hurricane Howard had hit the Dominican Republic, just off the nose of Mona Passage. It was a big storm now, one of the biggest of the decade. As he drove along the crowded freeway, he noticed the sky coloring up, shades of steamy orange low against the Everglades. There was some kind of electricity in the air. After all, it was hurricane season, still, humid, and strange.

*r*oberts parked in a pay lot under Biscayne Boulevard, then walked five blocks over to the FBI building on 39th Street. There was a fountain squirting tepid water on a statue of Cupid, and Roberts bought a hot dog from a vendor and sat near the fountain eating his lunch. Secretaries and lawyers mingled, smoking cigarettes and making small talk in the shade of overhanging oaks. Now and then, Roberts thought about Dolores Vega, wondering how much danger he had placed her in by showing up at her condominium, demonstrating that he was still alive. A bum tried to cadge him for a quarter, and Roberts gave the man a dollar just to get rid of him. What the hell, he thought, it was Hilliard's money anyway.

It was after one o'clock when he took an elevator to the fifth floor and checked in with Security outside the Agency offices. He was ushered through a security door overlooked by television cameras, then talked to by an electronic voice that asked him his name and the name of the person he wished to see. The voice allowed him into another sealed area that had a photo of Bill Clinton on the wall, some fake birds-of-paradise in a vase, fifteen issues of *People* magazine on a mahogany-veneer table in one corner, two blue-plastic chairs nearby, and an ashtray full of butts. There was a sign on the wall advising against smoking, and a series of commendation plaques.

Twenty minutes later, Roberts was ushered into another office by a young woman in a print dress who'd gotten a terrible sunburn over the weekend. Five minutes after that, Lawrence Littrow bounded into the room with the unmistakable animation of a cartoon character from afternoon kiddie shows. He had traded his seersucker suit for a plain gray Palm Beach–type, but his red face still expressed a casual cruelty. Littrow acknowledged Roberts, then led him down a long carpeted hallway and into a drab room with a table surrounded by five metal chairs.

"How's your prostate?" Littrow asked. Roberts sat while Littrow paced. The agent crossed his arms and adjusted the bow tie under his neck.

"Look," Roberts said. "I've got something for you. Maybe you can lay off the humor and get serious."

"I'm a serious person," Littrow said. "I looked at your sheet just now. On the screen, you're amazingly clean for such a shitbag-type person."

Roberts thought about leaving then. He wanted to fly home to Colorado and lie on his back in bunchgrass for two hours while a wild sky funneled his dreams southward toward the end of the valley. He thought about the first stone fly he would throw into a cold stream, where it would dart under a grass bank, trout holding there.

"You want it or not?" Roberts asked.

"I'm listening," Littrow said.

Like a good boy, Roberts began at the beginning, taking Littrow through his meeting with Hilliard, the assignment in Haiti, his experiences with the Tontons, the import business of Champagne Lambert, the connection to Pan-Carib through Port au Prince and on to Miami. About halfway through the tale, Littrow sat down opposite Roberts and began to pay attention.

When Roberts finished, Littrow asked, "What makes you so sure they're shipping contraband?"

"I've been to Hilliard's mansion in Bay Harbor. You can't build what he's built on the art business. I don't care how good the markup."

"And this Bobby Hilliard, what does he think you're doing right now?"

Roberts settled in for a long afternoon. He'd left some gaps in his story, though, failing to mention Dolores Vega, the Tonton he'd killed, the way he'd escaped from Haiti.

"Hilliard probably thinks I'm dead," Roberts said. "Maybe he hopes it, but he wants to believe. A couple of months ago, they sent another guy over there on the same trip. Guy named Raymond Cobo. They scared Cobo shitless, then killed him. He gathered up art, just like I was supposed to, but he never made it home."

"You can prove that?"

"I can't prove shit," Roberts said.

"Suppose you wear a wire for us," Littrow said.

"That makes great sense," Roberts said angrily. "Hilliard sets me up to kill me, then I show up wearing a wire. They'd take me straight out to the Everglades and bury me under a plastic sheet."

"Pan-Carib," Littrow mused.

"Don't you have any imagination?" Roberts asked. "Is wiring somebody up your only play?"

"Don't get huffy," Littrow said.

"One of Hilliard's boys is named Jimmy Glide. He loads and unloads Pan-Carib out at Miami-Dade. He came out of the Baggage Handlers' Union in Brooklyn. He used to work JFK."

"Now we're getting somewhere," Littrow said. "Let's assume they're smuggling cocaine out of Port au Prince. What kind of cargo do they use as cover?"

"The paintings, goddamn it," Roberts said.

"And how would that work?"

"They pack the paintings in Port au Prince. Lambert handles the formalities on the government side in Haiti, all the documents, bills of lading, inspection certificates and hiding the coke. When the plane lands in Miami, Glide unloads the cargo, but the invoices and bills of lading are delayed while he unpacks the coke, probably from the excelsior or the frames. When customs comes by, they've got clean Haitian paintings, and you know how busy customs is these days. Hilliard gets rid of the coke to middlemen, then takes the paintings to New York and unloads them on the black market. Hell, he could take the art to the West Coast or Japan, for that matter. He has his coke, which he sells, then he has his paintings, which he sells, too. As far as Raymond Cobo is concerned, Hilliard claims the man kept both the money and the paintings. He loses the art invoices. I screwed him up by actually paying the artists in cash before I left. That was the only difference between Raymond Cobo and me. That and Raymond Cobo is dead. I guess that's the biggest difference."

"Where do they transship the coke?"

Roberts shrugged. He had a good idea, but he wasn't ready to tell Littrow. "No idea," he said instead.

"I'd like to get you down on paper."

"I don't think so," Roberts told him.

"At least on tape."

"Not right now. I want to hear your thoughts."

Littrow tugged at his blue bow tie. It was silk, hand-tied, patterned with brown coconuts.

"Where are you staying?" he asked.

"I'll be in touch."

"Hey, I could hold you," Littrow said, smiling.

"You'll never bend me over again," Roberts said. "Don't even think about it."

The agent smiled malignantly. "Be in touch," he said.

*r*oberts spent two hours at the FAA Opa Locka office poring through the public records of Pan-Carib: safety reports, financial data, operating practices, accident filings. The owner was listed as Crazy Horse World Transport, Ltd., a privately held corporation doing business out of Grand Cayman Island, with a main office in Panama City. The registered agent was a Haitian named Ducette Margolis, whose stated office was in the Teleco building in downtown Port au Prince. It was Margolis who had personally signed all the notices and certificates issued to Pan-Carib, obviously a notary and front man.

Roberts ran through microfiches until he got a headache, then walked outside in the gathering dusty sunset and watched the sky bake to a purple haze, red over the Everglades, a touch of sparkling burgundy in the cumulus clouds above the ocean. Small planes cruised in for landings at the airport, and in the dim light, he could tell that a storm was building out over the Gulf Stream and that later there might be a big wind, though just now it was hot and dead calm, the humidity making him sweat salt bullets.

Roberts caught I-95 and rode the traffic over to Coconut Grove and ate dinner in a garden café down the street from where Dolores Vega lived. He took his time over conch soup, fresh-baked Cuban bread, a couple of Heinekens and a slice of key lime pie, freshly baked. He had left his car in a pay lot, and he walked three blocks over to the condo and pushed the buzzer. Dolores peeked out of the door, then pulled him inside as though he were a messenger from the Publisher's Clearing House.

"Where have you been?" she asked, hugging him almost uncontrollably. "I've been so worried about you."

"You sound like somebody's mom," Roberts joked.

He went to the living room and sat down on a plush couch decorated with beige-and-red roses. A red-plastic flamingo sat on a clear-glass table across the room, and there were spiderwebs of color in the flocked wallpaper. It had begun to rain outside, and water poured off the oaks and palms, clattering down to the asphalt in the street.

"I've been to the cops," Roberts said.

"I thought you might," Dolores said. She was still wearing her work clothes, a smart tan suit.

"I want to warn you," Roberts said. "I don't have much faith in the FBI. At least not in this one guy I met named Littrow. They'll check out Hilliard and they'll probably run you through their little computers. Light you up like a bug and look at your insides."

"I can stand that," Dolores said.

She got up and fixed them a tequila sunrise at a small kitchen bar, and they sat together on the couch while it rained hammers and sickles. Roberts sipped his tequila and thought about the first horse he had ever trained, a paint mare named Frantic Annie. He remembered the good dust smell of her flanks and the way she bit his arm when he offered her alfalfa from his hand. Dolores rose and stuffed a kitchen towel under the patio glass door to stop the rain from flooding inside, then came back and sat down beside him. He trusted her now, and he wanted her to know he trusted her. What he was doing could wreck her life, touch her in important ways. He knew how vital the gallery had become to her, and he wanted her to know how he felt about destroying it all. He felt like a traitor, but what could he do?

"I trust you, Dolores," he said finally, almost stupidly.

"Then you have to tell me," Dolores said. "You have to tell me exactly what Bobby is doing." She touched the edge of the glass with

her lips, but didn't drink. "Maybe I've turned a blind eye. That's possible, you know?"

"Bobby owns part of something called Pan-Carib. He flies paintings over here from Port au Prince. They pack the crates with cocaine, something like that. Jimmy Glide handles the loading and unloading of the planes. The export agent in Haiti handles all the documentation. As far as U.S. customs knows, a legitimate load of Haitian art lands. Glide off-loads the dope, then the customs people inspect the cargo. I don't know how it's done exactly. What a drug smuggler needs is a legitimate cover. That's their cover."

"I'm part of the cover," Dolores said. "The art galleries are a joke. My job is a fake."

"It isn't your fault."

"The paintings are window-dressing."

"I'm afraid so, Dolores," Roberts told her. He put his hand on her neck and rubbed the tension there. "I can't prove a thing, of course. That's not my job, anyway."

Dolores curled up her legs and sat on them. "These condos are built so cheaply," she said sadly. "Water always comes under the patio doors."

"Will you be all right?"

"Sure, fine," she said. "We started a gallery with art from South America and Central America. Do you think he was shipping in drugs even then?"

"I'd think so. The pipelines change every so often."

"It's how he got his house."

"His house, his cars, his clothing. Everything."

"But you don't know for sure," Dolores said.

"I told you I saw an apple painting on Hilliard's wall."

"I know the one. I've wondered about it."

"It's by Compere Duffault in Jacmel. Raymond Cobo purchased it on his trip. When Cobo disappeared, that painting disappeared with him. It's in a group that Hilliard told me had been stolen. He must have liked the idea of a wheelbarrow with rotten apples, the faces of generals on the apples. Or there was a bare space on his

wall. I can't explain Bobby, any more than you can explain Bobby. But the painting on his wall proves he stole it from Cobo, from the artist, whomever. It isn't a long jump to thinking he runs drugs from Haiti."

"But the documents. The paintings couldn't just disappear."

"The bills of lading are doctored by Champagne Lambert. False shipper, false consignee. No money changes hands, no bank documents, no bills of exchange."

"What are you going to do?" Dolores asked. "I've got to get away from the gallery."

"That's why I came tonight," Roberts said gently. "I know it means a lot to you, but you've got to quit. Make up some excuse, but leave there now."

Dolores bit her lip and smiled a false smile. "There are other jobs, aren't there?" she said. "I'm a tough girl."

"Sure you're tough," Roberts assured her.

Dolores put her head back on the sofa. Roberts touched her cheek, which was warm from tequila. He cupped his hand and caught her first tear.

*r*oberts turned his head just briefly when he heard the sound of a backfire on Calle Ocho and spotted the government-gray Chevrolet parked on the street half a block down from the condominium. He was angry at himself for being so stupid and careless, for wanting to see Dolores so badly that he hadn't watched out behind, for driving down I-95 in an otherworldly fog of self-delusion, a mist of incomprehension that now threatened to engulf the woman.

They had parked in the shade of an oak. Roberts walked down the opposite side of the street, passed a few cafés and open-air bars, exclusive Coconut Grove fashion outlets. He stood and looked at Lawrence Littrow, who sat behind tinted glass in the backseat of the Chevrolet, paring his fingernails with a small penknife. Roberts walked over and rapped on the glass. Another agent had driven, and they had left the engine on to run the air-conditioning with taxpayer's dollars.

Littrow tapped an electric button, and the window whisked down silently. Roberts could smell new-car aroma, plastic seats, air freshener.

"Let's see," Littrow said. "Dolores Vega from Santo Domingo. She runs about twenty-nine years old, resident alien, works at the Hilliard gallery in Coconut Grove. Walks to work. Not married, and hey, pretty damn good-looking. We haven't worked up her IRS or INS sheets, but we're on it."

"You're some crew of assholes and scum," Roberts said.

Sun streaked down through the cumulus clouds. The wind had

died after blowing all day, the way it often did after a big rain on the Atlantic side. It was so humid Roberts thought he might choke on the air.

"Why is it I don't trust you?" Littrow said.

"What are you doing here?"

"Get in," Littrow said, rolling up the window.

Roberts got in and sat in front, beside the driver, a big raw guy in a blue suit and red power tie. He shivered in the cold air, a contrast to the hot air outside.

"Leave her alone, can't you? She isn't involved."

"I have your word on that?" Littrow said. "Please, just give me a word and we'll flip off all those government computers and drop our entire investigation."

They were moving east along Calle Ocho, going slow through the midday traffic.

"Let me out of here," Roberts said.

"Come on, cowboy," Littrow said. "I've checked your whole jacket. I've checked her jacket. So what? I've done a quickie IRS on Hilliard. Let's say I believe you for now."

"You believe me?"

"I'm open to suggestion, anyway," Littrow said.

"So, you'll leave her alone?"

"I didn't say that," Littrow answered.

"Stop following me. Leave her alone."

"Tell me what you know."

"I've told you," Roberts said angrily. "I spent some time digging around an outfit called Pan-Carib, out of Panama City. You might check them out. Pay special attention to their flights out of Port au Prince. I haven't been able to spot a schedule, but I think they've got paintings piled up in Haiti, waiting to come to Miami."

"That's very good," Littrow said. "But we're going to need more than a bust at the airport. If we get a bust at the airport, we get some coke, but we don't get Hilliard. We need a way to connect the shipment to him. Maybe you could give us enough to take him down for murder. That would be great."

"I told you, I don't have any proof that he murdered Cobo, or had him murdered."

"Cobo was illegal, you know that?"

"Does that make a difference?"

They stopped at a light. Roberts watched a group of Cuban girls wiggle by in tight stretch pants.

"I just wondered if you knew," Littrow said. "We're trying to find something out about Cobo, but there isn't anything in the computer. You'd think the computer would know, wouldn't you?"

"Don't ask me," Roberts said. "I own a rotary phone."

The agent driving laughed dispassionately. Littrow looked out the window. They had circled the block and were going by Dolores Vega's condominium.

"How about that wire thing?" Littrow asked. "You show up wearing a wire and Hilliard will bust a gut talking to you about his operation."

"Can't be done," Roberts said. "Hilliard's goons and Tontons tried to kill me in Haiti. I show up and he'll finish the job. He wouldn't talk to me for anything. I couldn't even provoke it. He's too smart."

"Oh, come on," Littrow said. "You show up at his house and he just might tell you everything. Give you the grand tour just to show off. We'd be right outside the door."

"You have a great pitch," Roberts said. "Why don't I feel like buying what you're selling? Just bust the Pan-Carib shipment."

Littrow placed two arms on the backrest and talked into Roberts's ear. "Did you check the FAA flight records for Dade and Opa Locka on Pan-Carib?" he asked.

"I didn't get that far," Roberts admitted.

"You can call it up on the screen," Littrow said. "Pan-Carib had two flights arrive from Port au Prince last weekend. Rush jobs with last-minute flight plans. It's my guess the dope has been off-loaded already."

"You think the coke is in Florida?"

"That's what I'm saying," Littrow said. "That's why we need a wire. Otherwise, the coke goes bye-bye. Just like a puff of dust in the Wizard of Id. Now you see it, now you don't."

"I can't wear a wire," Roberts said. "Get your search warrant. Search the mansion. Don't ask me to do your job."

The driver pulled over to a stop in a bus zone. Littrow tapped a button and the knobs clicked open on the doors. Roberts got out and stood on the pavement. He was blocks away from where he had parked.

"Where are you staying now?" Littrow asked.

Roberts told him the Sandpiper Motel in Hollywood. It wasn't true, and Littrow probably knew it wasn't true.

*t*hat night Roberts checked into an art-deco hotel on Collins Avenue in Miami Beach. His room was on the eighth floor, overlooking the beach, sixteen square feet of moldy enclosure, a couple of plastic chairs, an end table next to a sagging double bed. For a long time, he sat in one of the plastic chairs drinking canned soda, one can after another, and watching moonlight on the Atlantic Ocean. It was three o'clock before he went to bed, and then he slept for only four hours, waking as the sun rose in the east, coloring his room drab rose.

He showered, ate breakfast in the hotel café beside the pool, then drove his rental Buick up to Bay Harbor and parked across from the post office. At ten o'clock, Jimmy Glide pulled up to the corner in the black Corvette and parked in a red zone, ran into the post office and came out carrying a bundle of parcels, letters, and newspapers. Roberts had rolled up the Buick windows and was listening to a Mozart concerto, thinking to himself how nice it was that the Hilliard household had a post-office box and checked the mail every morning at ten. He watched Glide get in the Corvette and head south and west and north, back to the mansion, where he stopped in the driveway, punched himself through the security gate, parked beneath a tamarind tree near the house, and then came back out the driveway. Roberts was right behind him, maybe by two hundred yards.

It was a beautiful morning, with a high, blue sky and puffy clouds roughing the horizon over the Gulf Stream. Traffic was light in midweek, and it was easy for Roberts to maintain his distance, two lanes over, heading down the Federal Highway with Biscayne Bay on his left shoulder and Miami stucco neighborhoods on his right. He concentrated on the Mozart, but couldn't help thinking about what he was doing. If Lawrence Littrow was right, the coke had already been delivered to Miami and it was time for Roberts to head back home. He'd informed the FBI, he'd taken care of his business in Haiti, he'd told Dolores. What more could he do? In his mind, he worked overtime trying to convince himself to go down to Dismal Key, take a look-see. But he was tired and he had one more thing to do. It wasn't his responsibility, was it?

Roberts almost choked when Glide took the Buena Vista exit and bypassed the FBI building near the water. He circled around Sabal Palm Road between gleaming white high-rises, the sun beating down on their towers, sending off shards of light as though a nuclear bomb had just been detonated. Gulls sat on pilings, and old folks pushed themselves around shuffleboard courts. Finally, Glide parked in the visitors' lot of a two-story deco building sandwiched between condos. Roberts stopped down the block, pulling to one side while Glide went up to the apartment building and was buzzed inside. Roberts listened to the end of the Mozart, thinking to himself that the building was a perfect place for a single flight attendant to live, only about fifteen minutes from the airport. It was nice, classy, and comfortable.

Roberts walked to the end of the block and found a pay phone outside a neighborhood grocery. He called Dolores, who told him he could come over, that she'd meet him at the condominium. It took him twenty minutes to get down to Coconut Grove and find a place to park.

On Saturday morning, Dolores had been crying. Her eyes were swollen into tight red fists and she kept rubbing them, as if that would do some good. She let Roberts in and they sat out back in the shade listening to the grackles play games in the oak trees. She was wearing a pair of white short-shorts, white deck shoes, a little

blue-and-white sailor blouse. Drinking coffee, they let time run between them like an invisible rope.

"There's a hurricane coming," Dolores said.

"I've read about it," he told her. "I've never been through a
hurricane before."

Suddenly she began to cry. He went to her, knelt beside her and
put an arm around her shoulders.

"Tell me what's wrong. You can find another job."

She spilled her coffee, some of it running onto the flagstones.
Roberts took a napkin and dabbed her eyes gently. He kissed her
cheek and told her she'd find something. She was talented. She was
strong.

"It isn't just that," Dolores said. "Some men from the FBI were
here. They gave me a pretty bad time."

"Goddamn it," Roberts said. "It's my fault. They followed me
here. You can't give them an inch. They'll take a mile."

"I know," she said. "I know."

"What did they say?"

"They asked me questions about Bobby. They wanted to know
about Jimmy Glide. I spent an hour explaining the galleries to them,
piece by piece. They made me tell them about the list of painters I
gave you and Raymond Cobo. One of them would ask a question
and then another would repeat it before I could answer, and then
they'd ask the same questions over again, only phrased differently.
They made me so frustrated. They frightened me, too."

"It's all right, Dolores," Roberts said. "Don't let them frighten
you."

"They don't want me to quit my job," she said.

"Quit now. Don't wait."

"I'm afraid. I'm not a citizen."

"You're a resident alien. You have the same rights we all have.
Don't let them kid you."

"They said I could be deported."

"That's nonsense. Let's go see a lawyer."

"I'm frightened, Mitch."

"I know, Dolores," he told her.

"I'm not just afraid of them. I'm afraid of Bobby and Jimmy, too. What if they find out the FBI has been to see me?"

Roberts sat close to her, holding her hand while she tried to stop crying.

"Are you going home?" she asked him. "Are you going to leave?"

"No, I'm not leaving," Roberts said. "I'm going to be here and help you through this. You can take that to the bank."

He smiled at the woman, thinking of his ranch in Colorado, how the sky in autumn would be pale blue above yellow grass, how the broom and bunch would rustle in the wind, how the smell of snow would be in the air. "I wouldn't leave you in this mess." He thought of a stream as clear as good glass.

"I could love you," Dolores said. "I'm not just saying that because I'm in trouble."

Roberts poured them more coffee and they listened to the grackles wrestle through another chorus. He didn't know what to say, he never did. And so he said nothing.

63

*r*oberts would later realize he had committed the sin of over-
weening pride.

Now as he wandered down neon-lit Collins Avenue after a dinner
of conch salad and Cuban bread, he was overcome by anger, the
relentless nagging dread of it inside his gut. Beachside, the neon
signs decorating cafés and bars were twinkling on in the dusky twilight, and the sky was coloring up again. Everybody on the street
talked about Hurricane Howard, said to be south of Santo Domingo
on a track to strike the Gulf, anywhere from the Keys to New Orleans. For all anybody knew, it could head due north and strike
Boston, or it could peter out and end its life as a tropical squall
above Bimini, pouring rain and bad vibes on deep-sea fishermen.

That day Roberts had picked up a Smith & Wesson he had purchased legally at a gun shop in Coral Gables. He'd spent some time
talking to FAA officials about Pan-Carib, and he had made two calls
to Lawrence Littrow, but the calls were not returned to his hotel on
Miami Beach. In order to pull Dolores through this experience, he
had decided to go public, come clean, cooperate with the authorities
in any way he could, maybe even to flush Glide and Hilliard for
the FBI, if that's what it took. But he couldn't find Littrow.

Then, just about dark, Roberts had the fit, he committed the sin.
He picked up his black Buick at a U-Park on Collins, just across
from Joe's Stone Crab, and headed south out of North Bay Village,
driving across North Bay Causeway in light evening traffic. Down

on Biscayne Bay, yachts and cigarette boats were playing in the shining sunset-lit waters, where the oranges and purples of evening were milling about like schools of fish. He passed Pelican Park and caught the Federal Highway just above Little River, where he could see gangs of kids hanging out, goofing and smoking reefers while it got dark. When he got to the Buena Vista cutoff, he found Sabal Palm Avenue and drove between groups of high-rise office towers, apartment buildings and condos where the purple ocean peeped between the structures. All the old folks had donned their evening wear and were out in a polyester-and-cotton Bermuda-shorts extravaganza, parading their white belts and white shoes.

The Clancy Apartments stood at the end of the block between high-rises, a 1920s-style art-deco stucco with plaster molding on the corners. It had been painted dark lime-green and its gardeners kept it well supplied with philodendron and palm.

Roberts parked out front and checked the mailboxes. There were four apartments, two on each floor, right and left, a service entrance to one side. The front doors were locked and there was no security camera. He walked back to the Buick and sat smoking a black cheroot until about ten o'clock, four hours of waiting, listening to classical music, hearing the crickets and mosquitoes as the sky darkened and the moon rose over the high-rises. Finally, Rosemary Collins came home just about the time Roberts decided she had a flight.

Jimmy Glide dropped her off in his black Corvette. She was wearing a short miniskirt of turquoise lamé, a light blue halter top, and a gray cashmere sweater draped over her shoulders. She looked like a college girl on spring break, moonlighting as a whore.

She kissed Glide through the open window of the Corvette. Then Glide sped down Sabal Palm, rounding a corner. The woman waved at the retreating car, then walked down the cement pathway toward her front door. Roberts got out of the Buick and hurried behind her. She turned slightly, like a sparrow cocking its head, saw him, tried frantically to open the door.

Roberts caught her just as she grasped the latch.

"We need to talk," he said. "Don't scream. Don't make any noise. I'll beat you senseless if you do."

She held her breath for a moment, then let it go. Roberts looked directly into her face and remembered her nostalgically as Miss Florida, his blond beam of sunshine.

"What do you want?" she asked, trying to maintain a tough front. Roberts pushed her against the metal frame of the door, partly to get her out of the overhead light.

"I thought we had a date. Tropical Lounge. You stood me up."

"Is that it?" she asked.

"What's your real name, anyway?" Roberts asked her. He had pressed her hard against the door. He could feel her heart race inside the halter top. He could smell white wine on her breath. "There are four names on the mailboxes. Which is yours?"

"Someone will come along," she said.

"You'd better hope not."

He knew he was scaring her now. He could feel fear through her clothes.

"I've got a boyfriend," she said.

"That really worries me," Roberts said. "That little scam out at the airport. The one where you find a businessman or traveler and steal his car. Was that something you dreamed up on your own? Or did you have some help? Did you do it just for fun? Or maybe it was Jimmy's way of having fun. Or maybe it was Jimmy's way of finding out if you loved him. And while we're at it, are you into coke?"

Rosemary Collins breathed deeply. "I don't know what you're talking about."

"Good girl," Roberts said. "You know, Rosemary, or whatever your name is, I could beat you until Jimmy wouldn't even recognize you."

She closed her eyes, opened them, seemed to have a hard time knowing what to say. "What do you want?" she asked, haltingly.

"I want you to tell Jimmy something," Roberts said. "I want you to tell him I'm watching. I'm waiting for him and his buddy. You tell him that for me." Roberts put his arm around the woman's neck and squeezed. She raised her hands and put them on his arms as he increased the pressure. "Tell Jimmy I want part of the coke,"

Roberts whispered. "That's the deal. I want a cut. Tell me you understand."

"I understand," she gasped.

"Tell Jimmy to meet me at ten o'clock tomorrow morning outside the post office in Bay Harbor. Tell me you understand."

"Yes, yes," the woman said.

"I'll kill you if you don't tell him," Roberts said. "Nod, if you understand."

She nodded, frantically, up and down, down and up. When Roberts was convinced he'd really scared her, he let her open the door and go inside. Then he drove back to his hotel on Miami Beach and drank two beers to settle his nerves.

*r*oberts drove over to Coconut Grove looking for Dolores. She didn't answer the buzzer, so he went to a pay phone and tried the gallery, but he had to leave a message. He walked up and down Calle Ocho, checking out the cafés and garden restaurants, but he didn't see her. When he drove over to the Escape Gallery, the windows were dark and the doors locked, and nobody came when he pounded the plate glass. He sat for a long time in an outdoor bar and drank iced tea with lemon, watching her condominium. Finally, about ten o'clock, his nerves shredded with caffeine, he switched to beer. About eleven, he drove to Miami Beach and went to his room to lie down. Every thirty minutes, he tried her at home, but got only the answering machine.

The next morning, he drank coffee by the pool and called her again. The gallery didn't open until ten, but he tried calling anyway, leaving a message. Down in the pool, a few early risers were swimming laps in the turquoise water, and five or six partyers were making their fun last with the dregs of a keg. The *Miami Herald* was full of talk about the hurricane, a front-page chart marking its progress through the Caribbean, down the spine of the Greater Antilles, skirting the south coast of Haiti, making its way across the Spanish Passage between Haiti and Cuba, now headed for South Florida. Outside the hotel, on Collins Avenue, traffic was thick, and a few hotel operators were busy tacking plywood over their glass fronts. Roberts didn't know it then, but in a couple of days, there would be a run on hardware supplies, groceries, gas, bottled water, food, heavy lumber. Even now, homeowners were making raids on plywood. There was an electricity in the air, part fear, part anticipation.

Just before ten o'clock, Roberts went to his room and dressed in jeans, a T-shirt, a pullover jacket to conceal the Smith & Wesson. He picked up his car at the lot and drove north on the Federal Highway and across Broad Causeway to Bay Harbor. Down in the marinas, yachtsmen and fishermen were securing their vessels and the birds had hunkered down on piers and wharves. There was a slight chop on the water and a gray glaze on the horizon, a yellow streak about twenty-five miles out above the Gulf Stream.

Roberts slid the Buick into a yellow zone across from the Bay Harbor Post Office. He could see Glide's black Corvette down the block, Glide leaning against the driver's door, dressed in his standard outfit: black muscle shirt with a Marlins logo, black drawstring pants, black tennis shoes. As always, he wore sunglasses. It made Roberts think of the Tontons, of how they imitated zombies, of how at night, Baron Samedi would whisk through the darkness collecting souls in his knapsack. Glide spotted him and walked down the block and stood on the sidewalk about ten feet from Roberts.

"How you doing?" Glide said.

"Okay. Yourself?"

"I'm doing good," Glide replied.

"You got my message?"

Glide put his hands in his pockets and shrugged in an offhand manner. "You're not wearing a wire, are you?" he asked.

"You want to strip me, give me a going-over?"

Glide tapped one lens of his sunglasses. "It really doesn't matter, pal," he said.

Roberts leaned his head out the Buick window. "I know how you do it," he said. "I know how you offload it in Miami. All I want is a cut. After that, you can keep on trucking."

"That's very nice," Glide said. "I don't know what the fuck you're talking about."

"Your girlfriend said different," Roberts lied. "She told me everything about the operation. She spilled her guts about the coke deal. She even told me about your little sideline with the stolen cars. You do that for fun? Or are you just a career criminal?"

Glide smiled knowingly. "There will come a time for you and me," he said. "I'm going to do you slow and easy and I'm going to talk while it happens. You're a loser, pal, but you don't even know half of it."

"What about it, Jimmy?" Roberts said. He put the Smith & Wesson on the ledge of the window, a black .44 that caught the sunlight and winked. "You tell Bobby I want a cut. I want it soon." Roberts laid the weapon down on the seat beside him. Glide had not moved a muscle. A few shoppers went into a bagel shop nearby.

"I want to tell you something," Glide said.

"I'm listening," Roberts said.

"You like little Dolores, don't you?"

"What about Dolores?" Roberts asked, now a little frightened.

"Tell me you like the cunt a little."

"Go ahead," Roberts told him. "Say what you have to say."

"Got your attention?"

"Go ahead, asshole."

"Dolores, she's taking a little trip. She's with Bobby now, and I think she's happy. But she could get unhappy real fast. It's up to you, loser. You make a move, you call a cop, you get too crazy, and she'll be unhappy. You don't want her to be unhappy, do you?"

"I swear to you—"

"Save it, pal," Glide said. "Just go back to your hole and take a nap. In a few days, you can see her again. She's a cute girl, isn't she? I like her. I've always liked her. She's got style. You don't want her to get unhappy, do you?"

"Where is she?" Roberts said stupidly.

"Don't worry, cowboy," Glide said. "Bobby told me you were a loser. He said you were a loser from the get-go. Bobby isn't wrong. I swear to you, anything happens and the bitch will get hurt."

"Just let her go," Roberts said.

Glide took two steps toward his Corvette, stopped and looked back. The owner of the bagel shop had come outside to hammer up some plywood over his storefront. "You and I will have a little talk soon," Glide said.

Roberts watched Glide go down the block and get into his Corvette. It seemed to Roberts that the air temperature had dropped a few degrees. A bank of gray clouds lay over the horizon, and the air smelled as though it had been soldered shut.

65

*r*oberts drove to Hollywood and filled his gas tank at a convenience store across from the Federal Highway. He went up to Las Olas in Lauderdale, just to see if Dolores happened to be at the unopened gallery, to see if Jimmy Glide was pulling his chain. The gallery was closed tight, no lights in the back, and a realtor's sign on the window offering the building for lease or sale. Stopping at a bar on the beach road, he tried telephoning Dolores at home, but only got the answering machine.

His fear now was profound. For a moment, he thought of calling Lawrence Littrow at the FBI, but he knew that Jimmy and Bobby were capable of anything, and he didn't particularly trust Littrow at any rate. He didn't know why he didn't trust Littrow, but it was enough that he didn't.

Roberts drove back to Miami Beach and parked in the U-Park across from Joe's, then walked the five blocks up Collins to his hotel. Under a gray sky, the sea was up and high-school kids were taking advantage of the big waves, boarding and surfing about two hundred yards out, catching breakers to the beach, paddling out, doing it again. All of the volleyball courts and beach bars were packed with drinkers, people enjoying the prospect of mayhem, turning the disaster into a party, danger mixed with adventure that sounded good when you heard about it on the news. The hotel bar was filled with "hurricane drinkers," getting themselves ready for three days of curfew and storm, when the streets would be empty and the airport closed.

Roberts went upstairs and opened the door to his room. He felt himself being lifted, his arm twisted from behind. There was a noise inside his head and he hit the floor hard, facedown. Somebody touched the cold barrel of a revolver to his neck and said, "Don't move, fucking asshole."

"Take it easy," Roberts said. He sensed two or three sets of feet near him. "Just take it easy."

"You are something else," he heard Lawrence Littrow say into his right ear. Roberts was rolled over onto his back as an agent patted him down. He had left the Smith & Wesson in the trunk of his rental car. "Sit up, prick," Littrow instructed.

Roberts got up and sat on the bed, back against the wall. Littrow was there in his seersucker suit, two others in black suits, yellow ties, standard-issue agents. Littrow put his gun in a shoulder holster and crossed his arms.

"Without any bullshit," Littrow said, "tell me what you did."

"I don't know what you're talking about," Roberts said.

"I wish I hadn't heard that," Littrow said.

"I don't know—"

"Get serious now," Littrow growled. "Think of something original and tell it to me now."

"I don't know—"

"Shut the fuck up, then," Littrow replied. "You're very close to being busted. Fuck with me and I'll do it."

"You're way ahead of me," Roberts told him.

Littrow leaned against the door. "Your pals Hilliard and Glide have gone. Tell me you didn't blow the whistle."

"Why would I do that?" Roberts asked. He sat quietly for a moment, looking at the shabby confines of the room, the paint peeling, cracked veneer on the tables and chairs, water-stained ceiling. "I wouldn't blow any whistle, would I? That wouldn't make any sense, admit it."

"They've got Dolores Vega," Littrow said.

"Jimmy Glide just told me," Roberts said.

"Where is she?"

"What's going on?" Roberts asked.

"You don't know, you fucking prick?"

"Come on, Larry, quit running a game on me."

Littrow put his hands on his hips. He looked at the other agents, who stared at Roberts.

"Dolores was wearing a wire," Littrow said.

"You bastards!" Roberts shouted.

"It was her choice," Littrow said. "She wanted to do it. She was happy to do it."

"I can really see that," Roberts said angrily. "So, did you do a number on her? Did you threaten her with arrest? Did you tell her you'd deport her? Did you start an IRS audit on her returns? What kind of pressure did you use?"

"Does it matter?" Littrow asked. "She was all wired up and ready to go. She had on her pack and her battery and we'd arranged for someone to follow her over to Hilliard's place on Bay Harbor. Then overnight, she's gone from her condo. Just disappears. Our guys showed up outside her condo that morning and she wasn't home. We went over to Bay Harbor and we found the mansion locked up tight and a For-Sale sign on the front lawn. We checked with the realty company and it went on the market yesterday. Nobody home, and an auction company is going over the furniture and art. We haven't got the wire and we haven't got our shipment of coke, and we haven't got Dolores Vega either. But we've got you. I have to think you fucked this up good."

"I talked to Glide," Roberts admitted. He didn't want to tell Littrow about Rosemary Collins, whatever her name was. "I didn't know you were going to wire Dolores Vega. Those guys tried to have me killed in Haiti and I took it personally."

"You took it personally," Littrow said. "Who appointed you Deputy Dog?"

"*I took it personally*," Roberts repeated.

Littrow shrugged and sagged against the door. The other agents had holstered their guns.

"So where'd they go?" Littrow asked.

"Brazil, who knows?" Roberts said, shaking his head. "Costa Rica. Where do bad guys go with their cash? What are you doing about Dolores Vega?"

"We'll take care of it," Littrow told him. "You don't go anywhere, you don't do anything. Do me a favor and stay away from me. You've caused enough shit. If Dolores Vega dies, it's on you."

"Don't give me that, you fuck," Roberts said.

Littrow's face turned red. "We'll find her," he said. He opened the door and let out the two agents. "We'll find her," he said and closed the door.

Roberts sat up and put his feet on the floor. From the street at beachside the sound of hammers and nails was louder now, people getting ready for the hurricane.

*r*oberts packed his bag and checked out of the hotel before noon. He had about fifty rounds of ammunition for the Smith & Wesson, some hiking gear he had purchased for the Haiti trip, a small carry-on for his overnight things. The traffic was thick in downtown Miami, and it took him forty minutes to get as far as the Rickenbacker Causeway through Key Biscayne. Below the long white bridge, the water was perfectly blue and hundreds of gulls wheeled in the slight breeze, tinting the sky a faint gray-blue. The breeze was ruffling the sails of a few yachts going into harbor near Virginia Key, and out in the cut channels he could see sailboats and launches being readied for the storm. Now the weather reports were becoming more urgent. It was the hour of decision for the storm. It could head west into the Gulf, or north to the Keys.

The traffic was against him, people heading out of the upper and lower Keys into the shelter of Miami. Roberts thought about Dolores Vega as he drove with the windows down. He thought about the nights they'd spent together in Haiti, first in the Holiday Inn, where they'd sat out on the veranda drinking rum punch, getting used to the strange sounds of the Haitian night. He remembered the touch of her at night, the smell of her, the way she made a little mewing noise in her sleep.

At Key Largo, he stopped at the Coast Guard station and tried to track down Lieutenant Ridley, but was told that the officer was out on storm patrol, catching up on hurricane duty, making sure warnings were posted, checking all the bays, inlets, shoals, and harbors where people might not have gotten the word. The young female duty officer assured Roberts that she'd see he got any message for him to come over to Dismal Key, or to meet him outside Jakob Liamsson's bait shop.

It was nearly four o'clock when Roberts finally turned down the dusty cedar-lined drive toward Liamsson's. He had used half a tank of precious gas and had decided he wouldn't try to fill the tanks again, because of the long lines. He parked in the lee of a cedar brake and walked around the bait shop to the wharf. He saw Liamsson in shade, struggling to lift a sheet of plywood and nail it over one of the windows that had no hurricane shutters.

"Hello, Jakob," Roberts called. The old man staggered back, almost dropping the huge sheet of wood. "I'm sorry I sneaked up on you."

"I can't hear shit no more," Liamsson said, grinning. He dropped the plywood and they shook hands. "You're just in time to help me gear up for the hurricane. I could use a pair of young hands to do the hard stuff. We can drink rum and ride her out up at the motel along the highway." He rubbed his hands together, trying to unknot the arthritis. "Hey, I thought you was in Haiti or some damn thing like that."

"Something came up," Roberts told him.

Liamsson stroked his thin beard. "You don't say?"

"Have you seen Bobby Hilliard?"

Liamsson folded his hands. "He came through here. I didn't see him, but I know he's over on Dismal. He took one of my launches and left a chit for the gas. He took the spare keys to the cabin. I had 'em on a nail over the door. I guess he took about twenty gallons of gas and some bottled water. Ain't nobody crazy enough to go over to Dismal in weather like this except that Bobby Hilliard. I can't help but hope he drowns over there."

"Jakob," Roberts said, "I have to go over to Dismal."

"That wouldn't be smart."

"You mean the storm?"

"Hell yes, I mean the storm," Liamsson laughed. "You want a cigar and some rum?"

Roberts declined the rum. They went inside the bait shop and Roberts dug a root beer from an ice bucket in back.

"I need the ten-footer," he said.

"Look," Liamsson told him, "I don't care one whit if Bobby Hilliard and his buddy drown, but I don't want you up and floating away along with that crew."

"I'm going to tell you something," Roberts said.

He walked his soda outside to the shade of a stunted oak. It had turned out to be a beautiful afternoon, not too hot, a slight breeze clicking through the palms, a good lemony smell in the air. Roberts couldn't name the color of the water if he had a million years. Six pelicans dropped through the air and landed on the dock.

"So tell me," Liamsson said.

"They've got Dolores Vega over there," Roberts said. "They run drugs through Dismal. They're holding her so I won't tell the police."

Liamsson looked across Florida Bay, rubbed his scabrous, bearded face, spit in the oily water at his feet.

"You sure about that?" he asked.

"I know she's over there," Roberts said. "They smuggle coke through Port au Prince and off-load it at Miami-Dade. They probably transfer it to Dismal and let somebody run it up to Flamingo. Bobby is moving out right now. His house in Miami is up for sale. His galleries are closed. This is his last big run before he checks into a nice life on the Riviera or in Brazil, some happy shit like that."

Liamsson chewed on his cigar. "Is there anything else you want to tell me?" he asked.

"I'm not involved in drugs," Roberts said. "I don't do drugs and I don't sell them. I found out about this in Haiti. I checked it out with the FBI. I have to do this alone because if I let the FBI handle it, they'll go in with helicopters and Dolores Vega will die."

Liamsson walked into the shack and brought back a bottle of rum. He uncapped it and took a long swig. "At most, you got twenty hours," he said finally. "Even if that storm don't hit head-on, you're going to have some big weather. You ever been through a hurricane?"

"It doesn't matter," Roberts said.

"You sure the cops can't handle this?"

"I had dealings with them in Miami. They'll come down with boats and planes. I don't think that's the way to get Dolores out of there safely."

"And you think you can do better?"

"I can't do worse," Roberts said. "Let's put it that way."

"You like her, don't you?"

"I really like her," Roberts told him. "But I'd do this even if I didn't like her so much. The FBI scared her into wearing a wire. These are guys who know her. They'll kill her once the coke is moved. She'll wind up like those Haitians we found out there."

"You think Bobby killed those Haitians?"

"Probably . . . well, maybe. It would make sense."

Liamsson stood and walked down to the end of the wharf, Roberts on his heels. "I drained all the gas out of her," Liamsson said. "Because of the storm. We'll have to gas her up and get some water. Like I say, you got maybe twenty hours, maybe less. And before that, it's going to rain and get windy. Takes us three hours to get out there and three to get back, that's six. Takes us an hour to get ready. Maybe you're out there an hour. That's only eight, but in eight hours, she's going to be high water and big tides and plenty of wind. We got time to do it, but if we miss or if the hurricane comes up fast, we'll drown."

"There's no *we* here," Roberts said. "You're not going."

"Sure I am," the old man said. "You think you can find Dismal and get back, especially when it starts to rain? Even if you get the girl, you'll lose her coming back in, and you'll lose yourself, too. Don't that make sense?"

"Don't bullshit a bullshitter," Roberts said. "If I head due south in the skiff, I'll hit the Keys somewhere."

"Unless you don't," Liamsson said.

"I can't risk you, too," Roberts said. "I've already put Dolores out there."

"You'll waste hours wandering around in the bay," Liamsson said. "You think Dolores has that much time?"

Liamsson was pumping gas before Roberts could reply.

67

*I*iamsson sat in the stern of the motorized shallow-draft skiff, guiding them through surreal reaches of powdery green water. They listened to a small transistor radio, an AM station out of Islamadora. The Miami Hurricane Center predicted the storm to come ashore near Lauderdale, but it was anybody's guess, a wave lash of sixteen feet, winds up to eighty-five miles an hour, enough to knock out plate-glass windows, scatter mobile homes, flood beachfront property. Alarms and warnings were posted from Jacksonville to Key West, and every ship was advised either to head for port or out to sea. Above them, a pearl-gray sky lay flat, and sudden gusts of wind skipped on top of the water, creating whitecaps even on the shallowest of shoals.

"You have anything in your head, son?" Liamsson asked. He turned off the radio and dragged one hand through the water. "I mean, do you have a plan? Or do you just figure to charge up to the front door like John Wayne?"

"I thought we'd circle Dismal and come up behind the Key. There's a mangrove stand and an inlet there where I used to go in the mornings to watch the egrets move."

"I know the place," Liamsson said. "We can run her slow for the last mile or so. We're downwind now, and I figure in the two hours or more it takes us, the wind will pick up. They won't hear us over it."

"You stay with the skiff," Roberts said. "If you hear anything wild, you head back to the bait shop and wait for Ridley of the Coast Guard. I left a message for him at Largo. He might be tied up for days, but I left the message anyway. Tell him I'm on Dismal if you have to."

Liamsson sat quietly in the stern, thinking and rubbing his scraggly white beard. He had brought along an oilskin packed with an old shotgun, some shells, a set of flares and a flare gun.

For an hour, they ran quietly through the bay. The sky grayed over and thickened, the humidity increased, and eventually the clouds above them began to stampede south. Roberts could smell the salt in the air, and a few drops of rain sprinkled his head. Liamsson told him to watch the seabirds, how they would be heading south toward land. Overhead, the terns, pelicans, herons, egrets, and an occasional osprey went past.

The old man turned them north-by-east, heading into a steady wind, chopping up through small waves. Spray doused them and they bounced hard enough to take on water.

"You never did tell me your plan," Liamsson shouted. "We'll tie up in the mangrove, then what?"

"What is it, dark in two hours?"

"You going to wait until dark?" Liamsson looked concerned. "That loses you two hours to the storm."

"I'll crawl over to the cabin, see what they're doing. They may let Dolores walk around. I don't think they'll expect us out this way."

"You think she's okay?" Liamsson asked. "I don't mean to bring up something bad, but those two are capable of anything."

"She's got to be okay," Roberts said. "She's got to be. I think they need her for now."

"I hope so, son," Liamsson said.

Forty-five minutes later, Liamsson throttled the skiff engine back suddenly. They were bouncing through chop toward low sand keys that Roberts thought he recognized. The day had become heavy and gloomy and suddenly much cooler. Liamsson told him that it was the edge of the big cold front, a boundary of low pressure on the near side of the storm. He killed the motor.

"I think I hear something," he said.

Both men were still, trying to hear. Wind rocked the skiff, sending up water to the gunwale, pounding the hull. Under the wind, barely audible, was the certain sound of another engine on idle.

"You think it's them?" Roberts asked.

"Has to be," Liamsson said. "Listen. That motor is off to the northeast, toward Dismal. By the sound of it, I'd say it's parallel to the island. What the hell would they be doing cruising at this time?"

"Their coke contact," Roberts said. "Nothing else. You remember those dead Haitians? Those were the buyers. I think Glide and Hilliard ripped them off. Now they're making another sale out here."

"You're just guessing," Liamsson said. "That makes it harder, doesn't it?"

"Not if it gets them out of the cabin," Roberts said.

"You want to go in?"

"Circle back the other way," Roberts said. "Get back in the mangrove like we planned. I remember where we found the Haitians. I'll go over and see."

"You do that and it adds forty minutes to our time," Liamsson told him.

"What choice do we have?" Roberts asked.

Great black fists of cloud whirled above them. It had stopped sprinkling rain, but it looked as though it would start again, harder. Liamsson listened to the radio quietly, but the station had been lost. The old man shook his head and turned them back west, circling Dismal from a new direction.

"You're going to have to be quiet," he said. "The wind will change around soon. It'll blow our sound right up to their front door."

"You ever been in a hurricane, Jakob?"

"Two or three," he said. "Small ones. Ones that didn't hit head-on. I got down here after the big one hit in nineteen thirty-six. I saw what that one did. I saw the houses knocked over and the high-water mark inland. We better hope this one isn't like that one."

Just as Liamsson finished his sentence, it began to rain, huge drops plunging like rocks from a gray sky.

a dull yellow sun rode the western horizon. Roberts could see it through the clouds, a gold halo sending thorns of orange and purple toward the zenith. It was a bizarre sunset, the likes of which he'd never seen before, an augury of mystic power.

Liamsson piloted them slowly to the north and west of the Dismal Key, the skiff chopping through heavy water as wind buffeted them from the southeast. The rain had stopped and started twice more since they'd sighted the Key, but as they turned toward the shoals north of Dismal, it stopped again and the wind died suddenly, leaving an eerie calm. The sun was lighting the belly of the sky, ribbing it with cards of color.

Liamsson turned the skiff south then, riding the waves toward the ragged mangrove shelter Roberts had camped in during his stay at the cabin, a secret place from where he could watch seabirds leave to feed in the morning, returning at night in huge white sheets of energy. The old man cut the engine and Roberts hopped into shallow, warm water and dragged the skiff onto a sandbar about ten feet from the beach. They were hidden to the south by dense mangrove and on the west by camelbacked dunes and palmetto waste. It had cooled considerably, so much so that Roberts wished he had a jacket.

Roberts offloaded the oilskin duffel and tucked his Smith & Wesson into the belt of his chinos. His tennis shoes were full of sand and pebbles, making his feet hurt. Then Liamsson hopped over the side as well and they slid the skiff under an arm of mangrove at the eastern edge of the cove.

Liamsson unpacked the shotgun, an old Remington Model 11, loaded it with two shells, then tossed a tarp over the skiff to keep it hidden and to stop the rain from dousing the engine.

"Crawl up into that mangrove and wait for me," Roberts told the old man.

"What are you going to do?" Liamsson asked.

"Take a look at whoever's on that boat. I'll crawl back down here and report to you. Like I said, if something happens, get the hell out of here fast."

"I'm coming along," the old man protested.

"No, please," Roberts him. "If I get in trouble, I want you to go to the mainland. You come along and we could both get killed. What good would come of that?"

Liamsson scratched his beard. "Then I'm coming to the top of the dunes. I can't stay down here in the dark like some damn crab."

Roberts sighed, nodded, checked his weapon one last time. He didn't want Liamsson coming along, but what could he do?

Together they splashed slowly through the mangrove, then up a sand hill for forty yards, across sea-grape and saw-grass dunes, then past forty yards of palmetto. The wind had risen again and it threw sand off the hills in a steady southeastern breeze. At the top of the dune, Roberts sat down and steadied his field glasses to the south. He could see a motor launch floating in shallow water, just about where he'd discovered the bodies of the Haitians. It was a twelve-footer—more or less—dual outboard with a small conning tower. He could see Jimmy Glide on the foredeck, the man in black T-shirt, black chinos, black deck shoes. He was talking with two men wearing cutoffs and baseball caps.

"It's Jimmy Glide out there," Roberts whispered. Liamsson scuttled to the top of the dune and laid his head over the side and looked.

Roberts looked back west toward the cabin. A light burned in one of the windows, probably a kerosene lantern. Another launch was tied in the estuary, the one Hilliard had taken from Liamsson's bait shop. Roberts couldn't spot Dolores, nor could he see Hilliard.

Liamsson lay on top of the dune, his shotgun cradled on his hip. "What are they doing out there?" he asked.

"Glide is doing his dope deal," Roberts said. "You got any idea where those guys might go after they buy the dope?"

"They'll go over to Flamingo," Liamsson said. "It's about sixty miles, give or take. The storm gives them cover. It's risky but smart, Glide and Hilliard will go back to Islamadora. They've probably got someplace to hide over on the Keys."

"Then they take the cash and leave the country." Roberts put away the field glasses. "I've got to take Jimmy Glide," he said.

"You make any noise and Bobby will hear," Liamsson said.

"You wait here," Roberts told him.

"What else can I do?" Liamsson tapped Roberts on the shoulder. "You be very careful," he said.

"Glide will be done any time now," Roberts said. "I'll catch him coming down the beach toward the cabin. Stay put."

One of the men on the launch started the motors. Roberts could hear the engines dance and swivel to life, a small puff of black smoke coming from the exhaust. Glide jumped down into the water as the launch backed toward the bay. As Glide watched the launch leave, Roberts sneaked down to the beach through fifty yards of waste and palmetto stand until he had reached a sheltered lee of palm thicket about ten feet from where Glide would pass on his way to the cabin. Now the air was as heavy as a woolen blanket, weighting down. There were about ten feet of beach to cross, so Roberts knew he'd have to confront Glide. The man came walking down the beach, not hurrying, just taking his time.

Roberts was five yards behind Glide, who suddenly turned. While Glide swiveled and ducked, Roberts came in hard and low, tackling him at knee level and putting him down on his back in wet sand. Roberts swung wildly and connected to Glide's right ear. On his back, Glide struggled to get up, but Roberts kicked him in the lower groin. Glide rolled quickly to the side and came up, landing a hard right on Roberts's jaw. Roberts went to his knees in a hailstorm of starlight, then dug a blow to Glide's stomach. For a moment, Roberts thought he'd snapped a wrist against the man's belt buckle, but then Glide grabbed a fistful of his hair and tipped him forward, Roberts now on his feet being dragged through wet sand, Glide trying to get Roberts down on his knees again. Glide hit Roberts twice more, glancing blows off the forehead and cheek as the men danced backward toward the water. Roberts hit Glide with a left, not a good punch. The man was muscled and hard as rock.

Roberts was being lifted when there was a sudden crack and Glide softened, his hand going limp, his knees buckling to the sand. Behind Glide, Roberts could see Liamsson towering over them both, shotgun in hand, butt-first. Then the old man hit Glide hard on the back of the head, the man going down face-first.

"I never liked that son of a bitch," Liamsson said.

Roberts felt sick. His jaw hurt where he'd been hit and his back ached from being bent nearly double. Liamsson hit Glide again, a glancing blow on the temple.

"He's had enough," Roberts said.

"Just once more," Liamsson said.

"Just once then, but take it easy."

Liamsson cracked Glide on the crown of his head and smiled, breathing hard after his run through the dunes. Roberts had not noticed, but it was raining now and both men were soaked. The sun had burned a hole in the sky and all the birds had disappeared.

*t*hey dragged Glide north, away from the beach, and stashed his body inside a palmetto stand about thirty yards from the water. Both men were exhausted, so they sat and looked at Glide while rain poured down from a gray sky. The skin around Glide's eyes had turned purple and a spray of blood was drifting down from the top of his head where Liamsson had hit him a third blow.

"I kill him?" the old man asked, slightly nervous.

Roberts leaned down and checked his heartbeat. It was there.

"You didn't kill him," he said.

"How long you figure he'll be out?"

"I don't know," Roberts said. There was swelling on his right jaw and his tongue felt as though it had been burned. "I don't have that much experience whipping up on people with a shotgun to the head. Do you?"

Liamsson grinned impishly and took a deep breath. "I'm flat scared," he said. "We've got to get Hilliard out of that cabin before he misses Glide. He's probably sitting on the front porch right now wondering where Glide is. After all, that motor launch is already heading north around the Key." They could hear its thin high-wire whine going away on the breeze.

"I was thinking the same thing," Roberts said. "I didn't get quite that far into my thinking, though Glide was a lucky break. Otherwise, they'd both be in the cabin."

"Or they might have gone," Liamsson said. "We got to get Dolores out of there."

"That's right," Roberts said. "Or we've got to get Hilliard out of there. One or the other."

Liamsson got to his feet and surveyed the beach. The rain pattered steadily down, big drops blown in on the southeastern wind. The bay spread out flat before them, all twenty miles of it to the Keys mainland just a single sheet of gray, with a chalky gray sky above.

"Let me circle around to the estuary in front of the cabin," Liamsson said. "Hilliard will be above to see me from the front porch. He'll come down to the beach. I know he will."

"Don't be crazy," Roberts said.

"It ain't crazy," Liamsson said. "Hilliard will come to the beach. He'll want to know why I've come over to Dismal."

"It's too dangerous."

"I can be around there in a few minutes," Liamsson said.

"He might shoot you just for the hell of it," Roberts told the old man.

"I'll tell him I've come to check out the cabin. He'll believe that. Hell, it's my damn job, ain't it? He'll walk down to the beach and I'll have a chat with him and you can see about Dolores. You'll have about five minutes to get down there. You go up to that cabin with her and Bobby inside and anything can happen. You think you can get lucky twice?"

"Maybe I can," Roberts said.

"Now listen," Liamsson said. "I like that girl, too. Besides, I'm tired of Nazis and drug cowboys and human shit like Glide. I'd as soon do it myself as let somebody hurt that girl. Can you understand that?"

"I guess I can," Roberts said.

"I'll get then," Liamsson said.

Roberts followed Liamsson across the dunes and watched the old man hop into the skiff. He pushed the skiff into shallow water about fifteen yards out.

"I'm going up the estuary," he said. "When I get inside the chan-
nel, I'm going to fire off a couple of flares and make some noise.
That's got to bring Hilliard down to the beach from the cabin. When
he walks down there, you go up to the cabin and save that girl. If
anything happens to me, you can try to take Hilliard if you need
to. If he gets me, you take him and his boat. It will be faster anyway.
I don't know what to tell you, but head south out of here. You'll
hit the Keys sooner or later. Get ashore as quick as you can and
head inland. The highway is two miles from shore, so find yourself
a building and get inside. I didn't want to tell you, but they're pretty
sure the hurricane will hit around Homestead. We'll get a big enough
blow here. You've got to be inland."

Roberts tossed over the line and watched Liamsson back out
north, then head west around the point.

"I'll be up at the cabin," Roberts shouted. "You be careful."

"You be careful, too," Liamsson called.

Roberts scurried up a wall of dune waste and trudged fifty yards
across a narrow inlet. The water was ankle-deep and skin-warm. It
had begun to rain harder and he was soaking wet, his jaw swollen
now to the size of a grapefruit. When he had crossed the inlet,
he hurried around a mangrove and then found his path back to the
cabin. For a moment, he thought about the night he'd spent on the
beach there with Dolores Vega, about the things they'd said, talking
about the stars, Haitian art, fishing for bones on the flats during
long, hot days, tuna-fish sandwiches, Dominican baseball players.
He found it amazing that he'd been able to talk to a perfect stranger
for most of a night. He felt a lump in his throat, the rise of abject
fear. What if she were dead? What if they had already killed her?

The first flare exploded like a blue glaze of broken glass. Roberts
watched it rise and then float on the wind, finally falling into the
vast grayness of the storm. He could see Liamsson turning the skiff
into the estuary in about two feet of water, the skiff moving shore-
ward slowly, the bow making ripples, the old man standing on the
stern and shouting into the wind, his words not audible to Roberts
from that far away. Something was causing Roberts's ears to pop

and buckle, the sounds diluted. The second flare exploded and star-fished like a nova. Liamsson was waving his arms and screaming like a banshee.

Roberts had made it to within forty yards of the cabin when he saw Hilliard come out. Bobby stood on the porch with an automatic weapon in his right hand. It was the crazy Bobby—a shock of red hair, tall, gangly as a snake, hopping nervously from foot to foot as though he were being burned.

"What are you doing, old man?" Hilliard shouted. He looked up and down the beach for Jimmy Glide.

"You've got to get off the island," Liamsson shouted back. "I came over to batten down the hatches. Didn't know you were up here."

"Get out of here," Hilliard shouted. He had come down to the bottom porch step and was standing there, holding the gun in his outstretched hand. Roberts kept hoping he would go on down to the beach, but he didn't. Liamsson continued to shout and wave his arms.

"Goddamn it, old man," Hilliard shouted. "Get the hell out of here!"

Roberts was almost directly behind the cabin when he saw Jimmy Glide stagger up the beach and raise a limp hand.

*h*e was two hundred yards down the beach, an apparition barely visible through a dense fog of rain. For a moment, Glide stood on the top of a dune, then stumbled down through the sand and lay facedown on the beach, his hand clawing forward as if he thought he could crawl to the cabin. Roberts prayed that he would stay down, that he had lost consciousness again and would lie quietly while Hilliard walked down off the porch. Hilliard seemed to be looking out at the estuary, flailing the air with his arms, trying to ward off the old man, make him go home where he belonged. It didn't look to Roberts as though Liamsson had seen Glide on the dunes. Liamsson had taken the skiff fifty yards up the estuary, making toward the beach, coming in to force Hilliard out. Hilliard was still standing on the lower porch step, one foot on the sand now.

Liamsson guided the skiff in. "You've got to get off this damn Key!" he shouted to Hilliard. "Haven't you heard about the storm? She's coming in now! Get out into your boat and I'll guide you back to the mainland. We've only got a few hours left! You'd best hurry on."

Roberts edged downhill toward the back of the cabin. He pulled the Smith & Wesson from his belt. Down on the beach, Glide raised his head again, his arm outstretched in supplication. Hilliard came off the bottom step and headed out to the beach. He was holding the automatic in his right hand, pointing it at Liamsson. Roberts circled back of the cabin and looked inside one of the open hurricane shutters.

Dolores was standing near the front window, her back to Roberts. She turned and saw him and seemed about to scream.

"Oh, my God!" she cried, hurrying to the window. She was wearing jeans and a man's long-sleeved shirt. "Oh, I thought they'd killed you!"

Roberts reached through the open window and touched her face. "Quick, climb out. We don't have much time."

"Bobby's got a gun," she said.

"I know, I've seen him out on the beach."

"Who's out there?"

"It's Liamsson," Roberts said.

"Jimmy Glide is down the beach. He'll be back soon."

"Just get out here," Roberts said. Dolores climbed over the window ledge and Roberts helped her down to the sand. Out on the beach, Hilliard had gone about twenty yards toward the estuary, where Liamsson was holding the skiff into the wind. Sheets of rain pounded down now, the wind making a deafening roar. They had become marbled with black, whirling tunnels of wind, like a surrealistic painting of itself. Roberts peeked around the corner of the cabin and could see Glide making his way slowly on hands and knees, an inch or two at a time. He was immersed in gray rain, a zombie in the dark.

"Bobby Hilliard," Roberts screamed through the rain.

Hilliard turned quickly, holding up his weapon. The rain was making it impossible for him to see clearly, the torrent blowing back into his face, a nearly perfect wall of water.

"Is that you, cowboy?" Hilliard shouted hoarsely.

"It's me, Bobby. Give it up."

"No way, cowboy," Hilliard screamed.

Hilliard stepped up the beach toward the cabin, sheltering his eyes. He bobbed down to get a better look and spotted Jimmy Glide on his feet about two hundred yards away.

"You ain't going to shoot nobody," Hilliard shouted.

"Don't count on it, Bobby," Roberts shouted back.

"You got out of Haiti," Hilliard said. It was matter-of-fact. "I thought they'd put a spell on you, some kind of damn hex or other. Black-magic crap. You must have held up better than Raymond. You got some special voodoo working for you?"

"I'm serious, Bobby," Roberts said. "Drop the gun."

"You can't kill me," Hilliard screamed at the top of his lungs. "I'm already dead. You didn't know that? I got killed years ago. I been dead all this time, ain't I? You can't kill a man who's already dead."

"Drop the gun Bobby, I mean it."

With one hand Hilliard stripped off his tank top. He had painted his body with daubs of white, hailstones in irregular shapes. He tugged at the emerald on his left ear and laughed hideously.

Roberts heard Glide fire a shot and saw Liamsson sit down hard in the stern of the skiff. Roberts fired at Glide, who had tumbled onto the beach on his stomach and continued to fire his weapon. Dolores cried out now, saying something that Roberts couldn't understand. Rain was hammering down on the tin roof of the cabin, hundreds and thousands of pings that confused the ear.

Liamsson rose and directed a shotgun blast at Hilliard, who turned and fired wildly up the estuary. Roberts fired twice then, once at Hilliard, who was fleeing toward the dunes, once into the wind.

"Come on, we've got to run," Roberts told Dolores. They hit the beach, and Roberts called out to Liamsson, who raised his shotgun and fired again, this time toward the dunes where Hilliard had run. Then the old man lay down in the stern of the skiff and did not reappear. "We've got to make it to the skiff. Don't stop moving. Stay on the inside of me so I can shelter you. If I go down, just keep running."

"Oh, God," Dolores said. "Do you think Jakob is all right?"

"Let's move," Roberts said.

They skirted the cabin porch and began to run in the rain and thick sand. Roberts could hear gunfire from down the beach, five or six sharp pops against a backdrop of wind and pounding rain. Dolores fell, got up, fell again, Roberts half-dragging her through the wet sand. He turned and let loose twice more with the Smith & Wesson in the direction of the other gunfire, but he couldn't see anything in the storm. Together they splashed into knee-deep water, struggling to keep their balance. The storm wind delivered the sound of more pops, maybe three, though Roberts couldn't tell for sure.

Dolores fell and swam, then rose and pedaled through water as thunder blossomed in the clouds. Roberts caught her and picked her up out of the water and they finished the last twenty yards to the skiff. He helped her over the side and fell in it beside her. Liamsson lay in the stern, his eyes closed. There was a bloodstain on his blue work shirt, a dark-red patch working its way through just beneath the left underarm.

Roberts made Dolores lie in the bow and he crawled back to Jakob.

"I'm all right," Jakob said. "You'd best start her up and get us moving south."

Roberts choked the engine and started it on the first pull of the rope. He circled the estuary and turned the skiff south, hearing Hilliard's weapon above the wind, a sequence of sharp reports. When they reached Hilliard's launch, Roberts put two bullets in the gas tank and moved them far out onto the waters of the bay. He could hear Hilliard screaming through the sound of the storm.

a hard wind blew rain in diagonals. Roberts headed the skiff due south and made Liamsson continue to lie down, while Dolores Vega took the helm. There was a hard chop and the skiff rose, then bounced down between waves, making a clap on the surface of the water. Roberts tried to look at the old man's wound and to help Dolores keep the skiff straight, hoping they wouldn't take on too much water.

"Hang on, Jakob," he whispered to the old man, whose breathing was stuttered. "Just relax and let me look at this thing." Roberts stripped off the work shirt. There was a delicate blue hole under the armpit. It looked as though it had gone straight through without striking bone or artery. Roberts wadded up the shirt and held it against the hole.

"Wind will drag you back south," Liamsson said. "You've got to hold her steady or she'll drift west."

"I'll take over for you," Dolores told Roberts. She was soaked to the skin, her hair plastered to her skull. She and Roberts switched places, Roberts taking the motor, Dolores Vega looking after the old man. She made him lean back against the oilskin duffel, trying to shelter him from the rain as much as she could. The day emitted an audible howl, a low rumble like a pack of wolves. The sound came from the north, somewhere behind them, past the edge of the dark horizon. Wind had pushed water over the gunwales, and Roberts began to worry about swamping.

"You'll have to bail sooner or later," Liamsson said weakly. He held one arm over his face, trying to shield himself from the rain, probably hiding his grimace. "She'll get so low in the water, she'll stall if you don't." He managed to kick a coffee can over to Roberts, who began to bail with one hand.

Fifteen minutes later, the old man lost consciousness. Dolores looked up at Roberts in horror and began to feel for a pulse. She signaled that she'd found it. "It's weak," she said to Roberts. They bumped through a large wave, and Liamsson opened his eyes. "Can't we hurry?" Dolores asked.

"We'd better not," Roberts said. "There's enough water coming in now. We go too fast, we'll swamp her for sure." He continued to bail, one coffee can full of water after another without letup. Rain fell in dark sheets, obscuring everything but the narrow confines of the boat, the old man prone, Dolores over him like a wing.

"Whatever happens—" Dolores began.

"Don't say it," Roberts cautioned her. They were shouting over the noise of wind and rain. "We're going to make it back to the Keys. Jakob is going to be fine."

Dolores hunched over the old man. "They made me wear a wire," she called.

"I know," Roberts shouted. "Littrow paid me a visit at my hotel on Miami Beach."

"They threatened me," she said. "They frightened me. They told me they'd implicate me. I could prove I wasn't involved if I wore the wire. I wanted to talk to you, but they were all over me. I could hardly breathe with them all around me."

"It's my fault," Roberts said. "They wanted me to wear the wire. I should have done it, but I didn't. I confronted Jimmy Glide, hoping they'd bolt and run. They did, but I didn't think they'd take you along."

It was raining so hard that Roberts could barely see her face, just three feet away. He was going dead slow, barely creeping through an area of shoals, hoping he wouldn't ground them and hove to get out and wade. Liamsson groaned and moved, Dolores holding his shoulders as though he were a child. Just then a few pelicans went over, low and hard.

"Pelicans," Dolores said.

"Going south. We're headed in the right direction."

"Who were those people in the boat on Dismal?" Dolores asked. "The ones who came up while I was in the cabin?"

"Glide's Miami buyers," Roberts said. "They came out to Dismal to buy coke. Liamsson thinks they take it over to Flamingo to avoid Alligator Alley. Dismal is the perfect place for a drug deal. It's isolated and you'd think it couldn't be approached. This was their last deal. The house in Bay Harbor is up for sale and the galleries are closed. Escape is for sale and the Lauderdale building has been put up for lease. I'm sorry, Dolores. I know how much it all meant to you."

"What's going to happen back there?" Dolores called, gesturing toward Dismal Key.

"I don't know," Roberts said. "I guess it depends on the storm. I put in a call to the Coast Guard on the way down. They'll be pretty busy right now. I think we're on our own out here."

Below the sound of the rain, Roberts heard another sound. He thought it might be engine noise, but he wasn't sure. He took a flare out of the oilskin duffel and sent a red one flying high into the rain. It exploded dully and showered down sparks, hanging in the gloom for a minute.

"I thought I heard something," he told Dolores. "I don't want to get cut in half by another boat."

"You're going to be fine," Dolores said to Jakob, who was breathing in great gulps, half air, half rain.

Roberts fired up another flare. He was having trouble with the skiff, now heavily loaded down with water. He turned and looked toward what he thought was south, but he wasn't sure of his directions anymore. Then, through the darkness, he saw a huge spot of light. Behind the spot was a bulky Coast Guard cutter, heading toward them. He stood up in the bow and began to wave his arms. The cutter made toward them and hove to about fifteen yards to their starboard. Roberts cut his engine back and waited. Ridley was standing on the bow of the cutter, wearing a yellow rain slicker and yellow rain hat.

"That you, Roberts?" he called out.

"We've got an injured man onboard," Roberts shouted.

"We'll get you," Ridley called. "Stand by."

Dolores touched the old man's face. "You see, Jakob?" she said. "You're home now. Everything is all right. There isn't anything to worry about. You're going to be fine."

She looked at Roberts, but didn't smile.

*r*oberts was sitting on a Naugahyde sofa on the third floor of the small community hospital in Islamadora. The windows on the south side of the hospital had been blown in by the force of wind, waves had come over the piers only a block away, along the waterfront, flooding the access roads for motels and convenience stores, swamping boats, ruining the beach. All of the electric lines in town were down, and most of the highways in and out were closed. Telephone service had been interrupted, and nobody knew when crews would be out in the streets, restoring service. Reports up and down the Keys were bad, trees down, boats wrecked, stores blown away by the gale. Even now, the hospital staff was servicing its rooms with emergency power from a gasoline generator, enough to light a surgical-team room, two patient wings, a small kitchen and cafeteria. There were rumors among the cutter crew that heavy wind had ripped through a mobile-home park in Homestead, killing dozens of people unlucky enough not to have been evacuated, wrecking housing developments, sending trailers and roofs flying, a blizzard of debris, broken glass, and vehicles.

"That's how it gets you," Ridley had told Roberts as they'd chopped through Florida Bay, heading east toward Islamadora and land. "It isn't the wind really, but the water and the debris. Flying glass like razors, a bit of tarpaper that cuts your face off and you can't see it coming, a sheared-off dowel that burrows right through your chest, cuts out your heart. You step on a downed power line, or even close to it in water, and suddenly you're toast. Most people are killed in a hurricane by drowning. I'll bet you didn't know that."

They had come within sight of Islamadora's north pier and the rain beat down in gusts. It was not fully night, just the ghost of late afternoon, a gray glow on the horizon to the west and the howl of the wind. "It'll get real quiet," Ridley had continued, "and then it'll blow like hell. We're going to tie up here and get old Jakob over to the hospital. We've got about three hours before it really hits."

Roberts had stood on deck and watched three guardsmen carry Jakob Liamsson away on a gurney. The old man had his eyes closed and his breathing was steady, if shallow. Dolores had stopped the bleeding, but they didn't know what kind of damage the bullet had really done. They'd lost his skiff in the wind and maybe they'd find it later, maybe they wouldn't. At the end of the pier, an ambulance had been waiting, its lights flashing in the gloom. Roberts hurried down the gangplank with Dolores, and together they'd ridden with Jakob across town to the small hospital. Streetlights suspended above the intersections were standing straight out in the wind, and all manner of things were blowing about—lawn chairs, garbage cans, newspapers.

When the hurricane hit, Liamsson was in surgery. Neither Dolores nor Roberts were allowed in the unit, so they waited outside in the half dark of forty-watt bulbs. The building shuddered and shook in the wind, and Roberts thought that any minute they might lose the roof. Water was seeping in through cracks under the windows, rolling in sheets down the back stairs. All of the carpets in the building were soaked, and the staff told him that the first floor was drowned in six inches of salt water, pieces of floating debris. Roberts was able to go to the north windows and look outside, the heavy wind knocking down palm trees at ninety miles an hour, wind groaning like a freight train, a sound that hurt the ears. Roberts sat on the Naugahyde couch with Dolores, wishing he had a cigar, something to do with his hands, anything to take his mind off the wind, and Liamsson in surgery. Twice the generator failed and the floor was plunged into darkness. But in minutes, the staff started it again and there was light.

About ten o'clock that night, a doctor emerged from the operating room. He was dressed in a green smock, green apron, a small green cap. He looked tired and was stripping off rubber gloves when he came over to Roberts.

"Your friend is going to be okay," the doctor said.

"Thanks, Doc," Roberts said. Dolores gave a weary smile.

"He lost a lot of blood and he's got a good hole through to the shoulder blade. The bullet dented some bone structure and ricocheted back up through the clavicle area. We went in and cleaned it out and he'll lose some movement in his left arm. It took this long because we were looking for bone chips. He'll be up and around in no time. Probably as mean as ever."

The doctor smiled and disappeared back into the operating room. Lieutenant Ridley came over and joined them. He was dressed in white, unbelievably fresh.

"They say Jakob is okay," Ridley said.

"That's what they say," Roberts agreed. "I want to thank you for coming out to get us."

"I got your message," Ridley said. "Duty officer radioed me just after you left. I remembered you from Dismal Key that time we found those dead Haitians. This have anything to do with them?"

"It's a long story," Roberts said.

"We've got ten hours," Ridley said. "Storm will fool around that long as least."

"It won't take ten hours to tell," Roberts said.

"It doesn't have to do with drugs, does it?"

"It might."

"How'd I guess?" Ridley laughed. "You might like to know we've been working those dead Haitians for weeks now."

"I didn't know that," Roberts said.

"Had our eye on Dismal Key as well," Ridley said. "You might be interested to know that those Haitians were connected to a little ring down in Miami. Small-time thugs, strong-arm thieves, just muscle on the wing."

"You do an autopsy?"

"Sure we did," Ridley said. "Both shot. One got it right in the back of the neck. The other was hit in the side and under the heart, like he might have made a run for it but wasn't quick enough."

"I know who killed them," Roberts said.

"I think I do, too," Ridley said. "This afternoon about four o'clock, there was a curfew for South Florida. The evacuation out of there was stopped and Alligator Alley east to west was closed. About seven o'clock, the sheriff over in Flamingo stopped a car heading out of town, going toward the West Coast. Rental car from some agency in Miami. He didn't like the look of the three guys in it, and they panicked. Sheriff took them down and searched the car and guess what he found?"

"Cocaine?"

"That would be right, sir," Ridley said.

"I think I can explain it," Roberts told him.

"I figure the coke was offloaded over on Dismal."

"I'm kind of hungry," Roberts said. "You don't think we could find something to eat around here, do you?"

"They've got some Jell-O down in the kitchen," Ridley said. "You that hungry?"

"I might be," Roberts laughed.

Just then, the building seemed to move on its foundation and the air compressed.

"You ought to see a *big* storm," Ridley said.

*r*oberts sat up with Liamsson through the night, sleeping in bits and pieces on a chair in a private room, Dolores outside on the Naugahyde couch. Every two hours they changed positions, Dolores beside the old man, Roberts on the couch. Toward morning, the old man sat up and began to talk, ate some Jell-O, bothered the nurses for sexual favors and a bottle of rum. Between them, they decided that Dolores would stay with him for the day and would wait for Roberts, who would run over to Dismal Key with Ridley.

That morning, Roberts and Ridley walked through the streets of Islamadora toward the north pier. Most of the palms on the island had been knocked down, and there were bits of them like splintered matchsticks laying in piles where they had been blown. Telephone poles were down, as well as electric poles, and there were no working traffic signals on the whole island. Even as they walked together through bright sunshine, work crews were beginning to clean up debris, fix power lines, unstop gutters and sewers, sweep up broken glass. The AM station in town reported that five people were missing and presumed dead on account of the storm. Roberts could have told them there were two others out on Dismal Key.

Ridley told Roberts they couldn't take the cutter, which had been pulled over to Key West in order to run supplies out to Dry Tortuga. Instead, they would take a motorized rubber dinghy borrowed from a construction crew at work on a jetty that had been damaged by the storm surge. The President had declared South Florida a disaster area and was sending troops, supplies, and money.

Ridley was wearing his standard-issue .45-caliber automatic. He'd managed to scrounge some food and water and had put them in a couple of plastic sacks. Roberts had borrowed some clean clothes at the hospital: a new pair of slacks, shirt, a ball cap to ward off the sun. They managed to get a breakfast of hot cereal and instant coffee in the hospital kitchen after the storm passed. Ridley had called the FBI in Miami and told them about the bust in Flamingo. Littrow said he'd be down when traffic got back to normal on the causeways. All their helicopters were tied up in the relief effort.

Out on the water, it was hot already. The bay was covered with floating debris, bits of lumber, palm fronds, scattered wreckage riding the placid, blue-green water. Ridley sat in the stern of the dinghy while Roberts rode up front, staring out at the sparkling Florida bay and the seabirds flying toward the north.

"Agent Littrow didn't say much about you," Ridley said. He cranked up the Evinrude and they topped over the waves.

"You tell him they busted the buys with the coke?"

"Yeah. He was upset. I guess he thought it was his bust."

"Oh, it was his bust," Roberts said.

"That's what I thought," Ridley said.

Roberts spent an hour telling Ridley the story, top to bottom, start to finish. They were riding shallow and fast as the sun climbed up high and turned hot. Roberts broke a hard sweat and covered his eyes, looking for a sign of the Key, the cabin, the dune where he'd last seen Jimmy Glide crawling over the wastes, Hilliard waving his arms down on the beach. He and Ridley chatted about life, horses on the southern Colorado plains, Wisconsin, where Ridley had grown up, the son of a Methodist minister. Ridley told Roberts he loved the Great Lakes the way Roberts loved the San Luis Valley. It was a matter of what you found to love, and how you behaved when you found it. Ridley said he couldn't believe the way coke dealers frittered away everything worth doing in life.

They'd just shared a cup of water when Ridley cut the engine to low idle. "We're almost home," he said.

Roberts looked at the cabin. It had no roof, and two of its hurricane shutters had been blown off, the porch steps covered by blown sand. It was obvious that water had rushed over the island, leaving wavy tracks of sand on the altered dunes. Ridley slid them up the estuary on full slow. Roberts scanned the horizon, noting that many of the mangroves had been flattened. He could almost see over the top of the Key toward the north and the empty bay beyond.

Ridley nudged him. From behind one small dune, Bobby Hilliard appeared. He was wearing pants but no shirt, and he looked as though he had been electrocuted, his skin bright red from the effect of blowing sand. He stood on the edge of the beach in bare feet, waving his weapon. He was screaming words that Roberts couldn't understand.

"Drop the gun now," Ridley shouted at the top of his lungs.

Hilliard screamed something unintelligible and fired a shot. Roberts and Ridley dropped to the deck and waited. They heard another shot, and when Roberts peeked over the gunwale, he saw Hilliard splashing in shallow water, running and then stumbling, falling, getting up and trying to make his way through the knee-deep estuary.

"What's with this guy?" Ridley asked.

"He thinks he's dead," Roberts said.

"He thinks he's what?"

"Dead," Roberts said. "He thinks he's already dead. He thinks he's invulnerable. Can't be killed. Protected by some kind of spirit medicine. Hell, I don't know."

Hilliard picked himself up out of the water and fired. There was a whine and a pop, the bullet going over high of its mark.

"To heck with that," Ridley said. "He's crazy, all right. But he's crazy from lack of water to drink and he's crazy from being scoured by blowing sand for six hours. I can't believe he survived out here all that time."

Another bullet pinged over their heads.

"Give up the gun," Ridley called out.

"It won't help," Roberts told him.

Ridley raised himself and fired once, carefully. Hilliard lay still, facedown in the shallow water, his head bobbing, half-floating. Ridley holstered his automatic and looked away to the south, where there was nothing but a blue glaze.

"Well, shit," he said. "Excuse my language."

"You had to shoot him," Roberts said. "I'm surprised he got out as far as he did."

"Probably lack of water made him crazy," Ridley said. "You can't go much more than two days without. Maybe he drank some salt water. That might be why he was so crazy."

Ridley guided the dinghy to within twenty feet of where Hilliard lay. They splashed through the water and turned him over. His face and arms, his entire upper body, had been sandblasted to raw skin, red and bleeding, the man's blue eyes swollen nearly shut, the eyebrows singed. Ridley floated the body in toward the beach and set it back on dry land.

"What are these white daubs on his legs?" he asked.

"Symbolic hailstones," Roberts told him.

"You must be joking," Ridley said. He went out and got the dinghy, brought it over, and hauled Hilliard over its side. They spent an hour looking for Jimmy Glide, but they didn't find any trace of him. They didn't find the launch either. Roberts hoped that Glide had been eaten by sharks by now. Maybe in a few weeks, some fishermen would find the launch, miles south, east or west, where it had been blown.

"Here's to the sharks," Roberts said, lifting his plastic cup of fresh water.

Ridley stared and said nothing.

*h*e was a Jacksonville boxer named Calvin Clinton and he'd been down sport-fishing in Bimini when he rented a nice pink Lincoln Continental for the ride up to Broward, where he knew a "lady friend" who enjoyed good-looking cars.

Clinton told Roberts it was nothing special, just a surprise for the woman, a former Miss Broward County, who'd lost her husband to prostate cancer and got lonely occasionally. They were perfect for each other, Clinton said on the phone, the boxer in perfect shape after all these years. And the lady was old enough to know better but she didn't, out on the town in blue polyester pant suit and a gardenia in her hair.

Clinton had gone over to Bimini on a cheap sports cruise. He'd fished for tuna and shark, then he'd caught a short hop to Nassau and had done some gambling on Paradise Island, a few passes at craps and some blackjack. After a week, he'd caught the sport cruise back to Miami and rented the pink Continental at a cut-rate agency on the grounds of the International Airport. He told Officer Martinez that he'd been sitting in one of the departure lounges waiting for his rental car, when a woman named Margaret Hatcher sat down next to him on a stool. She looked cool and blonde in her blue flight attendant's outfit, and they'd struck up a conversation about his pink Continental, fully equipped. About fifteen minutes later, the woman had invited him over to the Tropical Lounge for a drink. She said she'd go home first and freshen up, then she'd stop by the parking lot, where he should wait because she didn't like walking into bars alone. After he lost his car and wallet, Calvin found out that the Tropical Lounge was a gay bar. The bartender let him use the telephone, and Calvin waited for the cops outside under the faux-grass awning.

Roberts had been in Metro-Dade running records for two days when he ran into Calvin Clinton, one of sixteen others who'd lost their cars out of Miami-Dade International. He had talked Officer Martinez into letting him run the stolen-car records. Martinez barely remembered the case, but what did it matter to him if Roberts wanted to run records, stare into a green computer screen and go blind?

"I've seen so much of this shit it all looks brown to me," Martinez told him at the South Dade station house. When Roberts discovered Calvin Clinton and the Tropical Lounge location, Martinez expressed interest.

Calvin Clinton had driven down from Jacksonville to meet the plane, a two-o'clock from London, about twenty minutes late. They were standing at the gate drinking coffee, watching all the cruise passengers walk by in their Bermuda shorts. He stood about five and a half feet tall, gray hair, originally from New Jersey.

"They called me the Black Tornado," Clinton said. "You ever catch one of my fights?" he asked Roberts.

"I might have," Roberts replied.

"You believed the woman?" Martinez asked him. She was named Rosemary Reese.

"Hell yes, I believed her," Clinton said.

"You didn't think it was a little odd?" Martinez asked.

"This a racial thing with you?" Clinton said.

"It isn't a racial thing," Martinez sighed.

Roberts was reading the *Herald*, all about hurricane cleanup. The storm had caused two billion dollars' worth of damage, most of it in the northern Keys, southern Dade.

"What good would it do anyway?" Calvin said. "Me identifying her. That all you got?"

Martinez sipped his cold coffee. "You identify her for me right here in the airport. I've got five other cars that were stolen out of this airport. All of them connected to your blonde lady friend. We put all five of these cars with Rosemary Reese and she'll start to sweat."

"It's a long shot," Roberts said.

"It's what you wanted, isn't it?" Martinez asked him. "The other victims will give affidavits. She'll crack."

The flight was announced on loudspeakers. The three of them walked up to the arrival gate and sat down just outside the doors. A line of businessmen, tourists, kids with backpacks got off the plane. Hordes of visitors all ready to take advantage of the sun and fun of South Florida. Their trips had been booked for months and the hurricane wasn't going to stop them.

"Bitch took all my money," Clinton said. He had described the thief as best he could, solid guy with dark hair, black beard, built like a bear with black eyebrows. A light-heavyweight, maybe bigger.

"Tell me again what happened," Martinez said.

"I told you," Clinton said, exasperated. "I'm having me a drink in the lounge when she comes in and sits down. I can't help looking at her, good-looking bitch. We start to talk easy-like and I mention I'm on my way up to Lauderdale, got to pick up my pink rental. She starts telling me she'd like a drink after her flight and she says why don't we go over to the Tropical Lounge and get a quick one. What the hell, I'm thinking, good-looking bitch like that, why not? I say to myself, bitch up in Lauderdale can wait. Serves my ass right. I'm waiting in the parking lot like she told me, when some guy puts a gun on my neck. I get out easy-like and he takes my wallet and he takes my keys, then he drives away and I'm standing in the parking lot alone. Now, what am I gonna tell the Lauderdale bitch? I wait for a while and the gal never shows up for her drink. So, I call the Lauderdale bitch and tell her I lost my car. She says, you lost your car? What kind of shit is that? Then I called the police."

Martinez listened carefully, watching people come out of the arrival gate. Roberts nodded when he saw her, the woman in her smart blue-and-red uniform, wearing a Miss Florida tan, Miss Florida smile, a cargo door full of white teeth.

"That's her," Clinton said.

Martinez went up to the woman and took her by the arm. She stopped and looked very surprised.

"Man," Clinton said loudly. "I thought it was just coincidence, the bitch not showing up and all."

Martinez pulled the woman out of the line. "What's the matter, Officer?" she asked innocently.

Clinton and Roberts stood together, looking at her from about six feet away.

"You recognize these guys?" Martinez asked her.

"This is ridiculous," she said. "You'll be sorry for this."

"I'm already sorry," Martinez said.

Roberts smiled as Martinez handcuffed her. He waved as she was led away by the officer.

"How about a beer?" Roberts asked Clinton.

"Now you're talking," Clinton said.

*t*hey were at the veranda bar of the Hotel Olaffson, both of them
sitting on stools while merengue played in the background. Basil
Davis had brought them two rounds of rum punch on the house
and they were finishing the second, ceiling fans clicking above them,
stirring the humid air as the smell of charcoal drifted up from the
city. Dolores Vega was wearing a ridiculously huge straw hat, dark
sunglasses, enormous copper earrings that sparkled in the sun.
Down below, the city baked in direct sunshine.

Basil Davis finished talking to two American NATO types and
came over to the bar. He leaned against the burnished mahogany
and smiled.

"I didn't expect to see you two here so soon," he said. "But I'm
delighted. Quite delighted indeed."

"Business is better, I see," Roberts said, abetted by the rum and
the ceiling fan. Davis had his own rum, and they toasted Aristide,
the new regime, better times. "Perhaps you'll change over from
temporary interim manager to permanent interim manager."

Davis laughed heartily and downed his drink. There were a dozen
people at the bar for Happy Hour, all of them drinking rum and
eating roasted nuts. "Even the electricity stays on all day," he said.
"The Americans see to that. I think they're footing the oil bills."

Roberts finished his second rum and began to feel sleepy. They
had flown over from Miami on the three o'clock and it was late in
the day. Soon it would be time to take a nap, shower, catch some

dinner up in Petionville, where he would need a sweater for the cool night air. After the hurricane, he had stayed on in Miami, talking to the FBI. The Agency had located sixty Haitian works of art in storage at the Pan-Carib warehouse in Opa Locka. The works were being held as contraband, but Roberts was hoping he could get them released to benefit the owners, artists on Haiti and elsewhere. Littrow told Roberts that the government was going after the mansion, the cars, the boat, all the jewelry, every piece of garbage that Hilliard had owned.

Half an hour later, Roberts saw Virgil pedal up to the veranda steps on his bicycle. He parked near the pool changing rooms and climbed the steps. He was dressed in jaunty white pants and a dark-blue T-shirt with a photo of Michael Jordan on the front. The two exchanged hugs, and Dolores gave him a big kiss.

"I'm happy to see you," Roberts said. Virgil sat down between them, his feet barely able to touch the floor.

"Is it not dangerous for you, M'ser?" Virgil asked.

"NATO is in control of the police. I checked with Interpol and they think Champagne Lambert is on Martinique. He's not doing his customs thing anymore. Besides, I'm staying only a few days. I think it's safe, don't you?"

The bartender brought over some griots, small pats of fried bread with goat meat inside, a pink platter of freshly sliced mango, peanuts grilled over an open fire. Virgil ordered an orange soda, and together they watched the sun sink into the ocean, an extravaganza of mauve, orange, and pale blue tinged by charcoal smoke and diesel exhaust.

"How is your family?" Roberts asked.

"They are well, Mes-z-amis," Virgil said happily. "There is much optimism now that the generals have gone. We are happy to see Aristide in the palace."

"Have they gone back to America?" Roberts asked.

"Not as yet," Virgil replied. "There is much discussion."

"I'd like you to come to Miami," Roberts said. "I think you can get a student visa. Enroll in a junior college. Once you're inside the country, then you study, perhaps try to work, find a home for your-self. I can help you, sponsor you."

"I'll help you get started," Dolores said. She had found temporary work in a gallery at Vizscaya. It was not as important as Escape, but it was a place to start.

"Thank you, my friends," Virgil said. "I have thought of this very much. Every night for years." He sat brooding, his dark eyes ab-stracted into some unknowable distance. "But I believe I must re-main in Haiti. I think it is something you would not understand." He laughed daintily. "Besides, you have made me a rich man!"

"You earned it," Roberts said.

They went shopping, and Dolores selected an evening wardrobe for Virgil, red-checked pants, a green-satin shirt, new black shoes with platforms. They drove up to Petionville for dinner, the three of them sharing lobster, green salad, a chocolate cake doused with rum. They drove back down to the Olfaffson and said their good-byes on the veranda, where five or six couples were dancing to slow music. Roberts hugged his friend, and he and Dolores watched him pedal off into the night.

Back in the room, it was hot and airless. Roberts opened the French doors and they stood on the balcony looking down at the pool, a shimmering blue rectangle under moonlight. There was no wind and the crickets chattered wildly.

Dolores went to the bathroom and came back in her nightgown. She was so beautiful that Roberts could not believe his luck. For a long time, they stood at the window breathing in the night air, watching the moon rise over the mountains.

"It's beautiful, isn't it?" Dolores said. She put her arm around his neck and kissed his ear.

"At night, very," he said.

"Once I told you that I could love you," she said. "Do you re-member?"

"I remember," he told her.

But already a dark wind was blowing him home.